One

S arah was climbing the hill slowly, which seemed to her an odd thing when she noticed it, for probably never in her life had she been so eager to get to the top. But then, everything was strange today. She was dry-eyed when all the others—family, friends, and even strangers—were weeping openly. At lunch she had eaten a large cheese sandwich and drunk her milk as usual, while Lucy and her mother choked over the morsels of the choicest food the neighbors had brought in. She even remembered thinking that the milk was good now that the cows were back on clover. It was funny that cows could go on eating clover today just as they did yesterday. She looked down toward the Bensons' pasture and counted the black-and-white cows—or was she counting her own footsteps climbing the hill? Beyond the field, the mellow green of the woodland, and the rim of the sky bluer than she'd ever seen it. Clouds floating softly, ever so white, ever so light, just wandering around. That was it; the whole world seemed indifferent. Nothing cared about what had happened. Nothing, that is, except people. With people so terribly, awfully torn by grief, it would seem as if the world should be shaken by storm, slashed by lightning, cut by rain. But in every direction as far as she could see, the world was beautiful, and warm and living.

Only her father was dead.

She had reached the top of the hill now, the highest point where one gaunt pine stood alone. She leaned against it. Her father always laughed at that pine. Its branches began far up the

1

tall trunk and then reached out, long branches and short, in grotesque attitudes. He said that back in the lumbering days the tree had probably been passed over because it was so twisted and full of knots, but after it had stood alone for a score of years, no one dared to touch it. Every year it seemed mightier, with a kind of majestic awkwardness. The last time she had climbed this hill, her father was with her. They had raced and he had beat. His long legs carried him like seven-league boots and he dearly liked to go sprinting up a hill. His sandy hair was always tousled in the wind. They had stood together under this very tree while they got their breath. Her father had pointed things out to her, making wide quick gestures with his long windmill arms and his long lean hands. His hands! Suddenly Sarah leaned weakly against the rough trunk of the pine. The quiet numbness which had protected her all day was breaking apart. Her throat had gone dry, and something that hurt worse than pain pulsed deep in her chest.

She would never see her father's hands again.

They were the strongest hands she had ever felt. Long, strong fingers. And always such clean hands; cleaner than any ordinary person's. "Dennis Duncan has surgeon's hands," people said. She remembered a long time ago asking her father once when they were eating breakfast together whether he became a doctor because he had surgeon's hands or whether he got to have surgeon's hands because he was a doctor. Her father had said that the entire matter was settled by his *genes,* and as far as he knew the only time he ever exercised an entirely free will was when he proposed to her mother. He laughed to himself and then he explained about genes, but Mama, who was reading the newspaper at the table, said it was silly to explain things like that to a five-year-old child. Why, she couldn't understand them herself, Mama said, and learning all those big words would just make Sarah show off. But Sarah had understood. That is, she always understood as much as her father explained. And she didn't show off. Lucy could show off very

2

well indeed, and it pleased their mother. Sarah would like to show off sometimes, but she could never think of anything to show off about because everything she knew seemed so ordinary as soon as she knew it.

The pain in her chest grew worse until it seemed to fill her body with a vast and terrible aching. She tried to push her mind to remember more of these unimportant little things, to go on from one memory to another without stopping to think. If she could remember hard enough and fast enough, then she wouldn't know that her father was dead. There was the time he had bought her a new hammer and helped her to build a cart. And the time he came into her room at night to shut her window because the snow was blowing right across her bed. And the time, the many times, they had played duets together. There was the May morning a long while ago when they had planted marigolds. And then a few days later, when the little leaves showed green above the ground, an energetic six-year-old Sarah had carried a teakettle of boiling water from the kitchen to pour on the tiny leaves because her father had said it took heat and water to make the flowers grow. That evening they had pulled up all the wilted marigolds and planted new ones. Then her father explained about the sun's heat, and about playing Nature's game with Nature's laws. He often said that about playing by Nature's rules. She tried to remember other things he said, but she couldn't remember fast enough to stop this smothering loneliness. She could only lean against the rough tree.

Beside the pine, the girl seemed small and helpless, but she was really large for eleven years. She was tall and angular but not ungraceful. Whenever her mother commented on her large feet and her long legs, then her father would wink at her and say, "She takes after the Duncans; they're all tall. But her ankles she gets from Ma. The O'Malleys have good figures. Ma has the prettiest ankles I ever saw." Last Christmas when Sarah had come home from shopping for a party dress, discouraged and chagrined by her size, her father had taken her into his home-office and talked to her sternly about her good body. It was a fine thing, he said, to be long-legged and long-waisted, to be wide through the pelvis and broad of shoulder. He unrolled a great chart of a woman's body and talked about the bony framework and the importance of free movement. Good posture was almost a passion with him, but he believed that it came from mental attitude and not from rules or exercises. He talked a long time that evening; it was one of the best evenings of her life. Not only had she learned a great many things, but she felt graceful and beautiful and important, like a queen. Her father often made her feel that way, as if the house was too small, roomy as it was, and the town was too small and the hills were too small and maybe even the world was too small; as if she might leap from star to star if she had a mind to. Although he made people feel big, there was no one more particular than Father about little things: about little tasks like dusting and dishwashing and sweeping the porches. Her father ...

It was almost dark when Sarah was again aware of outward circumstances. Hours must have passed, but not as hours. They were only one large luminous moment in which she was remembering many things, although not for their own sake. Beneath the remembering, something within her was trying to make sense out of everything together. But as soon as she tried to think, nothing made sense. Only when she left off thinking, quick little flashes of understanding filled her with excitement. And all the time she was acutely aware of the shifting of sunshine and lengthening of shadow, the softening of color in the field, in the sky. Aware and not aware. All that long afternoon, little incidents she had never remembered before and would not remember again welled up within her, but afterward it was bits of the outer scene which stayed in her mind. White ducks in the Bensons' pond, looking very small and placid, like the toy ducks on a looking glass that her mother sometimes used as a centerpiece; wagons, buggies, and a few automobiles scuttling down the state highway like a procession of beetles; smoke spiraling from a chimney; clouds like cream puffs jostling one another in a blue dish.

She went slowly down the hill. It was no use to hurry now. Everyone was long since home from the funeral. Maybe they hadn't missed her with all the people coming and going in the house. Maybe they thought she was crying in her room. Her father always said it was a child's privilege to go to its room and stay there if there wasn't any work to be done. He understood the unsociableness of social people. Sarah was a sociable child; her mother often said so. Her mother said she was a lot of company. Thinking of her mother, Sarah quickened her pace. Until that moment it hadn't occurred to her that her mother would be dreadfully lonely now. She had thought only that her mother would be dreadfully bewildered; she wouldn't know how to make up her mind because she had always depended upon her big doctor husband for that. Or if he wasn't home, there was Grandma Vanderiet. Not to mention Grandpa Vanderiet, who had a firmer mind than any of them when he wanted to use it. Well, there were still Grandma and Grandpa Vanderiet. To be sure, they lived halfway across town, but a fifteen-minute walk was nothing when one really wanted advice. Maybe they would move nearer their widowed daughter now that she was alone. Sarah said the words over slowly: "widowed daughter," "widowed mother," "widow." She tasted the melancholy sound of them. Now her golden-haired mother was alone in the world. She tasted the sound of that too. Everyone should help look after her. But it was hardly possible that Grandpa and Grandma could move any nearer because a minister had to live in his parsonage and the parsonage was beside the church, and certainly the First Christian Church could not be moved even for a widow alone in the world.

It was dark when Sarah reached home, and the house was more brightly lighted than any of its neighbors. She thought she would walk around the house and decide which door would be best to come in through so that she might slip quietly into the room where the most people were; the more people, the less she would be noticed. As she cut across the back yard she saw two figures standing under the elm, a short slender woman and a tall, angular man. For an instant she couldn't remember ever having seen these two people before. Then a shaft of light showed them to be her grandmother and grandfather Duncan. They had arrived only in time for the funeral after coming from Nebraska alone on the train. Sarah hesitated. Until today she had not seen her Duncan grandparents since she was four years old. She could not decide whether to go on and speak to them now or to turn away quietly. Then from her early childhood some prompting of memory led her forward.

"There's Sarah now," Grandmother Duncan said. Her voice sounded glad in a quiet way, with no overtone of recrimination.

"We didn't know where to look for you, Sarey," her grandfather explained. He always drawled his words and he always called her "Sarey." She liked it. "Being new in the neighborhood, we didn't know where to look for you." He did not put his hand on her shoulder as her father might have done, but Sarah felt gathered in.

"Your mother has sent three or four people to find you, but everybody just asks someone else. We sort of thought you would come back when you got ready." Grandmother Duncan spoke quickly, but all of her words sounded round and easy, with no rough edges of worry left over from other times she had used her words.

"I went to the top of a hill," Sarah explained. "I went there instead of to—to the funeral. I went there—I went there ...." The impulse to explain brought forth no words.

"Everybody has to have a hill," said Grandmother Duncan.

They were walking toward the house. Grandmother Duncan was not as tall as Sarah.

"It's good corn weather," Grandfather Duncan said. "Tomorrow will be a hot day, but the crops can take it. I see you've had plenty of rain around these parts. This soil holds the moisture better than our black mud. Dennis always set great store by the soil in this part of the country. I'd like to have called his attention to that truck garden down the road, first turn left before the cemetery. It looked to me like—" So he talked on easily about the crops, mentioning her father as casually as he mentioned the beans and tomatoes. Twice he stopped short for the sparest instant, but when he went on his voice was steady, even hearty. Sarah didn't know why she suddenly wished she were a hundred feet tall so that she could reach down to pick up her grandfather and rock him to sleep.

Two

Grandmother and Grandfather Duncan, followed by Sarah, went in through the back door to the dining room where the people were. Her mother was sitting by the table, her head propped on her hands. She wore her best dressing sacque of pink china silk with great wide sleeves. Every time she put it on her mother wondered aloud whether it would wash. Tonight her face looked splotchy from all her crying, and her hair, usually so carefully combed, hung in wisps about her face. Lucy was sitting on a high tea chair beside her, patting her arm. Tonight Lucy looked younger than her nine years, younger and prettier and more golden-haired, Sarah thought gently. Crying never made Lucy's eyes and nose red, although she cried a good deal because she was so tenderhearted. Tonight she looked a little wilted.

The room was full of family and friends wanting to go on being kind when there was nothing more to do. Sarah found herself looking at them separately, which made each one seem strange, like a familiar chair in an empty room. Grandma Vanderiet still wore her black silk with the high collar. Her black silk was really a winter silk, but Grandma had insisted that nothing else was appropriate for the funeral. Grandpa had remonstrated. He was trying to get his congregation to be less heathenish about their mourning. He said death was a promotion, an occasion for solemn celebration. Grandpa himself wore his Prince Albert, and that was heavy too. Tonight he looked tired, but then Grandma always said he had never been as strong as he looked. He wasn't one of the round jolly Dutchmen. He was rawboned and thin, not too tall, with very blue eyes which seemed to see everything from under their heavy straw-colored brows. When people met him for the first time they had a way of turning to look into his eyes again. In his cheeks were creases that Grandma said had been dimples when she first knew him. He was a person more likely to smile than to laugh even when a joke was quite funny. Odder still, he was likely to smile when other people were sad or mad. Suddenly Sarah realized that if she could have been sure of sitting by Grandpa she would probably have gone to the funeral.

Grandma would remember everything that was said at the funeral. The preacher had come from the First Christian Church in St. Paul. Grandma would know if he had been unscriptural at any point. She was smart, was Grandma. Everyone said she could have been a teacher of mathematics if she had wanted to. She had made a wonderful record in college. But she didn't want to be anything except a good wife to Grandpa and a worthy servant of her Lord. All of her New England ancestors had been worthy servants of their Lord; that is, all she ever mentioned. Sarah thought of these things as she stood behind Grandfather Duncan looking at the roomful of people. If one thought hard about the people who were here, then one didn't notice so much that Father wasn't here.

Mrs. Rand was here. She was a nice size of a woman, cushiony to lean against. She walked light on her feet and she probably made the best fried potatoes in the world. Sarah looked eagerly at her face with its jolly freckles and pug nose framed by her flyaway crisp pale red hair. But Mrs. Rand did not look jolly tonight. She looked unstarched and heavy. Mrs. Rand always said that Sarah's father …

But Sarah turned quickly from the thought of her father to Rachel Rand, her "best friend" and the person she probably felt least near tonight of all people in the room. Rachel would think that Sarah should have gone to the funeral. No, that wasn't quite it. She would think that anybody's daughter should have gone to any father's funeral, and sooner or later she would explain it to Sarah. But to anyone else, she would declare staunchly that Sarah had a good reason for not going and she would shut her lips so firmly that you would never believe she didn't know what the reason was. Her own father had died when she was three, and her mother earned their living by sewing for people. People with the best materials took their work to Mrs. Rand. Rachel was twelve but not as tall as Sarah. A slender child with softly curling dark hair. She never did anything awkwardly. Rachel and Sarah had fun being together. Sarah felt her own smile, checked it in a grimace, looked at the other people to see if they had noticed. But they hadn't.

Mr. Ramsey, who was a lawyer and an elder in the church, was talking earnestly to Grandpa Vanderiet. Although he spoke in a low voice, he was excited and very emphatic, using his hands a great deal. Sarah drew away lest she overhear what he was saying. Mrs. Kraft and Mrs. Benson, who were neighbors who didn't care for one another but both cared for Mama, were bringing in hot coffee and iced tea. There was a great deal of food on the table. Sarah listened to each one urging everyone else to eat. But no one wanted anything himself; only if it would make the others eat, why, each one would force down a few bites. Sarah was hungry. She took a sandwich of Mrs. Benson's homemade bread.

Her mother saw the sandwich and then she saw Sarah. "Where have you been all day," she asked, but not as a question. It was more like saying, "That's right, there's you to think about too." However, Grandmother Duncan answered.

"She's been walking around with Thomas and me. We were looking at Dennis's peonies in the moonlight. Just last week he wrote about the dark red ones." She spoke lightly, and her black eyes caught Sarah's gray ones.

"Peonies and hollyhocks were his favorite flowers," said Grandfather Duncan, making "favorite" rhyme with "bright." "He always said a peony was a man's flower."

"He said dandelions were the prettiest wild flowers." Suddenly Sarah's eyes shone and she threw back her head. "Coming home from the hospital, we used to walk the long way round past Old Man Cooper's yard. It's just yellow with dandelions in the spring. Father said the Lord would probably forgive Old Man Cooper a lot of mistakes on account of his beautiful dandelions and peonies. He said anyone who raised a garden like Bill Cooper couldn't be all bad. Once—"

But Sarah's sentence snapped in mid-air and fell sharply to the floor. She had said the words her mind refused to countenance. *Bill Cooper couldn't be all bad.* Bill Cooper was responsible for the accident which had caused her father's death. People said, "Bill Cooper killed Dennis Duncan." That's what Mr. Ramsey was saying to Grandpa Vanderiet. In logical phrases of the law he was saying what half the town had sobbed for two days, "Bill Cooper should be hung." Bill, who just sat still on his own broken-down front porch, knew what they were saying.

Sarah's mother burst into fresh tears and shook in an ecstasy of grief. She had cried before, most of the time, indeed, since her husband's death, but this time it suddenly seemed as if she knew how useless her tears were, and cried for them too.

Mrs. Kraft leaned over her. "You mustn't," she said gently, sternly. "In your condition, you mustn't." But Sarah's mother had to cry.

Lucy began to cry, too, whimpering lonesomely. Tears ran down Grandma Vanderiet's face. Mrs. Rand sobbed, dry-eyed, and drew Rachel close to her. Grandmother Duncan walked over to Sarah and took the child's cold hands in her own small warm ones. She said nothing. No one seemed to be saying anything, although the room was far from still. Then Mr. Ramsey spoke out.

"Friends, I have just been saying to Mr. Vanderiet some action has to be taken about Bill Cooper. Sooner or later we have to decide whether such an irresponsible piece of human driftwood is to run at large to jeopardize other human lives."

Mr. Ramsey paused to let his words sink in. All eyes were focused exactly where he meant them to be, except Sarah's. She was looking at her shoes, thinking three thoughts at the same time: driftwood had to run at large—that's what made it driftwood; she would have to polish her shoes tomorrow; and Bill Cooper must feel awful today. The last thought held her. But Mr. Ramsey was saying important things.

"—some social responsibility. It all depends upon our point of view about Bill Cooper. Was he criminally responsible for Dennis's death and hence liable to the law? Or as an alcoholic should he be put in a psychopathic institution? I take it we agree he *is* responsible for the untimely death of our leading citizen." The last remark was not a question, but Grandma Vanderiet answered it.

"Yes, he is," she said, holding her head high like a fire horse. "He was drunk." With Grandma, drinking intoxicating beverages was high on the list of sins. Chewing tobacco, smoking, and swearing were high, too, but drinking was highest. Bill Cooper was not a habitual drunkard; he was one who went on sprees. Grandma repeated, "No one can deny he was drunk."

"The facts are known to all," Mr. Ramsey said patiently. "Dr. Duncan and his nurse, Miss Ruggles, are driving home at night from a case in the country. They are driving the doctor's own horses, Prince and Pauper, and they have just turned onto the main highway. Back of them comes Bill Cooper in a Ford. Where a good-for-nothing like Bill Cooper, whose family has been on the town for years, ever got an automobile, nobody knows. But let that pass. He sweeps round the corner, thirty miles an hour, and runs into the doctor's buggy. The buggy is thrown into the ditch, the doctor's skull fractured, as well as internal injuries. Miss Ruggles sustains some broken bones. Prince, the better of the two horses, has to be shot, and Pauper may be maimed for life."

The lawyer stopped with a gesture that shouted for justice and then wiped the perspiration from his face. No one had anything to add to the story except Grandfather Duncan, who said to Sarah, "Pauper's the better horse. From the time they were colts, Dennis said Prince never had the sense Pauper's got." No one else seemed to hear Grandfather except Mr. Ramsey, who stared at him coldly. But Grandfather was looking down at his own knotted hands.

Then Sarah's mother wiped her eyes with her wet little ball of handkerchief and spoke plaintively. "I know Dennis wouldn't want anything done in anger."

"No one is angry, Evelyn," Grandma Vanderiet said sharply. "Righteous indignation is a different thing. You might say it's a Christian virtue."

"No kind of anger is a Christian virtue," Grandpa answered resolutely. "We all know that Bill Cooper meant no harm and that he's never done any harm before."

"He's a menace," Grandma declared. "Any man who drinks is a menace. Bill Cooper has been a ne'er-do-well from the day of his birth, like his father before him. Lazy good-for-nothings, those Coopers. Sit in the sun all day while their neighbors are out in the fields." Grandma's voice was rising in crescendo. "Over and over again, Dennis befriended them. And now—and now—" But her voice had reached its highest pitch and could go no further even if she had the words. She turned to Grandpa with a look that said, "Now you take up where I left off." She often nudged Grandpa into speech with that look, but this time he did not take up.

Mr. Ramsey turned to Grandpa, too, but when Grandpa kept right on looking at nobody and saying nothing, Mr. Ramsey spoke out.

"None of us can set himself up to fathom the mind of the Almighty. We don't know why God allowed this tragic miscarriage of justice which takes the good man and leaves the sinner." This much he said in a fine sonorous voice. Then he added sharply, "But we can, and surely we ought to, keep such a thing from happening again."

"Why? Why, Mr. Ramsey?" Sarah leaned across the table toward him. "If God planned it all, why should we try to keep Bill Cooper from running down someone else? Maybe God plans for him to run over quite a lot of people." She was tense and white with wanting to know, for this was the thing which had confused her all day, which had kept her home from the funeral. *If* God planned her father's death, then they had no right to be sad. They should take it standing, as her father would say. And they would have to forgive Bill Cooper because he couldn't help being an instrument of God. Now Mr. Ramsey had put it into words, she saw at once that she had to get God straight before she could weep for her father or hate Bill Cooper. "Tell me," she begged, just as if she were alone in the room.

For the space of ten heartbeats there was no answer, and the roomful of strained faces looked blankly beyond each other, staring at the time-old question of untimely death. But such stark silence was too loud to bear. Grandma Vanderiet spoke. "People have to use common sense, Sarah. Even if we cannot completely know the mind of God, we can feel pretty sure that He doesn't want a menace like Bill Cooper jeopardizing the lives of Christian men and women."

Almost everyone looked gratefully at Grandma, not for what she said but for the asperity and assurance in her voice. After standing on the brink of an Answer, it was comfortable to be safely back among their own accustomed doubts and conclusions. Mr. Ramsey nodded approvingly. But Grandpa did not nod approval; his face worked; there was a thing he had to say. His words came out in little spurts.

"God has a plan, all right. A plan for each of us and a plan for Dennis. He has a plan for all creation, and the whole evolutionary process is part of His plan. It moves toward something. I believe that those who put themselves in His hands, dedicated to finding His will and carrying it out, will find there are no accidents in their lives. I think that in some way Dennis has finished what he came into the world to accomplish and God let him go on to more important things in a less hampered sphere. Missing him is our cross, but we have to take it up with confidence." It was plain, Sarah thought, that he had taken it up with confidence, although his share of this particular cross might turn out to be the heavy end.

Mr. Ramsey wasn't one to be turned aside from what he felt to be the main point of the discussion. He stepped into the middle of the room, his right hand thrust under his left coat lapel, as if he might be about to address a jury. "Friends and neighbors," he began slowly. "In humility this family has to accept their cross and carry it according to the will of God." That took care of God, and he could take a sharper tone with worldly affairs. "Part of their cross is the necessity to deal with Bill Cooper. But the family are too near their grief to have unbiased judgment." He paused and swallowed hard. Sarah watched his Adam's apple slide up and down. She felt certain it was not his grief that Mr. Ramsey found hard to swallow. His next sentence was crisp. "Therefore, I suggest to the family that the matter be left to legal counsel." He looked fixedly at Grandpa, as if defying him to defy the law.

Grandpa defied. "God is love as well as law," he said. "We have to be fairly sure we know the will of God before we proceed." And with that he walked out of the room—and out of the house. Sarah knew from experience that probably he'd gone off someplace to pray, maybe out in the country. Maybe he could get an answer in five minutes, and then again maybe he might be gone all night. By that time Bill Cooper might be locked up. She looked quickly at the other faces. They seemed to be agreeing with Mr. Ramsey. Couldn't they see that he wasn't the kind to decide for God?

"Listen, everybody!" she cried out. "Listen! Father *liked* Bill Cooper. He said Old Man Cooper was smart, too smart to work in a town that didn't mind supporting him. He said Bill Cooper was smart, too, and that's why he got drunk all the time, because he was too smart to be happy doing the only kind of work he knew how to do. Oh, I can't remember what he said, only he wouldn't want Bill Cooper locked up anyplace. He's— he'd rise right up from his grave and throw a fit, Father would. Mother, Grandma, Mrs. Rand, somebody say something."

"Miss Sarah forgets that we are our brother's keeper." Mr. Ramsey looked at Sarah, but he spoke to the world at large. "People aren't safe with a man like Bill Cooper running free."

But Grandfather Duncan interrupted him. He unfolded from the chair he had slumped into and stood up taller than anyone else in the room. His face was very white under its good country tan, and his hands were shaking a little.

"I've never been one to be very sure about religion. Back in my young days I was a wild one. Dorcas can tell you that." He looked down at Grandmother for quite a moment and then he looked at the wall over Sarah's head and went on. "I drank and I caroused around the country. Worked hard enough daytimes, never lazed back on nobody, but nights I cut out high, wide, and handsome. There wasn't a barn in three counties I hadn't danced in." There was neither pride nor regret in Grandfather's voice. He was hunting slowly for the thought he would come to in a minute. "Even after I got married—and nobody thought I was such shucks of a bet for Dorcas—even after I got married I didn't settle down fast. Not until our Mary died. She died sudden of typhoid fever when she was twelve. Twelve isn't very old, but Mary was born good and understanding and she joined the church young. She felt awful bad because I never went to church with her. Now and then she'd say, 'Pop, there's an empty pew you oughta fill.' After she died, the very day of the funeral, I said to the preacher—Parson McGuire, he was—'Parson,' I said, 'Mary's place won't be empty come Sunday.' And it wasn't. Every Sunday I've been sitting in that pew." Grandfather took a long breath and then he went on. "I've heard a lot of sermons from my place in that pew. I've passed a lot of collection plates and seen a lot of baptizin'. But I haven't never yet understood

16

the scheme of salvation. Not even when they draw it on a black-board. To me it don't even make sense about God sending His Son to die for me. Maybe some of you will think I'm an infidel, but I have to say it. I don't understand about God and His way. Now to me it seems like any God smart enough to make this world, not to mention the stars beyond, is just too smart to go around killing off men like my Dennis. I think God set the world spinning and then He made man the best He knew how. And then He said, 'Look here, men. I done my best to start you off, but the rest you got to work out by yourself. Because if I keep interfering and setting you right, why, then you won't never be men. You'll just have to take your bumps and figure out your own way of doing. May take quite a spell. But some-day you'll be grown up and then you and me can talk together.' Now if my figuring is right, if it's anything like right, why, then Bill Cooper running down Dennis is just a part of the growin' up. And there ain't much use in us locking up Bill Cooper, who ain't wicked and neither is he feeble-minded. Sarey's right. Dennis wouldn't want something awful done to Bill Cooper because we know he didn't set out to do no damage. And yet Dennis was too hardheaded to want Bill Cooper left chasing around the country to run down somebody else. So maybe all I've said ain't such a lot of help after all."

Grandfather Duncan sat down after the longest speech of his life. Sarah answered him directly, unaware for a moment of anyone else's presence. "Yes, it is a help, Grandfather. It's a big help." But she stopped as suddenly as she had begun. "Although of course—if Bill Cooper wasn't an instrument of God—why, then—Bill Cooper is—is responsible for his own self." Again she stopped short, aghast at her own words. Had her grandfather rescued Bill only for her to fling him back to Mr. Ramsey? She hadn't meant to say what she'd said. The words come out of her mouth as though they welled up from some inner place without stopping to be thoughts first. Her words often did that, and startled her with what they said.

"Bill Cooper *is* liable for some kind of drastic restriction." Mr. Ramsey snapped up Sarah's words, but slowly. Everything Mr. Ramsey did, even snapping, had a premeditated quality. Sarah had an urge to go over and pound Mr. Ramsey's thin back. From some place deep her anger was rising, and it frightened her, as it always did. Grandmother Duncan, clear across the room, must have sensed its coming, a good deal as one feels a draft even before the wind begins to blow, because she left Grandfather's side and came over to the place where Sarah was standing by the table.

Sarah turned and seemed to see her for the first time. Grandmother Duncan was a little woman and all brown. Dark brown hair parted in the middle and drawn into a great knot of braids at the back of her head. Her eyes were small and black and alive. Her face was brown and the skin was smooth and fresh. Her hands, which she now clasped tightly together, were small but strong. Something flashed between grandmother and granddaughter. Then Sarah heard Mr. Ramsey going on.

"—but if the family can come to no decision, then it becomes my duty, as I see it—and no man can exceed his duty as he sees it—it becomes my duty—"

But the family of Dennis Duncan never found out exactly what became the duty of Mr. Ramsey because footsteps were heard crossing the living room; sure dignified footsteps more loved in Wheaton than any except Dennis's own. Dr. Enrique Rivera stood in the doorway smiling at them.

"Good evening," he said gravely in spite of his smile. "I thought I'd drop by to see how Mrs. Duncan is feeling." Sarah liked the way he took her mother's hand and bowed low over it, as if he were greeting a queen, and then kept his fingers lightly on her pulse as he spoke to the rest of the people. "It's a very beautiful night outside. The stars surpass themselves. Just the other night as we walked home late, Dennis said to me that if he had his life to live over he thought maybe he'd be an astronomer."

Sarah thought that Dr. Rivera never looked handsomer than tonight. You would hardly guess he was such an old man, but the whole town knew he was half a century old because there had been a big reception on last Midsummer's Day, which was his birthday. He did not look old. His hair was scarcely gray at all, and he had a straight proud way of standing. He was neither fat nor thin, but rather wide and solid. Some people said he was a member of the Spanish royal family. Others said he was from New Mexico. But no one ever asked him. He wasn't the kind one asked. More than twenty years ago he had come to the Wheaton hospital direct from postgraduate work in Vienna. Now he was senior surgeon, and people came from all around, from big hospitals and far cities, to see him operate. His fingers were not long, as you would think, but very strong and quick. They were something else, too, but Sarah could not find the word "compassionate," so she only smiled at him. Everyone was smiling at him now, or to themselves.

"I always thought maybe Dennis should have been a painter," Grandmother Duncan said to Dr. Rivera, as if they were old friends instead of having met only that very day. "I declare I never saw a boy so quick to see pictures in everything. He was always wishing he had a paintbrush."

"He never did paint much, though," Grandfather Duncan said. "We've got some things he crayoned off when he was a boy. Seemed like after he got into high school there never was no time."

"He was always urging Sarah to draw," Mama said. "He thought she had talent."

"He'd have made a first-rate cook," Mrs. Rand said, smiling broadly. "How handy that man was around a kitchen!"

"I know he'd rather sing than eat," Mrs. Benson said. "If anybody else could sing 'My Ain Folk' the way he could, they'd have gone on the stage."

"My! He'd like to be hearing you say all these things about him." Grandmother Duncan looked proud, almost happy.

"Who says he isn't hearing?" Dr. Rivera asked quietly.

The looks which answered him were slightly startled, not because of his words but because he, who was not a religious man, had said them. But Dr. Rivera went right on. "Men like Dennis never die. You should know that."

Grandma Vanderiet nodded vigorously, but Sarah had a vague feeling that Dr. Rivera's words and Grandma's nod meant something very different. She wished she could ask Dr. Rivera more about his words. But he left no time for asking. He looked at his watch and said, "Mrs. Duncan needs a good night's rest, and I think"—his smile seemed meant especially for each person present— "that it's time for the neighbors to go home."

The women began to scurry around pleasantly, picking up dishes and hunting their hats. Mrs. Kraft bent over Lucy, who had fallen asleep with her head in her mother's lap.

"Let me take you upstairs, darling."

"I want Mama to go with me," Lucy said with sleepy stubbornness.

"Mama can't climb so many steps, darling. It isn't good for her. Put your arms around my neck and I'll pickaback you."

Sarah found herself standing by Rachel. A strangeness was between them. Even their words came over a distance.

Rachel said, "What will you be doing tomorrow?"

Sarah answered, "I'm going to wash my hair."

"Then I'll come help you dry it." After that they felt more natural and began to talk.

Mrs. Kraft came back saying that Lucy was sound asleep before she was undressed. Everybody was about to go home when suddenly Mr. Ramsey spoke out. He had been talking to Grandfather Duncan over in the corner while Dr. Rivera talked to Grandmother Duncan. Grandfather looked worn. Grandmother looked beaming.

"Friends, everyone here wants to do the will of Dennis Duncan, but we aren't just sure what Dr. Duncan might want. Now it seems to me—"

But Dr. Rivera interrupted Mr. Ramsey with a bow. Dr. Rivera could do that and make it seem as if he'd paid the interrupted person a compliment. "Thank you, Mr. Solicitor." Dr. Rivera always called Mr. Ramsey "Mr. Solicitor," although Mr. Ramsey had told him a thousand times that Americans said "lawyer." "I know what is in your mind, Mr. Solicitor. In all your minds. And that was really one reason I came over. You want to know if Dr. Duncan left any messages."

Now they all pushed nearer the table where Dr. Rivera stood beside Mama. He looked down at Mama and drew up a chair for her. "Dennis did speak, Evelyn. He spoke three times. When we lifted him from the stretcher he gained consciousness for a moment and he said, 'Miss Ruggles. What about Miss Ruggles?' I told him Miss Ruggles was hurt but not seriously, and he lost consciousness before I could say more. A few minutes later he began to mutter to himself. I was leaning over him with the stethoscope and got every word. He kept saying, 'Been drinking again … he'd been drinking … but he didn't mean to … friend of mine, Bill Cooper … friend of mine.' And the last time he spoke, just an instant before he died, he was fully conscious. He looked right at me and spoke in a strong full voice. 'Sarah's got to be something … something grand,' he said. 'An artist, maybe … wonderful.' Those were his last words, Sarah, and I want you to know that he said them with a clear mind and a happy light in his eyes."

Sarah stood alone, still and white, her eyes burning darkly, her whole body at attention. And yet not tensely. She was like the earth, long parched, waiting for the rain which, when it came, brought all the answers. Everyone looked at her, but this time even Grandmother Duncan made no move to go to her. She had no need of them. Besides, her mother was speaking to the doctor, hurt incredulity in her tones.

"Did he have no word, no message for me? After all—"

"Why, Evelyn," Dr. Rivera reproached her gently. "At his first stir of consciousness I told him we had sent for you, that you were on your way, that you would be coming in through the door any minute. His eyes were on the door when he died."

It seemed to Sarah that her mother should have known, without Dr. Rivera's saying it, because everyone knew that Dennis Duncan thought he had the world's one perfect wife. He never wanted her any different, even when she charged too many things at the store or forgot an important message. When Sarah was a little girl her deepest wish was to be like her mother because her father loved her mother so, but one day when they were all sitting together on the front porch, talking, she suddenly realized that she could never be like her mother because she was already like her father. Now her mother was weeping violently again, crying so hard that the table shook.

"I was too late, too late."

Sarah had a quick feeling, less a thought than an intuition, and entirely sympathetic, that her mother never cried so hard when she was alone as she did when someone was around.

Dr. Rivera nodded to the roomful of people. "She must go to bed." He turned to Mrs. Rand. "A half glass of water, please."

Everyone moved toward the door. Mr. Ramsey cleared his throat. "About Bill Cooper..." he began.

But Grandmother Duncan took the sentence in her own teeth. "About Bill Cooper," she repeated with almost lyrical finality, "my son has said the last word. Dennis called Bill Cooper his friend, and one doesn't deal out a jail sentence to a friend."

"I thought you'd feel that way, all of you," said the doctor without lifting his eyes from the glass into which he was dropping something from a tiny bottle. "I thought you'd want Bill to have a chance to rectify a great mistake. And he couldn't do that amid the recriminations of some of the good people of this town."

"Nevertheless, he is in this town," said Mr. Ramsey shortly, speaking directly to the doctor.

"*Was*, Mr. Solicitor. Was in this town." The doctor straightened up and looked at the other man tentatively, as if he were debating a diagnosis.

"What do you mean?"

"A little while ago I went to Bill Cooper's house. He was sitting on a stump outside the kitchen door, all slumped over, shivering and saying to himself, 'I liked the Doc a heap and Doc, he liked me.' Old Cooper hobbled up and down the yard with his big knotty cane, so mad that he choked on his own profanity, and every time he passed Bill he hit him with his cane. The womenfolk were gathered in the kitchen, sniffling about their terrible disgrace."

"The old woman was always sending Dennis funny little presents," Mama said, so much to herself that Dr. Rivera did not feel interrupted.

"I called them all into the kitchen and talked to them. Then I sent Bill away. Away from Wheaton." He spoke the last two sentences in a stern tone, almost clipping his words.

"For how long?" asked Mr. Ramsey caustically.

Dr. Rivera looked steadily at his questioner. "For ten years," he said shortly.

"And what makes you think he will stay for ten years away from the town which has always been his home and his chief support?" Mr. Ramsey had an ungentle patience in his voice.

"For one thing, I gave him enough money to go quite a distance," the doctor replied with an elaborate gentleness in his own tone, "and for another, I told him to stay away."

Grandmother Duncan gave a deep sigh. "That's fine," she said simply.

But Mr. Ramsey had not finished the prosecution. "I take it, Dr. Rivera, that you do not know it is something of a criminal offense to send a criminal wittingly into another locality where he may endanger other lives?"

"You don't say!" replied the doctor with so convincing an accent of alarm that Sarah was taken in for an instant. Then the doctor smiled at Mr. Ramsey and his smile held no guile.

"You have my word for it, Mr. Solicitor, Bill Cooper will not make his tragic mistake twice." However, it was the doctor's gesture rather than his words which brought the discussion to a close. He raised his hand, he lowered his hand, and the matter was finished. Sarah thought he looked like a king, or even an emperor. He gave Mr. Ramsey a look which sent him toward the door, not hurrying too much nor forgetting to tell Mama good night, but nevertheless out the door. Only he had to stop at the door because Grandpa Vanderiet was coming in. Grandpa came in looking happy, as if everything were all right now. Well, it was all right now, but how could he know? He was surprised to see Dr. Rivera, and he still didn't know what had been decided. But plainly enough he knew that the will of God was going to prevail. He asked Grandma if she wanted to stay all night again, and she said no, the doctor was giving Mama something to make her sleep.

To Sarah, Dr. Rivera said, "It's a long pull, my child, but you'll make it."

Sarah knew what he meant. Her life was dedicated now. It was something like becoming a missionary or a nun. You were set apart with a purpose. By rights there should be some kind of ceremony. She would have a ceremony! All by herself after she got to her room, she would have a dedication ceremony. She thought rapidly. She wished she had a silver cross, some kind of cross. To be sure, Grandma Vanderiet would say that a cross was popish and that a Protestant had no reason to traffic with Catholic things. Still, the Episcopalians used crosses and they were certainly Protestants because they came to the united services last summer. Anyhow, she liked the idea of a cross. In fact, she often wished she owned a slender gold cross to wear inside her dress on a chain. It was aristocratic in a kind of spiritual way. Now that she was dedicated, maybe she could get a cross someday. Tonight, at least, she would make a cross. She would make it out of two lead pencils covered with white tissue paper and hang it from her window shade, and it would look very beautiful in the moonlight. Maybe she should light a candle. There was a fancy candle on the upstairs hall table which might be borrowed. She wished she could put on her white dress, but a white nightgown would be safer in case, just in case, someone should come to the door.

Her room was a long, low room under the eaves, windows facing west and south. By leaving the door open into the hall she could also get any breeze from the east. But tonight she shut the door and undressed quickly. Almost surreptitiously she took out her best nightgown of fine muslin with narrow blue ribbon threaded through the embroidery of its square Dutch neck and short puffed sleeves. It felt cool against her body, cool and sweet like a scentless rose which smelled only of sunshine. Or did sunshine really have a smell? She stood still for a moment trying to remember, her gray eyes dark with the elation of her grief and the new purpose. Long brown braids hung over her shoulders. Oddly enough, the rather angular face with its wide mobile mouth, delicate nostrils, and high forehead looked younger than usual tonight, for all of its whiteness. She was very tired; too tired to know that she was tired, so she hurried to make the cross. She tied it together with a bit of blue ribbon pulled from the sleeve of her nightgown. Then she hung it from the window shade and ran the shade to the top of the window so that she could see only the cross against the night. After turning out the light she set the burning candle in its blue candleholder on top of her plump Bible on the window sill and stepped back to admire the effect. Moonlight slanting through the elm spilled splotches of brightness around the room. The room might have been the cell of a saint, she thought, except that there were a great many photographs on one wall. Beginning tomorrow she would live a more austere life. Tonight was the night of her dedication to Art in the name of her own father.

A knock sounded at her door. She blew out the candle, removed the Bible, and said, "Come in."

It was Grandmother Duncan.

"I thought I'd like to sit here for a few minutes—if you don't mind." Grandmother looked lonesome, although her smile was not sad.

"I don't mind," Sarah said gravely. Indeed, she rather liked the idea of her father's mother coming to see her just before the dedication. "Shall I turn on the light?"

"Oh no. No, indeed. I came because I knew it would be quiet and—and peaceful in your room. Did you ever notice how one room can be quieter than another even when there's no sound in either?" She laughed a little uncertainly. It was a very sweet laugh, Sarah thought.

"You can see the moonlight," Sarah said. "That's my favorite window, winter or summer."

"Climb in bed, child, and I'll just sit a few minutes." Grandmother drew the low rocker near the window and looked out. Sarah got into bed and pulled the sheet over her. The sheets were freshly washed and smelled of sunshine too. Sunshine *did* smell. But Grandmother was talking in a very low, far-off voice, almost as if she were sitting outdoors ... in the upper branches of the elm. Grandmother would be all right sitting in the elm. She was little and brown and the tree would not be disturbed by her. She was talking about the room Father had when he was a boy on the farm. It was a west room too. It had an old walnut bed of her grandmother's—how many "greats" would that be?—and Father grew too long for the bed, so they had to make new sidepieces for it and get a longer mattress. ... Funny about Father, he'd never be an old man now ... but he'd be the father of a very great artist and everyone would know him for a hundred years. ... Funny about Bill Cooper. Since he didn't have to go to jail he could live to be an old man and maybe have a straggly beard and a choked-off laugh with a few high snorts just like his father's. Funny about Grandmother with a white cross perched jauntily on her knot of dark braids.

Grandmother wasn't saying anything that needed to be answered so Sarah didn't answer.

Three

B y the end of August, Sarah felt that she had been studying painting all of her life and that Miss Moseley, instead
of being a contemporary of her grandmother's, had been
the companion of Titian, Rembrandt, Constable, Giotto, and
Leonardo da Vinci, all of whom must have grown up together
in some remote, convergent past when it was God's custom to
speak more directly to those whom He had singled out for
greatness. It never occurred to Sarah to doubt that she belonged
in this high succession, but she did sometimes wonder why a
soul so laved in sunsets as her own should have such difficulty
in matching the plain green of ordinary lawn grass.

But even the intricacies of color, under the direction of a
teacher who believed that the artist's best compliment to Nature
was to match its shades realistically a good deal as a dressmaker matches thread to goods, were less confusing than the so-
called simple matter of drawing a Grecian urn. When at last
Miss Moseley's oily encouragement turned rancid in sarcasm
and she told her earnest pupil that she might do better if she
would bring a water bucket to school and draw an outline she
was more familiar with, Sarah took her serenely at her word.
She brought the pail. She set the pail on the drawing stand. She
took her place at the drawing board. Certainly, as Miss Moseley
said, she knew by heart what a pail looked like, and besides, she
had the pail to look at.

"Now draw what you see," said Miss Moseley, clicking her
teeth into place with a cheerful sucking noise which became for
Sarah in after years the verbalization of a drawing pencil.

But Sarah could not draw what she saw because what she knew about a pail got in her way. Obviously, a pail sets flat on the table, so Sarah drew a straight line as a base. Obviously, since she could see into the pail, the top curves made an elliptical outline which she reproduced with geometrical exactitude. In trying to figure out what was wrong with the curve she realized that the bucket was not so squat as she had made it look on the horizontal rectangle of her paper. Surreptitiously she sidled up to the bucket and measured its height with her pencil, then its width at base and top. Out with the eraser as she quickly computed a scale for her drawing. Miss Moseley was not one to allow her pupils to waste paper. Let them erase and redraw until the paper wore through.

The drawing class was a daily affair, nine to eleven, and Sarah never skipped. It never occurred to her to stay home even for the all-day homecoming picnic, although she was very fond of watching old settlers greet each other. Grandmother Duncan was paying for these lessons, and Sarah owed it to her to be faithful. Besides, she was dedicated to her task of becoming a great artist.

Twice a week in the afternoon there was painting. Because it was summer and college was not in session, Sarah was the only member of the beginners' painting class. At the first lesson Miss Moseley gave, impromptu, bits from her lecture on "Color in Nature," just as if Sarah were in a class of college freshmen. Then she set Sarah to doing stereotypes of fruit and flowers. Evidently the colors appeared brighter to pupil than to teacher: the two could never agree on the color of an orange. One day Sarah brought to the painting class a strange vegetable called an eggplant. She felt a glow when she held the lovely smooth-skinned oval in her hands and had planned all night on how she would mix that luscious blue-red, more-than-purple, less-than-brown color. But Miss Moseley did not care for the eggplant. It was not a fruit and it did not go with flowers. Yes, some people painted vegetables, but largely as a pose, she said. Who would want vegetables hanging on a parlor wall?

It never occurred to Sarah to be discouraged. Miss Moseley's criticisms were so thorough and so varied that she felt she must be making progress or she could not merit so many helpful suggestions. There was no one to argue with. No one except Ernestina Tupper. Miss Tupper, aged nineteen, was a fragile-looking blonde who did canoes by marshy shores and moon-risings over limpid lakes. Miss Moseley was grooming Ernestina to enter art school in the city. Sometimes Ernestina had an impulse to help the long-legged girl with the long brown braids and the long inept fingers, but she always stifled the impulse because she believed that the way to get ahead was to mind one's own business and let as many sink as couldn't swim. And yet Ernestina did one kindness for Sarah. She said, "When you draw jugs at home, paint them. The paint gives you a kind of satisfaction." The paints did more than that. They made the jugs look more like jugs. Sarah would have liked to paint the jugs freehand without outlining first in pencil, but Miss Moseley did not believe in such haphazard procedure.

It was Grandma Vanderiet who shared most deeply Sarah's faith in her own destiny. Not that Grandma was an artist. But she had respect for Miss Moseley's thoroughness and high morality which, to Grandma, were qualities heaven always blessed. Miss Moseley had been graduated from art school and had come to Wheaton when Bryan College was founded. As a woman she seemed to have more than her share of joints, and yet she also had a kind of high-collared style about her. She had never been ill a day in her life, which she felt to be a personal achievement; hers was an upright character never made vulnerable by pain. Both she and Grandma taught Sunday-school classes, Grandma teaching the boys because she could maintain discipline, and Miss Moseley teaching the girls because it seemed as if girls should be exposed to art. Miss Moseley brought a great deal of art into her class mostly by way of the Perry pictures, which any girl could surely afford.

Grandma said to Miss Moseley in front of Sarah, "Our oldest granddaughter has real talent, don't you think?"

Miss Moseley said, "Her father was a brilliant man. But one has to develop a feeling for outline before she can make free with the paintbox."

Whenever her painting took more from Sarah than it returned, she went home and played the piano. The piano stood in the corner of the parlor, which was a comfortable room in spite of the spindle-legged matched furniture. The fireplace had blue tiles brought all the way from Italy, and there was a lovely vase more than three feet tall which one of Father's grateful patients had bought at the Thieves' Market in Peking; it was the color of American Beauty roses. There were a good many pictures on the walls, some good and some merely expensively framed, and a hand-painted skillet depicting a jolly farmscape. A huge fern stood in the front windows; its leaves nearly touched the floor. One had to be careful not to touch the points of the leaves or they would die. Sarah liked the room's rather stiff orderliness.

She loved the piano. The old rosewood case which had once belonged to Jenny Lind had brand-new works made to order for Sarah's tenth birthday present. Mama said that it was the most ridiculously expensive birthday present ever given to a child who wasn't a member of royalty or a millionaire and that she would object roundly except that she knew Dennis would get as much pleasure out of a good piano as ever Sarah could. He did. He played by ear, or by guess, he would say, so that when Sarah propped a duet in front of him and found him the key and gave him the first bar, he could hobble along with her on the first round, overtake her on the second, and on the third embellish the score. The private delight and public pride was the Overture to *William Tell*. After her father's death, a single chord of it would bring back to Sarah his living presence.

When her father discovered that, at the age of four, Sarah could play by ear also, he promptly took her to Miss Lillie

Tower, who taught music for music's sake and not for the sake of developing a prodigy. When Sarah got to be a big girl, seven or eight years old, people asked her to play for various occasions. Usually she went without comment, much as another child might run an errand to the grocery store. Compliments were just the things people said after music was played. For her, life came as it came. Toward seasons, weather, and the gifts of Nature she had the calm acceptance of a meadow. After her father's death, however, she seemed suddenly conscious of music as a thing apart, necessary to her like the food she ate. Because she had less time, being a serious student of drawing and painting, she looked forward to her hours at the piano.

But drawing and painting and practicing were not her only interests during the summer. One day in July, Rachel said, "I think your mother is going to have a baby." The two girls were shelling peas on the Duncans' back porch when she said it.

Sarah looked at Rachel in horrified amazement. Then she got up and went into the house where her mother was ironing. Yes, her mother did bulge a great deal. Strange she hadn't noticed it before. She went back to Rachel and the peas and the amazement.

"Yes, she is, I guess." Then after a pause, "I never saw a baby who didn't have a father."

"I—I thought babies had to have fathers or—or something was the matter," Rachel said without looking up. "I don't know what would be the matter because of course a woman has to have a baby when God sends it, but Helen Caldwell's hired girl cried terribly when her sister had a baby without a father."

Rachel sounded unhappy. She had wanted to spare Sarah this thing which she did not understand.

"Babies do have to have fathers," Sarah said calmly. "My father was the baby's father. He told me all about fathers a long time ago. Well, about a year ago." And then she told Rachel what she knew. She was not embarrassed. She used technical terms, but she did not know they were technical. They were the words her father had used.

"So that's the way it is," said Rachel raptly. "It's a very good plan. And you'd think that people would tell people." Sudden resentment came into her tone. "Why, you've known for a long time."

"I guess you were gone to your cousins' when my father explained a lot of things to me, and after that I never thought of it."

"Helen Caldwell knows. Quite a lot of the girls know things they don't let us in on." Rachel spoke gently, but the pea pods snapped under her fingers.

"Our baby will be something special," said Sarah eagerly. "Probably he will be a great man. A statesman or an inventor or a reformer or maybe the greatest doctor in the world. He'll be about six and a half feet tall."

"How do you know it will be a boy? That's something you can't be sure of until it's born." Rachel could speak with authority here.

"Ours will be a boy," said Sarah firmly.

Everyone seemed to share Sarah's conviction. That same afternoon Sarah said to her mother more casually than she felt, "Do you think the new baby will be a boy?"

Her mother burst into tears and hid her face in the roller towel which hung in the kitchen. "It's got to be a boy," she sobbed. "It's got to be, it's got to be."

Grandma Vanderiet came in at that moment, her arms full of parcels, which she dropped onto the kitchen table. "Of course it will be a boy. I've prayed every day. And you have all the signs, Evelyn, so hush that crying."

She patted her daughter gently on the shoulder, and after that Mama cried more comfortably and Grandma chatted more cheerfully. "Look, I got a bargain on a piece of Viyella for little flannel nightgowns." From one of the packages she shook out the creamy softness. Sarah loved the feel of it and buried her face in its folds.

"I can featherstitch," she said.

That night she began to help make baby clothes. Her stitches were small and even, although she held the needle awkwardly and did not use a thimble. She liked sewing these fine things. When a garment was finished it was finished. Nothing to erase, nothing to wish you had done differently.

The baby was born in early December on the night of the eighth grade party. Her mother had seemed as usual when Sarah kissed her good-by. The house had seemed as usual: warm, comfortable, but always waiting expectantly for someone to come in, someone tall and laughing whose clothes smelled vaguely of pipe smoke and ether and sunshine. When Sarah came home from the party at ten o'clock excitement met her at the door, although not a soul answered when she called, "Hello." No one downstairs, no one upstairs. Lucy's bed had been slept in, but there was no Lucy. No Anna in the kitchen. But Sarah wasn't frightened, although the thought of the baby did not come at once. The house seemed perked up.

Then Anna came in the back door carrying a jug of buttermilk borrowed from a neighbor. Nursing mothers should drink buttermilk. The fact that Mrs. Duncan would be two weeks in the hospital had not yet clicked. Anna was like that. Her ideas came one at a time and stuck. She was solid and Polish and valuable.

Now Anna hugged Sarah roundly. "Praise be to God, she's gone to the hospital. Dr. Rivera came for her himself. Your grandma's got Lucy over at her house."

Suddenly Sarah's throat went dry. Women did die when they had babies. Mrs. Wilcox had died and left four children besides the new one. Mothers died in books, or at least there were an awful lot of children in books whose beautiful young mothers had died giving them birth. Suppose Mama wasn't as well as she looked and the pink in her cheeks was some kind of fever. Or suppose the baby was born dead and Mama just turned her face to the wall and died of a broken heart. All the dire possibilities came flapping around Sarah's head like a flock of mad crows beating their silly wings over her. She reached out to Anna, who drew her into her arms just as if she had been Lucy.

"There, there. Everything's all right. Your mama's good and husky and none of her babies give her much trouble." The words were reassuring, or would have been had Sarah really heard them, but she was thinking that Anna's hands did not feel red and rough the way they looked.

"I wonder how big he'll be!" she said, drawing away from Anna. "The Duncans are all big men."

The telephone rang. Sarah ran to it, grabbed up the receiver, said "Hello," and then was afraid to listen. She thrust the receiver into Anna's hands but stood so close that she heard every word.

Dr. Rivera's voice said, "I'd like to speak to Miss Sarah."

So Sarah took the telephone, feeling neither afraid nor excited now, only knowing it was her task to take the message.

"I want to tell you," said the resonant voice with the elusive accent, "that you have a baby brother and that your mother is doing very well."

Childhood reclaimed Sarah. "How big is he?" she sang into the telephone. "And does he look like—like Father?"

Dr. Rivera's laugh made the telephone buzz in her ear. "He doesn't look like much of anyone yet, and he weighs three and a half pounds. But he's a fine baby."

He still weighed three and a half pounds two weeks later when he came from the hospital. And he was not beautiful. His little face looked old and puzzled. He had practically no forehead; his thick black hair grew almost out of his eyebrows. His nose was like a little beak, and his toothless mouth twisted into meaningless grimaces. Not even Lucy's warmest friends said he was pretty, but Grandma Vanderiet said she had seen other babies with practically no forehead who grew to be very smart men. However, Rachel told Sarah privately that Mrs. Kraft had said that imbeciles had no foreheads either. There was nothing

34

of the gossip in Rachel. She was just standing shoulder to shoulder with Sarah, letting her know the worst first, protecting her as a bantam hen might protect a large and trusting gosling. Sarah went right to Dr. Rivera.

It was a hot day. She walked the twenty-odd blocks to his office and then would not let the office girl send her in ahead of her turn. She wished Miss Ruggles were still there, but after she got over the accident Miss Ruggles had gone to California where her brother was a doctor in an orthopedic hospital. When Sarah finally proposed the question of the new baby's imbecility to Dr. Rivera, he said, "Nonsense, my child. He's as bright as a new penny and as strong as a little zebra. He's just little, that's all. Small bones, small hands, small feet, small all over. He won't be a big man, but he'll be a brainy one—if I know babies."

"He won't—be a big man—even when he's grown up?" That was worse, if possible, than not being quite bright. Real men were *big* men. Her father was a big man and his father was a big man. Duncans were big men. Bigness was part of being Duncan and great and good and different.

Seeing the look in Sarah's eyes, Dr. Rivera answered gravely: "A big share of the world's work is done by little men, my dear. There were Napoleon and Stephen A. Douglas, for instance. Certainly in these days we are too civilized to think that size matters. Or race or color or personal idiosyncrasies. Quality is the only thing to care about; texture of mind and personality."

Sarah nodded, her eyes wide and honest. She could see that what the doctor was saying was eminently true, but her heart could not give up its image. She felt sure that the baby counted on being a big man. She could see it in the way he waved his fists and hear it in the demanding tones of his cry, which was not high and shrill like most babies', but full of authority. The hard thing would be to make him understand that he would never be a big man. She thanked Dr. Rivera and went home.

No one said anything definite about a name for the new baby until he was three weeks old and Grandma and Grandpa

Vanderiet came over for Sunday dinner. Mama stood beside the baby carriage looking down and talking baby talk.

"Evelyn," Grandma said with asperity, "I never have believed in baby talk and I do not think you ought to use it on the child."

"She's only funning," Lucy commented. "She talks that way to him all the time and he likes it."

"It's foolish," Grandma insisted. "He's a human being and he deserves to be talked to like a human being. I'm sure I never talked baby talk to you."

"And I never talked baby talk to Sarah, either," Mama answered with a kind of pout which Sarah always thought was rather sweet. "But I did talk baby talk to Lucy, and I must say that Lucy's just as bright as Sarah. I don't think it makes a bit of difference."

"Maybe it makes a difference to the baby!" Sarah exclaimed in sudden inspiration. "Maybe *he* feels foolish even if we don't." Baby talk made her vaguely unhappy—like when a new girl at school wants to walk with her arm around your waist to show you are chums.

"It's time he had a name," said Grandpa, who felt that changing a subject was often as good as settling a matter.

"He has a name," Mama said, still pouting prettily. "There's only one name we could call him."

"What's that?" Sarah asked in sudden apprehension.

"What could it be but Dennis?" A rapt ecstasy shone in Mama's face.

"Oh no !" cried Sarah in an agony of protest. "You wouldn't! There's only one Dennis, and he was *Father.*"

All of them were surprised at her vehemence. "Don't be silly," Mama said, a little angry. "It's proper to name a son for his father."

"Not when he isn't like his father," cried Sarah. "Not when" her face was contorted with emotion— "not when he's little." Grandpa rose to smooth out this matter. He walked over to

Sarah and took her clenched hand. "Why, Sarah, he's going to be a fine big man just like his father."

"He's the image of his father now," Mama insisted. "Every expression, every movement, is Dennis himself."

"He's nothing like Father. Oh, I can't bear it. *I can't bear it.*" And Sarah, who never cried, ran weeping from the room. She went to her own room and threw herself on the bed, sobbing wildly, uncontrollably. Grandma went up to reason with her, but Sarah was beyond reason. If they didn't understand, there was nothing to say. Grandma went downstairs and sent Grandpa up. Usually Grandpa and Sarah understood one another very well. Grandpa said, "It means a lot to your mother to give the boy his father's name."

"But he won't want it, the baby won't. He'll know it isn't his." Sarah's face went deeper into the wet pillow as the heavy sobs twisted her body. Grandpa stood helpless beside her. These were no ordinary tears. He went downstairs quietly, but he couldn't go to the table where his wife and Evelyn and Lucy were eating dinner. He walked up and down the sun porch. When he went back upstairs Sarah was still crying passionately, as helpless in her own protesting misery as a young forest torn by cyclone.

He went downstairs again. "I am going to call Dr. Rivera," he said to the women.

"Nonsense, let her cry it out," Mama answered, not unkindly. "No one is going to tell me what to name my own child."

"She's been working too hard all fall," Grandma said. "A good cry will do her good. And then maybe she ought to let up on her art lessons for a while."

But Grandpa called Dr. Rivera. "I wish you would come right away. Sarah is crying too hard."

Dr. Rivera came right away. He went to Sarah's room alone. He pulled a chair beside her bed and spoke sternly. "Sarah, the baby won't be named Dennis. I can promise you that. Dennis isn't his name."

A deep sigh swept the child, although her sobs continued in racking spasms.

"There was only one Dennis and he is gone," the firm voice went on. "We have to let him go. We can't keep waiting for the sound of his footsteps, his voice. I know how it is with you, because I find myself waiting too."

Slowly Sarah sat up. Her face was swollen; even her long braids of hair were heavily spent. There seemed nothing of a child left in her.

"Maybe it would help if you knew more, and not less, about how great your loss is, Sarah." He sat for a while saying nothing. Sarah's sobs were still rhythmic and rasping, but she had ceased to cry. "When your father died, you lost more than a parent; you lost your security, your foundation. Your father stood between you and the hardness of the world. Now there is no one between you and extremity, between you and the precarious universe. Maybe someday you will find security again in the love of a man. I hope so, because a strong woman like you needs reassurance. One shoulder to lay her head on should be every woman's birthright, peasant or queen. But only the strongest will be of any use to you." He paused and then added, "You'll be in great distress if you accept a substitute."

Sarah's eyes, small and dark from weeping, clung to his face. She felt as if she scarcely needed his words to take in his ideas.

The doctor went on. "When you lost Dennis, you lost the one person who could have cut the underbrush for you and helped you to find your way in life—your own particular way. Now you'll be thrown back on trial and error. Your kind makes a lot of mistakes because a sense of duty nags at you and pulls you off the path which your own sound instinct might direct. Your father would have saved you from doing too many good deeds for other people before you found the one best thing which you were meant to do. It will be almost a miracle if you ever find your own way."

"Oh, I'll find it," said Sarah in a vibrant whisper. "Nothing will keep me from being an artist, you know. Nothing."

"That's what you think now, my child. At twelve. But you have other talents, too, and these will tug at you. And men will be in love with you, and sometimes you will have weak moments when it seems a better thing to fall into the pattern of life about you than to wait and work for something you cannot name."

Sarah shook her head and smiled. She felt very certain of her calling and just as certain of her single-mindedness. Both the doctor and the child sat silent, having reached the limit of all that words could do for them. The doctor went to the window and stood looking out for a long time. But Sarah did not know it was a long time because the moment was as full as a brimming cave after rain. When he turned to speak again, his words had more than their usual faintly foreign accent. "You will not be alone," he said shortly. "There is a brooding. Something which gives succor to those humans who will have its help." The brown, lined face showed sharply against the twilight window. Then a hint of irony crept into his voice. "But I would not spend much time—not too much time—at Grandma's church hunting for Grandma's God. Your grandpa, now, he may have an inkling."

Sarah did not answer. She knew what he meant. Quite suddenly she knew what he meant, although up to that moment she had never had a thought which Grandma could call unorthodox. He meant that most people were too easy about God. He meant that you deserved darkness unless you demanded light. But that sounded more like Grandpa quoting from a book or something. She lay back on the pillow, too tired to think further.

She stayed in bed three days and she ate everything that Anna brought to her and she slept a great deal and she thought about painting the furniture in her room and planting a garden next spring. And maybe getting out her dolls again and making them one more set of new clothes and then giving them all to Lucy. It would be fun to make the clothes. The third day the overt, physical sign of womanhood appeared, and Mama called Dr. Rivera to say, "You see, *that's* what all the trouble was about."

Dr. Rivera said lightly, "Women know everything." Then the mocking tone came into his voice. "Who shall say when the psychological precipitates the physical?"

Mama said, "I beg pardon?"

Dr. Rivera said, "Don't forget to give young Archibald two teaspoons of cool water three times a day."

Archibald was the name they had decided on for the baby. He was named after Grandpa Vanderiet for so many good reasons that Mama believed she herself had thought of naming him for her own father. Grandpa Vanderiet was self-conscious about saying the name himself. He felt a bit fatuous bending over a crib to call a squirming little morsel of humanity by his own well-worn and respectable name. He covered his embarrassment by calling the baby "Baldy," and the nickname stuck, much to Mama's horror. Lucy liked it; she said it all the time. "Look, Mama, Baldy has his whole fist in his mouth.".... "Baldy's mad. Anna laid him on his tummy and he's got his head clear up off the pillow, just screaming." Anna picked up the name from Lucy, and Grandma slipped quite unconsciously into the growing desecration.

Sarah wasn't always begging to hold her brother the way Lucy did. Lucy never came into the house without rushing to see whether Baldy was awake and trying to make him smile, while the truth about Sarah was that sometimes she scarcely thought of the baby for days at a time. She was learning to paint and draw.

Four

One morning when Lucy had the sniffles which Mama thought might be the beginning of measles or whooping cough which the baby would be sure to catch, Dr. Rivera came to call. Sarah was painting on the sun porch. She was absorbed in trying to make a bowl of oranges look the way oranges looked to her and at the same time the way they appeared to Miss Moseley. The doctor stood in the doorway watching her for some moments before she was aware of his presence. Then he said, "I see you do not like oranges."

"Oh, but I do." Sarah laid down her brush and smiled at him. It was as if, on the instant, she had slipped out of a dingy smock into a bright one. "I like them every way there is, even in custard, but I like them best with a hole cut in one end so that I can suck them. Do you?"

"But yes," said the doctor, picking up an orange, cutting the hole with his pocketknife, and handing it to her. The way he handed her an orange made Sarah feel grown up and wearing a red velvet dress with a train. Then he cut one for himself, and they both sucked their oranges contentedly and not very quietly.

"Now I can't paint any more," said Sarah, "because Miss Moseley told me to paint a bowl with at least four pieces of fruit, and there isn't any more fruit in the house."

"She's rather mathematical, isn't she? Maybe for you it should be four bowls and one orange. *Quién sabe?*"

"Not four bowls!" said Sarah in dismay. "I can't get the curve right on one bowl, and a jug is even harder."

"Come down to my house," said the doctor. "We have some very good jugs for painting. They aren't too, too symmetrical because they were made by hand. Carlotta will show you."

Sarah was surprised, but she did not say so. Carlotta was the doctor's wife, and everyone knew that the doctor's wife did not usually care for company. The funny thing was that she looked like a person who would like company. Once or twice a year she gave a very gay and very grand party and she looked lovelier than anyone else in Wheaton. But after the party, if anyone went to call, she could not see them because she was an invalid and lay on a chaise longue, wearing the most beautiful kimonos in the world. If they could be called kimonos. Certainly they weren't dresses. When Sarah was small she had sometimes gone to the Riveras' with her father, who dropped in several times a week to "have a cup of tea with Carlotta." Her father and Mrs. Rivera talked about painting and things he never talked about at home. In those days Sarah had never specially listened because she had no idea of becoming a great artist and talk about painting rather bored her. Instead she looked at the pictures in the big magazine that came from Paris, France, or she wandered into the library where the Riveras had more books than anyone else in town, even the high school reference shelves.

Now here she was going to call on Mrs. Rivera. By the time Dr. Rivera had gone upstairs to see Lucy and pronounced her ailment a "sneezling cold," Sarah had her paints put away and her hat and coat on. Dr. Rivera did not make house calls on most people; he operated in the hospital and saw special people in his office. But if Mama so much as spoke to him over the telephone he came as soon as he could. Usually nothing was the matter. Sarah supposed that was why he ate an orange before he went up to see Lucy. If something were the matter she knew he would sniff the trouble by the time he was in the front door and hurry like anything.

As they went down the street together Sarah said, "Perhaps Mrs. Rivera won't feel like having company."

"I think she will." There was an odd note in his voice. "Queer I never thought of it before." Then he added quickly, "She leads a rather lonely life, you know, and I ought to see that someone drops in more often."

Yes, it was queer, Sarah thought, that a man wouldn't have noticed his own wife was lonely. Anyone in town would be glad to go see her; even the most stylish ladies, because everyone said that Mrs. Rivera's father had been "fabulously wealthy" and that she had silver "worth a king's ransom." She had jewels too; Father had seen them. And she had servants instead of a hired girl. They were black, they came from Haiti and they talked French. Even now, after years of living in Wheaton, only one of them talked English, and he had to do all the buying. Everything about the Riveras was different, people said, than you'd expect to find in a Midwestern town of twelve thousand.

At the great carved door of the house Sarah waited while Dr. Rivera took out his key to open the only door in Wheaton that was ever kept locked in the daytime. They entered the stately hall where sunshine cut sharply through high leaded windows. The staircase was the widest and the longest Sarah had ever seen. On two great curves it swept to the top of the house, and its wrought-iron railing was a very different thing from the wooden banister, good for sliding, in other people's houses. The floor of the hall was of stone, but oriental rugs almost covered it. Some people in town had oriental rugs, but none so large as the huge black, red, gold, and violet one which covered the floor of the Rivera parlor. The Riveras did not say "parlor." They said "drawing room." This morning Dr. Rivera did not take Sarah into the drawing room. They went upstairs to Mrs. Rivera's sitting room. Although the door was slightly open, the doctor knocked. Sarah had never heard of such a thing. All the fathers she knew walked right into upstairs rooms which belonged only to wives and children. "Carlotta, I've brought a guest." He spoke with excitement and his eyes were merry. Sarah was excited too.

"Come in," said the voice of Carlotta from the far end of the room. It was a low, full voice with an odd, clear quality as quiet as twilight after rain. "I'm taking a sun bath."

Sarah could not see the owner of the voice because the high-backed chair was facing the great plate-glass windows which filled almost the whole south end of the room. The windows were now wide open. The doctor leaned over the back of the chair and kissed his wife's forehead. And not in a hurry, the way other men kissed their wives. He said, "Someone—and I mean *someone*—has come to draw a jug. One of our jugs, maybe a cobalt jug and maybe a bronze one. Or just a little yellow cream jug." He took Sarah's hand and led her around in front of the chair. "It's a long time since you've seen Sarah Duncan."

Sarah looked at the doctor's wife, who was snuggled to her ears in a white woolly coat with a white fur rug pulled over her lap. Her black hair was coiled on top of her head. Her face was very white, but not the thin white of a sick person. It was a lovely skin which one wanted to touch immediately and ever so gently. Her eyes were brown, not dark like the doctor's, but flecked with gold, and the lashes which closed over them when she looked down at her hands, as she had a way of doing, were unbelievably long and curling. Her lips were red. A dark, rouged red. No other woman Sarah had ever seen put something red on her lips. She was not beautiful in the way that a woman on a calendar or in a store advertisement is beautiful; her nose was too long and her cheekbones too high. But she had something about her which made one never want to stop looking. Maybe it was her smile. She was smiling now, showing her even white teeth.

"So you have come to draw a jug," she said, laughing. She took Sarah's hand in both of hers. "Well, you shall draw a jug. Let me see your hands. Both hands." She looked at them closely, bending back the long, supple fingers, feeling the cushioned tips of the fingers. "They are not ordinary hands," she said gaily, but with a kind of stern satisfaction. Then she turned to the doctor. "Since they are not ordinary hands, you may go now." She laughed up at him, too, and he laughed at her. They had a special way of laughing at one another, as polite as a party but as comfortable as a snooze by the fire. When he left he did not kiss her, as one might expect a husband to do on leaving for the day. He laid the back of his hand against her cheek for ever so brief a moment. For years and years Sarah remembered the warmth of that gesture.

"I would have said they were piano hands," she went on to Sarah. "But hands are made to do what the heart decrees. Push that button for me, will you, and let's get the windows closed so we can go to work. Tell me about your drawing. Who teaches you and what do you draw at home and do you use colored crayons? Tell everything. Everything all at once."

And that was the way the next hour passed—everything all at once and yet not jumbled or hurried. Hortense came. She was tall and burnt-almond color. She had a loose and hippy walk, but she moved quickly and did all the right things with scarcely being told. The windows were closed, the fire lighted on the hearth, her mistress's wraps put away, a table brought for Sarah, an assortment of jugs set forth on top of the grand piano which filled the west corner of this great room, and a supply of large creamy sheets of drawing paper put in Sarah's hands.

Sarah talked, with only a little steering. It was so easy to talk. She told about Miss Moseley.

"Why do you want to paint?" Mrs. Rivera asked suddenly.

Sarah stood up slowly before she answered. "My father expected me to be an artist." She moved toward the window and then told about her father's death. "But you must know all this," she said, as if she were only then aware of her own telling.

"But I could not know how he died for you unless you told me!" Both of them stood motionless for a moment, realizing there was no more to say or any need for more. Then Mrs. Rivera crossed to a small table. "Here is your vase."

It was three-sided and of a luscious honey color, shining but unglazed. She set it on the mantel above the fireplace. So Sarah began to draw and Mrs. Rivera went about some tasks at her desk. Another hour passed. By and by Mrs. Rivera came back to the drawing table and picked up the sketches.

"You don't feel like a jug," she said.

"I don't—what?" Sarah asked in astonishment.

"You don't feel like a jug. You see, you have to feel like a jug or how can you speak for the jug? The beautiful jug which stands so proudly on the mantel! It's not just doing nothing there. It's *standing*. It feels a relationship to the mantelshelf." She ran a swift finger down the sharp edges of its three sides, around the urgent eclipse of its mouth. And as she turned and touched the jug she talked about the making of jugs and the use of jugs, a fascinating hodgepodge of information which Sarah neither remembered nor forgot but understood.

"I will try again," Sarah said finally.

"Oh no!" cried Mrs. Rivera, frankly horrified. "Don't try. That spoils it. No one ever did anything by trying."

Sarah gazed at her blankly, her gray eyes wide and puzzled.

"Never mind." Mrs. Rivera smiled, and with the smile her mood changed. "Someday you will understand and then perhaps you will remember what I said. But if you do not remember, what difference does it make, just so you someday understand?"

"I understand *now*," Sarah said slowly. "That's the trouble. Some things I can do without trying, like playing the piano, but when I draw I have to try." Her tones were dry and flat, too stark for twelve years old.

"Try then," said Mrs. Rivera warmly, urgently. "But first we will have some luncheon."

They ate by the fire. They spent the afternoon by the fire. Where the time went, Sarah did not even wonder. The sun retreated behind a thick, opaque sky and snow began to fall in flakes so large and soft that one could see their separate intricate design.

"How slowly they fall." Mrs. Rivera was standing by the window, her eyes as eager as any child's. "Each one wants us to see him. They have no other immortality except as they catch our eyes, yours and mine."

Sarah knew what she meant, for she herself had often walked in the deep woods and stood before a cluster of slender, waxen Indian pipes or paused before a branch of scarlet maple and wondered, almost with a shiver of apprehension, what *if*—*what* if—no one had seen this lovely thing and it had passed wherever loveliness passes, unsaluted?

Hortense brought tea and toasted muffins on a silver tray which she placed on a low table by the window.

"No lights," said Mrs. Rivera. "Sarah and I—we have room for the twilight, don't we?"

The cups were the thinnest that Sarah had ever seen, and she wished that she could take one home to Lucy. Also, she wished she knew what was in the tiny sandwich she was eating. She could ask! And she did. It was guava jelly. Mrs. Rivera had seen guavas growing. She had seen lemons and oranges growing. She had seen palms and tall cypresses. She did not say, "I have seen these things"; they merely trailed through her conversation on her way to talking about a ship which lay at anchor through two moons because she wanted to go home on that ship and was too ill to be moved. Sarah wished she knew more of the story, but this time she did not ask.

After tea Sarah said suddenly that she must go home. Her consternation was the spontaneous embarrassment of a well-brought-up child who suddenly realizes it is dinnertime.

"But so nice a compliment !" Mrs. Rivera cried, clapping her hands lightly. "And do not worry, because I have already sent word to your mother that Enrique will drive you home before dinner."

"When did you do that?" The tone was a bit incredulous.

"When I was telling Hortense where to set the tea table." Mrs. Rivera laughed and then Sarah laughed. Since the conversation with Hortense had been in French, there was no guessing what had been said.

"Now maybe you will play for me—a little—yes?" Mrs. Rivera indicated the piano and then leaned back in her chair with the relaxed eagerness of one who awaits some good thing.

"Couldn't you play for me instead?" As soon as she had said the words, Sarah felt oddly self-conscious for the first time.

"No." The answer was so short and final that a sea seemed to spread between them. Then Mrs. Rivera recovered herself for the child's sake and spoke gently, naturally. "I almost never play any more, but I would love to listen. I am a good listener—one of the best." She shrugged her shoulders with mock modesty and laughed so gaily that Sarah laughed, too, and the ocean between them shrank again into itself, leaving only a friendly room. Sarah went to the piano.

"I do not know a piece about the snow, but I know one about rain." She played Chopin's Prelude in B Minor. There was a sturdiness about her playing larger than the thing she played and a delicacy which entirely escaped sentimentality.

When she had finished Mrs. Rivera said, "I see you understand the rain."

"At least better than I understand jugs." Sarah smiled at her.

"Or can it be that you understand the piano better than the paintbrush?"

"Oh no!" Sarah was plainly aghast at the idea. She tried to explain. Anyone could play the piano; almost every girl she knew took lessons. She happened to play a little better than some girls, just as they might cook or dance better than she. But painting was different, something special. It took a great deal of work to learn to paint, to become an artist. But she would work until she achieved. Her father expected her to. Her words were almost defiant, as if she were answering many long and threatening arguments instead of responding to a casual sentence.

Mrs. Rivera answered more than her words. "Don't be anxious, my dear. Your hunch is right that the biggest part of genius is just plain work. Many people are inventive, sometimes cleverly so. But real creativity begins with the drive to work on and on and on."

Sitting on the ottoman, Sarah hugged her knees and did not realize that she made no answer. She was realizing that she had the ability to work on and on and on. But this initial inventiveness, did she really have that thing? From smallest childhood she had drawn pictures to fit whatever story she was reading or telling. She and her father found the pictures vastly amusing, but her mother had once said that was because they looked so little like the thing Sarah meant them to be.

Her father had said, still laughing, "Maybe her pictures don't look the way a cow or a clothesline looks to you, but they look like those things *feel.*"

But what would be the use in drawing a jug, for instance, the way a jug felt, if the drawing did not look like a jug to other people! In consternation she spoke aloud. "All my work might be no use if I'm not really accurate."

Again Mrs. Rivera reached behind the hidden question. "Your father had good clean intuitions about people. He would never have said he expected you to be an artist unless he felt that you had the understanding of an artist. Everything else can be learned."

Reassurance flooded her heart. To doubt her own ability would be to doubt her father's wisdom, and that would be so incredible that even the thought did not form itself. "Of course everything else can be learned," she said simply.

"Play something else, won't you? It's the perfect time of day for music, you know." Mrs. Rivera leaned back in her chair and waited.

"If you want me to," Sarah said. "I'll play the 'Moonlight Sonata.'"

"That will be nice," Mrs. Rivera said.

Sarah looked over at her. There was a little something in her voice that sounded like a grownup speaking to a child who was going to try to do something it couldn't possibly manage. Sarah struck the first chord softly, firmly. At the end of the third phrase Mrs. Rivera sat up. The slow broken chords always gripped Sarah too; she once told Miss Lillie that they ached her. At the close of the first movement Mrs. Rivera looked as if she were about to speak, but Sarah went right on into the *allegretto;* she loved the swing of the second part; the simple chords made her think of trees bowing rhythmically to each other in a fine breeze. From the corner of her eye she could see that Mrs. Rivera was smiling in real delight, so she sped through the repeat with joy in her fingertips. At the third movement Mrs. Rivera jumped up from her chair and came over to the piano. Sarah's fingers were wings now, almost ethereally light, then growing more insistent without losing speed or fire. Here was music she could put her whole self into, body as well as mind. Maybe it was too big for her, but she could do it; she could more than do it; her fingers knew every note. Miss Lillie Tower saw to it that Beethoven was played with complete accuracy of note and time, but Sarah herself saw to it that a kind of wild desperation lifted the passages marked *crescendo agitato.* In the closing *adagio* she always wanted to cry, not a little, but with all her heart. She struck the closing chords as if she were signing her name with good firm strokes.

Mrs. Rivera did not say anything for a moment. Sarah smiled at her confidently. She had done justice to the music and she was neither proud nor humble about it. She'd had a good time. Then Mrs. Rivera laughed a little ruefully. "Of course you know that you took me completely by surprise. I thought you'd play something pleasant and play it well, but instead you gave me—music. Music with stature. I'm hunting for words and wondering which words to say to you."

"You needn't say any words," Sarah told her, grinning like a happy child. "Miss Lillie says that's why we have music—so we needn't talk. I like to play." So far as she was concerned, there was no more to be said. Naturally a person did well what she liked awfully to do.

The doctor came in cold and abstracted. All the time he was driving her home he talked heatedly about a tramp who had been found dying of pneumonia in a boxcar. There they were back again with the question as to which calamities were brought about by God's intention and which ones were the result of man's willful stupidity. Sarah thought of Bill Cooper, but she had never mentioned him before. This time she spoke out quickly, partly to escape thinking of the tramp, but more because she wanted to know about Bill Cooper.

"Do you know where Bill Cooper is?" she asked, without preamble.

"I do," the doctor answered, turning to look squarely at her. "Why do you ask?"

"Because I often think of him. Sometimes I think my father would not like having him cut off from his folks and his garden with one—one stroke."

"With one stroke of the social guillotine." Dr. Rivera spoke sternly, but he smiled at her. "He is not cut off from gardening. Will you keep a secret if I tell you? Bill Cooper is now working for the Board of Charitable Institutions of the State of Minnesota, and his particular charitable institution considers him their prize gardener. The superintendent of that institution has a passion for blue morning-glories growing over high fences, and Bill can make morning-glories climb to heights of fence or telephone pole which no morning-glory ever reached before."

Sarah smiled and then gasped. "You don't mean he's been put in an institution! Not such a rover as Bill Cooper."

"I mean he is employed by an institution and paid with the state's good money. Some of Solicitor Ramsey's money is no doubt lining Bill's bankbook this minute. And Bill is no longer a rover. He lives on the grounds and arrives at work an hour before the check-in. After supper at night he prunes a few leaves and on holidays he works with his flowers some more."

Sarah's eyes shone. "Father would chuckle, wouldn't he? To think of Bill Cooper reforming!"

"Nothing so drastic as that," he remonstrated. "I'm not sure that Bill has exerted any special will to change. He's just got a chance to do what he wants to do and plenty of it. When he first arrived the other workmen didn't know he wasn't supposed to be respectable. They expected him to work regularly and he eased right into their expectations."

"Does he still drink?" Sarah asked, still smiling. "I mean, does he sometimes go on a spree?"

"If he does, it hasn't been reported to me. I'm inclined to think that your father would say that Bill Cooper, at fifty-six, has come to himself."

When the doctor left her at her door he did not say, "Come again," but Sarah knew she would be going again. Something new had come into her days.

Five

March came in like a lamb. One day there was an abundance of crisp white snow well packed for sliding, and the next day the same snow slumped and sagged in gray patches while sleds waited in pained surprise by doorsteps suddenly alive with spinning tops. The world seemed straining at the leash, sniffling at spring, eager to be off and going places—Sarah with it. She and Rachel began to talk about graduation dresses.

Regardless of tantalizing weather, school went on as if there were some distinction in merely going on. But life began to deal out a number of amazing *firsts* for Sarah. A boy walked home from school with her. He was not merely one of the boys she had always known who happened to catch up with her and walk a few blocks. This was a new boy named Leslie Sando who had just come to town with his father, who had bought the paper mill. Leslie's mother was dead, so he and his father lived in a hotel, which was certainly a strange way to live, ordering your own meals three times a day. Leslie was not as tall as Sarah, but he was one of the most alive boys she had ever met. He walked around a room as if he had a thousand little springs instead of bones inside his skin. His hair was also made of coiled springs, blond and almost too thick to part. His eyes were blue, his nose was thin and aristocratic. Altogether he was handsome, as well as quick in arithmetic. Sarah was quick in arithmetic too; it was their first bond. After school one day

Leslie stood at the gate waiting for her. He said, "Say, can you play the piano?"

"Some," Sarah said. "Why?"

"Because then we will play duets." He said it as if there was nothing strange at all about a boy's liking to play the piano.

"Oh," Sarah said with a rush of gladness. "My father and I used to play duets."

"He was a doctor, wasn't he? People have told us about him." Then Sarah talked about her father freely, happily, for the first time.

The spring was marked also by a falling-out she had with Rachel; the only falling-out she ever had with Rachel. It came over a book called *The Trail of the Lonesome Pine,* which was probably the most interesting book written in the world up to that time, although *Paradise Lost* with pictures might be a bigger treat for scholars. They had been reading the book aloud, and on this Friday night they took for granted Sarah's going to Rachel's house for supper and all night so that they could go on reading. But when Friday night came Sarah had a sore throat.

"Sore throats are frequently contagious," Mama said as she mixed a strong gargle of vinegar, salt, and hot water.

Sarah said tensely, "I will turn my chair toward the wall while I do my reading, and when we go to bed I'll sleep with my back to Rachel."

"You'll turn over in your sleep," Mama said serenely. "Here, gargle this."

Sarah, who seldom argued, used all the persuasion she had. Finally Mama had enough of talk and turned to her sharply. "What's the matter with you lately? I declare, you seem more childish all the time instead of more grown up."

The words were not true, as both of them knew.

Sarah said, "One person can't know everything."

It was the first time she had ever spoken to her mother in such a tone, and so no one was surprised as she.

Her mother turned in astonishment and then said emphatically, "You may go to bed. Now."

Sarah went. She undressed and went to bed without opening her window and lay looking at nothing, feeling more stunned than angry or hurt, but feeling definitely worse about the book than about what she had said.

By and by her mother came in without knocking, bringing a bowl of hot soup. "I hope my eldest daughter is ready to apologize," she said. "It's hard enough to have to raise children alone, unaided, without having the oldest one use such language to her own mother."

"I suppose it is," said Sarah without emotion.

"Is that all you have to say?" Her mother set the soup on a small table beside the bed.

"No," said Sarah in the same colorless voice. "I would also like to say that I do not care for any soup."

"Sarah Duncan!" Bright red spots burned in her mother's cheeks. She was rather pretty, Sarah thought.

Driven on by something quite outside herself, Sarah added, "I could say that you spoiled my evening, but you already know that."

"You'll be sorry someday." Her mother began to cry. "You'll stand beside my coffin and look upon my still face and say to yourself, 'I'd give my right arm to have my mother back so that I could apologize to her.'" She was crying in earnest now, sitting on a stiff straight chair, sobs shaking her shoulders.

For once Sarah was not very sorry for her. She wished she were. She got out of bed, trailing her long flannel nightgown, and walked over to her mother and patted her shoulder. "I do apologize," she said earnestly. "I'm sorry I was impudent. I'm sorry you have a hard time raising us. When Baldy grows up he will be a great comfort to you."

"But he will never know a father! Poor little boy with never a father's hand to guide him!" Her mother sobbed on from sorrow to sorrow. "And when he is grown he will get married and go off and I will be left alone. You'll never know what it is to be alone." Sarah did not know what to say to that.

Talking about being lonely seemed a more naked thing than being lonely. But in a way Mama's case was less sad this way than if she were lonely in secret. "There, there," she said. "You'll always have us. Lucy will be the one who gets married and goes off. She'll marry a very rich man and you can travel with them to foreign places, and when you come home Baldy and I will always be waiting for you."

Mama began to dry her eyes. "Do you know," she said between sobs, "I think Baldy is beginning to look more like his father. He has the same way of stretching his arms over his head."

After that Baldy led the conversation until the doorbell called Mama downstairs, leaving Sarah with the lukewarm soup. Mama's parting injunction was, "Now put your light out early and take a nice long sleep."

Sarah drank the soup, walked around the room in her bare feet, tried not to think about Mama and certainly not about Father, automatically took the book from inside her desk, crawled into bed, and began to read. She had not intended to read ahead of Rachel. In all the books they had read together, neither had ever read ahead of the other. But on this night she read quickly, avidly, in a kind of unhappy rapture.

Shortly after ten o'clock she heard her mother start upstairs. Quickly she turned out the light, settled herself into her pillow, the book well under the covers, and began to breathe regularly. Mama always said that no child could fool her on the matter of being sound asleep because sleeping children breathed deep regular breaths. Sarah knew that waking children could do that, too, when they had their minds on it. Of course if Mama had ever said, "Sarah, are you sleeping?" then she would have answered, but Mama never asked on account of thinking she already knew. The door opened and shut. Out came the book.

In the morning Sarah slept late. When she wakened she felt very well indeed and went downstairs two steps at a time.

"Mama, I read my book last night instead of going to sleep like you told me to."

"Why, Sarah, I'm surprised at you," said her mother absently. "Wash off your finger in alcohol, rinse it in the glass of water, and come here, will you?"

She waited in evident excitement while Sarah did as directed.

"Now run your finger along Baldy's upper gum and tell me if you feel something which might be a tooth."

Sarah felt it, ever so tiny and sharp but unmistakable. "Isn't he too young for a tooth?" she asked in genuine surprise.

"Much too young," Mama said. "He's barely four months. Call your grandma."

Thus, so far as her mother was concerned, Sarah's impudence and disobedience were closed matters. But there was still Rachel. Somehow the thought of Rachel did not overwhelm her until she started toward the Rands'. What could she say to Rachel? Of course she *could* go right up to Rachel's room and begin to read where they had left off the last time they read together. But no, she couldn't do that to Rachel. Suddenly the enormity of what she had done began to dawn upon her. She could not bring herself to say, "Rachel, I have read our book." It would be easier if she had to say, "Rachel, I lost the opal ring you inherited from your aunt."

By the time she reached the Rand house she felt all gone. Rachel was sweeping the porch and called out the minute she saw Sarah. "Hurry up! I've got every bit of my work done and we can start reading right away. Mama's fried a whole batch of doughnuts. They're rolled in sugar, too." She squeezed Sarah's arm and pulled her into the house.

"Wait. Wait, Rachel, I have to tell you something first." Sarah pulled away and stood against the newel post. She twisted her long brown braids around her hands, as she did only in times of deep distress. "I read the rest of our book. I read it all. I went to bed and …" But she couldn't go any further.

Rachel stood stock-still. She looked at Sarah, incredulous, then walked slowly upstairs without once turning her head.

Sarah went home. She went to her room and just stood, not doing anything, not even looking out of the window. Pretty soon Anna called that it was lunch time. Sarah went downstairs. She ate her lunch, but she could not talk. Her mother said, "You look sick, Sarah, even if your throat is better. You'd better go see Dr. Rivera."

"No, oh, please, no!" Sarah begged. Dr. Rivera would insist on knowing the real trouble and she could not tell him. In the afternoon she got out her paints and then as quickly put them away again. A crook could never paint a great picture; that's what Miss Moseley had said. In the evening, after dark, she walked over to the Rands' house to see if there was a light in Rachel's window, but there was none.

Sunday morning dawned as sunny as a dandelion. Millions of little grass roots were humming in the earth. Ordinarily Rachel would have come dancing in a full quarter hour before Sarah was ready for Sunday school. They would have laughed and chattered and then gone off together. Today no one came.

"I wonder where Rachel can be," Mama said.

"She's prob'ly scared of Sarah's sore throat," Lucy suggested.

"How is your throat, Sarah?" Mama took her eyes off Baldy long enough to tie Lucy's hair ribbon and to look at Sarah's pale face. "I declare, you don't look well. I wonder if you hadn't better stay home."

Sarah thought maybe she had.

The day dragged on and night came again. People said that trouble could be forgotten with time. But Sarah knew that no matter how long life might last she would never feel happy with people again. And certainly she would never feel happy alone. How could one hide from oneself?

It was half an hour before schooltime on Monday morning

when Rachel appeared at the door of Sarah's room, wearing a crisp blue Peter Pan, her dark curls tied back with a stiff blue bow. She did not smile, but her words rushed out eagerly, like a stream which knew it was falling on parched sands.

"Sarah, listen! I got up early this morning and burned the book in the stove. Now we have to pay the library for it and here's my half of the money." She laid the money on Sarah's desk.

"No! You can't pay for any of it." Sarah was bewildered with joy. She thrust the money into the pocket of Rachel's blouse. "I will pay for it." From the desk drawer came her small savings bank. She turned the combination lock rapidly, took out the money, and buttoned it firmly into the patch pocket of her own skirt. "We have time to go to the library before school."

"But, Sarah, I burned the book. You see—" Rachel looked at her friend and stopped. "All right," she said. Then slowly, "Let's don't even talk about it again."

They never needed to talk about it again. By the time they reached the corner they were talking happily of other things. Each was restored to herself.

Six

One perfect day in April, Grandpa Vanderiet had a funeral which became for Sarah a lasting landmark of the spring. It was the first time she ever noted that some people do things differently from the way one's own people do things and there is nothing really *wrong* in the difference.

Grandma said, "It seems strange having such an aristocratic funeral in our church. You'd think they would have an Episcopalian funeral, except that Marcia was always very loyal to the church of her fathers and she wants her husband to be buried here."

Marcia Furness had moved away from Wheaton before Sarah was born, but the tales of her clothes and her suitors still lingered. Everyone knew she was not a church person any more, but how could she be when her husband owned race horses and country estates and had to entertain important people all the time? Everyone felt that if Marcia had remained in Wheaton she would also have remained faithful to her church.

Sarah did not intend to go to the funeral, although Mama said she had better get over being so afraid of death that she could not even go to a funeral. There was nothing to fear about death, Mama said, when you believed in heaven and immortality. Mama put on her black broadcloth suit with the black satin waist smocked in pale pink—because Grandpa continued to feel strongly on the matter of a Christian's not going into mourning.

But Grandpa need not have worried about Marcia's husband having a too black funeral. There was no black at all. Just before the funeral Grandma called Sarah to come over quickly; she had something to show her. What she showed her was that the coffin was a lovely silver gray and that the flowers heaped upon it were not white lilies but spring flowers—daffodils, tulips, hyacinths, and a huge wreath of trailing arbutus which made the church smell like woods after rain. Instead of potted palms there were branches of pine. The seats for the mourners were roped off with yards of wide soft ribbon the color of cream after it has been poured into a dish of wild raspberries. No one in Wheaton had ever seen a funeral like this one. Grandma said afterward that you could almost call it an informal funeral.

At supper that night Mama said that a dozen of Marcia's friends, all of whom had crossed the continent with her, had taken part in the services. The only thing Grandpa did was to pray, and very well. Four of Marcia's friends made up a quartet and they sang some of her husband's favorite songs—which were not hymns. Among other things, they sang "Somewhere a Voice Is Calling" and "Danny Deever." Grandma said that if she had known what they were planning she would have suggested putting sacred words to those same tunes. The only hymn they sang was "Beautiful Isle of Somewhere," which was a very good hymn, to be sure, but had no mention of Jesus or of the church. Later in the service a friend had stepped out from his pew, walked down front but not onto the platform, and told about the life of Marcia's husband and how much people loved him. When he sat down another friend stood right up where he was and said he would like to tell a story about this man who was supposed to be dead. The story was about a young chap who worked in a bank and forged a check and was going to be sent to the penitentiary, when along came the president of the bank and talked to the young forger, and then talked to the judge and got the forger freed and put him right back to work in the bank at a more responsible position. The man telling the story said, "Forty years ago this dead man was president of the bank and I was the young forger." Mama said it was very dramatic because the man did not raise his voice and neither did he weep. The story would be in all the papers, Mama said, because this man was now a millionaire known to all. After the service at the cemetery Marcia and all her friends went to the station and took the train back to the West Coast. No one stayed to see about the tombstone or to have a weeping willow or a thorn hedge planted on the lot.

But Sarah did not need to be told how Marcia looked because she had not only seen her, she had talked with her. It was at the corner drugstore where Marcia had stopped for some headache medicine. She wore a dark blue dress of soft wool and a coat to match. Sarah was near enough to touch it because she was buying horehound drops at the same counter. Marcia was a tall woman with a dry brown face and a wide mouth and a long nose and scraggly eyebrows. She was not handsome. But for days after, Sarah wanted to be exactly like her when she grew up. Marcia had looked at Sarah and said, "Horehound! I had forgotten about it. Thank you for reminding me." Her voice was deep and husky and exciting. Sarah had said, "Please take some of mine." Marcia said, "Thank you, I will." And she laughed, even though this was the day and hour of her own husband's funeral. She said, "I lived here when I was a girl and my mother had tansy in her garden." Sarah said, "There's still some there." So they talked about the garden and about the Carnegie library and the bakery and the way spring came to Wheaton, until a friend of Marcia's, a little woman dressed in gray, came into the drugstore and said, "We didn't know what had happened to you." Marcia said, "I met a friend whose name is—" "Sarah Duncan," Sarah had replied. "Yes, it would be Sarah," Marcia had said. "I couldn't bear it if you had said Edith or Jeanne or Katherine." All Sarah said was, "Good-by. I hope—I hope you will be *all right.*" And Marcia said firmly, "I shall." Then she took Sarah's hand in her two gloved hands and said, "He was a great man, you know. I mean a great man to live with. That kind never lets you down, even *after* he dies. That's the kind you must marry, my dear. I'll think of you sometimes."

She went out the door with her friend. Sarah went home. It was all rather strange. She never told anyone because there was nothing to tell.

The next day after the funeral Grandma came over with lengths of the wide satin ribbon which had roped off the mourners' pews. She said cheerfully, "This will make perfectly beautiful sashes for the girls. I'm dividing it around and sending some to your cousin Annie's girls. We don't want too much of it here in town."

Sarah took her piece gratefully. It was more than three yards long and as nice to touch as to look at. Later in the afternoon she showed it to Rachel, who admired it almost longingly, although there was no envy in Rachel.

"You take it, Rachel," Sarah said. "I want you to have it."

Rachel demurred, but Sarah insisted. She could find no way to tell Rachel that she had something better for herself because she had talked to Marcia and really did not need the ribbon. Rachel understood only that Sarah felt it important to give her the ribbon and she took it.

A month later when Mama found out that Sarah had given away her ribbon she scolded her, but Sarah insisted staunchly, "I gave it to Rachel because it was really hers. It looks like her. I don't need anything I haven't got."

"But you need pretty things yourself," her mother said, irritated with Sarah and with herself for not being able to make Sarah understand such things. "Your red sash is fraying." Her mother's voice came querulously from the clothes closet, but Sarah didn't hear her. She was wondering what her own words meant, "I don't need anything I haven't got." They were some of the words which came up from deep inside her and said themselves without stopping to be a thought.

Early in May of this, her first year without her father, Sarah made two discoveries which for her were the great discoveries of life so far. And yet when she tried to put them into words so that Mrs. Rivera would understand, there was again almost nothing to say. It was a day of steady, insistent rain so that by late afternoon pools stood in every hollow of sidewalk and street and the trees were sodden with their weight of dropping leaves. Almost no one was out when Sarah walked down the entire length of Elm Street on her way from her music lesson to the Rivera house, but if there had been people she would not have seen them any more than she saw the puddles of water or felt the rain. She was thinking of Miss Lillie Tower because it was Miss Lillie who made her aware of these two new things.

Miss Lillie Tower had been Sarah's music teacher for eight years now, and she had been other people's music teacher for a long time before that. Sarah supposed, vaguely, that she had been a music teacher since the Civil War because Miss Lillie's mother talked a good deal about the Civil War and one felt that wherever Miss Lillie's mother had been, surely Miss Lillie had been there also. Miss Lillie loved her mother. She never went to the store without asking her mother whether it would be all right to go. If she changed the part in her hair she explained, "Mama wanted me to try it this way." She said, "No, I don't go out very much, but that is because Mama and I have such good times at home." They did everything together—cribbage and checkers, crocheting and tatting, puzzles, cooking, reading, making beautiful beaded portieres out of strips of colored paper cut from magazines, rolled, and varnished. They did everything well.

When Miss Lillie was a child she had had a dreadful sickness which the doctors now said must have been infantile paralysis. At the time the doctors had not seen the child until the worst of her illness was over because her mother did not believe that a child could not move her legs if she wanted to; she thought the child was stubborn. After the illness the doctors said that the child would never walk and that she could never use her hands either. But they reckoned without Miss Lillie. She learned to pull herself up a rope with her hands. She learned to climb a tree. By and by she learned to walk, but with a very marked limp. She decided that, although her legs might never be much use to her, with her hands she could earn a living, and so she learned to play the piano and began to give lessons when she was sixteen. She had been giving lessons ever since. This much everyone knew about Miss Lillie.

Miss Lillie was a good music teacher. She never expected her students to become concert pianists, and they never did. But she made them like to practice so that all the mothers were grateful. If pupils wanted to take lessons after they were in high school, they naturally went to Professor Green at the college. He charged more.

On this day of the gray persistent rain Miss Lillie looked smaller than usual. She was naturally tall in stature, but some days she looked smaller. Sarah watched her as she raised the window shades by the piano. Her hair was the same dry-hay color it had always been; her nose was always slightly pinched and her deep blue eyes too large for her face. Whatever she wore looked like the same dress. Still—even if she was not beautiful or stylish, even if she did not crack jokes and laugh a lot as Professor Green did, she made a person glad when it was music-lesson day.

Sarah played her scales, melodic minors, accenting thirds. Miss Lillie listened critically, frowning slightly. Then she spoke sharply. "Play them again and don't pause between scales and don't break your rhythm. Someday you will have to play them twice—three times—as fast." When Sarah had finished she said, "Now the Bach Two-hand Inventions. Twelve, Thirteen, and Fourteen, from memory."

"Oh, but I haven't played them since Christmas," Sarah objected.

"Will you do as your teacher directs or not?" This was not the usual Miss Lillie at all. This was no usual lesson. Sarah played the Inventions. Even while she was playing she knew she had never played them so well. She wished someone could hear her. While the last chord still lingered she looked at Miss

Lillie, who had been walking restlessly around the room. Miss Lillie was angry! She looked, thought Sarah, suddenly somewhat frightened herself, as if she might explode.

"The technique is good," Miss Lillie said hotly. "Anyone can see it is good. Nothing sloppy, nothing sentimental, nothing weak."

"Thank you," said Sarah in amazement.

"Thank me for what? In a month, two months, you will either quit taking lessons or you will go to Professor Green. Isn't it so?"

"Why — why, yes. I suppose I will quit. That is, I'm going to be an artist, you know, and Mama says there's no sense putting time and money into something that won't help me to paint."

"And when your mama said that, what did you say?" Miss Lillie bit off the words.

"I said I supposed she was right. But I—I thought maybe something might happen so that I could go on taking lessons. Just for fun, you know. Just enough to—to go on." Sarah knew that something was the matter with her words. She felt rather blank.

"Let me tell you a thing or two," said little Miss Lillie, bearing down on her like a miniature dreadnought. "Nothing will happen unless you make it happen. You have to fight for all you get. You have to take what you want. You have to be selfish."

"But it is true that I'm going to be an artist, and pretty soon now I have to quit doing anything else. I have to quit going to parties and reading so many books. I have to quit the piano too. Because I'm going to be a painter."

"Don't be stupid," cried Miss Lillie, who probably had never said anything mean in her life before. "Don't be childish. Painting has to feed on something. All the arts feed on one another. Music fills your soul; it gives you something to paint about. Tell me this: when it is time to draw and you don't feel like drawing, what do you do?"

"First I practice for a while on the piano. It loosens me up in some way."

"That's because you're good on the piano. You know what you're doing, however imperfectly. Sometimes when you play the piano you look quite beautiful. Are you going to quit something that makes you feel and look like *yourself*?"

"But, Miss Lillie, playing is only for *fun*. Father always said we play the piano because we enjoy it. But being an artist is serious business."

"Everything worth doing is done because we enjoy it. You won't be a great painter unless you paint for enjoyment too. Cling to the things that are fun for you, the things that make your soul feel bigger. They are *your* things, and the other things are not your things."

Sarah sat still, thinking; winding her braids around her hands. It was true, playing the piano was her favorite thing to do. If she didn't have a piano she would feel as queer as if she didn't have hair—and she had always felt a great sympathy for Samson, who became weak when they cut off his hair. A person thought with all of himself, she believed, and if someone cut off his hair there would be less of him to think with. At least there would be less of *her*. In a way, the piano was a part of her too. One did have to keep the things which were one's self. By and by she spoke. "I understand, Miss Lillie. And I will keep on taking lessons."

"Maybe you'll have to fight for them," Miss Lillie said.

"I don't think I'll have to fight," Sarah answered slowly. "My mother wants me to have whatever's good for me."

"That's what you think. That's what you've been taught. But let me tell you that your mother is your worst enemy. She'll make you good instead of great. I can see it coming because you're like me. My mother made me good and useful. She made me quit everything except giving music lessons. And now I'm nothing at all. If I'd kept some other things, too, then maybe I'd have been a real musician. I had it in me." Miss Lillie sat down abruptly, like a jackknife going half shut. Just as suddenly she began to cry. She did not cry tears but dry consuming sobs. Then Sarah knew that while the things Miss Lillie had said about music and painting were true things, true for anyone, still she was really talking about herself. She stood up slowly and went over to Miss Lillie.

"What happened?" she asked, sitting down on the wide arm of Miss Lillie's chair, but not touching her.

In short sentences which had no emotion in spite of the sharp sobs which broke them apart, Miss Lillie told about her childhood. She told about her illness and about the way her mother had later done her best to make an invalid out of her, had begged her not to try so hard to walk, not to use her hands. "Mama will take care of you, darling." And then, when she had learned to get around again, to look after herself, her mother had lost what money they had. Her mother had said, "Now you will have to look after me, Lillie. I have no place else to turn. We have no one but each other." Her mother had not explained what the lost investments were, but she never again had so much as a nickel unless Miss Lillie earned it and gave it to her. At the time the money was lost, Miss Lillie had a sweetheart named Harold Johnson. She was only seventeen, but he was twenty-five and had a good job in wholesale groceries. He said that on her eighteenth birthday he would ask her mother for permission to give Miss Lillie a ring; he was proud of a girl who had overcome many handicaps and could play the piano so well. But after they had no more money Miss Lillie's mother explained to her that it would not be fair for him to have to support two women. "And if you are going to make a living by giving music lessons, you don't have time to go to parties with a boy." She said the same to Harold. Miss Lillie never found out what else her mother said to him because he never came any more.

"Now I'm fifty-six and my mother is seventy-eight. She will live forever. Her mother lived to be one hundred three. When my mother is one hundred three I'll be eighty-one. You can't do much after eighty-one." The even drabness went out of her voice and anger came back. "It's thinking about my own life that makes me tell you to hang onto all the good things you can. If you want music lessons, demand them. Let your mother be the one to go without. If she still can't pay for lessons, make me give them to you free. Get all you can from everybody, and don't let anybody run your life."

But Sarah was no longer thinking about music lessons. She was thinking about Miss Lillie. She must do something about her! That is, she must find the person who could still give Miss Lillie a chance. She felt vaguely important as well as weighed down by what she had heard. Of course Miss Lillie had not intended to make her feel responsible, but if something about a person draws out one's heart, then one has to do something.

The music lesson was over and she was walking down Elm Street in the rain before she realized that she had left the house and that she had discovered this thing. Once inside the Rivera house, she gave her raincoat and rubbers to Adolph and went directly to Mrs. Rivera's sitting room.

"*Mon Dieu,* my child, your hair is dripping. Come by the fire. Sit down. Something exciting has brought you here." Mrs. Rivera had that way of sensing an excitement before it expressed itself in words.

"Why, my hair is wet!" She began to unbraid it. "I guess it is raining pretty hard. I want to tell you something. Would you believe—" And then she stopped short.

"Tell me what? Why do you pause?"

"I—I just remembered that what she told me was—was just told to *me.* I never thought about that when she was telling it. I only thought that I would come to you and you would think of something to do."

"I might still think of something to do if I know what person and what trouble is worrying you." Mrs. Rivera leaned back in her big chair, looking so at ease that some of the tension slipped from Sarah also.

"The person is Miss Lillie Tower, my music teacher."

"I know her. She is the best musician in town. And by all odds the best teacher."

"Oh, but Professor Green!" Sarah said.

"Oh, but Professor has the artistic temperament of a China poodle." Mrs. Rivera snapped her long white fingers and disposed of Professor Green. "Miss Lillie Tower might have been a real musician."

"That's just what she said!"

"I'm glad she knows it."

"I'm not. It doesn't make her happy to know it because when her mother is one hundred three Miss Lillie will be eighty-one."

"And so?"

"That's what I'm not sure I should tell you, now that I'm here. She thought I needed to know something and she had to tell me a lot about herself to make me understand. But anyway, now that I know about her, I have to do something. That's a funny thing, isn't it? The person who knows what is needed is the person who has to do something."

Mrs. Rivera was not smiling now. "It might be called fact number one about life. But can you do something?"

"I don't know. And still I must." Suddenly Sarah's face brightened. "If I can't think of what to do myself, why, then I'll tell you! But I don't think I ought to tell anybody if I don't have to."

Mrs. Rivera nodded agreement.

"There was one other thing. Do you believe that a person can paint better if he also writes poetry or maybe plays the piano or something like that?"

"It's usually that way. At least it is usually true that a person of high creative ability can express his creativity in more than one form. Take Da Vinci, for instance. Painter, engineer, physiologist, sculptor, architect—what else? Sidney Lanier was the greatest flautist of his time, perhaps the greatest our country has known, but he lives for us today as a poet."

Sarah thought for a moment. "But maybe they would all have been greater in their own line—even greater than they were—if they'd put all their time on one thing."

"Let your own heart bear witness. What are the pastimes, the pursuits, the interests, which make you feel most like painting? What keeps you buoyed up so that you long to grab your brush quickly? Those are *your* things to do."

"But that's exactly what she said! Miss Lillie said almost those very words." Deep gratitude rang in Sarah's voice. She felt as if someone had made her free of something which she did not know was binding her. "She said that I don't have to give up everything to be an artist!"

"You'll give up plenty. You'll have to forfeit ever so many of the pleasant ways of wasting time. Even worthwhile interests will have to be pushed aside. You'll give up trips you want to take and people you want to be with. But the few things and the few people you can't give up—they belong to you. If you gave up too much, then you wouldn't have anything to paint about."

"That's nice," Sarah said simply. "I'm glad it's like you say, because of course it is like you say."

"It's true for everyone, but that doesn't make it true for you until it happens for you." Mrs. Rivera smiled up at the earnest girl still standing by the fire.

Sarah smiled too. "I learned two things today. I learned about a person's being responsible for another person and about the arts feeding one another."

Mrs. Rivera's smile died away. She looked into the fire for several moments without answering. Sarah watched her face. The older woman had a way of seeming to withdraw into a far place and then of coming back refreshed. She spoke slowly, as if hunting for words.

"It's almost too bad you learned both those things because they are the two things in life which cancel out each other."

"I don't see what you mean. They're such different things. It's like canceling an apple against a sailboat. One and one make

71

two, but apples and sailboats don't affect each other much. They're just two kinds of things."

"But we're not talking about things. We're talking about forces. Becoming a creative artist and becoming a socially minded individual responsible for the world's woes—those are likely to be contradictory forces. You see—when the artist becomes too tender-minded of human need he cannot be hard-shelled enough about protecting his own time and energy. The two concerns pull in opposite directions."

"I can see that," Sarah said, undisturbed. "It's plain enough. With most of my time I will work at my painting, and with part of my time I can help people. I see that you can't let one thing crowd out the other."

Mrs. Rivera laughed once more. Her laugh was always gay. "I know you *see*. You see with your mind, and as you say, it's plain enough. But wait until your emotions begin to battle. Then all you see won't help you much."

Sarah did not feel worried and she surprised herself by quoting a book she had just read. "You know Bach himself said, 'In the architecture of my music I want to demonstrate to the world the architecture of a new age and a beautiful social commonwealth.'"

"Excellent! If you can demonstrate through your music and not get too mixed up in reform while still expecting to be a great musician—why, then you may be a great musician." She smiled at Sarah and Sarah smiled back, feeling very grown up, drying her hair before the fire and quoting Bach. She looked down at her own long hands and felt as if she could manage anything.

After the Fourth of July nothing happened. Carefree days chased one another across the calendar, and neither Sarah nor Rachel could guess where they went. Only Baldy made this summer a little different. Baldy, and the fact that the family listened less frequently for the quick steps of Father coming up the path and were more lonely in the sudden moments when a familiar sound or smell or phrase brought back his presence. They knew now that missing Father was for keeps.

The painting lessons went on steadily. Miss Moseley was as dogged as her pupil; she was always waiting in the art room at the college when Sarah arrived, and Sarah arrived at the same time every day. She taught Sarah to take good care of her palette and quickly smothered her notion of using a big sheet of plate-glass for mixing paints the way Mrs. Rivera had showed her. Once she said to Sarah, "After all, who is your teacher?" and Sarah felt the question was so fair that she never mentioned Mrs. Rivera again. It was somewhat confusing, however, to have two people so sure of different ways of doing the same thing. Miss Moseley believed in taking great care of one's paints and never wasting, while Mrs. Rivera would say, "Never be mean with paint. Use all you want. An artist can't afford to be stingy with anything." Miss Moseley added medium to her tubes of color. Mrs. Rivera felt it was terribly important to get the right consistency of color early. Miss Moseley felt that painting should grow out of drawing. Mrs. Rivera was irate at the thought. "Drawing grows out of painting," she would insist, "just as grammar grows out of writing and speaking." Sarah thought that remark did not make too much sense because certainly one studied grammar in French or German before he attempted conversation. All the high school girls said so.

The big moment of the summer's lessons occurred when Sarah saw a white bowl sitting in the sunlight and wondered how to paint a highlight which was certainly whiter than white! Then she was plunged into a sea of new experience. Everywhere she looked there were highlights and shadows and new linear patterns. Working in a room, walking down the street, wandering in the woods, sitting on the porch, she found herself surrounded by patterns of light and shadow. Every color had its shadow, color, and every shape its shadow shape which often shifted before one could mark off its outline. Miss Moseley said that the study of grays came in the last half of the second year's work and Sarah was not ready for it yet. But whenever she was alone, or at church, or wheeling Baldy, Sarah kept figuring on the problem of painting a highlight on something white until she stumbled onto the notion that the original white would have to be a little, ever-so little, gray. If she should ask Mrs. Rivera, she knew that out would come the gray crayons and they would be off for a wonderful time. But it did not seem fair to ask her. Certainly a teacher knew more in the end than the most enthusiastic of amateurs, and Sarah had an almost superstitious respect for taking the proper steps in proper order exactly as the teacher directed. This much Miss Moseley had made plain: there were no short cuts to Art, and the Artist had to apply himself faithfully.

Sometimes Sarah wished that it were Rachel whom her father expected to be a great artist. Rachel had no interest in painting, but if she had, Sarah knew that she would learn quickly and easily. Then Sarah could look after her and explain things to her. But it was not Rachel. Her father hadn't mentioned anyone else. Only herself.

Seven

Sarah decided to stop to see Grandpa on the way home from high school. He could be more help in gathering source material for a history paper on Robert E. Lee than all the book lists in the library because he had studied history since he was a boy. But Grandpa was not at home. Grandma thought he must have gone calling and would Sarah be sure to remember the young people's social on Friday night. Sarah thanked her, secretly hoping she could forget the social because she always felt silly playing games. Then she went next door to the church. On this unseasonably warm September day Grandpa might very well be sitting right in his own study reading a book. He was.

The study of the church was his real study. It was shaped like a boxcar because the architect had meant it for a storeroom, tucked away by itself back of the pipe organ. One went up six dark steps and down a very narrow, dark passageway to reach it. The bulb in the hall light was always broken or borrowed by someone. Grandpa didn't mind. He knew his way, and besides, he tried to keep this study for studying and not for visitors. He had another study at home, called "the library," which was the place for visitors because Grandma could bring in little cakes and fruit juice, which often helped a person to decide to join such a friendly church.

"I like this room, Grandpa. Whichever chair I sit in, I feel like it's the best chair." The one she was in now was low and deep so that her knees were up and her head was back and she was comfortable.

"I've sometimes thought we should have a national bonfire of all the chairs which no one likes to be caught sitting in. Think how much happier the whole country would be after the fire. Fewer divorces, reduced delinquency, more people in church. Although, of course, more than half of the church pews would have to go into the flames." Grandpa tipped back in his swivel chair. He was a noble-looking man, Sarah thought, with his fine, high forehead and his keen blue eyes.

"Grandpa, I need help on Robert E. Lee. If you could …"

"Sarah!" Grandpa was on his feet, going to the magazine table. "I have something for you. It's in the new *American*. A poem called *If* by Kipling. Listen to this." Then he read the poem aloud in his best manner, which was very good indeed.

When he had finished, Sarah was leaning forward, looking hard at Grandpa, but thinking to herself that while no doubt these were the things everybody should be faithful to, still for herself she liked the *Song of the Banjo* better. It made her feel sadder and, somehow, more *good* than this poem about goodness. Something must be the matter with her.

"I'd—I'd like to copy it," she said slowly. "I'll make a copy for Rachel. And a copy for Baldy. Baldy should grow up with a copy right over his bed!"

Grandfather nodded. But instead of feeling happy because she was passing a good thing on to other people, she felt unhappy. Actually she would be passing on something she didn't want herself. It was confusing.

"Sarah," Grandpa said sternly, "you are not saying what you think." Then his blue eyes twinkled. "You are playing up to me."

"I guess I am. Heavens! Maybe I'm not really an honest person at all." Then she told him what she had been thinking about *Song of the Banjo*.

"They are better lines," Grandpa agreed, and began to quote. Sarah joined in, and between them they pieced together half the poem, having a wonderful time of it. Finally Grandpa said, "All of us are younger sons finding our way home. The fortunate thing is that no matter how far we wander, the tug is there."

"Not for everyone, Grandpa. Leslie Sando's father doesn't believe in God. He says that even the watch argument that preachers always use—about a watch needing someone to make and wind it in the first place—he says even that argument is a thing you can't prove." She was sitting up straight now, twisting her braids around her hands. "I wish I knew a few more logical arguments for God."

Grandpa went over to a shelf and took down a book, blew off any possible dust the way he always did, hunted for a passage, and read it aloud to Sarah in French. Then he translated. "'It is the height of folly to try to measure infinite love by limited knowledge.' This is a sentence that has helped to make my life," he said. "Fénelon wrote it. He was a priest who dealt with the profligate court of Louis XIV. One of the most brilliant men of his time and one of the simplest. I'd call him a saint. He wrote some letters of spiritual advice to Madame de Maintenon. She was—"

"I know her," Sarah broke in eagerly. "For thirty years she ruled a king. She wasn't as beautiful as many others at the court, but she was witty and wise and she had so much common sense that His Majesty used to turn to her in council and ask, 'What does your solidity think of it?' After she was married to the King she founded a school for poor girls, and many of them loved her more than their own mothers."

When Sarah paused for breath her grandfather remarked, "She has to be judged in the light of her times, and all of the pages of her record are not bright. But just the same Fénelon considered her a seeking soul."

"If Fénelon wrote to her, I'll read what he said."

"Maybe you'll translate the letters someday and give them to us in English. Listen to this: 'Thou art nearer to us than we are to ourselves.'" For some minutes Grandpa continued to turn the pages, reading a sentence here and there, but Sarah had almost ceased to follow what he was saying because she had suddenly seen what he was. A seeker! Grandpa was trying to make sense out of life, just as she herself. Moreover, there was a way in which books meant more to him than people did, just as they did to her, and for the same reason. Most people didn't get you anywhere; when they left, you were just the same as when they came in. None of this exciting stretched feeling. Now she realized that she had often seen Grandpa trying politely to bow callers out of his own door while Grandma held onto them.

As if he were aware of her thoughts, Grandpa went on reading. "'It is not right to stay with a person to whom we can be of no use when we might be meeting others productively.'" That's what she wanted—productive friends. More people like Mrs. Rivera and Dr. Rivera, like—well, even like Miss Lillie. And like Leslie. More people like Grandpa himself. People who shone out.

"'God has not placed you under a bushel but on a candlestick,'" Grandpa was reading; "'so that you may light all those who are in the house.'" Grandpa did that. More than the Riveras, more than anyone she knew. When people came to him in true need he had all the time in the world. They might be intelligent people or ignorant people, even stupid people, but if they had a need they were his people. He was reading as if the words mattered terribly to him, almost as if he had written them himself. "'Within me it is thou who doest all that I do of good. I have felt a thousand times that I could not of myself conquer my disposition, nor overcome my habits, nor moderate my pride, nor follow my sense of right. Without thee I am only a reed blown by the wind.'"

He broke off suddenly and snapped the book shut. "Thank you, Sarah, thank you. You see, I have no one to read to, and an appreciative audience makes me a little drunk."

Sarah's eyes, wide with appreciation, were her best answer. "Grandpa, I think you are quite—" She caught herself. She had almost said "lonesome," but she changed it to "—wonderful."

He would not really want anyone to know how lonely he was. Not that loneliness was a weakness. Grandpa seemed twice as strong to her as he ever had before.

She was nearly home, still turning over in her mind the afternoon's talk, when it occurred to her that they had never got back to the arguments for God. Arguments for God seemed silly alongside Grandpa. But that wouldn't help Mr. Sando. Maybe she should lend him the book. Still smiling at the picture of big burly Mr. Sando reading Fénelon in French, Sarah went into the house.

"What kept you so late?" her mother asked. "I was worried about you."

"I stopped to get Grandpa to help me with my history."

"How were they?" Her mother was feeding Baldy and asked the question absently.

"Fine. He gave me a poem." Sarah produced *If*.

And now the poem drew forth the kind of respect it deserved. Her mother read it to herself and then she read it aloud to Lucy and Anna. During supper she set the children to learning it by heart. After she had gone to her own room to study, Sarah heard her mother downstairs reciting it aloud. Sarah knew without asking that when Mother lead the devotionals at the missionary meeting on Thursday, this poem would be her climax. It never occurred to her to wonder what her mother would do with Fénelon, although she read French fluently.

On October twenty-first Sarah was thirteen years old and she had a party. Everyone said that getting into one's teens was an important event. The family gave her presents, especially books. Her mother gave her *The Calling of Dan Matthews* by Harold Bell Wright. Mama had read it first and said that something new and noble had come into American literature. Grandpa gave her *A Certain Rich Man* because he thought that William Allen White was a great man. He said that one fourth the people in Emporia, Kansas, had bought that book because they valued their leading citizen so highly. Nobody gave her

The Man in Lower Ten by Mary Roberts Rinehart, which was the book she wanted most.

The party was a success. Everybody helped, but Sarah herself worked hardest at it. She found herself doing her best for every single person there, and she had thought to herself that she was getting quite unselfish. It was exciting, being unselfish in such a popular way. Nevertheless, she wished they would go home so that she could read one of the new books.

Being in high school brought none of the great changes she had expected. To be sure, the classes went from room to room instead of staying in one place, but the boys and girls were just about the same group she had always gone to school with. The same ones were smart and the same ones were slow. In class or out, they made about the same remarks you would expect them to make, except Rachel, who always said the honest thing if she knew it, and therefore frequently startled people accidentally. Except Leslie, too, who often had ideas which had not occurred to anyone else, even the teacher. There was something nice about routine days which neither offered nor lacked excitement.

Eight

On an ordinary day along in the first week of February, there came a telegram. The delivery boy said that it came from Nebraska, but beyond that he would not even admit that he knew what it said because the telegraph company was very honorable and never told what it knew.

Mama had gone to a silver tea at the church and Sarah, Lucy, and Anna all waited anxiously for her return, passing the unopened envelope from one to the other. So far as they knew none of the relatives in Nebraska was sick. A few weeks ago a horse had stepped on Grandfather Duncan's foot and crushed it rather badly, but at the last writing he was doing very well.

Just when Sarah had decided to take the telegram and go to meet her mother, her mother came in. She looked pretty in her gray box-pleated winter suit with the stiff white embroidered shirt-waist. It seemed too bad to give her a telegram. But she was very brave. She did not hesitate, but opened the envelope quickly and read aloud, "Father's foot gangrene amputation necessary wants to see Dennis's boy wire." According to Mama, it meant that Grandfather's foot was very much worse; bad enough so that if it was not cut off his very life would be threatened, and he wanted to see his grandson, the one who would carry the Duncan name. He wasn't going to have the operation until the baby got there.

"We will go tonight," said Mama calmly.

"Who will go?" asked Lucy. "Who is we?"

"All of us," Mama said, no more excited than if they were going to a church supper. "Sarah is a great favorite with her Duncan grandparents and Lucy should be there too."

Then Mama began to move. She telephoned to Dr. Rivera, who said that he would buy the tickets and come after the family himself in his own car at seven o'clock. Grandma Vanderiet came over to help pack. Anna brought up the freshly ironed clothes and helped with Lucy's bath and gave them all some supper. Mama did not forget a single thing. Father would have been greatly surprised because he used to be the one who remembered.

On the way to the train it was Sarah who for once did most of the talking. Someplace far inside her chest her heart was numb with apprehension, but she felt that if she could keep gay and unconcerned, then Grandfather's operation could not be serious. Lucy sat still, looking really elegant in her Sunday coat and leggings, and a hat with fur edging perched on her blonde curls. Mama would take no chances on the weather. Baldy was wrapped in so many layers of blanket that he looked like a boarding house washing.

They had to ride in a day coach as far as the Twin Cities. Once settled on the train, Lucy did not lie down and take a nap the way Mama wanted her to, but sat up straight, holding her doll and looking around. The man across the aisle gave her practically a whole box of toasted marshmallows out of which he had eaten only one. Sarah expected her mother to return the candy firmly, but Mama said that Lucy could keep it because the man was plainly a gentleman trying to be kind. The book which Sarah had planned to read on the train had been left behind through a mistake for which her mother felt responsible, so she called the newsboy and selected *When Knighthood Was in Flower.* It was a novel and therefore interesting, she said, but it was also full of English history so that no one need be ashamed to be seen reading it. Sarah was absorbed at once, but underneath her avid joy in a new book she felt guilty in enjoying herself so thoroughly and resolved to stop at the end of each chapter to think about Grandfather for a while. By the time they changed trains and boarded the Pullman it was the Princess Mary who dealt gently with Lucy in the matter of sitting up in their berth to swing her doll in the hammock. The book and the mood lasted all the way to Nemaha, so that it was a very grown-up Sarah who stepped off the train and fell with a gesture of gracious condescension into the arms of Uncle Bill McMann. He kissed her soundly and laughed aloud over her tallness, so that everyone on the platform heard him.

Uncle Bill was the husband of Aunt Ag. He was short and compact with hard muscles. His eyes were small and brown; his hair was curly and brown. He said that Grandfather Duncan was holding his own and refused to have the leg taken off until all the family got there.

Grandfather Duncan's house was white and stood in one corner of a quarter-block yard with a white picket fence around it. As soon as Lucy was out of the carriage she flew down the walk toward the front door and stood admiring the frosted glass with its etching of doves trailing scrolls of clouds. But no one came to the front door. Grandmother was waiting at the side door. Later, when Lucy asked Grandmother if the front door was stuck shut or something, Grandmother said of course not, but why should anyone want to come in through the cold hall and parlor? Sarah loved the dark cold parlor. She remembered being allowed to play in it with her coat on if she was sure to remind someone to pull down the shades when she came out so that the roses in the carpet would not fade. As soon as she had opportunity she slipped off to it to see if it smelled the way it used to—a smell halfway between the way leather smells and the way crackers smell. There was the organ just where it used to be. It had two rows of stops and a lamp stand at each end of the music rack.

Today the family were all in the back parlor, which was also the dining room on the rare occasions when Grandfather and

Grandmother did not eat in the kitchen. There were four large windows forming an oblong alcove in which stood a huge wicker plant stand with tiers of geraniums, begonias, fuchsia, and other blooming things. The largest picture on the wall was one of President Garfield because he had also belonged to the Christian Church. A base-burner with isinglass doors heated the room as well as the big bedroom which opened off it. Grandfather was in that bedroom.

Sarah did not want to hear about Grandfather's symptoms, which all the family were talking over. Talk would not help. She wandered unnoticed into the kitchen.

The kitchen was a grand room. Inside the door was a small lattice affair with pegs upon which were hung fascinators of various colors and a short fur cape which looked like a collar without a jacket. Sarah remembered how her father would wrap that cape around her on a cold winter's evening. Also near the back door stood the washstand at which Father used to wash her hands and face before meals. She poured some water from the gray granite pitcher into the basin. It was soft cistern water just as it used to be! She lathered her hands with soap that looked like mottled pink marble and smelled like geraniums. It seemed as if Father would surely come swinging in all ready for a breakfast of fried potatoes, eggs crisp around the edges, thick slices of salt pork which were his favorite, hot soda biscuits, and something called hominy which was white like little marbles and tasted like laundry soap.

Aunt Jane called out.

"What are you doing out here alone?" Then she came over to Sarah and squeezed her hand and said, "All day, since we knew you were coming, I've been seeing him too."

"You can go in now and see Grandfather," said Mama, who was just coming out of the bedroom, holding Baldy in the crook of her arm. Mama was not weeping; she seemed very cheerful. Everyone seemed cheerful—in a sad way. They liked being brave. Sarah felt small and shrunken.

When she stepped in the room Grandfather said, "Hello, Sarey," and his voice had a faint boom to it. He was pale and gaunt, but he did not look weak.

"My goodness, Grandfather, I thought you were sicker than this." She sat down on the chair by his bed and then leaned over and kissed him with a loud and jolly smack, the way he had taught her when she was a little girl. He was Grandfather, after all, and not a strange sick man.

"You don't think I look bad, Sarey?" He took her hand in his long, strong, bony one.

Sarah squinted her eyes and nose, as she often did when trying to concentrate. "You look a little pale in a brown way, but I think that's partly because you have on a white nightshirt instead of a blue work shirt, don't you?"

"I keep telling them I'd be all right if I could get into my shirt and pants." The boom was in his voice again.

"I'll sneak you a blue shirt, Grandfather. And I'll tell you something else. You've got your hair combed too nice. You look like Sunday." She leaned over and tousled his hair lightly. "Now if you could just smoke your pipe a few minutes to cover up the medicine smell, why, you'd just about be like yourself."

"By cracky, I would," Grandfather said. "They've kept that pipe away from me so long, I plumb forgot what it was I kept missing."

"Where is it?" Sarah asked.

"I know where one of them is. Right in the pocket of my overalls, hanging inside the woodshed door." He laughed out loud and heartily.

Aunt Jane and Aunt Ellen hastily stuck their heads in the door. "Get out," their father shouted. "Sarey's putting me to sleep. Can't I get me a little nap?"

Sarah slipped out. When she returned Aunt Mily stood by the bed holding a glass of water, Aunt Jane was combing her father's hair, Aunt Ag was once again rearranging the bottles of medicine on the dresser.

"Out with you all, I ain't got no time to waste," said Grandfather, trading on their mood of imminent disaster. "Sarey and me's got to have a talk. After all, she's Dennis's oldest girl."

Aunt Milly sobbed and Aunt Jane patted Sarah's shoulder, although she had to reach up to do it.

"Close the door," said Grandfather. The aunts closed it as on a last rite.

"Here it is." Sarah giggled as she took the pipe from inside her blouse. "I brought the tobacco too. Shall I fill it?"

"No woman can pack a pipe right," said Grandfather, trying to hoist himself a bit on his pillow.

"I can. My father taught me. You shush and see if I can't." She sat down by the bed, took out the bag of Bull Durham, and set to work, using her thumb quickly and firmly. Then she put the pipe in her mouth and lit it. "There," she said. "It draws like a chimney."

Grandfather took a puff. "I swan!"

"Father taught me when we used to drive in the country and he had to keep both hands on the reins."

"Sarey—" He puffed thoughtfully for a moment. "How do you feel about this here foot of mine? Doctor says it's got to come off. Case of dry gangrene and they can't stop it. I might last out several weeks yet, but in the end it's me or the leg. Now what gets me—" He stopped short.

"Well?" said Sarah with something of her father's sternness in her voice. "What gets you?"

He went on quickly. "It ain't the matter of not having a leg. Other people have stumped around on a cork leg and I reckon I can. It's a case I heard your pa tell about once. Man got his leg cut off—in fact, Dennis done it—and it was a good operation. Then about three days afterward the nurse came running down the hall after Dennis. The man had up and died without warning. A blood clot got caught in his heart."

"Maybe that's true," said Sarah, "but I should think with a man like you, why, Nature would just about be sure to do everything right. You aren't in a stew in your own mind like the men that count money all day in the banks or run around collecting bills. I've often heard my father say that a man has a lot better chance if he doesn't stew."

The door opened. "What on earth—" cried Aunt Milly. "Father! Ag! He's got a pipe."

Aunt Ag, Aunt Nancy, Uncle Al Squires—all of them streamed in. Grandfather waved them back with his hand. "Call your ma."

Grandmother came quickly. She just stood at the foot of the bed and waited for the talk to stop.

"Dorcas, we're cuttin' her off this afternoon." Grandfather indicated the leg propped up under the covers.

The aunts all spoke at once. It couldn't be done this afternoon. He had to be taken to a hospital and the doctors would give him medicine and things the night before the operation. "You can't have anything on your stomach, Papa," said Aunt Nancy with finality.

"There's mighty little there now, and such as there is is going to stay. Call Doc." He looked right at Grandmother. Grandmother looked right at him.

"All right, Thomas. I guess the time has come."

"I'll call the doctor," Uncle Al Squires said.

"I'll call him myself," Grandmother said.

All afternoon Grandfather smoked his pipe and grew stronger. He had an argument with practically every person in the household and he won all his arguments. The worst one was over what should be done with the leg after it was amputated. Aunt Ellen first raised the point. She was a worn-looking woman of forty-five, an invalid who had taken more kinds of medicine than anyone in Nemaha. But whenever there was something special like a wedding or having Grandfather's leg cut off, she would get off her couch and move around as strong as anybody. She warned them all that she would collapse later, but not while she was needed. She certainly looked a long ways from collapsing at the moment, but then she was excited about what should be done with the amputated leg.

Uncle Bill McMann said that a leg should be properly buried on account of the Judgment Day when the dead should rise. Aunt Nancy said that for goodness' sake that was a funny thing for Uncle Bill to say when he wasn't even a church member. Aunt Ag said gently that neither was Aunt Nancy's husband a church member but he no doubt hoped to rise from the dead. Aunt Nancy felt sure that if Uncle Nat could have left his busy law practice in California to come to Grandfather's bedside he would certainly say it didn't matter what happened to the leg; just throw it away. Still, Aunt Jane asked, where would you throw a leg? Aunt Milly thought it ought to be buried in a little coffin all its own. Where? asked Aunt Nancy. In a graveyard? And would you have a service read over it? Then Mama spoke out strongly and said that she believed in the resurrection but she thought that a God powerful enough to raise the dead would not be confounded by a misplaced leg. Sarah was proud of Mama.

Grandfather heard the talk even with the door closed into his bedroom, where he was not resting at all. He called for Aunt Ag because she was the oldest and he said, "Ag, my leg is to be put in a box and buried someplace at the foot of the slope in the garden. Then after your mother and I are both gone, you can move the box to the cemetery if you want to."

Uncle Louis said the old gentleman might just as well have his way because you couldn't suit all the girls even if each of them donated a leg.

After school the cousins began to come in. Sarah couldn't remember who belonged to whom, and no one explained it. There was Cousin Earl, who owned the creamery and was married to a woman named Ramona, who had a great many freckles and a cheerful, loud voice. They had two small boys, but they left them home because Grandfather had seen them plenty of times. Cousin Timothy was a farmer and lived on the farm next to Aunt Ag, which was very convenient for the women when thrashers came. He did not have any children yet, but Sarah thought his wife must be going to have a baby soon or else she had lost her shape very young. Aunt Ag's twins were there, too. Ernest and Arnold, whom their families called *Ern* and *Arn*. They were twelve years old but short like their father. Sarah liked them and they liked her. Not that she or they had more than said "hello" to each other, but she knew at once that they would get along first-rate and she hoped she could stay at their house for a few days.

Aunt Milly and Uncle Al had brought Jackie, who whimpered and wanted something all the time, until Uncle Al said cheerfully that he was fed up and would take the brat home, and Aunt Milly said how could he say such a word about his own child, and Uncle Al answered that she ought to ask how could they have such a child. No one was mad at anyone; they were just talking; they didn't even mind very much that Jackie whimpered. He was spoiled. Ruby Simpson came in after high school. She was the most stylish of all the cousins. At sixteen she was practically a young lady with her hair done up, but that, said Uncle Eph, was one thing he did not approve of. Ruby only patted his arm and called him "old darling" and told Sarah that when she got a little older she would understand how hard a father could make life. Aunt Nancy had not brought her three daughters, Anabelle, Beatrice, and Clara, from California, but no one was more present than they. This day of Grandfather's operation crowded more impressions into Sarah's heart than she could remotely assimilate all at once, but they remained untarnished in the grab bag of memory.

By four o'clock the house was transformed into a hospital, with huge white lights installed in the kitchen and two nurses, a pretty red-haired one and a large pock-marked one, taking Grandfather's temperature and being very calm in a clean, starched way. All the aunts and uncles came in to wish Grandfather luck. Some said "good-by" by mistake. Mama brought Baldy in for Grandfather to kiss. When it was Sarah's turn to go in to speak to Grandfather she felt her throat getting dry and her head seemed a long way from her feet. However, she gave her voice an urgent everyday tone and said, "Listen, Grandfather, hurry and get through this business because I've just got to have an easel, will you? I can draw on a table, but when I start to paint there isn't any place to prop my canvas, and if you could make me a stand I'd get along a lot better."

"This is no time to talk about a painting stand," the pretty nurse said sharply.

"Why not?" asked the large nurse easily. "If she needs a stand, why shouldn't Mr. Duncan make it for her? He doesn't saw and hammer with his foot, does he?"

Grandfather looked at her hungrily. "That's right, I don't."

"How many days before you could get at it, do you think?" Sarah wheedled.

"Two or three, maybe. Tell you, Sarey, take a look in the woodshed and see if I've still got a couple of light one-by-sixes." He raised himself on his elbow and looked, Sarah thought, as if he might be just waking up from an after-dinner nap. She didn't know what one-by-sixes were, but she walked out briskly, stopping only to call back in a good natural voice, "Listen, Grandfather, could I use some of your nails if I need them?"

"Let Sarey have what she wants," said Grandfather to Aunt Milly, who was tiptoeing in.

The large nurse followed Sarah out and Sarah turned to her. "You look after him, won't you? He kind of hates it, you know."

"You bet," said the large one with inelegant directness. "What's a leg these days?"

Sarah was glad when Mama said, "Aunt Ag has to go home to feed the chickens and Uncle Bill has to look after the stock, so I think we will just go out there and spend the night."

Uncle Bill was chewing tobacco hard and fast, even if he was in the house. He didn't want to see the kitchen fixed up like an operating room. He wanted to get outdoors. Aunt Ag, at the last minute after they all had their wraps on, thought maybe she should stay, but Uncle Bill said he could drive her back the whole eight miles in forty-five minutes.

They all climbed into the spring wagon set low on runners. There were two seats, but the girls preferred to ride with Ern and Arn in the hay on the floor of the sleigh. They sat facing each other, girls on one side, boys on the other, buffalo robes over all. Already Grandfather's operation seemed something that had happened quite a while ago.

Nine

Even in the rush of leaving home before daylight, Aunt Ag had put a good fat hen into the black iron kettle on the back of the coal burner in the living room, and when the family arrived home there was dinner almost ready, smelling better than good. Everything had its own special smell which, added together, made "Nebraska" seem to Sarah all her life one of the most fragrant words in the English language. There was the tangy odor of the pink geraniums on the kitchen window sill, Uncle Bill's strong old pipe on one corner of the washstand, corncobs and kindling already snapping into blaze in the cookstove, a pantry full of peach pickles and homemade dills, and—

But Sarah couldn't smell and look and feel and taste fast enough. If somehow she could only paint all of this exactly the way she felt it, there would be a picture for Miss Moseley! The thought made Sarah laugh to herself and then try to explain her laugh to Aunt Ag, who had given her eggs to beat with a flat wire egg beater.

Aunt Ag understood. To look at her, Sarah thought, one might not guess she would understand about painting. She was a woman of considerable size and no special shape, soft as a cushion if you bumped into her, but so strong that back in the days when she and Uncle Bill were just starting out, she used to go right out and drive the hayrack if a hired man got sick. Uncle Bill liked to tease her now and to call her a "weak sister" because she used an electric cream separator and—of all highfalutin ideas—an electric churn.

Aunt Ag had never painted, but she had ideas about painting. When Sarah told her about Miss Moseley, she said, "Well, don't take anybody's advice unless it shouts what you were already thinking."

"But advice is telling you things you'd never know by yourself."

"Oh no, it isn't. You really can't use advice unless it puts you on the track of the thing you would naturally do anyway—in time. Advice is temporary. Everyone has his own work and his own way to do it, and when he finds that, then he doesn't need advice or teaching any more. He only has to work."

In the two weeks that Sarah stayed at Aunt Ag's they had many talks about painting. On the second morning after Grandfather's operation, when he had been declared out of danger and doing nicely, Ern, Arn and Lucy went off tobogganing on Old South Hill while Sarah, longing to be off with them, dutifully set out her paints and paper. A blizzard, as prophesied by Uncle Bill, had blown in earnest for two nights and a day, so that it was impossible to go to town, but Aunt Ag or Mama called Grandmother on the telephone about once an hour. This particular morning Mama was bathing Baldy in a small washtub set on two chairs beside the coal burner.

Mama said, "Sarah, you shouldn't try to work on vacation. After all, you're only thirteen and you don't have to make a living with your paintbrush yet."

"I have to learn," Sarah said in her most moral tone and with a set of her mouth reminiscent of Grandma Vanderiet. "Miss Moseley told me not to get out of practice while I was away. I think she'll be pleased if I could match the color of this pink geranium just right."

"I don't see why you don't just take her the geranium," Mama said a little crossly.

"In a way—in a way," said Aunt Ag, who was watering the plants, "a picture of a geranium is better than a geranium because in a picture you see not only the geranium but you see

Sarah!" She smiled at her lanky niece and Sarah smiled back in amazement.

"Why, Aunt Ag, that's true and it's kind of a deep thing to say."

Sometimes it was difficult for Sarah to work in the living room where everyone talked all the time. She tried the parlor, but it was colder than outdoors. She tried the big bedroom off the parlor where Mama and Baldy slept. In the bedroom there was a small corncob stove which was lighted every morning while they dressed, and the heat lingered for an hour after breakfast. Sarah thought it was one of the nicest rooms she knew. The great walnut bed had a feather-bed mattress and quilts of intricate design. At the other end of the room there was an immense clothespress, and Aunt Ag loved to tell the story about the time when she was a little girl and Father was a little boy and they played calaboose in that clothespress until one fine day when Father got mad at his little sister Jane and locked her in the press and left her for a whole morning while the family looked everywhere for her, down the well, in the silo, and over in the gypsy camp. When Father finally came home from the neighbors' and let Jane out, Grandfather whipped him because Jane had cried herself sick. But Father bravely said he didn't mind being whipped at all and went whistling from the woodshed to the house, even though the switch had left marks on his bare legs. Grandfather did nothing by halves, but neither did Father. Later on he had made Jane a doll-house which Aunt Jane still kept.

Sarah decided to paint a picture of the bedroom itself. Then she could keep it forever. She chose an angle that included not only the clothespress but the south window through which could be seen a stark brown sycamore and, inside the room, the marble-top washstand with its beautiful washbowl and pitcher intricately ornamented with violets and rosebuds. She spent a great deal of time on the sycamore and even more time on the ornamented pitcher. Later, when Sarah showed Miss Moseley the painting, Miss Moseley said, "You can't make a picture out of a clothespress, but the pods on the sycamore are very well done and the washbowl and pitcher are really amazing, my child. It must have taken a great deal of time to copy those decorations so faithfully." Sarah flushed with praise and took the picture to Mrs. Rivera, who propped it on her mantel, studied it from every angle, and said, "You should be spanked for the time that must have gone into ornamenting that horrible pitcher and bowl, but the big old clothespress—now you have caught the essentials of structure there. The clothespress has *action*. I could open its doors and expect a story to step out at me." Sarah was pleased again and told her the story about the clothespress. But she was also much confused. Everybody said a different thing, and in both praise and blame she was inclined to agree with them all, which resulted in anything but a happy frame of mind.

Probably the nicest picture she brought home from Nebraska, Sarah thought, was a bowl of eggs. It was a blue crockery bowl containing white chicken's eggs, pale green duck eggs, large, speckled turkey eggs, and one tiny bantam egg. She had seen the bowl of eggs on Aunt Ag's kitchen table, some wisps of straw still clinging to the freshly gathered eggs, and had sketched them quickly with a pencil, afterward trying water color.

The days went by too quickly at Aunt Ag's. In the evening they took turns playing checkers with Uncle Bill, who cheated openly, his face solemn and his eyes twinkling, and then assumed an air of outraged innocence when you caught him. Catching Uncle Bill was much more of a game than the checkers. Sometimes Aunt Ag would get out the big iron kettle and pop corn which Arn and Ern had raised themselves. Sometimes she made popcorn balls by adding homemade corn syrup and kernels of black walnut. If the children wanted walnuts, they had to crack them, using a hatchet on the thick black shells. Some days Lucy visited the one-room country schoolhouse, carrying her lunch in a tin dinner pail just as her cousins did. She was very popular. She could run fast and she was polite. Even the big boys stood around for her. When she came home and talked about the school, Sarah decided to visit also. But she never did. She was too shy to go where she would probably be the tallest person in the room.

For ten days the snowdrifts and the cold weather kept all the children from going to town. Only Uncle Bill and Aunt Ag and Mama drove in to see Grandpa, who was doing well. Then Mama said it was time to pack up to go back to Wheaton. Sarah was sorry to think of going. She liked being with Aunt Ag, who worked all day and yet never seemed to be working at all. Aunt Ag no more complained of her work than she complained of her ample waist; both were hers. Reluctantly Sarah began to pack. But Lucy did not want to help to pack even as much as her own doll clothes. She said that her eyes hurt and she wanted to lie on the big leather couch with an afghan over her.

The next day Lucy had the measles. Probably she had got the measles at school. Arn and Ern and Sarah had had measles, but there was Baldy to think of. After discussing a dozen plans, it was decided that Mama would take Lucy in to Grandfather Duncan's where there were no other children.

During the next two weeks Baldy became a person. When Mama went away he was just a baby, fourteen months old, running around actively, saying a few words, but a baby. He stood by the window and watched his mother, with Lucy bundled in a bear rug, drive off with Uncle Bill. Sarah watched him, wishing she had paid more attention to the way one amused a baby. By and by he hunted his A B C picture book, brought it to Sarah, leaned against her knee, and said, "Read." She read two pages and when she shut the book as if to stop, he said, "Read." So she read to the end of the sixteen pages. Then he climbed into her lap. He was small and wiry and did not snuggle down but leaned raptly over the picture book. When she had finished he turned the book over and said, "Read." So she began for a third time, looking at her small brother in large wonder. His interest made her excited, too, so that each time she read the book it was a new book. They read the book complete eleven times. The twelve years between them was never again of great moment.

During the next few days Baldy learned new words so fast that Aunt Ag became worried. She spoke to Sarah cautiously. "My mother had a little sister who learned to talk too young. She could sing whole songs when she was a year old, and she died of brain fever." Sarah looked quickly at Baldy, who was pushing around some big blocks which Uncle Bill had made for him. He did not seem to be ailing with those red cheeks and quick movements. His face was sharp and intense. Perhaps he should be outdoors more. Quickly she bundled him into his coat and leggings. Together they made a snow man. Baldy copied all her movements. He learned to say "buttons" and "forehead."

At the end of another two weeks the snow was nearly gone, so quickly had it become March and spring. Mama came back to Aunt Ag's, leaving Lucy in town for a few more days. Baldy seemed gravely glad to see her, but he did not talk much. Mama simply did not believe all the things Aunt Ag told her about his sentences.

Just before supper a thunderstorm came up. Uncle Bill said it was too early for a thunderstorm, but the thunder drowned out his words. Baldy was standing in the middle of the floor when the first clap sounded. He stood very still, clutching his book, and his frightened eyes went from one person to another. Mama called from the kitchen, "Don't let it scare the baby." Sarah said, "It's just thunder, Baldy. It's a big noise in the sky." She spoke firmly. The sky had darkened quickly, and Aunt Ag brought in a lamp and drew the shades so that they would not see the lightning. The thunder grew louder and nearer, then all at once a terrific peal seemed to envelop the house in its roar. Mama flew into the room and grabbed up the baby, but Baldy slid from her arms and ran to Sarah. When she picked him up he was trembling but he did not cry. Sarah held him so closely that one breath seemed to do for both of them. In a few moments the storm was over, and when Ern flung open the kitchen door they saw that the great elm in the barnyard had been slashed in two.

The next day Sarah went to town to look after Lucy, who was now up and playing around the house somewhat wanly, while Mama got a rest out at Aunt Ag's before starting home. In the evening, after Lucy was in bed, Sarah sat with Grandfather and Grandmother by the base-burner in the back parlor. These were the best evenings of her life up to that time.

Grandfather was dressed now and looking like himself, although more gaunt. His left trouser leg was empty below the knee. By and by he could have a cork leg, but at present he used crutches. The first thing he had done after he was up and around was to make Sarah her easel. He liked to whittle as well as carpenter and was now making a set of doll furniture for Lucy. Grandmother brought the tall parlor lamp and put it beside Grandfather, then she sat in her small rocker on the other side of the lamp. Sarah sat opposite them in a deep hickory rocker with a thin cretonne cushion. Grandmother was piecing a silk-and-velvet crazy quilt, but Sarah did nothing. They sat this way every evening.

"My goodness, I'd forgotten all about Deborah Howe's green velvet suit," Grandma would say, holding up a patch of bright green mottled velvet. "Remember it, Thomas?" Grandfather remembered. He chuckled.

"Why do you laugh, Grandfather?" Sarah's rocker creaked in anticipation.

Then Grandmother would tell the story of a hard-working girl, plain as a piebald horse, who took herself off to high school before there was a high school in this country, and finally married a lawyer who drank. She stuck to him through thick and thin for fifty-five years.

"She must have been terribly in love with him," Sarah said.

"I don't know if she was so much in love with him as she

just wasn't in love with nobody else," Grandfather said. "There's a difference."

No one said anything for a few minutes. The silence was more friendly than most people's conversation.

Sometimes Sarah prompted one of them. "Tell the story about when you were a bride, Grandmother."

So Grandmother would begin back in Virginia, where she lived in a white house with tall pillars, and she'd tell about the skylarking son of the Duncans who hadn't even begun to settle down when he was twenty years old. Egged on by Grandfather, she'd tell about the courtship and the wedding and about the way her own mother never shed a tear when she climbed up beside her young husband on the front seat of a real covered wagon and started for her new home in Nebraska. Two rooms, the house was, "smelling sweet of new boards and sunshine."

"But I built her a parlor the second year. First parlor on the Old Muddy was your Grandmother's. I said I'd marry a lady and I'd keep her a lady," Grandfather said stubbornly. "Had an awful uphill job sometimes; she was ornery as a mule."

"He wanted me to stay in the house no matter what might be going on in the field," Grandmother said complacently. "The year the grasshoppers came and Thomas broke his arm and your father had the whooping cough, I took things in my own hands a bit." Grandmother snapped off her thread with decision.

"All she done was put in a second crop of buckwheat by herself. Otherwise we might of starved. Plenty around us almost did." Sarah looked over at Grandmother. She was very small and very, very, well—Grandfather had said it when he called her a lady. Everything about her was clean and sweet and fine. Grandfather was looking at her, too, and Sarah saw the look in his eyes. Grandmother looked up and saw the look also. She said, "Silly." Sarah thought it was the nicest thing a woman ever said to a man.

Some nights they talked about politics and William Jennings Bryan, whom Grandfather and Grandmother knew well. William Jennings Bryan had said that if Grandmother were only a man he'd have put her on the ticket with him. Sarah said that Grandpa and Grandma Vanderiet were Republicans, but she doubted if Grandpa Vanderiet knew what was happening to the tariff or he would no doubt switch over. Other nights they talked about great important things like trusts and interstate commerce and parcel post and what would happen if China should ever become a republic. Grandfather said, "Your grandmother is pretty radical. I have to hold her down." Grandmother snorted and told Grandfather he'd better drink some hot milk and go to bed. But Grandfather said he could not go to bed because his foot itched.

"Scratch it," Sarah said practically.

"I can't," Grandfather answered plaintively. "It's my left foot that itches."

"But your left foot—your left foot—" It didn't seem polite to say "is buried in the garden," but plainly he had no left foot.

"It itches just the same," Grandfather insisted. "You may say it's nerves which used to lead to my foot, but I say it's my foot."

Sarah could hardly bear to see the evenings slipping by so fast and listened anxiously every morning when Grandmother phoned to find out about Mama's cold. Sarah had no wish ever to leave this house. Everything about it suited her: the windows that could be raised only after one pulled out the two little pegs at the side, the red tablecloth on the kitchen table, the silver-and-cut-glass canister on the cupboard, the neighing of the horses and the cackling of the hens down by the barn, the aunts and cousins coming in to discuss the news of the town. But most of all, just Grandfather and Grandmother, being their own two selves. Or were they two selves? Their roots were so tangled together in their yesterdays, their branches so intertwined, that they cast one shadow; one great protecting shadow on the bright hot roadway of the hurrying present. It was a great thing, Sarah thought, to have people like them belonging to you.

Ten

After the spring in Nebraska summer seemed uneventful, but somehow October was an exciting month, although not one single thing happened out of the ordinary. Perhaps it was only the weather; each morning came along as fresh and independent as a girl in a starched shirt-waist. Sarah found that being a sophomore was not too hard, and she was doing better with her painting. She had been studying now for more than two years and she could look back and laugh at the jugs. But nevertheless there was a long stretch ahead. Maybe fame would not come before she was forty. Fourteen from forty left twenty-six years to go. But eventually the day would come when Miss Moseley would stand beside her easel and say, "My dear, I can teach you no more. You have gone beyond me." Then Sarah would say, "All that I am I owe to your patient teaching." All her life she would send Miss Moseley flowers on her birthday—odd, to think of Miss Moseley having birthdays—and she would make sure that the reporters mentioned Miss Moseley when writing the early life of Sarah Duncan.

Also, she would have them mention Miss Lillie Tower. The reporters should say, "Sarah Duncan's sensitive soul was always greatly moved by music. Indeed, the two arts, painting and music, fed one another. They sometimes vied for first place in her affection." (That was a dreadful thing to say; she did not really mean it—painting must always come first.) "Miss Lillie Tower was Sarah Duncan's music teacher as long as Miss Duncan lived in the quaint little city of Wheaton."

Miss Lillie Tower seemed happier than she used to be. Sarah had finally thought of something to do for her. Or rather Mrs. Rivera had thought of it after Sarah had been forced by her own unresourcefulness to turn for help. Mrs. Rivera said that there was not a single music teacher in all of their neighboring village of Taylortown with its twelve hundred inhabitants and new consolidated school and that Miss Lillie should have a class there one day a week. Taylortown was only thirty miles away, but the train connections were so poor that she would have to stay overnight in the hotel.

Miss Lillie said she could not possibly leave her mother, whereupon Mrs. Rivera got in her car and went to see Mrs. Tower. Sarah was with her and she knew that Mrs. Rivera had never looked more queenly at any of her receptions. She wore a taupe velvet suit; the ostrich feathers on her hat paled from cerise to taupe, and their tips curled over the beautiful black hair knotted at the back of her head.

At first Mrs. Tower said quaveringly that Miss Lillie had never spent a night away from her for forty years and she wouldn't know what to do without her daughter. Mrs. Rivera said that maybe Mrs. Tower would have positively to make Miss Lillie go to Taylortown, but it was a fearful and a wonderful thing to have a will power like Mrs. Tower's. After a while Mrs. Tower said that there was no sense in a grown woman hanging back and leaving it for her mother to make all the decisions. When Mrs. Rivera rose to leave she bowed to Mrs. Tower as if Mrs. Tower had done her some great favor such as giving her half a duchy, then she took Miss Lillie's hand in hers, as strong as a vise, and practically dragged her into the entry. She set her teeth and hissed at Miss Lillie, "Now you get out and go or I will poison every pupil you have in Wheaton and you will starve." She kissed Miss Lillie good-by and left her in happy tears. On the way home Sarah said, "Miss Lillie is afraid to go to Taylortown and ask people for their children, and I think she is afraid to stay in the hotel alone."

"Of course," said Mrs. Rivera, as if it did not matter. "But she will get over being afraid, and then every Tuesday will be a Roman holiday for her. Miss Lillie is a ninny, but she is also something of a love. Besides, I have already sent word to certain people in Taylortown that it would be a good thing for their children to take lessons of Miss Lillie."

Later Miss Lillie told Sarah that she simply could not understand how word got around so fast that she was at the hotel ready to begin a music class. So many children came that she was afraid that later on she might have to stay two days in Taylortown, and not a single mother complained about her price.

Quietly Miss Lillie had begun to bloom a little. Sarah had found out how she spent her evenings—that is, if her mother had a caller to visit with—and all the rest of her spare time too. She played Bach. For her there were three kinds of composers: the poor ones, the great ones, and Bach. For all she was a small person, she had large strong hands. Indeed, her big hands embarrassed her and she wore long sleeves with cuffs pointed down over them and tried always to hide her hands in her lap. But when she played Bach she forgot about her hands; spanning ten notes was easy for her. She could strike a firm chord with thumb and little finger and then use the middle three fingers for intricate designs, just the way Bach would have expected her to do. Sometimes Sarah wondered if it wasn't hard for a person born with Bach-fugue fingers to teach the children of Wheaton and Taylortown all day long. Or was it? Miss Lillie was always pointing out that Bach himself was bound down by routine duties and yet thanksgiving ran through his music with irrepressible joy. Every pupil she had knew about Bach's life and works. Maybe the incessant teaching gave her more understanding for Bach. It made her free time freer.

November was so cold and rainy that Grandma Vanderiet said she understood for the first time what a trial it must have been for Mrs. Noah to spend forty days hand running in an ark without a single day fit for hanging out clothes. On the long rainy afternoons Mama read a great deal. She said that *The Winning of Barbara Worth* was a nobler book than *Queed*. And that whoever this H. S. Harrison was, he did not have the deep understanding of human nature that Dickens and Harold Bell Wright had. Baldy played and let her read. His mind was always someplace else than where one thought it was. Now that he was almost two years old, he talked as much as he wanted to. Sometimes he merely sat still on the front step and looked at the leaves falling off the trees. Or he might lie on his stomach for a long time watching ants. He spent hours following Sarah around with his books, which Mama said were too old for him. But Grandpa said that some souls were born older than others. Mama said, "That's silly," and Grandpa said, "Yes, isn't it? But there's nothing we can do about it except give each soul its proper bill o' fare." To hear Grandpa talk, you'd think Baldy was older than his own mother.

The last Sunday of the month was the rainiest day of all. The world seemed a gray and sodden thing beyond the hope of sun or cheer. Sarah went to church because it seemed the only decent thing to do when so many people would surely stay home. But Grandpa talked about baptism, which seemed an unnecessary thing to do on such a day. Moreover, they were a long time getting away from the church because some woman whose son had run away wanted to talk to Grandpa. So dinner was late and Anna was cross and the roast was hard and dry.

Just at the end of the cheerless meal the telephone rang. It was Adolph, the only one of the Rivera servants who spoke English, calling to say that Mrs. Rivera would like to have Sarah come to tea to meet a friend.

"Oh, but, Adolph," Sarah answered in some consternation, "does she mean a party?"

"Only one friend," answered Adolph's reassuring English accent. "I think if I may say so, Miss Sarah, that you will feel quite at home."

"I'll come," Sarah said a bit dolefully. "And thank Mrs. Rivera very much, Adolph."

She dressed with care in her newest dress, which was a fine French broadcloth of powder blue, trimmed in braid. The skirt was long, too, down almost to her ankles, because even if she was only fourteen she was the tallest girl in her class. She wound her braids around her head in an almost grown-up fashion, and Mama lent her one of her best handkerchiefs. She looked at herself in the mirror. The whole effect was very stylish and really rather grown up. The rain stopped abruptly and she walked happily down the avenue.

The guest was an odd but distinguished-looking man with a tremendous head of brown hair. Mrs. Rivera said, "Tony, this is our friend Sarah Duncan." Sarah said nothing. They were calling this man "Tony," but certainly—certainly—if pictures and posters could be believed, he was Josef Aronowitz, first violinist of his day. First violinist of the world! Although she could think of no words to say in greeting, Sarah smiled and shook his hand firmly and looked him evenly in the eye, for she was as tall as he.

"She's a winsome girl," cried Tony with enthusiasm. He did everything with enthusiasm, as unforced as the rapids of a river. "Come, you shall see the house with us. Can you believe that I have never been in the house of Carlotta Rivera before?" He slipped his right arm through Sarah's, as he had his left through Mrs. Rivera's, and they walked three abreast to the dining room. Dr. Rivera followed, leading the way! For plainly neither his wife nor his guest knew quite where they were going, so pleased were they to be together. Dr. Rivera looked so happy he was shining. Everybody talked at once. Everybody but Sarah.

"Look, Tony, Enrique matched my mother's silver. The tray, the sugar bowl, they are exactly like the other pieces—yes? A silversmith in Genoa knew the pattern. His great-grandfather had worked on the original things. See how he has hidden the tiny coat of arms under the falcon's wing."

Tony looked and admired. He exclaimed in half a dozen languages at once. He looked at the gold-and-blue icon above the teakwood table. He took the Dresden ladies from their shelf. He rang the fragile wineglasses, all shapes and sizes, and only the laughing restraint of his hostess kept him from arranging them into an orchestra. Finally he turned to the doctor and clapped the older man on the shoulder. "Enrique, my boy, you are taking care of her! I always said she should have everything, and she has. Only a few mortals should have such things because only a few mortals can transcend fine craftsmanship."

"It's all very simple here." The doctor spoke modestly, but he was as pleased as anything. "It's not half she was used to."

"It's everything that matters," cried Carlotta, stepping away from them. "Nothing can bring back my mother—or my father—but—but, Tony, Tony—" Pity and terror were both in her voice. Sarah drew back by the doctor, and protectingly he took her hand. The woman by the window in her long white wool dress, ebony beads with a cross around her neck, eyes burning, lips scarlet, cheeks grown whiter than the gown—later across the intervening miles and years, Sarah remembered her exactly as she was then. Only for a moment the enveloping tenseness held them together, motionless. Then Tony went to Mrs. Rivera and took her in his arms and brushed back her hair with his hand and said comforting syllables which were scarcely words. Dr. Rivera looked grateful, and Sarah's throat ached almost past bearing, and then everything was all right again. They began to talk.

They all went together into the kitchen, where Mrs. Rivera was as charmed as a child showing off the electric gadgets. Tony worked the egg beater and wanted something to beat, so the doctor brought eggs which Sarah broke into two blue bowls, yolks in one, whites in the other, "in case the cook should want to make a cake." Tony laughed at her for being so clever and so canny. Everybody laughed at everybody, and the doctor munched a hard dry roll.

Then it was late afternoon and they were up in Mrs. Rivera's own sitting room by the piano. No one said, "Tony, will you play now?" but Tony took his violin from the case and tuned it as he walked around the room.

"How about giving me an A, Sarah?"

Sarah gave him the key. Mrs. Rivera lay back on her chaise longue, eyes closed with their unbelievable lashes flecking her cheeks. She was smiling at Tony's banter, and waiting. The doctor took the big chair by the fire. Sarah had decided on the stool near the window for herself because there she could see all of them and watch the sunset too. But Tony was talking to her.

"What shall we begin with, young woman? Because of course you shall accompany me. I am in a mood to be accompanied."

"Not me!" cried Sarah in complete consternation.

"But who else? Certainly not Carlotta, who is much, much too lazy, and besides, I have come a thousand miles to look at her just as she is now. And not Enrique, my lad, who doesn't know a single note—except a bank note. By simple induction, or shall we say subtraction, the duty falls on your young shoulders. Which, by the way, are very good. Broad but not too square. One day, Carlotta, you must put her into dark red velvet. Let me see! What shall it be?"

Then she noticed the huge pile of music stacked on a table by the piano. Across many of the covers *Carlotta Sandoval* was written in a large, firm hand. Had that been Mrs. Rivera's name and had she once played those accompaniments for some violinist? It was now plain to Sarah that they had been telling this Tony about her piano playing. No doubt they had told him that she played for the high school orchestra and that she was now paying for her art tuition by accompanying Professor Richter when he practiced on his violin. She wished to goodness she had not been so conceited and told Mrs. Rivera that Professor Richter had said he'd like to have her play for him in public because she followed him better than Professor Green did, except—of course—it would not look well for a young girl to be accompanying the head of the music department. Tony had now found what he was looking for. He put it before her. It was Mendelssohn's "On Wings of Song." Sarah frowned. She liked the piece a great deal, but he had probably chosen it because he thought that was all she could play.

She played it easily; the notes flowed smoothly beneath her fingers. And it was fortunate he had chosen a familiar piece because something in his tones made prickles go up her spine. This was no ordinary violin. This was no ordinary playing. In his own mind Mendelssohn must have heard his music played as Tony was playing it. When they came to the end Tony said, "Hm," and no one else said anything. So Sarah did not say anything, either.

He handed her Grieg's "To Spring." Now there was a thing she loved to play. The accompaniment was much harder, but she knew the runs and her fingers always had themselves a good time. They were off and it was more exhilarating than a frosty morning. This time when they had finished he said, "I see! I see!" She did not ask what he saw. These were people who took their music for music's sake. And then he handed her Franck's Sonata in A Major.

She felt weak. To be sure, she had played it before, but only two or three times; she had meant to work on it before Professor Richter called for it again. The first part was easy, but in the second movement she might get lost entirely. Tony sensed her hesitation. "Nonsense, young woman! Have you never heard Ernest Newman's dictum: music that is worth playing at all is worth playing badly?"

"But not the bad and the good—me and you—at the same time!" Her hands were folded tightly in her lap.

"Ah! But the good redeems the bad." He was laughing at her. "You've never played with a master before. Come, I will share with you." He threw his head back, fully aware that he was a master, and yet there was no conceit in him. Sarah looked into his honest eyes, gray-green, with highlights of copper. She had never seen such eyes. But then neither had she ever seen a body of such compact vitality, nor hands so quick and strong. They were like her father's hands! She sighed, turned back to the piano, and, at his nod, began to play.

Tony walked around the piano and turned his back to her, but something invisible and strong flowed from violin to piano. Even in the second movement when the accompaniment grew difficult, her fingers sped surely and she struck the chords firmly. He had turned toward her now. Occasionally he held her back with a nod. Before the third movement he beat out the time for a moment with his bow. The piano led out, slowly; then the violin sang its call. Her chords were her answer; it seemed to her that her hands would have known what answer to make had no accompaniment been written. As she touched the last soft note of the *fantasia,* a pain of regret swept through her. No matter how many times she might play this same sonata, it could never be this way again. And then they were off for the last movement. Her part was strong and lively; it was, as he had said, something outside her experience to play with a master. His assurance flowed into her. Her fingers found their way in a kind of ecstasy of assurance. She was buoyed up, carried along, on the swift current of the music they were making together. For it *was* partly her music. She could never make it alone, this vibrant, poignant, daring thing which filled the room and raced onward to the stars, but neither could it exist without her. It was bigger than she was, and when the violin stopped she would be small again, but never so small as before.

A swift crescendo to the closing chord, and Tony laid down his violin. Bow in hand, he turned to Sarah, but for a full moment he spoke no word. *"Mon Dieu!"* he said in a whisper sharp with excitement. "The girl is born to accompany. The technique one can learn, but *simpatico*"—he gesticulated with his bow—"*simpatico* is from the gods. How old are you?"

"Fourteen." Her voice was eager, but her eyes were anxious. What was he going to say that made her hands turn cold before he had spoken?

"Who did you say teaches her?" He turned to Mrs. Rivera abruptly.

"A local music teacher who might have been a musician." Then she explained Miss Lillie Tower.

"She"—he indicated Sarah with a toss of his head—"she must have the right teacher at once. Koenigstein in Minneapolis will be her man. He is genius for work. How many hours a day does she practice?"

"Only one or two except when the day is rainy or the summer long. She is in high school, you see."

"She must have more hours at the piano." He spoke almost angrily and then turned swiftly to Sarah. "Do you think you can learn in your sleep?" Back to Mrs. Rivera, "School, yes, in its place." He shrugged his shoulders, gesturing rapidly with his bow, including them all. "But these are the years for technique. Speed and strength—they come early if they come at all. How old were you when you began?"

"Four," said Sarah. It was all she could think of to say.

"Ah! Very good. Let me see your hands." Frowningly he laid down his bow and examined her hands as carefully, as impersonally, as a surgeon, flexing the fingers, bending them backward, pinching the cushioned tips, feeling the muscles of her forearm. His frown disappeared. Holding her hands lightly in his, he bowed from the waist, clicking his heels together. "Mademoiselle l'Artiste, I salute you." He kissed her fingers lightly. Then turning again to Mrs. Rivera, who was now sitting upright on her chaise longue, as excited as he was, "I shall take her with me to Koenigstein tomorrow, yes?"

Sarah rose unsteadily and went to them, reaching out to them as if they were unwittingly destroying something fragile and precious, something alive. "But, please—you see—you see, I am going to be an artist."

"Of course we see!" Tony smiled his wide and dazzling smile. "Have we not just been saying, 'She is the artist born?'"

"I mean—I mean I am going to be a painter. I am going to be the kind of an artist who makes pictures. My father expects me—I mean he planned for me to paint. To paint awfully well."

"So?" Tony looked at her quizzically. Then at Mrs. Rivera; then at the doctor. "Can she paint?"

No one said anything. The doctor stood up. "We don't know, Tony. She is very young and she has not studied long. I am not a sufficient judge and Carlotta is not sure."

"What do you mean, Carlotta is not sure?" He turned impatiently to her. "Can she or can't she?"

"Really I am not sure, Tony. After all, she is only fourteen." There was pain again in her voice. Sarah felt it.

"Then she can't," Tony said shortly. "What are we wasting her time for? If she could paint, you would know."

"That's not certain, Tony." Mrs. Rivera went over to Sarah and took her hand, for all the world like a defiant child protecting the rights of a playmate. "She has no gift for line and movement. I think she has no real gift for color. But her energy is amazing and she has improved greatly in two short years. You have to make allowance for what temperament and determination can do in a long future."

"Bah!" said Tony shortly. "You know she has a gift for the piano. You are uncertain about the brush. And yet you stand wasting time! Is life so long and a gift so ordinary that the swift-flying days make no difference?" His scorn included them both; it was not gentle.

Sarah walked away from them all and stood beside the piano. She seemed taller than before and older, genuinely older. "I am going to be a painter. It's true that I love to play the piano. Perhaps I like it better than painting because I played with my father, and it comes more easily to my *fingers,* and I'm happy playing. But I am going to be a painter." Her voice took on a stubborn note. "People can learn to paint if their minds

111

and eyes and hands are good. No one could make me give it up."

"No one is trying to." Tony's voice held exaggerated patience. "You have to do your own giving up. Everyone has to give up his own sins, his own mistakes, his own second-bests. Someone who knows must examine your work. If you cannot paint, you may as well cease trying. If you can surely paint, you must go on. If there is a middle ground of perhaps and maybe, why, then"—he shrugged his shoulders—"perhaps and maybe."

"Who will know?" the doctor asked. His eyes were on Sarah with the expression of the diagnostician. "Now that we have raised the question, we must answer it. I wish it might have waited another year or two. Fourteen is very young."

"Fourteen is too old to wait. Blodgett would be a good person. We will send her to New York." Tony was as cool about the matter as if he were sending her to the kitchen for a cup of coffee.

"I think not," Mrs. Rivera said thoughtfully. "Blodgett is a fine artist but a less fine judge of character. I want someone who is sensitive to personality, someone who can see the plant in a single cotyledon."

"Then Aylesworth. He is a great man, but he had protégés who are even greater and he has made them so." Tony spoke to the older woman, but his eyes were on Sarah. "There may be a dozen in the land, perhaps even fifty, with just as much talent as this girl, but we cannot find them. And probably they cannot find themselves. This one we have found. She will grow up slowly, but we can wait for that. Only let us make no unpardonable mistakes now."

"We will find the right man, Tony, and we will find out the truth." Mrs. Rivera did not smile, but her voice was at ease again. Sarah felt better too. She sat down in a chair near the doctor. He reached over and patted her shoulder.

"You have not even heard her play alone," he said.

"Oh no!" Sarah sat up stiffly, like a puppet pulled into position by a too swift hand.

"Never mind," Tony said lightly. "I do not make mistakes; not about musicians. Mistakes about cards, yes. About women, it could be. About horses, but always. But not about musicians. I will play myself."

He picked up his violin and began to play softly, walking around the room as he played. Plainly he was abstracted; his expression changed and shifted as if he were holding conversation with a roomful of people. By and by his face cleared and he turned and bowed to them as if they were a full concert audience. "Ladies and gentlemen, I would like to play for you the Mendelssohn Concerto in E Minor." He smiled at Sarah and added, "Without accompaniment." Then he struck the first note and they were no longer three separate people and he was no longer an artist on an imaginary platform. They were the world without form and the stars without courses; his was the hand that reached into chaos and gave them design. They were the earth before any green thing had sprung from it; he was the miracle of sun and rain and time. They were the clay and he was the potter ten thousand years ago ... yesterday ... tomorrow ... there was only *now*. When he came to the end of the concerto, no one spoke because he did not expect them to speak. If words would have done, then why the violin? After a bit he played again, this time Wieniawski's "Legende." Now he seemed to be drawing the music from them directly. They were three wells, Sarah thought, and he would have gone thirsty if he could not have reached into them. No, he was a flowing fountain into which long lines of parched travelers would come to dip cups. They—the three who listened here—were the springs which fed the fountain. Or were the real springs still far beneath and beyond them all, and were they only the channels through which the water flowed? The emptier one became, the larger the flow. Apparently Tony knew that he could not make this music without them, because when he finished playing, he looked slowly from one to the other and said, "Thank you for giving me that music." Mrs. Rivera smiled and saluted him with her hand.

Dr. Rivera smiled, shifted his position, and said, "One can work a long time on such a diet." Sarah did not smile and she did not speak. She waited for him to go on.

And he went on. Darkness came, but no one saw it, although at some time Mrs. Rivera lit the tall candles on the table and the doctor put another log on the fire. Finally—after hours, or was it days, or was it no time at all?—Tony was playing Bazzini's "La Ronde des Lutins," and they were all laughing with the goblins and no one knew how or when their mood had changed. It was like having a scene shifted without disturbing the players who, when they saw that the scene had changed, began to say different lines because now they were different people. The line which Tony said was, "Carlotta, my angel, I am starving. I am weak with hunger."

He flung himself on the couch, calling loudly, "Adolph, Hortense, Manuel—Heinrich, Elsa, Fritz—Marie, Francois, Romaine, George, Anna, SOMEBODY!"

Hortense came and the lights went on. Adolph came with a tray and small glasses. Sarah was given a sip of sherry, and Tony stopped his banter to propose a toast, "To stubborn little Sarah, who will someday come to herself!"

"To Herself!" Mrs. Rivera cried, holding her glass high.

"To Herself!" the doctor said.

Sarah thought quickly of Bill Cooper. Everybody, high or low, had to come to himself sooner or later. If a person didn't manage to get there in this life, then he had to make it in some other. She said nothing, but she smiled at them happily. What a big silly she had been to think that these people would pull her from her path. They were the kindest people she knew. Suddenly she decided to leave off studying Latin the next semester and begin on French. French, and German, and by and by Spanish and Italian. Everything. She wanted to know what they were saying to each other so gaily. Were languages nothing to them at all that they must speak a different one for every mood and never know that they had changed? But still, they never left her out. Each one called on her in good plain English to say that he was right and then went on talking without explaining what he was right about until another beseeched her help. Finally a perfect torrent of words carried them to the dining room, where the buffet was covered with many things, some of which Sarah had never eaten before and could not name.

Eleven

In the weeks which followed the visit of Josef Aronowitz called Tony, Sarah doubled the time she spent in Miss Moseley's studio. She listened to everything Miss Moseley said; she did exactly as she was told. She spent all of her spare time at home perfecting what Miss Moseley felt to be a sense of proportion. At school she did not study less because there was something within her which made it hard to be content with a poor recitation. Also, she did not quit her music lessons. She told herself that she did not quit because she had promised Miss Lillie to go on. But there was another reason which she could not quite put in words: as a painter she meant to be better than the best she could achieve at the piano. Her days were very full. She grew thin.

It was in January that Mr. Templeton came. At first Sarah did not realize that he was the man who was to render final judgment on her possible ability as a painter. One day she walked through the main corridor of Goethe Hall, the fine-arts building at Bryan, and noticed a poster on the bulletin board announcing that Harry B. Templeton, portrait painter from New York, would lecture on Thursday evening. The lecture was open to the public, but Sarah knew there would not be a large public to hear a lecture on "Tendencies of the Modern French School." The notice also stated that Mr. Templeton would meet the art students in Miss Moseley's studio on Friday at four. Well, she would go to that too. Even though she was younger than the college students, she knew some of them and she would not feel out of place. Having thus disposed of herself, she was free to wonder about Mr. Templeton. She asked Miss Moseley about him, and Miss Moseley said that he had pictures in the Metropolitan Museum in New York and in many other Famous Places. Miss Moseley said that Bryan College was very lucky indeed to have Harry B. Templeton. He was going to spend a whole afternoon looking over the work of the students.

"Why? Why on earth would he come to a little college like Bryan and look for talented students here?"

"Bryan may not be a large college," Miss Moseley said coolly, her lips set in a straight line, "but certainly it is a school with a very fine reputation. No doubt some big art school in the East is looking for talent. I always say that the very best way to uncover talent is to teach the essentials but to leave the creative student free to follow his own bent."

"Yes, ma'am." But Sarah felt that "Yes, ma'am" did not denote particular comprehension, so she said, "Yes indeed," with animation.

Miss Moseley was pleased. "When he sees your work, Sarah, I am sure he will feel you have made great progress.

Then Sarah had an inspiration. She said, "I wish he could see all of our work without our names, Miss Moseley. You know, like they do in contests for exhibits."

"That's a good idea," Miss Moseley agreed. "And also a very professional procedure."

The afternoon before the public lecture Sarah happened to stop at the Riveras' on her way home from her music lesson. She had been working on Chopin's Etude in E Flat Major, Opus No. II, and she didn't like it. The extended chords were all right, but somehow the piece sounded to her like a lot of wild geese. At best it was a music-box affair and a sissy one at that. But Miss Lillie liked it. Sarah wondered what Mrs. Rivera would say. What she wanted to work at was something that would recover a little of the nameless excitement she had felt when playing with Tony.

117

Tea was being served in the sitting room when she came in. She caught a glimpse of Mrs. Rivera's Alice-blue velvet tea gown, with cream-colored lace on the deep, pointed collar. She hesitated. "Adolph, perhaps you had better tell Mrs. Rivera it is only me."

"That's all right, Miss Sarah. She told me if anyone else came she was not at home."

Sarah could never understand that about Mrs. Rivera. How could she say she was not at home when any visitor who stepped inside the door might hear her laughter? Hers was a kind of laughter which made anyone else's seem forced and heavy.

Mrs. Rivera put out her hand and drew her forward. "This is Sarah Duncan, Mr. Templeton. She is a special friend of Enrique's."

Mr. Templeton was a genial man. He had a Vandyke beard and close-cropped gray hair which fit his head jauntily, like a plush beret. His blue eyes were deep-set under the heaviest eyebrows Sarah had ever seen. He seemed like a very big man when he was sitting down, but when he stood he was scarcely up to Sarah's shoulder. It was his body which was large; his legs looked as if he had surely stepped out on the wrong side of bed and walked off on his little brother's underpinning. Fortunately, it was quite all right to laugh because he was laughing too. He was laughing because he had been so bored at the thought of coming to Wheaton, Minnesota. "I tell you frankly, Mrs. Rivera, it was the terms of your husband's letter which persuaded me, not my interest in the budding genius of Bryan College. To think what I would have missed!"

Then Sarah knew who Mr. Templeton really was and why he had come.

The next afternoon she went to the students' private tea and exhibition. She wore her second-best dress, which was brown and did nothing for her. Today it seemed very important to wear a dress which hid her real self and yet made her feel like herself. Only a couple of dozen students came to the tea because most of the younger ones did not care to come and some of the older ones had important things to do, such as basketball practice and rehearsal for the cantata. After the assembled group had drunk their lukewarm tea and eaten their peanut butter sandwiches, the class followed Mr. Templeton around the room from one student's exhibit to the next.

Most of the younger pupils' work he passed over with a few jolly comments. "A jaunty house this chap has made. Nothing holds it to the hillside except a cocklebur on its roof, or is that a chimney? ... That child has a nice sense of color—not afraid of his blues and reds and yellows."

Then he began on the older students' work. "Good sense of structure," said Mr. Templeton. "This lad should be given larger canvases and encouraged to use more paint. He's niggling a bit and it's not his nature." He and Miss Moseley fell into an argument about the use of barns in a landscape. He felt that it was very unimportant whether or not a barn held an important place in the picture; Miss Moseley felt it was very important that a barn keep an unimportant place.

"Number 12 has missed his calling," said Mr. Templeton. "He doesn't care whether he paints, and we do not care whether he paints." The class laughed. Howard Powers took art because it was a painless way of gathering enough credits to play football.

"Number 13 has some real understanding of perspective. I want you all to note—" And then he talked for ten minutes about the picture of Number 13, who was shy little Helen Richter standing there among them, red as a poppy and so happy that you wanted to walk over and touch her.

Number 22 was Sarah. By the time he came to Number 22, members of the class were beginning to drop away, especially those whose pictures had already been commented upon. Sarah hoped she looked casual, but her mouth was so dry she could not speak and her hands felt so far away that she dared not lift them even for the steadying effect of winding her own long braids about them.

"Number 22," said Mr. Templeton. And then he said nothing. Twice he started to speak and seemed to change his mind. "Well, I'll tell you," he offered. "Number 22 is no artist. He never will be an artist. But Number 22 will be somebody. If I had to hazard a guess, I would say that Number 22 will be an inventor. He should go a long way." This was the first time he had mistaken the sex of the painter.

"Why do you say that Number 22 is no artist?" Miss Moseley asked quickly. "Number 22 is one of the hardest-working students I have ever had, and he comes from a very talented family."

It was nice of Miss Moseley to maintain the fiction of sex. The other students who were listening were amused. Not one of them guessed how much these remarks mattered to the tall Duncan girl who could do so many things well.

"I know he is hard-working and I know that hard work is part of genius. There is a bit of daring in his landscapes—that windmill, this clump of maples—but he does not have a feeling for relationships, and plainly he has no more perspective than a cross-eyed kitten."

"Why, Mr. Templeton!" Miss Moseley's voice rose in honest protest. "Look with what care he scales his trees toward the horizon."

"That is just what I am trying to point out. He has *learned* something of perspective, but he has no feel for it."

The conversation lasted for several minutes. Sarah heard every word of it and yet she did not hear. She felt like a phonograph record taking down a foreign-language lesson which she could later play back word for word without understanding a syllable of it. Except, of course, that she understood that Mr. Templeton did not think she could ever be an artist. Then with the others she made the rounds of all the other pictures. She answered Miss Moseley's questions about Grandma's cold and about the chicken-pie supper. She thanked Mr. Templeton, and she only laughed when he asked her which pictures were hers.

She walked home by herself, ate her supper, told Anna how good the soup was, and read Baldy *The House That Jack Built*.

The telephone rang. It was Mrs. Rivera herself—although she almost never talked on the telephone—saying that the car would come for Sarah because Mr. Templeton must leave that night. They were waiting in the library for her. Back in her childhood when she used to come with her father, some of her happiest hours had been spent here sitting on top of the little ladder which coasted around the room, dipping into this strange volume and that. She was glad that the staunch little ladder was there tonight among these people whose voices seemed to come over a distance.

Mr. Templeton had a whole portfolio of her drawings and paintings, all that had been hung on the wall at the college and many other bits besides. "I called you a boy, didn't I, Sarah! Well, madam, that's a compliment. It means that you have vigor and a nice indifference to detail." Then he held up a painting of a cloisonné vase. "To be sure, this is nothing but detail, but I lay that to the septuagenarian who teaches you. Not that the old girl hasn't genuine strong points, and I quite agree with her insistence on form."

Mrs. Rivera said, "Miss Moseley is like an equestrienne teaching horsemanship on a wooden horse."

Mr. Templeton laughed heartily and scolded Mrs. Rivera all in one breath. "Miss Moseley has taught Sarah faithfully as far as she can teach. Which is far enough to show whether or not the child has genuine talent."

He turned to Sarah. "Fourteen is not very old and two years is a very short time. I am not saying that you cannot learn to paint. I am not even saying that you cannot learn to paint well. You might become a teacher of painting in a college like Bryan. Sometime you might take Miss Moseley's place. You might have your pictures hung in local exhibits. Sometime you might be hung in some Midwest exhibit at the Art Institute of Chicago. It is impossible to say who may be shown in Chicago! But I think they will not buy your pictures for the permanent exhibit. Won't you sit down?"

Sarah sat down. They all three sat down by the table upon which her drawings were spread. In an odd way Sarah felt that she had heard these things he was saying at some other time or place. She seemed to anticipate them, almost sentence by sentence, and to hand him just the picture he wanted before he asked for it.

"If you were merely drawing for pleasure, as most girls draw, I would say to go right along. It will bring you much pleasure, and I hope that you will go on. Or if you were the kind of girl who dreams today that she will be a great artist, and tomorrow dreams that she will be a great modiste, and the next day plans to be a great singer of opera, and when she is eighteen marries a wealthy manufacturer of billiard balls—why, then I would say, 'Let her daydream.' But Mrs. Rivera tells me that you are not like that, and she also tells me that you have rather remarkable talent at the piano. If she is right—and to be with her for a day is to believe that she could not be wrong—then it becomes important for you to put your energy and your time where they will bring you the most return. Is it not so?"

Sarah nodded. Logic was logic, however far it might be from truth.

"Now let us look at some of these pictures." Honestly and gently—but without tempering his judgment to her wishfulness—he pointed out her fundamental needs. When he was through he bundled her drawings together, slipped them into their case, and handed them to her as one might wrap up a dress which had grown too small and should be passed on to one's younger cousin. Without seeming to change the subject, he began to talk of students he had had, of students he had watched. Before any of them realized the evening's passing, it was time for his train. Both Adolph and Hortense flew to get his things into his bag and him into the car which had just brought the doctor from the hospital. Dr. Rivera took Sarah under his arm, more or less, and together they escorted Mr. Templeton to the train, and then the doctor took her on home, talking cheerfully of many things. When she was alone in her own room, she sorted out her pictures. A few of the best she kept in her portfolio; the others she tore up and dropped into the wastebasket. She went to bed and to sleep. The next day she dropped into Miss Moseley's room when no one else was there and she said, "Mr. Templeton was right about my painting. He was right about your being a good teacher and Bryan College being lucky to have you, and he was also right about my not being the material great artists are made of."

"Did he say that about me?" Miss Moseley was pleased and Sarah was pleased. She never liked Miss Moseley so thoroughly as at that moment.

"I really need all my time on my schoolwork, and I think I won't take any more painting lessons until I get to college."

"I shall be sorry to lose you, Sarah. Not many of my students take their work so seriously." Miss Moseley looked almost sad; her new plain shirtwaist seemed suddenly too big for her. "I will really hate to have you stop."

"Well, I'd be sorry if you were glad!" Sarah leaned over and kissed Miss Moseley on the cheek, which startled her as much as it did Miss Moseley, and then they both tried to say something at the same instant, and by the time they got their sentences untangled each had forgotten her remark, so they went on to talk about the Valentine party which the men of the church were going to give to all the women and girls. It was something unique which would surely make the other churches sit up and take notice.

The next day was Saturday, and Anna decided to wash a pair of blankets. Sarah went to the basement to help her put the blankets through the wringer, and she caught her finger so that it was rather badly pinched. She looked at it wonderingly. She had certainly not pinched it on purpose, but she was oddly grateful to it for getting itself pinched. The next day she told

Miss Lillie that she would have to discontinue her music lessons for a time. Why she should want to give up music along with her painting she could not have said, except that there seemed to be something vaguely disloyal about continuing.

Twelve

After Sarah quit painting and taking music lessons everything else went on as usual. Sometimes she found herself standing in the middle of her own room saying words in her mind, "I just failed. That's all. My father thought I had something that I didn't have." She got into a way of lingering before his picture in the living room. Sometimes she thought it looked at her disapprovingly, which was more satisfactory, somehow, than its occasional look of compassion.

Winter lingered late that year. On the first of April there was still snow on the ground. Sarah's mother looked up from breakfast to say, "For goodness' sake, Sarah, you have got so thin that you are positively skinny. You study too much." Mama looked a little anxious. "I think you should see Dr. Rivera."

Sarah laughed and turned to her geometry. But a few days later she did go to see Dr. Rivera. "There is a little rough place on the back of my neck and it itches," she told him.

Dr. Rivera did not look at her neck. He looked at her face. It was not always good, he felt, for an outsider to disrupt the struggle of a sensitive personality at work on its own inner problems. He picked up a crystal paperweight and held it against the light, studying it intently.

"Are you going to tell my fortune?" She smiled at him with the same anticipation which had marked her as a child.

"No, not your fortune," he answered, returning her smile only with his eyes. "I want you to help me with my own fortune. What I mean is—Carlotta. I think she needs a change."

"You haven't taken a trip for a long time."

"And I can't take one now. I can't get away."

"She wouldn't want to go without you."

"She never has, but she might. She might if she thought it was good for someone else."

"Who could it be good for?"

"You. You've got a touch of neurodermatitis."

Sarah looked startled. "What's that?"

"The patch on the back of your neck."

"But you haven't seen that yet!"

"I don't need to. You're the type to have neurodermatitis now and then. It's just a substitute for losing one's temper or for lying down on the job. There's a kind of conceit behind it too. Sometime I *will* tell your fortune. But first I need your help."

"But I have to go to school! And I wouldn't want Mrs. Rivera to go to a great deal of trouble for me. And I'm not either conceited." Indignation and concern struggled in her voice.

"Of course you are conceited, my dear. You're too proud to act as tired as you feel."

"But I'm not tired."

"Then you're too proud to feel as tired as you are. Anyhow, I think we could cook up a good case of overstudy or growing pains, don't you? I want Carlotta to get away."

Sarah responded to the urgency in his voice. "I'll have rabies if you want me to. But I can never think of anything she could need that she doesn't have."

Then Sarah saw Dr. Rivera's expression tighten and his upper lip twitch slightly at one corner, as if he were in pain. When he spoke, the foreign accent was suddenly marked and his sentences were short and formal. "Carlotta's father was a distinguished sculptor. You would know the name. He was also a great patriot in Argentina. Her mother was a beautiful and fragile woman. At eighteen Carlotta had everything a girl could wish for or imagine. She was also painting with ability. Her talent for the piano was a good deal like your own. She knew great and good people in many parts of Europe. Life was a treasure chest into which she had only to thrust her hands." The doctor paused. When he spoke again, all feeling had gone from his voice. "That was true at eighteen. At twenty she was an orphan with her health broken and a weight of memory to crush a weaker spirit. Someday Carlotta will want to tell you about her people. Until then I can only ask you to understand when you have no facts to go on."

"I do—understand."

The doctor nodded slowly. He had always known that she would.

Two days before spring vacation began, Sarah found herself looking out of a window from the top story of the Astor Hotel. All New York seemed spread before her.

"Look how many people are on the streets! Do you suppose there is a parade someplace?"

"My child, you'll fall out of the window," Mrs. Rivera answered from the pages of the morning *Times*. "Skirts are fuller and hats are jauntier. The moment has come to go shopping."

"Let's don't shop. Let's find Central Park and take a walk instead."

"And you, *ma chérie*, almost fifteen years old! Beware of a woman who does not care for clothes. Flee from her. She is pestilence!" She rose from her chair and called to her maid in the adjoining room. "Hortense! Hortense! Draw a bath for Miss Sarah." To herself she continued, "I shall wear the tan velours. We will leave the hotel in half an hour." Then to Sarah, "Pin the braids around your head and wear the blue suit. It is easy to take off and on. *Mon Dieu*, shopping is no child's play."

But before the day ended Sarah thought it was better than child's play. It was fairy play. Her mother had given her a modest check for spring clothes, which, administered by Mrs. Rivera's capable hands, bought quantities of loveliness beyond her dreams. Beyond even Rachel's dreams, and Rachel had a penchant for planning the proper outfit for every occasion.

How Rachel's eyes would shine when she saw the soft rose negligee with silver slippers whose buckles matched the silver clasp on the gown's crushed chiffon girdle. "To look beautiful at home doing nothing—with no one to see you—that is the first lesson—do you say the A B C's?—for a girl-child to learn," Mrs. Rivera said as she leaned back in the comfortable chair from which she directed the assembling of the wardrobe.

"I should get something simple for school." Sarah was bewildered by the fragile lavender loveliness of a dinner dress and an enchanting yellow linen for mythical garden parties.

"You need everything simple. Simplicity is your style. But fabric and cut—that's where imagination begins." Then to the attentive attendant, "Now we will see cottons for school. Piqué, crash; stalwart, tailored things for an often careless young woman."

In the late afternoon, as they left the milliner's and took their places in the waiting automobile, Sarah spoke hesitantly. "Mrs. Rivera, I can hardly think my mother's check bought so much."

Mrs. Rivera smiled disarmingly. "I tell you frankly—it did not. I added here and there a dollar or two. And do you know why? Because I am waiting eagerly for a chance to give you a very hard scolding."

"To scold me," cried Sarah with alarm in her voice. "But you have only to tell me what you want me to do differently."

"Lean back and relax, my child. That is why the dear God made motorcars—so that poor, harassed women might relax in traffic." She herself might have been sitting at a concert. "My scolding has nothing to do with your manners. It is aimed at the years ahead and the clothes you will wear in all of those years. I am going to scold you for thinking that clothes are not important." She laughed softly, gaily.

Sarah leaned back, smiling. The scolding sounded exciting as well as inevitable. It would come when it would come.

That night they went to the theater to see *The Pink Lady*. It was Sarah's first musical comedy. More than a year ago Rachel

128

had seen *The Chocolate Soldier* at the Metropolitan Theater in St. Paul when she had gone on a trip to visit her aunt. Later, when she described the performance, Sarah had felt that rhapsodic Rachel was overimpressionable. But now in the fourth row center, looking up into the eyes of Hazel Dawn, illusion was complete. So far as Sarah was concerned, there never was a heroine so lovely, so spontaneous, so captivating as the little Pink lady, nor a hero so much worth waiting and conniving for. Nor a fat man so amusing in his writhing disappointment. And certainly no music so haunting.

When it was over she walked out of the theater in a daze of pastel emotions, seeing no one. But a great many people saw the tall, starry-eyed girl walking beside a woman of such distinction that men unconsciously straightened their shoulders and women remembered something more far away and long ago than youth or beauty.

Once back in their hotel rooms having their hot chocolate, Sarah thought aloud: "I wonder if I could really sing. My voice goes quite high."

"Even if you had the voice, you aren't the type." Mrs. Rivera took a generous bite of sandwich. Her husband often said that Carlotta's apparent fragility was altogether deceiving because she ate as she spoke, with ample directness.

"How can one be sure of her own type?"

"She can't. But I can. I have a gift." Mrs. Rivera smiled.

"Don't you ever make a mistake?" The question was too urgent to be impudent.

"You'd rend all the musical-comedy seams, my child. You'd sing of love when the tunes and the lyrics called merely for sentiment."

"The Pink Lady was beautiful." Sarah sighed—a long sigh flavored with chocolate.

The next day the *Titanic* was sunk.

Sarah saw the headlines and refused to read further. Mrs. Rivera read the entire paper, missing no detail.

"How can you?" Sarah asked.

"How can't you?" the older woman returned. "It's life."

"Some of life I can get along without. We might as well skip as much pain and suffering as we can. Especially when we can't do anything about it."

"*You* think so?" The mellow voice went hard. "Suffering is the essence of life. Only the coward tries to escape it. To understand is to bear! It is the final service."

"I'm not sure that I know what you mean," said Sarah, picking up the paper almost sulkily.

"*Mon Dieu!*" cried Mrs. Rivera, bending over the girl in sudden warm affection. "I would spare you if I could, but I can't, and so I would prepare you."

"For shipwreck?" Sarah asked, smiling.

"But yes!"

After that Sarah read all reports avidly. Read and wanted to talk. "At eleven thirty-eight there was no one on the bridge." She seemed to share the bewilderment of the man in the crow's nest sighting the iceberg and unable to get any response from the bridge. "They were going two thousand feet a minute, and he had to climb down and go hunt someone to report to."

At the moment of Sarah's remark Hortense was brushing her mistress's hair. Mrs. Rivera stayed her hand, rose, began to pace the room. "Failure at routine duty—it was the sentry's dozing at a small and very secret meeting which caused my father's—tragedy."

Sarah did not know what to answer. Her face was tense with the compassion she did not know how to express.

"Someday I will tell you," Mrs. Rivera said, as much to herself as to the girl.

After that they talked no more about the *Titanic,* but there was no escaping its multiplied tragedies unless one escaped the city, the country, the civilized world. It was Sarah's first personal experience of a world event.

For two weeks impressions crowded in so fast that Sarah remarked at breakfast one morning, "I feel like a brown bear storing up the food I'm going to live on during hibernation. You know I can't digest this fast. And I feel as if I've only had a few bites of the Metropolitan Museum even after three mornings."

Mrs. Rivera's eyes lit up happily for no reason at all that Sarah could see. But then she had not seen her own disconsolate face on the first morning when she had walked through that great gallery where her pictures would never hang. And now here she was, talking impersonally, even gaily, about the gallery.

During the days that followed, their pursuits were as varied as the temperamental spring weather. With each new experience Sarah blithely planned a new life, and each new day Mrs. Rivera blithely planned with her. The last afternoon was reserved for a concert by the great Peter Petruski, "triumphing for his eleventh consecutive season as the world's foremost master of the pianoforte." Sarah had been noncommittal when the tickets were bought. Once she had even suggested canceling the concert in favor of a trip to the Statue of Liberty. But on the afternoon of the concert she dressed happily enough, chattering at random about Baldy's excitement over the books she was taking to him, about Rachel's surprise when she knew the Italian bracelet was for her. But actually she was aware that she was chattering. She felt as if she were hammering a bright shell for herself, something that would shut out the engulfing enjoyment which she feared would roll in on the tide of the music. She had begun to realize that she missed her music far more than her painting and she felt a kind of acute disloyalty in the realization, as if she might have been good at painting if only she had managed to generate this inner glow about it. But the idea of transferring her allegiance had never crossed her stubborn mind. Right up to the door of Carnegie Hall she chattered. Once inside, however, she could not think of anything to say. Excitement choked her, although there was nothing in her experience to warrant this tense anticipation.

Peter Petruski was a tall and lanky man who smiled gravely at his audience before seating himself at the piano. When seated, his apparent awkwardness gave way to symmetry, and Sarah felt suddenly that if he did not strike a note, nevertheless she had heard music. If some people fall in love before a word is spoken, why couldn't one fall in music before a note is struck? After he struck the first chord, she had no more conscious thoughts. Even during the intermission when Mrs. Rivera talked about his recent achievement in presenting the entire 169 works of Chopin in half a dozen recitals, Sarah really did not hear what was being said. Sitting there starkly alone, although amid so many people, she was being wrought in a crucible of sound and emotion and insight more volatile than thought. Moreover, she knew that she was being made again, and irrevocably. When they had left the Hall and were in their cab riding across Fifty-seventh Street, she spoke. "It's all right now, but I would like not to talk about it for a while."

So they had a gay supper at Lüchow's, where some German students sang lustily and there was small chance for conversation. Finally, late that night, after the last packing was done and Hortense had gone to bed, Sarah said, "Is Mr. Koenigstein still in Minneapolis?"

Mrs. Rivera nodded. "I wired to him early this evening asking for an appointment day after tomorrow."

Sarah was not surprised. After all, a person seemed to have so little to do with her own future. Life merely flowed on like a river bearing one out toward the sea; struggling against its current or trying to hurry its pace—both were equally useless. She stood thinking for a moment and then impetuously went toward the chair where Mrs. Rivera was sitting, fell on her knees, and buried her head in her own arms, leaning, nevertheless, against her friend. There she cried out the last tears of her childhood, unaware, like a child, why she was crying.

Thirteen

New Year's Eve, 1912, Sarah and Rachel came home from a party to spend the night together in Sarah's long room under the eaves. The party had been gay and Rachel was ecstatic. It was her first party date with Leslie Sando. Sarah had gone with a junior named Doran Rites, a tall, athletic chap whose conversation most of the girls thought very witty and Sarah found about as humorous as playing an Uncle Josh record over and over. Both girls knew that Rachel had had the better deal, a fact which rather worried Rachel.

"I still can't understand how Leslie happened to ask me when you didn't already have a date. There's something queer about it, Sarah." Rachel's honest eyes, still shining, were perturbed.

"It isn't queer at all, you goose. He *likes* you. He's taken you a dozen places lately. Why shouldn't he ask you to the party?"

"But he hasn't taken me to important places like a dance. Just home from Glee Club or off tobogganing." Rachel stood uncertainly, one slipper and stocking in her hand, looking down the happy weeks behind her.

"I declare, Rachel," came the muffled voice of Sarah from the folds of the dress she was taking off over her head, "you don't seem to realize you're the prettiest girl in school."

"Oh, I know I'm pretty, all right. And don't think I'm not grateful. Sometimes I just thank God that he gave me good skin and curly hair. I've almost got to be pretty because I'm certainly not smart." Rachel's happy voice went on, "I try to tell myself I should be glad he asks me and not keep wondering why."

"You've been a honey-pot from the cradle and you should be used to it by now." Sarah liked to tease Rachel, who took so little for granted. Rachel's popularity was one of her deep satisfactions.

"But Leslie is different. Besides being more brainy, he's more sensitive. Do you know what I mean?"

Did Sarah know? No one so well. Ever since Leslie first moved to Wheaton he and she had been friends of a particular sort by virtue of their common interests and because each seemed somehow to bring out the other. It wasn't that they ever specially went out of their way to be together. They would just find themselves together, walking home from school, rehearsing a play, practicing a duo-piano number for convocation. Then during the fall Leslie began to ask Sarah to go places with him until she rather took it for granted that he would ask her. On the day before the Halloween party they were walking down the big front steps of the high school, when a clownish little boy happened to notice that Leslie was much shorter than Sarah, and yelled, "Hi, Shorty! You hafta stand on the step to kiss yer girl." His companions took up the cry, "Get a stepladder, kid," "Where's your stilts?"

It was all over in a minute. The raucous laughter trailed off across a vacant lot toward the ball field, leaving Leslie standing awkwardly, scarlet to his hair. Sarah went on talking about their history class, apparently as unconcerned as if the small boys had been a flock of sparrows. But all the way home they were conscious of nothing else except the fact that Leslie was undeniably shorter than she was. He came exactly to her shoulder, and the chances were not great that he would grow much taller because he was small-boned.

The next night she and Leslie went to the Halloween party together as planned. They talked just as usual, except that there was no fun in it. Sarah felt as if she had the proportions of a giraffe. On the way home she hunted in vain for a topic of conversation. Finally, after a half block's pause, Leslie said, "Tell me more about your father," and Sarah wondered if he knew that he was the only one to whom she could talk freely about her father. She began to tell about an instrument her father had invented for use in spinal operations, but Leslie interrupted to ask, "What did your father look like?"

"Oh, he was tall and—and—" She finished the sentence, but he had caught the break in it.

After that he never asked her to go anyplace. A dozen times, at school, at a picnic, at a skating party, she had been on the point of saying, "Listen, Leslie, it doesn't matter that you're short and I'm tall. It only matters that we are friends." But each time she hesitated. Maybe he didn't miss their talks the way she missed them. Maybe he'd think that she thought he was going to fall in love with her, which, goodness knows, she didn't think at all. Maybe he didn't know that Baldy was going to be as great a man as ever her father was, and Baldy was so small that some people called him a midget. Maybe Leslie didn't care about tallness, anyway.

Thinking back over all these things took so little time that Rachel was still repeating her conversation with Leslie. "—and I said, 'Sarah and Doran are the best-looking couple here,' but he said, 'Doran's such a dumb egg.' Do you think he's really dumb, Sarah? Some girls think he's a lot of fun."

"He's wonderful," said Sarah, striking an attitude of adulation with her hairbrush in one hand. "I know he's wonderful because he told me so himself."

"You mean he's too conceited?"

"After all, he's handsome as a Greek god—the girls are always saying so, and the news must have leaked through to him by now. And he's one of the fastest high school runners in the state."

"I don't think you like him." This tentatively, as much to a jar of cold cream as to Sarah.

"Then you're wrong, angel. I think he's probably the best dancer this side of the Prince of Wales, and why he ever took me to the party I don't know." Sarah yawned and tumbled into bed.

Rachel's face was unexpectedly serious. She walked over to the bed and looked down at Sarah. "Sometimes I wonder—I just wonder if the Riveras aren't going to make life sort of hard for you, Sarah. You expect so much. Boys in high school or even in college can't be like Dr. Rivera. And goodness knows when you'll ever meet another woman as—as exotic as Mrs. Rivera. Not to mention their famous friends. You don't want to let them get you used to expecting things you can't have." This was a long speech for Rachel. She wasn't too well satisfied with it, but these were things she'd wanted to say for a long time.

Sarah lay still with her hand shading the light from her eyes. She answered slowly. "If I can't have their kind of friends someday, why, then I don't want any." She removed her hand just in time to see an expression of consternation on Rachel's face. "But bless you, you're their kind, Rachel." She sat up in bed. "You're their kind because you're honest and beautiful, and Leslie's their kind too. Someday we'll get all of our own kind of people together and run the world."

She laughed. Rachel laughed and felt better.

Not long after that Rachel went with Sarah to the Riveras' one afternoon when Miss Lillie was to be there also. Sarah had just returned from her lesson with Koenigstein and wanted to play for them Beethoven's "Sonata Pathétique," which she had been working on for months. Only this week had it come through. Eventually there came a time when a piece of music was no longer something one had learned but something one had become. Miss Lillie was now also studying with Koenigstein, and under his direction she still gave Sarah one lesson a week. "If you call it a lesson," Miss Lillie would say. "I merely check up on her." But it was more than that; Miss Lillie had abject regard for fidelity to the composer's intentions; every note must be played as written. Her two most insistent admonitions were, "Make it clean," and "Make it strong." Sarah always remembered a thing Miss Lillie had said about a Bach prelude. "The two hands have to be independent as a man and wife who are successful in cleaving unto each other."

Miss Lillie's devotion to Bach had made her an immediate favorite with Koenigstein; with her he never flew into one of his famous tantrums. "He's plumb crazy about her," Sarah reported to Mrs. Rivera today.

Miss Lillie blushed and then calmly announced, "He loves me for my Bach. Next to having a great passion comes a common passion. And in this case I prefer the common passion, thank you!" This was the new Miss Lillie, speaking right up when she'd a mind to.

For all Sarah had been so keen to play the "Pathétique," it just did not suit her today. She stopped in the middle of the second movement. "Double tarnation, this is what comes of my wanting to show *off*. I don't get into it."

"I know what you mean." Rachel's eyes were on Sarah's face in apparent forgetfulness that anyone else was present. "Some days the music is too big for you like a too large dress that you'll grow into by and by, but other times it's too big like a forest fire you can't stop."

"And *I* know what *you* mean," Mrs. Rivera said in such candid delight that Rachel was not at all embarrassed by her own unexpected comment. Then they were off in animated discussion, first of Beethoven and then of Brahms.

"I read that he was forty-two before he ever produced a symphony," Sarah said incredulously. "It seems dreadful to get so late a start."

"Forty-two!" said Miss Lillie. "Why, that's still young. Just a boy, you might say."

"My stars," Sarah said, "if I thought—" And then she caught sight of Miss Lillie's and Rachel's expressions, each saying such different things. She laughed and they all laughed.

"Play some of the Chopin you used to play," Rachel asked, "the one we called 'Twas then, your hand in mine.'"

"She means the Number 3 Etude in E Major," Sarah explained. "It begins slowly and we used to think it sounded like Grandfather's clock. Rachel liked the way the two hands chase one another up and down the keyboard. Once we even wrote words to it. Isn't that dreadful?"

"But no," said Mrs. Rivera. "There is an age when we all need words to our music. Or printed descriptions in our programs. Some of us never outgrow it."

"I'm one," said Rachel honestly. Whereupon Sarah saw Mrs. Rivera look at Rachel with appreciation and Rachel smile back warmly. Something almost like tears rushed to Sarah's throat and she wanted to fly over to hug them both. Her friends were friends!

They never became intimates, Mrs. Rivera and Rachel, nor Mrs. Rivera and any other of Sarah's interests in high school, home, and church, but Sarah began to feel less as if she were living in two separate worlds.

In the spring Mrs. Duncan went away to a church convention, leaving Sarah in charge of the household, assisted by Anna and her twenty years' experience in the family, advised at least three times a day and the last thing at night by Grandma Vanderiet, and warmly supported by all the neighbors. Lucy and Baldy had promised to mind Sarah, and Sarah had promised not to hold Lucy up to any unwonted standards of conduct. Sarah felt her weight of responsibility. She wanted not only to do well but to make the occasion a memorable one. She expected to be the Lady of the Manor combined with certain Florence Nightingale characteristics and perhaps a touch of Elsie Janis.

Almost immediately Lucy asked to have her best chum, Kitty Lou, over to spend the night. Kitty Lou was a scrawny child with the emotional stability of a soda fizz, but she always had a lonesome look, so Sarah said yes.

"In fact," Sarah said, "since it is Saturday, you can have Kitty Lou and Anabelle and Jane. All three of them can stay all night, and you may use Mama's room. Like a house party."

"Oh, Sarah! Not really!" Lucy whirled around and around in her excitement. "And will you play with us?"

"Of course I will if you want me to." Sarah mentally folded up the three magazines she had planned to read in bed. Responsibility had its price and she would pay it.

She then turned to Anna. "Anna, if you want to go to your sister's you can just as well give us a picnic supper and we will stack the dishes afterward."

Anna was pleased too. She demurred only as much as was seemly, but not enough to persuade Sarah to change her mind.

Baldy caught onto the fact that joy was the order of the day. "Shall we bring Penelope in the house, Sarah?" Penelope was the goat his grandfather had given him. "I would like very much to teach Penelope to sit in a chair."

"Maybe it would be better to take the chair to Penelope," Sarah suggested. "All in all, it seems to me that a chair would be more useful in the garden than a goat would be in the parlor."

Baldy debated the matter seriously. "Other people could sit on a chair in the garden, but we couldn't very well have other goats in the parlor. For one thing, we don't know any other goats, do we? Why do we know so few goats?"

"Maybe we should look around for goats that Penelope could chum with. But first we must put the medicine in your eyes, young sir."

Baldy had contracted a mild infection which the doctor had said was not as pink as pinkeye but needed attention. Three times a day Baldy leaned his head back over the tub while his mother dropped in the Argyrol. He did not like the ordeal and invented excuses to get out of it.

"Oh, but not today, Sarah, because we are having company and the medicine makes my face streaked."

"I'll tell you what! We'll have a surprise!"

"What kind?" Baldy looked up at her with such keen anticipation that Sarah wanted to make it a genuine surprise.

"Bless you"—she gave him a quick hug—"I was going to say
I would surprise you by washing your face to remove the
Argyrol. But now I've thought of something you'll love—love—
love to see."

Baldy skipped upstairs ahead of her. "Hurry then. Hurry."

Sarah hurried after him. He looked so cute bending backward over the tub, his brown eyes snapping up at her! Almost
with one gesture she took the medicine off the shelf, leaned
over, and kissed both his eyes. "Now I'm going to drop this
medicine so fast that you'll never know what happened.
Ready?"

"Ready," shouted Baldy.

With a swift, accurate movement Sarah dropped the medicine in both eyes.

Baldy screamed. Frantically he grabbed at his eyes and ran
headlong against the wall, shrieking wildly.

"Baldy! Baldy, what is it?" Sarah tried to pick him up, but he
writhed away from her.

"It's fire in my eyes." His small face was contorted in agony.

Sarah looked at the bottle; it had no label; then she smelled
it. Iodine! Then with sudden strength she grabbed up Baldy and
ran downstairs. Anna had gone; no one was home. Minutes
mattered and the telephone was often slow. She ran out of the
house, toward the hospital, the shrieking child in her arms. To
the first passer-by she called, "Phone Dr. Rivera I'm coming." In
the middle of the second block a car overtook her. Three minutes later she reached the hospital and put Baldy in the arms of
Dr. Rivera, who stood waiting in the doorway.

"Iodine in his eyes. I did it."

"You're all right, Baldy," the doctor said.

Perhaps it was the sure voice, perhaps the strong arms—
Baldy drew a long breath without the frantic scream. A quarter
of an hour later, when a hypodermic was beginning to relieve

the pain and the eyes had been cared for, Dr. Rivera turned to Sarah.

"I'm not sure, Sarah. I don't know how old or how strong the iodine was. There is nothing I can do except wash out the medicine and wait a while. If the iodine was strong and hit the cornea directly, there may be permanent damage, but I doubt it. At least there is a good chance that the eyes will clear up in time." His words, like his gaze, were direct and without dissimulation.

Sarah's response came as a whispered question. "But he might—he could—be blind for life?"

"There is that slight possibility but not, I should say, a probability. Tell me how it happened."

"I don't know. I picked up the bottle from the shelf where the Argyrol has been standing for days." Her throat was dry and she spoke with difficulty.

"Those things happen. Tell me, shall we send for your mother? When Baldy wakens and can't see and finds himself in pain, he may be hard to handle."

"We can't tell her." Terror was in Sarah's voice, followed by dull acceptance. "But of course he will never want me to touch him again."

"Nonsense, my dear." Then more sternly, "Sarah, if the boy should be blind, you will be his one resource. How the accident happened won't matter after a while. Even if it were criminal negligence on your part, or on the part of someone else, Baldy's need will be for inner resources and you will have to furnish these resources."

"He has Mama," she replied almost sullenly.

"I know how you feel. You think you've done a thing so dreadful that there is no place left for you in this world. That's partly the reaction of the young, who think of life in terms of finalities. But unfortunately you can't transfer the responsibility to your mother for the most final of all reasons—she can't take it."

"What do you mean? She'd give her life for Baldy."

"I'm sure she would. She would gladly be arms and legs for Baldy, and eyes, too, as long as she lived. But she can't direct his mind because she doesn't have his kind of mind."

Sarah made no answer for a moment. Then her eyes filled with tears. "Here we sit—philosophizing—while he"—she indicated the child asleep on the couch—"is going blind."

Nevertheless, some of the acute agony was eased by the doctor's quiet analysis. He had said the things she must eventually figure out for herself, as both of them understood.

"Philosophizing is better than sentimentalizing the way you are trying to do." The doctor rose and bowed to her. "Will you call me when he awakens?" In the doorway he paused. "I think it is probably more fair if we let your mother know there has been a small accident."

"I can take care of him." There was eagerness in her voice now.

"But after all she is his mother and she will not want to be spared. I will get her on the telephone and make sure not to alarm her."

He closed the door after him, leaving Sarah to her thoughts. But at first she had no special thoughts. She watched Baldy, who occasionally drew a sharp sigh in his sleep. She noted that the fingers were long on his slender little hands. Moreover, his hands were clean. Oddly enough, as the reputation of little boys goes, he liked his hands clean and washed them himself. But there was a cuff of dirt around his wrists. He had spent the entire morning digging in the back yard in an attempt to reach China.

It was only last week he had first heard of China, and ever since his questions had been incessant. "Do they walk on their heads, then, when our side of the world is up?" But before Sarah could answer, he had laughed at himself. "We don't walk on our heads when their side of the world is up." Grandma Vanderiet had overheard the remark and said she did declare she had never heard of a three-year-old child who made such intelligent observations. *Grandma would have to be told about his eyes!* An early fly was buzzing up the windowpane. Did he know what he was doing, that fly, or did he buzz mechanically like Baldy's toy donkey? *Baldy couldn't see his toys any more.* Dr. Rivera's desk was always neat, no matter how many important papers he had to sign. Some people's signatures were worth a lot of money. Take Robert Louis Stevenson, for instance. And Stevenson was ill all the time he wrote his exciting stories. *He was ill, but he could see. How would Baldy learn to write? And when he was old, could he remember the color of the sky?* Once in a sermon Grandpa had said that some anthropologists held that primitive people did not distinguish blue in the sky. The Psalmists never mentioned the blue sky. But the Psalmists understood about God. *If there was a God would he let Baldy go blind?* Would God be more likely to listen to a prayer said in a church? *If all the people of Grandpa's church prayed, could they heal Baldy's eyes?*

Baldy stirred. Not yet awake, his hands went to his eyes. He whimpered and turned over, Sarah got up and began to walk up and down the room. How many objects in the room could she remember without looking? By keeping her mind on the game she didn't have to think at all. Then Dr. Rivera came back and spoke in a natural voice. "Isn't he awake yet?"

At the sound of his voice Baldy woke up, sat bolt upright, laughed as if he had had a dream, caught himself, and cried out, "My eyes hurt! I can't open my eyes."

Dr. Rivera picked him up. "Listen, young fellow. You've had an accident and your eyes are hurt. You can't see out of them for about a week."

"Why? I want to see. They hurt."

"We're going to play a game. We're going to see how many things you can do without opening your eyes. I'm going to take you home in the car, and after you get home Sarah is going to wash your face, which looks just like an Indian's, all streaked with brown medicine. And then the doorbell is going to ring three rings—you count them—and when you go to the door there will be a delivery boy with ice cream. Three colors of ice cream, chocolate, vanilla, and strawberry. Now the trick is for you to eat the ice cream without looking at it and see if you can tell by the taste which color you are eating."

"All right," Baldy agreed, sliding down onto his feet. "C'mon, Sarah." Then in surprise, "But I can't see to walk!"

"Take Sarah's hand. She can see and you can walk."

So they went home, making a guessing game of the street noises and the number of steps from the car to the house. The ice cream came and proved a shining success until the last few bites, at which moment Grandma arrived.

"Baldy!" she called from the front hall. "Baldy! Baldy!" She was climbing the steps, practically sobbing his name at each step.

Sarah ran into the hall. "Grandma, you mustn't." She took her grandmother's arm. "He's quite happy now even though his eyes hurt, and we have to talk about other things in front of him."

But Grandma was only partially restrained. She knelt beside Baldy with her arms around him. "How did it happen, pet?"

"What?" Baldy was energetically scraping his dish. "What happened?"

"Your eyes," his grandmother moaned, ignoring Sarah's gesture.

"I don't know. I can't see anything, but I can guess very good, can't I, Sarah? They hurt."

"How did it happen?" Grandma demanded sternly of Sarah.

"I don't know. I just don't know."

So Grandma turned detective. But she never found out how the iodine came to stand where the Argyrol had been unless Anna might possibly have made the mistake in her weekly round of what she called righting up the bathroom.

When his mother reached home at ten o'clock that night Baldy was sound asleep, hugging his stuffed flannel donkey.

Sarah was sitting beside his bed in the dark. Mama turned on the bed light and looked at him. She began to cry, saying over and over, "I shouldn't have left him. I never should have left my boy."

Sarah comforted her.

Finally Mama drank some hot milk and went to bed, still crying intermittently. The last thing she said was that she would gladly give Baldy one of her own eyes if the operation could be performed. Sarah knew she meant it. Mother love was a very wonderful thing. Mama went to sleep.

Fourteen

Sarah went to her own room, thinking over her mother's remark about giving Baldy an eye, but obviously if any eyes were to be sacrificed they would be Sarah's own. If Dr. Rivera's operations on the brain were as miraculous as people said, then surely he could safely transplant an eye. He could do anything. Not only were more and more patients coming to Wheaton, but there seemed to be a steady trek of surgeons to watch his operations. Miracles came from his hands. He made his own instruments to perform these feats of almost microscopic delicacy. Surely he could take an eye from Sarah and make it Baldy's.

She tried to picture herself as the blind one. From early childhood when her father had brought a blind piano tuner to the house, blindness had seemed to her life's greatest disaster. But it wasn't. Causing blindness to someone else was worse.

Walking softly down the dark hallway, she went to Baldy's room. If he wakened and wanted anything he could easily call his mother, for the door between their rooms was open, but she wanted to sit beside his bed. He sighed in his sleep. Moonlight flooding through the window made his face look white and thin. His small pointed chin was very firm. It might need to be firm.

She tiptoed to the window and opened it wider. Low in the eastern sky Arcturus hung full and red, scarcely dimmed by the moonlight. She leaned out. Cassiopeia was almost overhead. Her father had told her that Cassiopeia was the first constellation he knew the name of. Back on the farm in Nebraska a peddler had taught it to him. The peddler was named Abraham. He had a hump on his back, as well as a pack. Abraham would wash his face only in rain water. Every spring he brought Grandmother Duncan some new kind of flower seeds. On each visit he stayed one night with the Duncans and taught the children one new constellation. Where was he now, this kind old peddler whom she had never seen but knew so well? Where was the freckle-faced boy, Dennis Duncan? Someplace beyond the eastern stars? She knelt beside the window, letting the spring breeze blow through her long unbraided hair. By and by the moon disappeared in the west. The stars moved slowly across the sky. Baldy stirred and asked for a drink. He took one swallow and was asleep again. She stood for a while looking at him numbly. When she went back to the window, the first faint presentiment of dawn was paling the stars; the branches of the trees grew darker, more distinct. There was no longer any breeze. Nothing stirred and there was no sound. Night and day were in balance. For a moment she understood something she could not name.

Sarah did not go to school the next week. Baldy needed a great deal of attention in spite of the fact that he was an independent little human and quickly learned his way around. In the midst of his play he sometimes fell to thinking, as was his curious custom.

"Sarah, I'm homesick." He had lately learned the word and liked it.

"Why, Baldy, how can you be? We're all here. Who are you homesick for?"

"I'm homesick for God."

She gathered him quickly into her arms. "I'm homesick, too, but I never know what for."

"How can you be homesick for nothing?"

"I don't know!" She laughed and hugged him so tightly that Baldy laughed, too, and took advantage of her good nature to ask if he might blow his horn, which was the most deafening

147

noise he knew how to make. Sarah fled from the room at the first blast. When she came back, he was interrogating his mother.

"Does everyone in the whole world wash on Monday?"

"I don't know." Mama looked up absently from her accounts. Then with more decision, "But I don't know why they wouldn't. It's the logical day to wash, and the common people are likely to be logical. That's what makes a democratic nation great."

Baldy was impressed and went on building a tower of blocks he could not see. Sarah was impressed too. Just when you least expected it, Mama would seem to be very wise about something.

But Baldy was not always content in his darkness. "*When can I see?*" he would demand, sometimes staunchly, sometimes whiningly. The latter was the more distressing. Sarah could not bear to have him become a whiner. She told him stories. She took him to walk, but only around the garden or over to the Rands' where passers-by, most of whom were acquaintances, would not ask questions. All the days were long and the nights were even longer. There was nothing much that the doctors could do until the swelling and exudation had gone from his eyes.

On the morning of the fourth day Baldy got up on the wrong side of bed. He was usually independent of all assistance in putting on his clothes, but this morning he refused even to try to put his arm in a sleeve. "Why should I? I can't go anyplace."

At breakfast he demanded to be fed, completely ignoring Sarah's best inventions of games. Finally his mother became exasperated. "You're acting very naughty," she said to him as she left the dining room. "Even a blind child can be polite."

"What's blind?" he demanded.

It was left to Sarah to explain.

"Can't a blind man see *anything*? Can't he see big trees and churches? Can't he see teeny-weeny ants? Can't he even read?"

"Everything is dark to him."

"Sarah!" His voice halted. The small face looking up at her was twisted with a horrible incredulity. "Sarah! *Am I blind?*"

He slid from his high chair without a word. "I'm going upstairs," he said with infinite dignity in his quavering voice. He felt his way along the wall. Sarah heard his footsteps down the hall, up the stairs. Some instinct told her that Baldy wanted no intrusion. A few minutes later she followed to the door of his room, which was closed. She leaned against the wall and waited for some sound of activity within. After what seemed an interminable time there came the mighty pounding of iron on iron. She heard her mother rush in from her own room.

"What on earth are you doing, Baldy? I didn't even know you were in here."

"I don't want my bed any more." Baldy's voice was firm. "I'm going to break my bed down and bust it." Another whang of his hammer on the iron bed.

"Stop it!" his mother cried in alarm. "You'll break the bed to pieces."

"That's what I said," Baldy insisted stoutly. "I'm going to break it up and take it to Penelope." The door beside Sarah opened and he escaped into the hall.

"I'll go with you," Sarah offered, reaching for his hand. Baldy gave it to her willingly enough, and they hurried downstairs. On the back porch Sarah paused. "We can't go out. It's beginning to rain. Let's—"

But Baldy broke away from her and ran down the steps. Straight across the back yard he ran, across the kitchen garden toward the goat. He was untethering Penelope by the time Sarah reached him.

"Baldy! Baldy! How did you get here so straight?" She tipped back his head. The swollen eyes were half open. In his anger he had forced them open and *he could see.*

After that it was only a matter of days until his eyes were well again. No operation was necessary, no medicine. Finally Mama could laugh about the whole affair. "It was a drastic cure," she would say, "but he had no more trouble with pink-eye."

Baldy himself occasionally referred to "when I was blind—remember?"

But Sarah never referred to those days by so much as a word. The only difference they seemed to have made was that from then on she called her young brother by his full dignified name—Archibald.

The day after Archibald recovered his sight—and his temper—she sat down at the piano and practiced for five hours without a break. She ate her lunch absently, did an errand for her mother, went back to the piano, and worked on, until Anna's insistent voice called her, for the third time, to come to dinner. The next day she repeated the pattern, and the next.

Mama said, "What's come over you, Sarah? It's high time you went back to school. Baldy's going to get well and you aren't doing much for him anyway."

"I don't think I'm going back to school. I don't have time for it."

"You can't do that!" her mother said in consternation. "You can't even be a music teacher without a high school education. I'm going to talk to Dr. Rivera."

"I'll talk to him myself, Mama. But I can't go back to school yet. I've just caught onto something."

She had caught onto the fact that she and the piano were one, that she could tame the instrument, infuriate it, beat it to submission, or coax from it such melody that her own heart could not make room for the miracle her fingers wrought.

That night she hurried to the Riveras'. Mrs. Rivera was in her sitting room playing a kind of solitaire with chess, which was a game of her own invention.

"I came to thank you for the flowers," Sarah said, still breathless from her rapid walk. "For the red roses which came each day while Archibald was—hurt. I don't know what I would have done without them."

Mrs. Rivera waved her to a seat. She did not ask for details about the child. She said, "I hear you have been practicing very hard."

"How did you know that?"

"Your Anna told it to the grocer's boy and he told the garageman and Adolph overheard it and told Hortense, who told me."

Sarah laughed. "It sounds like an international conspiracy. But I have been practicing. Mrs. Rivera, my technique is awful. My fingers are all thumbs. I can't run a scale that suits me. I think I'll quit school."

"Let's talk to Enrique." She rang the bell for Hortense, who called the doctor from his study.

He came in singing, nor did he stop until he had come to the end of his "Toreador Song," whereupon he flourished his imaginary sword and bowed to the ladies. "I have mistaken my career," he said dolefully.

"He really has a very good voice," his wife said fondly, "except that he cannot carry a tune—what do you say?—in a basket."

"My darling! My love! You've picked up idle gossip from the servants."

"Well, then, you can carry a tune but you carry it through so many keys that the most expert accompanist—even our Sarah—could not follow you."

"Then we need better pianists." The doctor pulled a chair near the fire and sat down.

"That is what Sarah has come to talk about. She wants to quit school."

"Hm!" The doctor looked at Sarah and then into the fire. "Hm!"

"I can't tell you how badly I need the time." Her voice was urgent. "I practice a whole day and learn practically nothing."

Mrs. Rivera leaned toward him as if she, too, were seeking a favor. "Time is really of the essence."

"But so is content," he answered slowly. "Education is not all in the schools—we know that. But the friends of your own age are in the school. And a musician has to know many other things besides music."

The two women said nothing. After a time the doctor spoke again.

"Perhaps for a while it will be a good thing if time to practice is hard to extract from the day's studies. Just so long as you are sure to extract it."

"But teachers pile on so many unnecessary things that don't get you anyplace."

"Ah, my dear young woman," Mrs. Rivera said, "not all studies are worth doing well. Some assignments it is your ethical duty to slight. Languages you need, but mathematics—" She shrugged her shoulders.

"Fie upon you, Carlotta!" the doctor said. "Mathematics are for fun. They give her mental exhilaration."

"They give you mental exhilaration, my sweet clown. They give me spiritual dyspepsia."

"You see," laughed Sarah, "even you two cannot agree. Now me—I really like math. But then, there's nothing I don't like, at least part of the time. That's the trouble. I like my work and I kind of hate to do it poorly, and there goes my time."

"The battle is on," Mrs. Rivera said. "The long, long battle."

A few days later Sarah was called into the principal's office and told that a practice room had been arranged for her use and that she was to have three free periods each day. Soon the news went around the school that Sarah Duncan really had ability. Someday she might become a genuine concert pianist who went from city to city in full evening dress playing to packed auditoriums. Or if not that, at least the best music teacher Wheaton had ever known. Sarah herself never thought of the second alternative, and she dreamed less frequently of the first. Mastering her music for its own sake had become a goal, but no longer a choice. It was marrow in her bones.

Fifteen

On the night of Rachel's graduation from high school the two girls were up in her bedroom, where Sarah was helping her dress. The dress was made of fine white voile with real lace insertions and inserts of lace medallions above the wide hem. The neck was cut too low, Rachel thought, but Sarah said nonsense; anyone with a perfect neck and lovely slim shoulders would be a big silly not to look as well as she could. The short puffed sleeves stood out like butterflies. Rachel said that if Sarah honestly thought everything was all right, then she would just enjoy looking the best she could. She smoothed her hair into place, only to have it escape again in ringlets at neck and temples.

"You look like a French bonbon," Sarah said, "and I know who would like to gobble up the bonbon for himself."

With sudden earnestness in her voice Rachel said, "Sarah, I have to tell you something." She went to the little box she called her jewel case and took out a ring. "It's a little-finger ring," she explained, laying it in Sarah's hand. "Made in Italy. The blue is a kind of enamel inlaid in the gold. Who do you think gave it to me?"

"Leslie, of course." Sarah held the exquisite little circle to the light. Then she turned to Rachel. Amazement and incredulity colored her voice. "You're really engaged?"

"No, I'm not." Rachel smiled with an up-quirk of her mouth, as she did only when making fun of herself. "I couldn't very well be engaged to Leslie with this ring because he doesn't know anything about it. It was his father who gave it to me. And the funny thing is that lately I've thought his father disapproved of our going around so much together. You know how he wants Leslie to go East to college and how Leslie wants to stay here. They've argued so much about it that last week they quit speaking and ate their meals in silence. I felt so dreadful that I didn't even want to tell you."

"When did he give it to you? Just today?" Sarah sat down on the big tufted footstool.

"He gave it to me late this afternoon. I was downtown hurrying like everything when I almost bumped into him on Main Street. He asked me if I could come up to their apartment for a minute. I was almost too surprised to speak. You know what a big man he is and how he takes it for granted everyone's going to do what he says. I'd never been up there except that time Leslie had the International Relations Club, remember? It's such a nice place, you can hardly think there isn't any woman living in it."

Sarah nodded.

"I sat down in the big red leather chair where he told me to sit and I felt like a child brought in for a scolding or something. Then he excused himself and went into his bedroom. I just sat. By and by he came out and said he had a small graduation present for me. He said that when he first met his wife she wore a little ring her father had brought her from Italy. The ring always fascinated him, he said, because it was so very small and so beautiful. Then he slipped it on my little finger. He laughed and said he never thought he'd be putting a ring on a girl's finger again, but I could see he was just laughing to cover up something the ring made him feel. He said I was to wear it tonight but not to mention it unless Leslie asked about it. Somehow, I wanted to put my arms right around him, but of course I didn't. I just thanked him, and not very well either." Rachel leaned against the door and looked down at Sarah so thoughtfully that Sarah felt a quick little stab of realization that Rachel had grown up. Then Rachel said, "What do you make of it, Sarah?"

"Quite a bit." Sarah spoke to Rachel, but she looked out of the window into the twilight sky, wishing she knew how much to answer. Then she turned back with a wide smile. "You might say I know the other half of the story. Leslie told me. It wasn't just a little trouble he and his father had. It was big trouble. It began over his father's wanting him to go to Williams College and also wanting him to cut all ties with Wheaton. Maybe Leslie didn't tell you that part. His father wanted him to cut himself off from home completely so that he'd be free to choose what he wanted to do with his life and not feel he had to come back here to work in his father's mill. He was sort of bending over backward, Leslie thinks, because it was so plain he wanted him in the business. He tried to make Leslie promise he wouldn't write to you or me or anybody for two years. But Leslie wouldn't promise."

"Leslie's terribly stubborn." Both pride and distress were in Rachel's voice.

"Both of them are stubborn. Yesterday they got very stubborn and Leslie said he wouldn't go away to school at all. His father said then he wouldn't give Leslie any college money. So Leslie said he didn't care; he could make all the money he needed, and his father said he would have to make all he needed because he would redraw his will that very hour and exactly one dollar would be all Leslie would ever get. And when he said that, Leslie just walked out of the room. What's more, he didn't go back last night. He stayed at the Y.M.C.A."

"How terrible." Rachel sank into a chair and stared incredulously at Sarah. "Families just don't have fights like that in real life."

"That's where they do have them. But don't look so ghastly, as if you didn't know the rest of the story, goose. The ring is his way of begging Leslie's pardon. He knows Leslie will see his mother's ring on your little finger."

"You mean—you think he meant it as a message to Leslie? I thought he surely wouldn't be just giving me a ring like this."

Rachel looked so immensely relieved that the years seemed to drop away and leave her a child again, playing dress-up.

Sarah laughed up the scale and down. This was a time to laugh. "He gave you the ring, all right, Rachel, but he also meant it as a message to Leslie. You'll find out what."

"What will I find out?" Rachel looked a little frightened. It was one thing to be waiting for a joyous, inevitable moment and another to realize the moment was just around the corner. "You don't mean—you don't think?"

"Of course I don't think," Sarah answered firmly. "Why should I think? I'm not graduating from high school."

"I wish to goodness you were." Rachel followed the bypath back to the well-trod trail of discussion as to why Sarah had dropped behind her class. "I wish you had stayed home last semester and done your physics and graduated with us where you belong."

Sarah shook her head. "It was better to spend six weeks in New York and to hear concerts and be coached five times by Rachmaninoff. Rachel! How could you weigh Rachmaninoff against a course in physics?" Such large dismay loomed in Sarah's gray eyes that Rachel leaned over and kissed her soundly, a good deal as one might kiss an unhappy child. Then both girls looked at the clock and made a dive for Rachel's white coat.

"See you from the front row," Sarah called to the departing heels clicking down the stairs. Outside a car was honking. It was nearing time when the graduates should be gathering behind stage in the gymnasium. Sarah realized that she, too, must soon be on her way. According to the program, she was to play Debussy's "Soirée dans Grenade." But instead of going home for her coat she walked to the open window and stood looking out. Everything was still. This was day's blessed moment. The big maple stood silent, its leaves relinquishing their identity to the peaceful anonymity of twilight. She hadn't told Rachel that early this afternoon she herself had gone to Mr. Sando in his dusty little office at the mill and asked to see him alone. She had walked right up to the boss of the mill and said, "Look here, Mr. Sando, do you really want to lose your son? I am Leslie's best friend probably, and I know what he's like. He's like you."

Mr. Sando had said, "He is, isn't he?" At first he said it in amazement. Then he said it over as a statement of fact. The third time he chuckled. "He is, isn't he!" Then he laughed right out and patted her on the shoulder. He stood up straight to his full height of six feet four and said she was wonderful. She laughed too. That was all there was to it. The telephone rang, he waved her good-by, and she was outdoors again right where she'd been three minutes earlier. On the way home she realized a thing that Leslie had probably never put into words: when a grown boy stands a scant five feet seven it is hard to have the same nature as his father who is six feet four.

The affair of the ring came off according to its destiny. Rachel reported it faithfully the next morning as Sarah helped her pack away her graduation dress. Leslie had said, "Where did you get that ring?" and Rachel had told him. Then Leslie had laughed for a long time, just the way his father had laughed. He said, "My father's just like me. That's why we have such a time." He hadn't mentioned the ring again all during the evening or on the way home. But when they reached Rachel's own vine-covered porch they had sat in the porch swing and watched the moonlight spilling a melody of grace notes through the trellis onto the porch floor. Leslie had said he could pick out the melody of the notes. They were the first bars of the *Lohengrin* wedding march, he said; he could hear them in the distance, but definitely drawing near. That was the first night he had kissed Rachel.

Toward noon Sarah and Rachel went off on an errand and they met Leslie on the street. He was laughing. "Last night when I got home to the hotel I rapped on my father's door and what do you think I said?"

Neither girl could guess.

"I said, 'I'm sorry I'm late, sir, but Rachel and I were talking over courses, and we both think Williams has more to offer than Bryan. That is, for my purposes.'"

Only Rachel's and Leslie's new "understanding"—her mother thought them too young to be engaged—marked this summer as different from last summer. Sarah practiced many hours each day, went to Minneapolis to take her lessons of Koenigstein, spent long evenings with the Riveras. Sometimes on a Saturday morning she helped Anna make preserves. She liked measuring and weighing with care; she liked waiting for exactly the moment when fruit and sugar lost their separateness and became a new thing. Often when an afternoon seemed too warm for practicing she and Rachel sat together on one another's cool back steps and drank lemonade, as they had done since doll days.

The next winter was at once the busiest and the most routine of Sarah's life. At sixteen she was a young woman in looks, with the long-legged tallness that swings along with easy grace. Her face seemed a little too long to be called oval, a bit too angular to be beautiful. She wore her long braids of chestnut hair coronet-style around her head. Mama said she was lucky to have all that hair of her own. Coronets were fashionable, and a recent hair-goods advertisement in the newspaper had priced a false braid at $6.98, which was certainly more than Sarah could afford, Mama said, the way she was using her money for music lessons.

Koenigstein, Sarah said, was the one man in her life. Mama, who had once met Herr Koenigstein on a trip to Minneapolis, said that he was certainly not much to look at but he did have a lot of personality. In repose, Koenigstein was a meek-looking bald-headed man, neither tall nor short, lean nor fat. His eyes were intensely blue, seeming to turn black under intense emotion. His nose was thin through the bridge and then spread to a jolly three-cornered bottom which gave a jaunty look to the face in repose. But analyzing the face of Koenigstein was as profitless as trying to synthesize his personality traits. Something always eluded the observer. How could he demand so much of Sarah—sometimes an inhuman amount—and then suddenly, in the midst of a particularly good lesson, order her off for a month's vacation? How could he, but he could. Sarah, on her part, accepted his least suggestion as her order of the day. She never answered back even when he was wrong. Nor was her respect colored by fear of his displeasure. Once he had told her that she was the only pupil he had who was not afraid of him. How could she be? Both understood that his mind and his skill were her reservoir; whatever she could draw was hers. She could draw a great deal.

Sixteen

To Sarah it seemed odd to have Rachel in college, absorbed in interests which were apart from her own. Sarah herself continued to go three times a week to the high school physics laboratory to make up her course, but definitely she doubted if she wanted to go to college. It was a broken bone that changed her mind. A broken bone and the opportunity to read a few books. Late in the winter she slipped on the icy steps of the church and snapped an anklebone. While she was laid up Grandpa brought her one book which Mama said was no book at all for a young girl to read. It was the story of the white slave trade by Elizabeth Robins. Grandpa said everybody young and old should read it. He was so stirred up that he took the train and went in to a meeting of the Twin City Ministerial Association and asked what they were going to do about vice in Minnesota. Many of the ministers had read the book, and they were grateful that the question had been raised by this energetic pastor from Wheaton. They talked about the social gospel and went to work on the parts of their cities known as the Red Light District.

It was during that reform campaign that Grandpa got acquainted with Archbishop Ireland and reported that the Archbishop was a gentleman. Grandma snorted at that. But Grandpa replied that a good many Catholics lived exemplary lives according to their standards. Moreover, the Archbishop was also a fine scholar. He had seen a little book in Grandfather's pocket, a *Spiritual Guide* written by a man named

Molinos. They had fallen to talking and Grandfather had quoted a sentence from Molinos: "Man may, indeed, open the window; but it is the Sun himself that must give the light." The Archbishop had said he didn't think there was another Protestant in the Twin Cities who could have quoted that book. Grandpa was pleased but also, he told Sarah, he was miffed that the Catholics did not know there were scholars among Protestants. He said that no church had a corner on the inner light, but that if he had to single one church out for honorable mention it would be the Quakers.

"Maybe you should have been a Quaker, Grandpa."

He shook his head. "Like most people, I was born into my church, and on the whole it suits me. We Campbellites can use our own critical minds on our own experience and travel as far as we're able without a soul to bid us halt." Grandpa began to pace up and down the room, head back, fire in his eyes. "I tell you, Sarah, you can't shift responsibility onto anyone's shoulders. Follow the best trail you can find, and then if you come to a dead end, blaze a trail for yourself. Somebody has to do it, and it might as well be you and me."

That was Grandpa for you, Sarah thought proudly. What a lot of trails he'd blazed even in her day. People said Wheaton was too small for a good lyceum course; Grandpa said Wheaton was big enough for the best. People said Wheaton schools were as good as any; Grandpa said they weren't good enough. He pioneered with his church too. When the Foreign Christian Missionary Society decreed that the First Christian Church of Wheaton ought to give four hundred dollars to missions, Grandpa said nonsense, First Church would support its own missionary entire and complete. Grandpa did nothing by halves. He was the first man at a fire, right after the engine and before the hook and ladder, and the last man to leave a ball game. Yes, and the only man to visit people who had smallpox in the pesthouse.

Sarah thought her mother seemed glad to have her home to talk to; she came in often on unimportant errands. But one day when she came up to Sarah's room to leave a message she suddenly collapsed in a chair. "I don't feel well," she said. "I just don't feel well." Then she began to shake with a chill.

Sarah hobbled out of bed and called Anna. Anna got Mama's wraps off and helped her to her own room, but before she could get her into bed Mama was delirious. Dr. Rivera arrived, looked at her, felt her pulse, and said, "Pneumonia. And she is a very ill woman."

He called for a nurse. All at once Sarah found herself head of the household, with Archibald and Lucy to look after, custard to bake, oranges to squeeze, dishes to wash. But none of these things mattered; they were only the things one did with one's hands while the mind went its own bewildered way.

Mama was very ill indeed. Her temperature climbed to 105, and there it hung. Her breath came in deep rasps. In the middle of one night Dr. Rivera arrived with an oxygen tent. Cylinders of the precious gas were set beside the bed, and a little tent with a small isinglass window was put over Mama's head. A second nurse came to watch her breathing; she sat with her fingers lightly on Mama's pulse. Sarah sat in a stiff straight chair on the other side of the bed. She did not know that her own ankle was throbbing, nor that her hair was disheveled and her eyes red from lack of sleep. She only realized at last that her mother was a woman with a life to live. Before that time Mama had been Mama. One loved her and gave her presents, ran errands, looked to her for advice. Sometimes one rebelled at a restriction and inwardly called her unreasonable, old-fashioned, even silly about such things as never crossing one's legs in public. But she was a fixture in life, like the furniture, the house. Now all at once as she sat watching her mother's contorted face, she realized that here was a person with struggles of her own. Her mother had disappointments and ambitions. She had personal plans. And now Dr. Rivera was bending over her anxiously because she might die.

On the ninth day Grandpa came as usual immediately after breakfast. Grandma had been there all night, supposedly sleeping on a cot in Archibald's room because he had picked up a cold and might throw his covers off, but actually she had stood in the corner of Mama's room most of the night, a gray, shrunken person with nothing to say. Watching her standing there, Sarah was also aware that Grandma was a person too. She was a woman whose only daughter might be dying. She was a woman who gave her energy unstintingly to help others. All her funny ways were kindly ways, really; they were her ways for making people happier both now and ever after. A great lump rose in Sarah's throat. She wished terribly that she had realized sooner that Grandma was a woman too. Finally, at daylight, Grandma had gone back to Archibald's room and was still sleeping. Grandpa's voice wakened her.

On this morning Grandpa had not come in quietly. He came up the steps whistling, and fairly boomed out to Sarah, who was standing in the dining-room door, "How's your maw? How's my girl?"

Sarah looked at him blankly, too amazed to shush his loud tones.

Grandpa smiled and tweaked her ear, for all the world as if she were five years old again and this was Christmas. For a second Sarah wondered if he had gone crazy. He read her thought and sobered down. "Listen here, Sarah," he said in a quieter but none the less jubilant voice, "your mother is going to get well. She passed the crisis just before dawn this morning."

"She hasn't even come to the crisis yet," Sarah told him dully.

Grandpa stood looking at her. Then he spoke slowly. "I'll tell you a thing you won't understand. Neither do I. When your mother first took sick I began to pray for her. I spent a lot of time on my knees. I prayed that the sickness would leave her. Health is good and goodness is part of the nature of God. I prayed with faith in the power of God to make her well. And each day she got worse. Couldn't God hear my prayer? That's what I asked myself. Is my life so feeble that my prayer has no strength? Won't He answer? And then last night, as I knelt by my chair in the study of the church, I realized that maybe He was answering. Maybe He was saying *no*. It hadn't occurred to me that if He heard my prayer He would say no."

Sarah sank into a chair, but without taking her eyes from Grandpa's face. He was saying something more than his words said. He went right on.

"When I realized that maybe He was saying no, I got up off my knees and thought for a long time. I stood by the window in the dark and looked out. There were no stars. Just cold black night. For a moment I thought, 'This is what Evelyn is stepping into.' Then in a sort of flash I seemed to see the world as it looks to the eyes of God—as clear by night as by day. I saw the snow in the yard and the frozen ground beneath and I saw more. I saw the grass in the frozen ground, its greenness waiting. I saw the daffodil bulbs at the corner of the yard, each with a flower biding its time. I saw the whole of spring beneath the sheet of ice and I saw other springs to come. Do you know what I felt then?"

Sarah nodded, her eyes still glued to his face. "I know a little, I think."

"I hope you do," Grandpa said. "I felt plain silly, that's what I felt." He snapped his fingers. "I felt as silly as a puppy trying to tell his master how to run his business. I felt so silly I could have clopped myself on the head. If God could look after the frozen earth and bring forth daffodils and plum blossoms and arbutus and fishing worms, I guessed He could look after my child. So I said, 'All right, Father, have it your way.' I shrugged my shoulders, as if I'd let a burden slide off at his feet. 'She's your daughter too,' I said. 'She's done pretty well here on earth. Maybe you feel she's ready for promotion. Maybe her spring is about to come. Maybe you've got a better idea than mine.' So I sat in the chair by the window—that chair you like—and I thought how it would be for her to take off. I thought of the way my mother, just before she died, insisted she was seeing a wide blue river with green hills on the other side and people waiting.

I thought of the joy on her face and the way she squeezed my hand and whispered, 'It's all right. It's better than good.' You might almost say I went with your mother across the river, I saw it so plain. And then do you know what happened?"

Sarah shook her head. "How could I know?"

"You couldn't," Grandpa said, his eyes twinkling. "Because nothing happened really. But all at once I knew she was going to get well. All at once I knew that when she did go, everything would be fine, but this wasn't the time. She's still got work to do here. I was glad for us, and I said, 'Thank you, God. I don't understand your reasons, but I'm glad she's staying awhile.' And then I added a thing I didn't need to tell Him. 'But it was all right, either way,' I said."

Grandpa went over to the sideboard and took an apple. "You'd better eat some breakfast," he advised her as he took a big bite of it. "You look worn out. We've got to let your grand-mother know she can lay aside her grief."

But Grandma did not lay aside her grief. No one did but Grandpa and Sarah. Grandpa continued to be exuberant. Sarah only felt dazed, but no longer filled with anxiety. It seemed to her that this day was a bad dream from which she was trying to waken but could not come to full consciousness until the dream was dreamed out. Dr. Rivera came every hour. He said Mama was reaching the crisis. He took Grandpa, Grandma, and Sarah into the hall and told them the outcome was extremely doubt-ful. His face was drawn; he used no extra words. Grandpa looked so jaunty that Sarah was afraid he would make a flippant remark, but he didn't. He said, "There's an old saying that it's always darkest before the dawn, so we'll just bide the dawn."

Grandpa was right. Mama's temperature fell suddenly. She was very, very weak, but she breathed naturally and fell asleep. Now everyone beamed softly, but Grandpa outbeamed them all.

Sarah spent a lot of time with her mother during her con-valescence. A fine unspoken bond seemed to hold them. They were friends. Maybe they would never be intellectual companions, but that did not seem important. Mama talked about recipes; she had a good appetite now. Sarah enjoyed her mother's debating with herself how much nutmeg Mrs. Benson must have used in the custard she sent in.

For her part, Sarah told her mother about a book she was reading, and when her mother said it sounded dull, she only smiled without feeling there was a barrier between them. The book was called *An Interpretation of Dreams,* written by a man named Sigmund Freud. Both the Riveras had read the book. Mrs. Rivera said it was a great book and that more would be heard of that man. Dr. Rivera said there was no doubt something in what Freud said, but for himself he would rather base his analysis of a person's needs on his waking thoughts than on dreams. Mrs. Rivera said gaily, "My dear, you are simply shutting your eyes to the number of images of yourself that might greet you from your patients' dreams." The doctor said, "Carlotta, it is to keep you out of other men's dreams that I have you walled within my castle, drawbridge up."

Finally, just before the cast was taken off her ankle, Sarah read a book which whetted her intellectual appetite and then she announced that she had decided to go to college. The book was *The Business of Being a Woman,* by Ida M. Tarbell. When she laid it aside she had come to a firm conclusion that she wanted more understanding to speak forth. All the knowledge in the world seemed inadequate. She wanted to study in gulps—chemistry, biology, history, literature, and all the languages human beings spoke. She did not know that many other young women of her day were also being borne into adulthood on this same high tide of self-assurance which is neither modest nor conceited, but simply life at its zestful best.

Seventeen

June 28, 1914, made no impression on Sarah or on any other member of the family. Only Mrs. Rivera, Sarah remembered later, had especially noted the newspaper headlines. Sarah was having dinner with the Riveras, and Mrs. Rivera had said, "The world can bear the loss of the Archduke Ferdinand and his wife, but that sullen Slavic province of Bosnia cares not at all for the welfare of its new stepmother, Austria-Hungary." Sarah also remembered wondering if anyone else in all Minnesota had ever spent a day in both Sarajevo and Wheaton. It was that casual thought which marked the day as different from any other of the summer.

Along toward the first of August a note of warning came into Grandfather's sermons. He said it was ominous for diplomatic relations to be broken off between Serbia and Austria-Hungary. Even though everyone knew that world trade held the nations in too close a grip to permit an actual war, still it was poor business for any country to go so far as to make public avowals of blame. A democratic country such as the United States, he said, could well frown upon this hysterical cheering for Emperor Francis Joseph and Emperor Wilhelm, while the idea of crowds kneeling before Emperor Nicholas at the Winter Palace was almost idolatrous. Still, he said, America had plenty of sins of her own, what with Sunday movies and Sunday baseball.

One thing, however, gave Grandpa hope that summer. The country was gradually growing dry. For Grandma's birthday

Mama gave her a small enameled pin made to look like the white ribbon of the Women's Christian Temperance Union. Grandma even picked up a temperance joke from Baldy and surprised everybody, including herself, by telling it at Aid Society. In Wheeling, West Virginia, she said, a saloonkeeper named August realized he would be out of business the first of July, so he painted a sign over his store, "July first will be the last of August."

Before school opened Sarah and Mrs. Rivera went again to New York. Mrs. Rivera had a feeling in her bones, she said, that Paris might be cut off from America one of these days, and she wanted to see her dressmaker, who was also an importer. The doctor said such talk was hysterical, but he always encouraged his wife's fondness for beautiful raiment. Sarah went along to hear a series of summer concerts by a young German who would soon be leaving America because the Kaiser was calling all young German males home. But the concerts were a disappointment. She had a new feeling that if she only had the German's technique she could play better than he.

The thing that impressed her most on the trip was New York Harbor. Crammed in together were British, German, French, Dutch, Spanish, and Italian ocean liners, tramp ships, freighters, hookers, emigrant carriers—all with ensigns flying. Some of the ships were loaded and ready to go, blue peters aloft, but one couldn't help wondering if they would ever reach their destinations, or would they be like the North German Lloyd's *Kronprinzessin Cecile*, which had left New York bound for Germany with ten million dollars in gold and was glad enough to make Bar Harbor, Maine, in safety?

Although gruesome commentaries on trench life were beginning to appear in the press, Sarah, like President Wilson, felt that the war was a barbarous unreality upon which a civilized Christian had best turn his back. To register undue interest was, in some mysterious but real way, to give life to a nightmare. There were just too many good reasons why all of Europe could not be at war in this modern day.

In the fall of 1914, Sarah entered Bryan College. Dr. Rivera felt that she should go away to school; insularity of mind was a more permanent deformity, he said, than anything chronic arthritis could produce. Mrs. Rivera said he was right completely—when was he not right?—but that Sarah had a temperamental idiosyncrasy against insularity, just as some people had a natural immunity to smallpox, and this was no time to leave Koenigstein. Mama agreed with Mrs. Rivera; they not only discussed the matter daily on the telephone but went back and forth to talk in person. Mama tried to get Grandpa on her side, but Grandpa thought Sarah should go to Leland Stanford and study under David Starr Jordan, the greatest college president our country had ever known. Sarah herself felt that each college catalogue she looked at seemed to offer something important and decisive for her career. Finally she did the obvious thing and asked Koenigstein what he thought about her going away for a couple of years. He responded sourly, "Are you going to be a musician or a college professor?"

Sarah said, "You know the answer."

Taking Sarah's hand in his, he tapped her knuckles gently with his forefinger. "You stay by the old man until he bids you lief to go."

The next two years were happily uneventful. College studies were interesting but not demanding. Neither students nor professors at Bryan thought much about the fact that besides carrying the usual load Sarah was practicing three or four hours a day and making her regular trips to Minneapolis for lessons. At his end of the line, Professor Koenigstein paid no attention to college.

Sarah got up each morning with zest for the day. Sometimes, standing naked in her room, she looked at her own firm body and thought what a good thing it was to have flesh and bones; what a lot one would miss if the body were made of light waves or some other unsubstantial substance. She let down her long brown hair, brushed it hard, and loved the feel of it over her bare shoulders. Skin was a wonderful invention, and she was glad her body had no blemishes. When she looked at her face she sighed. Definitely she was not beautiful. Her mouth did not suit her at all; it was too large. She wanted a small mouth, cupid's-bowed in a fashion to draw men's eyes. Not that she felt any need of men in her life at present, so long as she had a date for a dance, but when she got around to being seriously interested in men she did wish she could be the clinging type with a somewhat lost look. Scrutinizing her face, she naturally looked her worst and always left the mirror a little depressed, but the depression never lasted because she soon forgot what she was depressed about.

To Sarah the war was an academic problem, a terrible example of what happened to a capitalistic society which put politicians instead of economists and sociologists in power. To Lucy, who was a honey-pot for buzzing young males, the war was merely something far away and long ago. But to Archibald, every battlefield was right next door. At six he read like a boy of ten, and he and Grandpa had long consultations over European maps. They read aloud Wilson's notes to England and her replies. Grandpa said when you came down to cases, the United States had more bones to pick with England than with Germany, but public sentiment was seldom logical. There was one odd thing about Grandpa's interest in the war: he did not believe anybody could win. "Whoever wins is bound to lose," he would insist.

One day Sarah asked the question that had not really occurred to any of them before. "Are you a pacifist, Grandpa?"

He did not answer at once. Then he spoke slowly. "I don't know," he said. "A pacifist sounds like someone who doesn't believe in his government. But I don't see how a man can love his enemies and fight a war."

Toward the end of April an interesting family named Kane moved to Wheaton. There were Mr. and Mrs. Alexander Kane and a son named Alan. Actually the Kanes were an old family in

Wheaton. The great-grandfather, Cyrus Kane, had homesteaded a double section of land even before the state had been divided into counties. The grandfather had built one of the first modern farm homes. Alexander Kane had grown up in that commodious farmhouse; he had attended Wheaton Academy, which later became Bryan College; then he had gone East to Yale and Harvard, both. The general impression in Wheaton was that Alexander Kane had received degrees from more colleges than any other man in Minnesota, that is, if one counted all the foreign universities where he had studied international law. People who knew about such things said that there was no more brilliant international lawyer on either side of the Atlantic than Alexander Kane.

Now Alexander Kane had come back to Wheaton to retire. He had three reasons for returning to Wheaton to retire: first, he wanted to write a three-volume history of international law. This reason probably accounted for the eight thousand books which came with him, and also for the highly insured documents which continually worried the Wheaton postmaster. The second reason for coming to Wheaton was that his lungs had given a little trouble of late and he liked the Wheaton climate. He felt, indeed, that if the whole world had the Wheaton climate there would be no wars, and he had his arguments worked out in terms of barometrical pressure and social ecology. The third reason why he returned to Wheaton was that he liked Wheaton. At the time of his return to the scene of his boyhood he was an extremely personable man of sixty-two. His hair and close-cropped Vandyke were gray, but his brown eyes snapped like a boy's, his tanned cheeks were ruddy, and his step buoyant. When he walked in the country he wore a beret.

Alice Kane, his wife, was a dozen years his junior. She was slender but fairly broad of hip and shoulder; both sturdy and aristocratic in bearing. Her black hair was straight and inclined to fly, and she made no attempt to put it up on kid curlers. Her features were sharply cut, her eyes very blue. She spoke with a

Boston accent, walked like an Englishwoman, shopped for groceries with New England thriftiness, kept an immaculate house, worked in her garden, and hunted out complicated references for her husband. Everybody in Wheaton liked Alice Kane at once.

Then there was Alan Kane. Sarah did not see Alan Kane because he came only for a week of spring vacation, which was a time she spent in Minneapolis with Mrs. Rivera, attending two concerts by Josef Aronowitz called Tony and having some of the most wonderful days of her life. Tony and Koenigstein were friends, but when Sarah played for the two of them they contradicted each other's criticism and glowered at each other horribly. Mrs. Rivera laughed and called them jealous boys. By the time Sarah returned to Wheaton, Alan had already gone back to Yale.

It was Rachel who reported on Alan. He was twenty, she said, and tall.

"Tell me more," Sarah begged, laughing at Rachel's enthusiasm. For herself, those days in Minneapolis were more important than any man.

"He has wavy brown hair and eyes," Rachel went on.

"Remarkable! I've never seen wavy eyes myself."

Rachel ignored the remark. "He's handsome, Sarah. Not a little handsome, but very, very. And no more conscious of his good looks than a good bookbinding is conscious of its leather.' She stopped, pleased with her comparison.

Sarah was pleased too. "You're getting literary, Rachel. You sound more like Leslie every day. How is Leslie?"

But this was Rachel's time to talk about Alan. "He is a very natural person. He doesn't seem to be trying to please people, but he's the kind that old ladies would pour out their troubles to."

"Children and dogs go for him," Sarah supplied. "When he walks down the street small boys playing ball send a fast one his way."

"How did you know?" Rachel said earnestly. "I know you're spoofing, but it's a fact."

"And what am I supposed to do about it?" Sarah was vaguely irritated by this talk of Alan Kane.

"Nothing. But he is coming here to college next fall. You'd think he'd stay at Yale when he is already a junior, but he explained to me that he thought he'd get more out of reading under his father's direction than from taking pre-law courses at Yale."

"How modest of him. And how bighearted to condescend to Bryan." Definitely Sarah had had enough of this talk.

"Funny how you can think people are just made for each other, and then they rub each other the wrong way," Rachel said. "When I told him about you he seemed kind of bored."

"That makes two of us." But just the same, Sarah was interested in what the Kanes were doing to an old house they had bought. It was a nondescript brown house, somewhat run down, built in a vaguely colonial style. Three months later when the Kanes moved in, it was a white house, shipshape as to plumbing, wiring, shutters, and flagstone walks, and there was no longer anything vague about its being colonial. She had not seen the Kane house in finished state, however, because very unexpectedly in the middle of June she had gone off to Cape Cod with the Riveras. Mama had been glad to have her go; sometimes she grew a little tired of the constant practicing, and yet she had begun to feel that maybe Sarah was destined to be more than the head of Bryan College Music Department and ought to be free to practice as much as she wished. Koenigstein had been glad to have Sarah go also. He said she could memorize the Grieg concerto while lying on the beach; he was a great believer in memorizing without the instrument.

The trip had come about unexpectedly. At dinner one evening Dr. Rivera had looked up from his dish of strawberries to announce that Carlotta needed sea air. Mrs. Rivera had protested that she never felt better in her life and would not leave her own house and garden if she came down with smallpox and double pneumonia. Then Dr. Rivera had said it was his own health he was concerned about. He grew tired, he said, with the least exertion. Having watched him run up two flights of stairs without a puff, Sarah merely lifted an eyebrow. But Carlotta immediately called Hortense to prepare an herb bath, ordered Adolph to telephone to Minneapolis for a Swedish masseur, and herself made eggnog with old Kentucky brandy. The next day Dr. Rivera had decreed it was Sarah who needed the salt air. For two years she had gone to college, studied with Koenigstein, and practiced like a steam-driven calliope. By the time she was twenty-five, he said, they would have a jibbering old woman on their hands. Rest was imperative and at once.

The short of it was that all three, in the best of health and spirits, were soon settled in a sprawling and commodious Cape Cod cottage. The household machinery, lifted bodily from Minnesota to Massachusetts, was not even jarred. Each day as soon as a leisurely breakfast was over, the doctor disappeared into the little room he had set up as a workroom. There he had all sorts of contraptions of steel and wire and blade from which he was fashioning new contraptions. Such, at least, was his story, which he embellished by reporting fantastic tales of his own inventions: a flying trapeze for trained fleas, a perpetual-motion machine that could be operated only by the grin of a Cheshire cat. About his real endeavors he had nothing to say, but both women knew he was working out new instruments for operations of amazing delicacy. Sometimes he went off to spend the day with the local veterinary, but if surgery were performed there he made no mention of that, either.

And why this pressure for better instruments? Why had he taken a whole summer out of his practice to work on instruments and to recondition himself physically as if he were preparing to enter some Olympic event? Neither woman asked the inevitable question: Is it the war he's getting ready for? Far beneath their conscious minds both knew the answer.

Ostensibly their days were serene. Long mornings on the sand in the sun; long afternoons with their books on the shady veranda; long evenings of moonlight and music, when Sarah played in the dark such things as she wanted to play—and the war was an invention of newsmongers. Anyone who read the newspapers should realize that the world was fast becoming too civilized for a serious war. Look at the amazing new telephone service which now spanned the continent. Look at the Federal Reserve system which had gone into operation with farm loans at only four to five percent. There were now more schools and more good roads in the U.S.A. than any nation in history had ever known before. The tariff had been revised downward. Railways engaged in interstate commerce had reduced the working day to eight hours. The Panama Canal had been opened and four battleships had gone through its locks. Undeniably, in America these were days of national improvement and social good will.

To be sure, at times the tragedy of Europe lapped the very shores of America; an angry lapping, as if a tidal wave had sent its precursors of imminent disaster. Carlotta, who read everything and lived everywhere, devoured three daily papers with avidity and then called on the others to listen and take heed. But even when she paced the floor in wrath or grief, Sarah sensed that her emotion was one step removed, like the tearing of heart one feels at the theater. The greater the tension became and the faster the diplomatic notes flew between the United States and Germany, the farther Sarah felt from this fantastic war which could not be but was. As the summer wore on the sense of detachment was underscored by the way Mother Nature outdid herself in the lavish affection of her mood, as if she would heal inevitable wounds before they were made. For two long weeks the sky preened himself in blue doublet and golden armor, flirting his white plumes in the faces of the lovely, languid earth. Sarah observed and participated in the miracle of the abundant summer. She knew that in some unfathomed depth she was getting ready for something too. Something besides the war. Something overwhelming, exciting, inescapable, something larger than she had known before. She might be playing Brahms or diving into the surf or merely eating a gooseberry when the presentiment of a new dimension in life came upon her. But there was no use in trying to analyze an event, or an advent, which had not yet occurred. It would come when it would come.

It came in mid-September on the day she returned to Wheaton.

Eighteen

From the day Rachel entered college everyone knew that she posted a daily letter to Williams College and received one in return. Nevertheless, she dated the boys, football heroes and grinds. With her heart in Massachusetts, she was everybody's little big sister. No one was prouder of her popularity than Leslie. On the third morning after school opened she chanced to sit down on the wrought-iron bench in front of Old Main to read her morning letter. Up the path from Science Hall came Alan Kane. Up the path from the music building came Sarah. Sarah did not see Alan and Alan did not see Sarah until both stopped in front of Rachel, almost colliding as they did so.

Alan said, "I beg your pardon," and looked at Sarah. Then he said, "Oh, it's you."

Sarah looked at Alan. She said, "Yes, it's you too."

Rachel began to introduce them properly, but she insisted afterward that neither paid any attention to her, so she finished her letter. An exaggeration, Alan said. He took only a fleeting glance at Sarah, enough to see that here was a tall girl with level gray eyes, a sprinkling of freckles across the bridge of her nose, a generous mouth, and a crown of smooth dark braids. Here was a girl looking exactly the way he knew a girl would some-day look to him, only he could never afterward remember how he used to picture the right girl before he met her. At the moment it did not seem so complicated. Sarah, for her part, saw a pair of brown eyes, warm with humorous understanding, a fine forehead, thick black hair parted to the right, and a smile.

Also, for the first time in her life, she saw a shoulder as something to lay a head against. Not that her head was tired. It was only acting strangely.

They must have sat down by Rachel and after a while Rachel must have gone off to class and returned, because they were still sitting there when she came down the walk asking if Sarah was going to have lunch at the Commons. In the intervening time Sarah and Alan had taken care of many incidental matters, such as their denominational allegiance, Sarah being an unquestioning member of the Christian Church, often called Disciples of Christ, and Alan being a questioning member of the Episcopal Church, often called Church of England. Also, they had disagreed over woman's suffrage. Sarah felt it made no great difference to the future of democracy whether women voted or not; there were other ways of exerting pressure than through the ballot. Alan felt that women not only should have the privilege of voting but that it was their duty to demand to vote. The responsibility of voting, he said, would encourage them to weigh their opinions and express their conclusions. Sarah thought of her own two grandmothers and laughed. Before she knew it she was telling Alan about Grandfather and Grandmother Duncan, about her father's childhood, and finally about Bill Cooper, who raised blue morning-glories in a charitable institution.

Alan was a wonderful listener. He lit his pipe and leaned back, taking in everything she said with such wholehearted enjoyment that she suddenly realized she was talking better than she had ever talked before. She even heard herself turning a clever phrase, the way she and Rachel used to imagine Madame de Staël's conversing in the drawing rooms of Paris. Aware of her thought, she stopped, almost blushing.

"What is it?" Alan asked, smiling also. "I don't see anything funny about Bill Cooper, an ex-drunk turned gardener when exiled from home. You're holding back something." He leaned over and tapped her arm with the stem of his pipe. "Come through."

"I'm laughing at myself for talking so much," Sarah answered frankly. "It isn't like me to babble. Somehow I think you're to blame."

"I hope I am. If I'm ever any good as a lawyer I'll have to be able to make people talk." So then they were off on the subject of law. International law. Now it was Sarah's turn to lean back and listen, fascinated at what appeared to her his broad experience. He had traveled in England and on the Continent. When he was fourteen he had gone to school for a winter in Geneva while his father straightened out an intricate legal matter regarding freedom of the seas. Alan, too, knew that he was talking well. He plunged into the history of the case, beginning with Grotius, who had got himself put into a Dutch prison back in the early seventeenth century for advocating safety zones of travel across the high seas. Seven years in prison, wasn't he, and finally smuggled out by his wife in a supposed box of books? Alan's courteous half questions—"Am I right?" "Is this your impression?" "Doesn't it seem to you?"—made Sarah feel that she, too, was a cosmopolite. Here was someone Mrs. Rivera must know.

But she had got no further with the Rivera household than describing Adolph when Rachel came across campus toward them with her question about lunch. Rachel was looking very pretty in her crisp blue linen dress. The skirt frankly showed her ankles and an inch or two more. Rachel was often more daring than Sarah, and this matter of short skirts was one instance. All at once Sarah wished she had worn something smarter than a brown crash suit. How could she know that she never looked prettier in her life than she did at this moment?

"Let's all go to my house," Alan said, as if it were the most natural thing in the world to walk in with two girls for luncheon. Rachel demurred. One let one's folks know, didn't one, and found out if it was all right? "Not at our house." Alan said. "We just add a couple of trays."

And that was exactly what they did. As the three came into the wide colonial hall, Flossie Foss, the Kane's ample-bosomed maid, was bearing a tray toward the library with Mr. Kane's salad, soup, and sandwiches ready for him. Mrs. Kane was already eating from her tray out on the sun porch, where she could comfortably prop an open book against a table lamp. The book was David Grayson's *Great Possessions*. Sarah had read it. By the time Flossie Foss reappeared with trays for the girls, Sarah Duncan and Alice Kane were voluble friends. Alan, balancing on his tray a mountain of sandwiches, a pitcher of milk, and half a dozen odds and ends from the icebox, took the girls out to lawn chairs in the back yard, where they could eat in the sun without being seen from the street. They went on talking, Sarah and he, feeling all the more alone because Rachel was present.

Rachel realized that on the third day of classes Sarah would either have to get herself registered and her class card signed or pay a fine. It was enough of a lapse to have returned to college two days late. But balancing one consideration against another in her wise little head, she said nothing. Plainly here were two who were meant for each other, and if Sarah were only half as interested as she looked, maybe she wouldn't give her entire life to art after all. How she wished she could write a letter to Leslie right now. Well—they wouldn't even notice if she took out her notebook and idly wrote a few lines.

They did not notice. Sometime later when they went into the house to the piano they did not mind her staying behind to finish her letter. Through the open window she heard the strains of Chopin's Waltz in A Flat Major. Sarah must be feeling gay; she was turning out those little fillips with an air. Really, Sarah was at her best. She went right into the arpeggio étude, the one she always loved to play. Swiftly and evenly the chords flowed. After a breath she struck up Liszt's "La Campanella." This would tickle Leslie; Sarah was turning on the works; her little finger went to town on the trills. And now, for goodness' sake, Rachmaninoff's "Polka." At that Rachel was drawn into the house.

Sarah saw Rachel as she slipped into the room and nodded as she lit out on De Falla's "Ritual Fire Music." This was really Leslie's piece, and Sarah was slapping it off in his heartiest manner. Sharp, often dissonant; boom-de-day! No wonder Archibald took to a war dance whenever he heard it. And after the "Fire Music" came Steinberg's Etude in C Minor. Why all this brilliant stuff? Being a pupil of Koenigstein, she usually stuck close to the old-time classical repertoire. After a moment's pause Sarah must have decided she needn't shoot off all her Roman candles because she eased into Mendelssohn's "Rondo Capriccioso." Mr. Kane asked for the name of each piece if someone didn't tell him, but this one he recognized. It had an air like a song, he said; even, quiet, light, delicate. Sarah seemed to change as she played it; she looked winsome, young, sweet.

Finally she said, "For the last one, I'll play Beethoven." Mr. Kane motioned to Rachel to come sit on the davenport beside him. They were old friends, having met early in the summer when he was out for a jaunt in the country. A white kitten was snoozing in the crook of Mr. Kane's arm, but when he saw Rachel he snuggled into her lap. Mrs. Kane smiled at the picture. She was sitting in a deep chair at the far end of the room, shading her eyes from the bright rays of the late afternoon sun but evidently preferring to sit exactly where she was. Was she watching Alan or Sarah? Alan was standing in the doorway listening with his eyes, and Rachel wondered if he had been standing all this time. He did not move at all.

With the last notes of the "Appassionata" Sarah stopped playing. She sat for a moment with her hands in her lap. Then she said without apology, "I played a long time, didn't I? Sometimes music is like that."

"Maybe great music is always like that," Mr. Kane said.

"And what is time anyway except a cup for our filling," Alice Kane said. "But it's only occasionally there is enough to fill the cup to the brim."

Sarah smiled over at her. Alan came and stood beside the

piano. "Where does such music come from?" he asked, looking down at Sarah.

It was his father who answered. "It comes from the musician. There is no other place it can come from."

"But which musician?" his wife queried. "The composer or the performer? You will say both."

"Neither," Sarah said quickly. "I don't think the composer or the performer has a thing to do with it, really, except to get out of the way and let it come."

"That's what I think," Alan said. He hunted for his pipe, found it, and began to pack the tobacco. "All this summer it has kept occurring to me that the most important thing any person can do is to get out of the light. Get out of his own light, I mean. Most of the time we let our shadows block off the sun. It takes so much not-doing to accomplish anything." He grinned at his father. "Am I clear, Dad?"

"You are not," his father answered with some asperity. "Sarah gave us music because she had skill, and skill comes of incessant work. Granted that an artist needs some initial equipment of brains and temperament, it's the skill that makes the music flow. Isn't that right, Sarah?"

"It's partly right," Sarah said. "That is, one has to have enough skill to be able to catch what's coming in. I mean—it's like a telegraph operator; he can't interpret what's coming in and he can't send the message on unless he knows the code and has the telegrapher's dexterity. But the message itself is a different kind of thing."

"Nonsense again," Mr. Kane said. "The musician's melodies well up from within him. That's his world."

"You're right." Alan nodded his emphatic accord. "His world is *within,* but the within can be augmented by the *without.* Definitely the *without* has the same nature as the *within,* and the two may sometime be one. For some people. I hope someone understands me!"

"I do," Rachel said emphatically. "I understand you because

last year I took a course in comparative religion. It's what the Buddhists mean by the Atman and the Brahman, God emanent and God encompassing. Coomaraswamy calls it 'The multiplication of the inexhaustible One and the unification of the indefinitely Many.'"

At that Sarah literally opened her mouth, Alan smiled broadly, and Mr. Kane slapped his knee in delight. "I surprise myself," Rachel said, rising. "I didn't know I understood it when I learned the chapter almost by heart. If we don't go, Sarah, the fire whistle will blow seven counts for lost children."

The girls walked home briskly. Supper smells spiced the friendly street. Birds darted about on the last forgotten errands of twilight. A man out watering his lawn called to his neighbor that the German U-boats were getting pretty damn cheeky sinking ships exactly at the three-mile line along the Eastern coast.

Nineteen

Alan said that as a musician he was a good basketball player. The only instrument he played was a comb wrapped in tissue paper. One evening at Sarah's house he demonstrated his skill, whereupon Archibald demanded a try. After that Archibald's cohorts began on combs until the neighborhood rang with a raucous rendition of "The Stars and Stripes Forever."

As a basketball player Alan was certainly a question mark in the coach's mind until he realized that young Kane's apparent abstraction while playing had nothing to do with his teamwork. He merely had an odd faculty of appearing to be absorbed in something far away, but actually he was quick as a squirrel and usually managed to land on the right spot at the needed moment.

During his first week at Bryan husky Bud Lempke had nicknamed him *Doc*. "Why do you call him that?" Sarah once asked Bud as he sat down beside her in sociology class.

"It's that accent! Hawvahd, don't you know," he told her. "But look here, Sarah, don't get me wrong. Doc can't help what he was born with. You won't find him a bit standoffish."

Sarah didn't. And yet in the usual meaning of dating she and Alan seldom went places together. When there was a concert, Alan was likely to escort his mother. For a public lecture, if the speaker happened to be first-rate, he came with his dad. On Sundays he went to the little Episcopal church. Nevertheless, there was seldom a day when he and Sarah were not together. The things they did were unimportant in themselves. Sometimes they went for a hike in the country, leaned against an old stone wall, and talked on and on until one of them happened to notice that a sharp north wind had risen and the sun was sulking off to bed under gray blankets. Then they would walk rapidly back to Alan's house, build a big fire in the fireplace, and roast apples.

Sometimes it was Sarah's house they went to. Alan liked dropping in on Anna's day off, when it was Sarah's turn to get dinner. Once he said that if she ever wanted to give him her daguerreotype, he wanted her done up in a crisp white apron, peeling yellow carrots into a blue bowl.

Their conversation was not heavy.

"Raw carrots taste exactly like they smell," Sarah said.

"Potatoes don't, though. Raw potatoes smell like an empty medicine cabinet, but cooked potatoes smell like washday."

"The best cooking smell in the world is navy beans boiled with ham," Sarah said. "Especially if there is a dish of thinly sliced onions nearby."

"No, the best cooking smell is clam chowder over a driftwood fire."

But Sarah had never made clam chowder.

"Great guns," Alan said, "maybe you've never sailed a little twenty-foot yawl!"

"From your tones you'd think I'd never eaten with a fork." Sarah turned the frying ham with unnecessary vigor and splashed the hot fat onto her fresh pink apron. "Probably you've never driven four horses, but I have. It was out on Uncle Bill's farm."

"Something's missing out of my life." Alan tipped back in the kitchen chair, prepared to listen. So Sarah swung open the gates to her childhood.

Little things drew them together a good deal as tendrils of grape intertwine on a trellis. Coming home from a basketball game one night, they caught the reflection of a street light in a pool of rain and stood for some moments just looking at its quiet loveliness. After a bit, there being nothing to say, they walked on. That was a thing to remember always.

One day Alan said, "Little big moments never get into the biographies, do they, not even in footnotes. But there was the time we saw the juncos arrive and the time we found the wild white orchises and the time we went to the country and saw the haystack fire."

One day Sarah said, "I'm not as good a musician as you think because I seem to play better when you're here, and it worries me. It makes me wonder if I'm drawing something from you to make my music, and that's a kind of cheating."

"No, it isn't cheating," Alan answered, blowing a beautiful smoke ring. "It's merely reciprocity because I never make good smoke rings when I'm alone."

The war was everybody's news of the day, but it seldom intruded on their private conversations. Sometimes Sarah wondered, with a feeling of self-reproach, if the reason they spoke so casually about the war was because it existed in their minds but not in their hearts. Intellectually they knew that all this carnage and horror was happening right now, and yet from some hidden citadel of common sense the answer seemed to be that of course the war was not real: if it were real, then everybody, everywhere, would be doing something about it. Besides, many people believed that any day now the papers would declare the terms of peace. To dwell on the atrocities of war was to postpone the mood of peace.

Lucy was the one who talked freely of the war. What was more, she worked for the war. She was a college freshman now and, according to Alan, the prettiest girl on campus. Plenty of the boys felt the same way. Sarah worried a little about Lucy and then scolded herself for worrying. She could never put a finger on an instance when Lucy had gone out of her way to draw masculine attention, and yet there was something about Lucy that seemed definitely in need of a following. But then who wouldn't have a following, Sarah asked herself, when golden curls topped a saucy face with eyes as blue as gentians and twice as innocent as any child's?

Lucy was busy all the time, getting a Red Cross chapter started on campus, putting on benefit dances whose proceeds went to Belgian orphans, selling chances on an automobile for the Elks Club—proceeds for disabled French soldiers. The chances sold best downtown. Lucy was the Elks' most successful promoter until one night when Grandpa Vanderiet found her standing at the door of a fashionable restaurant that sold liquor, offering chances to the patrons as they emerged in happy frame of mind. Grandpa took Lucy straight home. Sarah and Alan were there in the living room doing their trigonometry when Lucy blew in on a gust of snow and fury. Alan tried to appease the fury by telling her she was much too pretty to be downtown at night. She looked like something off a calendar, he said, with the trailing blue plume on her hat and her white party furs. Just the same, Sarah thought he looked a little worried about Lucy. After Lucy had stormed off to bed he said that maybe a good girls' school would be a wonderful place for her. A girls' school was used to handling the high-spirited type. For a moment Sarah almost envied Lucy. No one ever called her the high-spirited type that needed looking after.

Nothing pleased Sarah more than the way Alan and Grandpa hit it off. For that matter, Alan and Grandma got along mighty well. Lucy said that Alan brought out Grandma's feminine nature. Grandma prettied herself up when he was calling for Sarah at her house. Also, she drew him into literary conversations and quoted Emerson to illustrate points which, Lucy said, she planned out during the day. For his part, Alan liked the bright-eyed little woman who had such a mind of her own. But Grandpa, he said, was a buddy. Grandpa knew how it felt to be young with the world before you. No place but America, he said, could produce a minister who read the New Testament in Greek and also acted as chief executive of a booming common-stock company known as a local church.

About the middle of December, on an afternoon of heavy blinding snow, Sarah and Alan stopped in at Grandpa's study. It was his real study, the long narrow room back of the pipe organ. On the west side of the room the three high windows were almost obliterated by the driving snow. Beneath the windows were bookshelves Grandpa had built himself. At the south end of the room two long narrow windows looked out into the churchyard. It was beside these windows, Sarah recalled, that Grandpa had stood on the night Mama was about to die; here he had seen the daffodils beneath the ice and known that life and death were but seasons on the calendar of God. The east side of the room was also lined with bookcases reaching to the ceiling. This was a really choice library, Alan said. Grandpa said that collecting it had been slow business. How slow, Sarah had never before realized, but Grandpa must have gone without things to get those books. Grandma had gone without things too; she sputtered a lot at Grandpa, but there was nothing she wouldn't sacrifice for him. Grandpa had read all of these books. For him, they were alive. Although he lent his books generously, it hurt him to have one gone overnight. He was aware which book was missing from each empty place. In the southeast corner of the room stood an old-time Franklin stove with a coal fire burning brightly in its open grate. Sarah and Alan took off their big coats and overshoes, and Grandpa pulled chairs nearer the fire.

Alan took some cards from his pocket. He had been waiting, he said, to show them a poem he had just discovered. The poet was Rupert Brooke, an English chap, who had been killed some time ago in the war.

> "If I should die, think only this of me:
> That there's some corner of a foreign field
> That is forever England ..."

Something in Alan's voice was very moving as he read the last phrase—"and gentleness in hearts at peace, under an English heaven."

Grandpa said, "There is the poet, dying for those he knows and loves and also for those he loves but does not know."

Then Sarah spoke out with such sharpness that both men were startled. "Poetry confuses as well as clarifies. This Rupert Brooke makes England synonymous with the rich earth, the flowers, rivers, sunshine, and friendly laughter. But what about the rich earth of Germany? What about the German flowers and the laughter of German friends? Friends are friends in anybody's country. Germans and Austrians are dying for those they love also."

Alan answered almost as sharply. "Germans are not dying to protect their families as the English are. The best you can say for the Germans is that they are willing to die to get more power for their Kaiser."

"Oh no," Sarah said. Her head was thrown back and she sat very still and tense, only her eyes moving from one face to the other. "On both sides men die for the same thing. No matter how they work up to it, they die for an abstraction they call their honor. It's always been that way. They don't think about the right and wrong of an immediate situation. If they did, the English would sometimes have to fight with the Germans against the Russians and the Germans would sometimes have to fight with the Russians against the Austrians. Nobody in a war can fight for the right straight through. You see—" Sarah stopped as precipitantly as she had begun, amazed at her own vehemence.

All that Alan had held back even from himself during the past months flared up in him also. "When a man knows his home and country are threatened, he doesn't stop to argue. He defends. Later, perhaps, with his family safe, he can talk sense into the head of the enemy."

"But you can never talk sense to a man you have knocked down and stepped on," Sarah insisted. "Not even if he started the fight. Once you've beaten him up, he can't take in what you're saying." She turned to Grandpa. "You tell him," she implored. "It's your business to speak for God, and God doesn't answer evil with evil."

For a moment Grandpa did not look at either of them; only at the fire. His voice and his words came haltingly, not as if he waited to clear a thought, but as if he held back knowledge they could not bear. "I do not speak *for* God, Sarah. At best I can only speak about Him as I know Him. And as I know Him, He does not, as you say, answer evil with evil. In a sense He does not answer at all. That is, not in the way of sending victory to an army. He answers only with Himself and He is love. Himself He gives to all, both saints and sinners. Wouldn't any father do the same for his children, good or bad?"

"No, any father would not," Alan answered emphatically. "There are occasions in which my father would join a posse to bring an evil son to justice."

"And who shall say what justice is?" Grandpa looked from Alan to Sarah. "Especially for a nation made up of hundreds of thousands of individuals. Two men fighting side by side may not be fighting for the same cause nor in the same spirit. For the erring son, in war or out, there is only one answer, and that lies in making him feel his kinship with his brother."

Alan went over to the fire, raked together the live coals, put on more fuel, then filled his own pipe and lit it. Sarah, watching, did not see him. She saw only that if what Grandpa said were true, the innocent might have to take an awful beating. Slowly she put her thoughts into words.

Grandpa said, "Sometimes in these north woods we chop down a wide strip of trees and plow under the land so that a forest fire, finding nothing to burn, will go out of itself. There is a passivity like that. A few of the early Quakers had it. Someday there will be an unconquerable people willing to be conquered in order to teach the conqueror the meaning of kinship."

Alan heaved a big sigh and smiled. "Now you're talking in millenniums."

Grandpa smiled too. "I'll admit the Germans might first have to conquer the world. But in time they'd find out what Talleyrand meant when he commented that a victor can do anything with a sword but sit on it. Ultimately they'd discover that even as conquerors they couldn't govern without the good will of the people. And as soon as they set to work cultivating good will they would be caught in the net of their own good will."

"I'll never see that day," Alan said. "With the present *modus operandi* of the Germans, most of the conquered would be ground beneath the Prussian heel."

"I don't think I'd mind too much," Sarah said, almost with a sense of relief. "I'd rather be dead at someone else's hand than to have to use my hand to kill."

"That's because you're a woman," Alan told her. "Your logic is colored by a woman's dread of spilled blood."

Grandpa answered for her. "Maybe her dread of spilled blood is colored by a woman's fierce logic. It's my experience that women are the logical sex. What we call their intuition is often their logic working at high speed."

Alan caught the flare in Sarah's eyes. "Logic or no logic, I'm glad you're a woman," he said. "And I'm not going to risk your being one of the remnant. I'll fight for peace at my own terms."

Grandpa picked up the St. Paul *Dispatch*. "It doesn't seem as if we're looking very hard for openings toward peace. If our State Department had no other aim but peace, they would probably be finding a way right now. And I presume it is also true that if the American people had no army, no navy, and no munitions plants they would be exerting tremendous pressure toward peace. Any people who forswore retaliation would no doubt become inventive in the ways of peace."

"But we're not enough of one mind for that procedure yet," Alan said. "We see to it that mediocrity climbs in the saddle, and then we gallop along behind. I'm one of the gallopers, I guess. Although I believe the things you say, still I don't know how to work them out. And so I'll probably take the stupid way with the rest. I won't see how not to."

"Oh no!" Sarah protested. Then she caught the baffled look in his eyes. "Christmas may bring a miracle."

"At least it may bring a blizzard," Grandpa said, going to the south windows to look out at the whirling flakes. "And a heavy winter may slow down the fighting and give us more time to think." There was a forced optimism in his voice. Pity seemed to cloak him as he stood there in the dusk.

Sarah refused to be drawn into its mood. She stomped into her high overshoes and Alan knelt to fasten them. "I'm going to make apple dumplings for dinner, and you're both invited."

Grandpa shook his head. "We have a board meeting." Then he turned to Alan. "She makes 'em so big that each dumpling fills a soup dish. And then she drowns them in vanilla sauce and cream."

Alan tipped back Sarah's head and looked into her eyes. "I'll think of apple dumplings when I'm on the firing line," he told her with a grin. She smiled back at him. Each of them knew they would not again discuss the meaning of the war. But they had never felt so near as now that they were separate.

They went out into the driving snow. Dark was fast closing them in, two bewildered humans in a whirling world of white. Alan was holding Sarah's arm, how tightly he did not know, drawing her protectingly against him. Over the corner of her fur collar turned up against the cold, she saw only the curve of his cheek ruddy and hard where the wind stung it. Already the snow was piling into drifts which would be higher than their heads before morning. They braced themselves against the storm and walked as fast as they could.

Twenty

O n a Monday afternoon in February Sarah left school
early, intending to stop in to see Mrs. Rivera. She wanted to show her a picture of a blue velvet dress which
she had seen in *Vogue,* a lovely thing with full waist and gored
skirt, long, rather tight sleeves. She could see herself in that
dress. There was also a dark red suit with gray squirrel trimming.
Anybody would look twice at that suit. She could just hear Alan
saying gravely, "Wait till I borrow some smoked glasses."

She stopped in her tracks. Whatever had come over her? Of
all shoddy things! Deliberately planning clothes to catch the
masculine eye. She shook herself, almost as a collie might, and
mentally shredded the blue velvet.

When she arrived, Dr. Rivera was still at home. To be sure,
he was just starting out the door, but when Sarah came he
returned to the sitting room where his wife was sitting by the
window. "It's an odd thing, but I just said to Carlotta that I was
in no mood to go to work today. I said, 'I am in a mood to sit
in a big chair and have Sarah play for me,' did I not, my love?"

"He did, indeed, Sarah. And you know what it will be: some
Brahms."

She did not have the heart to refuse, so she pocketed her
mood of irritation. "The first piece I ever played for him was
Brahms," she said. "It was right after Archibald was born. I was
memorizing the good old A-flat waltz when he came into the
house, and he stopped at the parlor door to listen."

"That's right. And I said to myself, 'The long-legged one with the freckled nose, she has music within her.'"

"This is another dance, then. A Hungarian dance in D-flat major. Remember you once said that in good music the masculine and feminine elements were well married?"

The doctor looked surprised. "Did I say anything so clever?"

"You did, and here it is: big bass chords and a good lilting treble. Dignified but not above a fine swirl of skirts."

When she finished Dr. Rivera called, "Bravo! Here I am past due at my office, but my patients will gain by the delay. Perhaps one more Brahms will cure them entirely."

Mrs. Rivera said nothing; she was not one to feel that comments must trail after music. Sometimes Sarah played for an hour and Mrs. Rivera made no comment at all.

"This is another Hungarian dance, in A major. I like the way it climbs up the keyboard and still keeps waltzing, but I'm not a bit sure I'll remember it."

And she did not remember it. Suddenly she remembered the blue velvet dress instead. Then she began chastising the notes, and soon her fingers lost their way. "I'm sorry, but I'm filled with ire today. When it boils up it ruins the music." She left the piano abruptly.

"And for whom is the ire meant?" Dr. Rivera asked, walking over to his wife's side. "Is it perhaps for a professor? Or for the weatherman? Or for the increasing menace of the submarines?"

"It is against myself," Sarah said. "And do not ask me what caused the temper because I would be ashamed to tell you."

The doctor only smiled and kissed the tips of his wife's fingers. "I shall be leaving you," he said to her. "The lady"—he turned to Sarah—"with the tiger." He left.

"Perhaps you should play out your ire," Mrs. Rivera suggested casually. "Is it not Heine who says, 'What life takes away, music restores'?"

"Not today. Today, if you don't mind, I'm going to walk in the country and I hope the drifts are deep. I hope I get caught in a drift and flounder around and freeze half the skin off my face before the Valentine Dance." She spoke with such ferocity that Mrs. Rivera rose and went to the old-fashioned bell cord.

"I am ringing for protection," she said.

Almost instantly Hortense appeared.

"The small box on my dressing table," Mrs. Rivera told her. And then to Sarah, "Something came from southern France today, and I fear that not many more will come our way. This is only a very small thing to cater to your weakness."

Hortense returned with a little flat box. Sarah opened it and slowly lifted a square of fine white linen. "It's a lovely, lovely thing," she said softly. "I don't know what a fine handkerchief does to me, but from childhood it's been about my favorite present. A Christmas when I didn't get handkerchiefs, along with a book and a box of stationery, was just a Christmas lost for me."

"These are your valentine. And that reminds me that I have thought up your costume for the party. Tomorrow we shall assemble it."

"Please don't," Sarah remonstrated. "I have decided to go as a goose girl. Just a plain cotton dress and no trimmings at all. Archibald has an old toy goose I shall drag on a string."

"You made up the goose girl this very minute! I think you are doing penance for something. It is a mood I know well. There is always a man behind the mood, and I think he is right now coming up the walk."

Sarah looked out of the window. Alan was cutting across the street, making for the house with long determined strides. She started to say, "No, there is no man," but refused the subterfuge. Instead she said lamely, "Now whatever is he coming here for?"

"Why, you impolite young minion, and why would not a handsome young man come to call on me? I who have worn this beautiful tea gown only to entice some admiring eye? Would you have a rose to bloom in vain?"

"It is beautiful," Sarah said. "I've started to tell you so a dozen times. It's the most luscious sea green I ever saw." To herself she was thinking, "*She* dresses for the men, but she does it to give them pleasure and not at all to call attention to herself. She dresses with the same care and excitement with which an artist paints a picture. That's different." Aloud she said, almost nervously, "I have to hurry on. You see, I left a book at Grandma's."

If she heard, Mrs. Rivera paid no attention to the remark. Alan had come into the room. He was fresh and cold and obviously pleased with himself. To Mrs. Rivera he said, "Excuse my icy hands. My dad says this is the kind of weather that toughens people and makes them live a long time. I tell him if they live a long time it's a cold-storage principle and who wants to live in cold storage?" His eyes took in the gown. "I wish I had words for a woman like you, but the world has so few women like you that one's words get little practice."

"You're doing very well for an amateur," Mrs. Rivera assured him. "Perhaps diplomacy should be your field, is it not so, Sarah? 'Oh, the new Ambassador to the Court of St. James,' we will say. 'We knew him when he was a young law student battling the cruel winters of Minnesota.'"

"Who is your silent guest?" Alan asked, indicating Sarah. "She looks like a girl I knew in college, only the one I knew was a great talker who never sat still. The girl I knew had a way of dashing out of class when the first bell rang out and sprinting down the main drag at such a clip that one supposed, of course, she had been called home for a family crisis. But when one reached her home, she was not there at all. No one knew where she was. One had to cudgel one's brains and then trudge from one place to another looking for the wayward one."

"Now I am crushed" Mrs. Rivera said. "How vain of me to think the future ambassador had dropped in for a cup of tea with me."

"Frankly, I had no notion that a day so bitter could bring an occasion so delightful," he assured her. "I thought I was off on a wild-goose chase."

"That's me, I suppose," Sarah said. "And you are quite right. I am a goose. But a goose in flight again. I hope you'll both excuse me because I simply have to go on."

The consternation of the other two was voluble, but somehow it only made Sarah more determined to leave. Her mind was snapping comments at her. "This is the kind of woman he needs. Someone with charm like Mrs. Rivera. But since when did you become so interested in a woman for him? First you plan your clothes to take his eye and then you plan his life." Aloud she was saying, "I'd love a cup of tea and a date sandwich, but honestly I must go on."

In the end she stayed, of course, because it was plain that Alan intended to leave with her, but she added no charm to the occasion. Alan and Mrs. Rivera were in top form. Together they might have been the classmates and Sarah the rather stuffy chaperone. Or they might have been a pair of courtiers in the days when repartee was an art. Sarah knew wit when she heard it. But she had nothing to contribute.

Finally it was time to leave. "I'm sorry I'm so stupid today," she said to Mrs. Rivera. "I'm not really unappreciative of the company. It's myself I don't like."

Mrs. Rivera saw a sort of bafflement in her eyes. "Yes, you are stupid," she said. "You are a very stupid young woman but looking very well in that bright blue blouse. I do declare, you seem to pay more heed to your clothes of late, and that makes me think you may yet make a great success with your music."

Sarah blushed. Blushing was simply not her way.

"The lady is flustered," Alan said. He was much amused and patted Sarah on the shoulder as he helped her with her coat. "I must take her out in public more often," he went on. "A musician who expects to dwell in the public eye has got to get used to compliments. No private life for Miss Duncan. Always her public to think of."

Sarah said, "Big silly !" and her voice sounded as usual, but her mind kept on gibing, "Understand? He's trying to tell you not to put on these blushing acts around him. So far as he's concerned, you're a professional musician. And then you sneak up on him with your ideas about blue velvet gowns."

Fortunately for her mood, the wind was bitter and they faced into it, so that conversation was difficult. "Look here," Alan said, "I've been chasing you around in order to talk about the Valentine Dance. I thought maybe we'd celebrate and go all out for something fancy."

Sarah said, "This hardly seems the time to celebrate. Did you see the article in the *Literary Digest* about the submarine toll?"

Alan looked surprised. Not at the news but at Sarah. What was the matter with her today? Maybe he did sound adolescent, talking about a dance while the world was afire. But he couldn't discuss war in the teeth of this gale. So he made a casual answer and they pushed on. Sarah was thinking, "Now he'll think I'm a schoolmarm; can't even discuss a dance like a normal girl."

Rounding a corner, they ran smack into Grandpa. He had on his long fur-lined coat with his fur-lined cap pulled down over his ears. His blue eyes were shining. A great guy, Grandpa, to be out on a day like this and having himself such a good time. But Grandpa's excitement was not pleasure in combating the elements. He was mad. He had been to the jail to see a farm boy who had been driving when intoxicated and run down a cow. He was mad at the saloonkeeper who sold the drink to a minor and also he was indignant with the township which licensed the saloon.

"Come home with me now, the two of you, and we'll plot a reform," Grandpa offered.

Sarah was on the point of accepting when she remembered her avowed haste to get home. Just the same, meeting Grandpa in a worse mood than her own was a help. After they left him she chatted amiably so far as the wind permitted any remarks at all. But she did not ask Alan in and she said she wasn't sure she could even go to the Valentine Dance. She might have to go to see Koenigstein. She thought Alan never looked so handsome as when he turned to leave, plainly disappointed.

That night she went to her room early. "What's the matter?" Lucy asked. "Is your throat sore?" Lucy was sitting by the dining-room table sewing hundreds of tiny red hearts on a dress of white tulle. She had made the dress herself. It seemed obvious that Lucy would go to the valentine costume party as the queen of hearts. "She's more Alan's type," Sarah thought. "She's pretty and altogether feminine." Then her mind hooted, "There you go again. Alan's interested in law, not women. He won't be interested in women for years and years. And when he is, it will be some lovely English girl, probably, someone with honey-colored hair and a fine English complexion. Someone who has traveled and—"

"I declare," Lucy said. "You work too hard, Sarah. At your age a girl shouldn't look like a tired dray horse."

Sarah went off to bed. A dray horse! "What's the matter with you, Sarah Duncan? Look right at yourself. Are you in love? Have you gone off the deep end about the first handsome boy who ever paid attention to you?" "Nonsense, he isn't the first. I never lacked attention when I wanted it." "You never really wanted it before. But now if you don't see Alan for a whole day, you think the sun forgot to rise. You drag him into all your conversations. You go out of your way to hunt up Rachel, and the only reason you ask about Leslie is because she'll get you talking about Alan. Alan thinks such and such. Rachel knows it, too. Probably she's already written Leslie that you're head over heels in love, and he'll come home expecting to find Alan dogging your footsteps and instead he'll find you mooning about a blue velvet dress." "He will not. I'll go to the dance as a goose girl. What's more, I'll practice harder. It takes time to go to the Kanes'. It takes time to talk to Alan. He isn't really interested in me anyway. He'd die of shock if he saw me figuring on blue velvet."

She went to bed. But not to sleep. She reminded herself that love was a thing people didn't need to fall into until they were good and ready to get married. If she ever married it would have to be after she'd made a name on the concert stage. Best thing would be to go to Minneapolis and skip that childish Valentine Dance entirely. What if she was vice-president of the class? A vice-president was just a spare tire. Some people fell in love and didn't know it. But she had caught herself in time.

She fell asleep. But she dreamed, and in her dream she was trying to swim across a wide choppy lake while eating a hamburger sandwich which must not get wet, and all the time she was calling to a flock of wild geese flying high, trying to convey a message in weird cries geared to the Morse code. One goose was Alan with blue velvet wings.

Twenty-one

Sarah went to the Valentine Dance. She had three good reasons for going, but the first of the reasons was the only one she discussed with Alan. The class president, good old Shorty McKnapp, came down with the mumps. As vice-president it became her duty to lead the grand march.

"My mother was a great old figure leader in her day," Alan said. "You'd never guess she was right in the social whirl at Vassar, now would you?"

"I wouldn't," Sarah said. "She isn't the type."

"Just the same, she used to go to dances at Dartmouth and Amherst and was quite a belle. Whatever Mother did, she did thoroughly, even dance, and that's how come we'll make their eyes pop with the fancy figures for the grand march."

Sarah wanted to catch the mumps also; she just wasn't the type to be belle of anything. But she wasn't going to let Alan think he had a dud on his hands. This was their first big date together. Maybe she'd have but one big date in her life, and if this was it, she'd make it good. That was her second reason for going to the dance.

She dressed at the Riveras', but she had Alan call for her at home. That was partly because Mama liked to see how the girls looked. On this night, however, Mama had a graver concern, and that concern was Sarah's third good reason for going to the dance. The concern was Lucy.

Lucy had a date with a pale-faced youth named Eddie Hawkins. From grade school days Eddie had hung around Lucy, but she would never have anything more to do with him than eat his candy. Now why, on tonight of all nights, with the best dance band in the state engaged to play, why did Lucy suddenly announce she was going to the dance with Eddie? And why did she put all this time on an elaborate costume? "Time and money both," Mama said. "She even borrowed next month's allowance. Something makes me uneasy."

Questions addressed to Lucy brought forth conversational answers. "Oh, sure, I know Eddie's a dud, but faithfulness deserves a reward now and then."

"He isn't your type, though," Mama had insisted stubbornly.

"My type's the type with money who can show me a good time," Lucy had answered, giving her mother a hug. "Eddie's folks do have money. And I can wind Eddie around my little finger."

Mama had got a little stern. "Lucy, you wouldn't lead Eddie on when you didn't mean anything by it and he did? That's flirting."

"Why, Mama Duncan!" Lucy had said in mock surprise. "I'm surprised you'd even think of such a thing."

On the night of the dance, when Alan came into the sitting room where Sarah was waiting, he practically gasped. Having planned to be cool, charming, enchanting, but remote, she heard herself expostulating childishly, "I'm not really the Spanish type, but I couldn't resist the dress."

"Neither can I," said Alan.

It was her first black gown, this Rivera heirloom of lace over silk. The silk was corded with fine lines of gold, and the lace was flecked with almost miscroscopic brilliants. Over a comb of gold filigree with turquoise she wore a mantilla of black lace threaded with gold in intricate design. From her ears hung long turquoise pendants, and the fan she furled and unfurled after the fashion of Mrs. Rivera's coaching was a delicate thing of black lace and kingfishers' feathers.

"You look like a queen, doesn't she, Mrs. Duncan?" Alan bowed from the waist with a gallant flourish of his plumed hat.

"Maybe there's more reason for my dressing like a pirate chieftain than the fact we had the costume in an old trunk. Maybe it was my ships that plundered the cache of a robber baron and brought home those turquoise trophies. Gosh all hemlocks, Sarah—"

"Maybe we should be leaving," Sarah said. She called to Lucy, but Lucy only hung over the banister in her old pink kimono. "I won't be ready for hours. My stars, you look elegant, Alan. If you'd asked me, I'd have been ready on time, too, but for Eddie I think I'll be good and late." Something in her words made Sarah uneasy again as she went down the steps.

Everyone said the dance was undoubtedly the most gorgeous affair ever put on at Bryan College. The decorations, made by the nimble fingers of the junior-class girls, transformed the bare old gym into a summer garden of tissue-paper wisteria growing on white trellises, with huge potted palms from the funeral parlor, artificial orange trees with stuffed birds from the historical society's exhibit, colored bulbs of low wattage, and, over all, a marvelous sky of blue cheesecloth which practically hid the overhead rafters. The band played "Tipperary" in march time, waltz time, and tango. The saxophonist was also a baritone soloist and gave them "Where My Caravan Has Rested," followed by "Rolling Down to Rio" and an especially masculine number, "Give a Man a Horse He Can Ride." Finally Sarah and Alan led the grand march through a maze of figures that held together in unprecedented fashion.

But for Sarah the nicest part of the evening was the way the boys cut in on her dances; she supposed they did it because she was vice-president of the class. Even Rachel, a daring pierrette in stiff skirts barely below her knees, had no more cut-ins than she. It almost seemed as if the basketball team turned out in alphabetical order to take her off Alan's hands. "Look here," he said to one of them, "do you think she's the team's mascot?"

"You don't like, do you?" big Bill Tuper had called back.

"Not very much." Alan looked as if he meant it. Sarah was glad. If she was going to take herself out of his life, she'd certainly be pleased to have him notice she was missing. All evening she had such a good time that she forgot to be cool and charming. In fact, she felt heady with good time. Alan was practically shadowing her as she was whirled from one escort to another. Maybe she was crazy, but she loved it.

It was one o'clock when the orchestra struck up "Home, Sweet Home." One o'clock was a very late hour for a Bryan College function, but at that, Sarah was in no mood for the dance to end. Only occasionally one knew while having a good time that these were never-to-be-recaptured moments. For the last waltz the lights were turned low, according to custom. Alan held her closer than anyone had ever held her before. They did not talk; everything in the world that was treasurable seemed gathered in with them. The war and all dutiful tomorrows were out of focus.

When the dance came to an end he still held her for a moment. "Look at me, Sarah." But Sarah would not look. It was like asking someone to look into the sun, or was she herself the sun, or was she going to have a sunstroke right here in the middle of the dance floor? She put out her hand to steady the world, but what Alan saw was a pre-emptory gesture, and what he heard was a matter-of-fact voice saying, "We must look for Lucy. My goodness, I don't believe I've seen her since the grand march."

They looked and they asked, but there was no Lucy. Finally Bill Tuper told them that he had seen Eddie leaving alone about an hour ago. "So that's why she came with Eddie," Sarah thought. "He was someone she could ditch." She found Rachel, and the two of them held consultation in the dressing room. How could they tell her mother?

"You come home with me, Rachel, and when Mama hears us talking maybe she won't specially miss Lucy's voice."

"Maybe Lucy just didn't feel well and Eddie took her home and then came back for a while by himself."

But Lucy was not at home. Mama called out, "Is that you, girls?" and Sarah said, "Yes, Mama. Rachel's going to stay all night." They decided to wait until three o'clock before telling Mama anything. Every little while Sarah went to look out of the window which had the best view of the street. When the clock struck three she said to Rachel, "If she isn't in sight now, I'll have to call Mama or Grandpa." But a car had stopped down at the corner. A man in a dress overcoat and a bowler hat got out, followed by a slight figure in a long dark cloak. They came toward the house, the man walking unsteadily and waving his white muffler like a flag. The girl was laughing and trying to stifle her laughter. As they drew near the house the man tiptoed elaborately and kept his finger to his lips. At the foot of the steps Lucy turned him around and gave him a little push in the direction of his car, then came up the steps ever so quietly and let herself in almost without a sound.

Sarah met her at the top of the steps and followed her to her room. Lucy slipped out of her cloak. She looked almost disheveled, and the first thing she did, even before she took off her dress, was to grab the cold cream and start removing the color from her too bright cheeks. "Well, sphinx," she said to Sarah, "I could do with some sleep."

"Where have you been and who was that man?" Sarah asked gravely.

"I've been to a wonderful party," Lucy told her from the folds of cheesecloth with which she was removing the cold cream. "None of your tissue-paper flowers for decorations, either. And the man I was with knows his way around. He's no rah-rah college boy."

Sarah helped pull the white dress over Lucy's head. The tiny hearts looked wilted, and there was a long coffee stain on the skirt.

"What's the matter, Miss Prim? Are you afraid your fine Alan Kane won't approve of your sister's friends?"

She did not answer but left Lucy standing in the middle of the room holding a slipper in each hand.

It was to Grandpa that Sarah went the next day.

"The Elks had a dance," he told her. "Didn't you see the account in the paper? Lucy's young man was probably one of the McGinty crowd." He frowned; then he sighed, and finally he smiled. "There's nothing the matter with that crowd, Sarah, except they're cheap. Young McGinty got a divorce recently and he's marrying a redheaded girl from St. Paul. Her father is one of the beer barons. He was divorced himself last winter."

"Grandpa! You do get around," Sarah said. "Whoever'd think of your knowing the society news? I don't think I've ever met anyone who's been divorced, although I know about plenty of people who have."

"I do get around, as you say," Grandpa acknowledged. "I know about the McGintys because I was called to the hospital to see one of them one night."

Sarah looked at Grandpa's fine lean face. The lines were growing deeper. He had a little stoop. She'd never noticed that stoop before; maybe it was only a morning sag.

"I'll find out about Lucy's young man and I'll have a talk with Lucy," he went on. "Sarah, do you realize we've broken off diplomatic relations with Germany? Gerard's been recalled, and German ships in American ports have disabled their engines."

All in all, Sarah went home in deep depression. What she wanted was to see Alan, but she'd firmly made up her mind not to see him. Last night was only a dream. She must think about her music and her responsibility to her father. Not since the day of his funeral had she wanted her father so much. He'd know what to do with Lucy and he'd tell Mama to let Archibald make two grades a year if that's what the principal said he ought to do. You can't stifle a good mind, he'd say, and it's not only wicked but useless to try. Father would even understand about falling in love before you were asked and about knowing you mustn't fall in love for years and years, even if you were asked.

At school she went directly from her classes to the practice room in the music building. That night when Alan telephoned she told Anna she was washing her hair—and then had to wash it. The next evening she picked up Miss Lillie and dragged her over to the campus to play two-piano numbers until midnight. They had a wonderful time with Saint-Saens's "Variations on a Theme of Beethoven," and there were sometimes as much as three minutes when Sarah never thought of Alan at all.

Miss Lillie said, "You look fagged out, Sarah. Maybe it's too much to go on with your music while you're in college."

"You mean that maybe it's too much to go to college while I'm in music," she corrected.

Then Miss Lillie broke into a torrent of words, the way she had done only once before in all the years Sarah had known her. "Listen, Sarah, love matters more than a career. Have a home. Have a family. Take security. Take affection. Take your good time. What does a career matter? When you look around you—"

But Sarah answered, almost coldly: "Nobody's offered me any love, Miss Lillie. And if I ever give up my career it will be because I am dead. Let's call a cab, shall we? It's too cold to walk."

Twenty-two

For all her big talk to herself about putting time on her music, Sarah telephoned Koenigstein to tell him she would like to skip her next week's lesson. In fact, she'd like to lay off until after mid-term exams the end of March. Koenigstein answered shortly that anyone who wanted a vacation could take a vacation. Maybe Mozart treated himself to little vacations. Maybe Paderewski took holidays when he did not feel like work. He could not say because the holidays did not appear among the opus serials. But whenever Sarah would decide to return, would she please bring a book of little sonatinas and they would start her training all over.

Sarah practiced five hours that day.

All in all, the next week was the most miserable she had ever experienced. Everybody else was doing well. Grandpa must have talked to Lucy because a change seemed to come over her. She dug into her studies and went singing around the house. Archibald skipped a grade, and the complaints about spitballs and comic drawings stopped automatically. Mama read the paper she had prepared for the Monday Club—*Advance on the Suffrage Front*. Just before dinner, while the glow was still upon her, she called Alan and thanked him copiously for getting the material for her paper from his father. They chatted endlessly. Sarah stopped peeling potatoes in the kitchen and listened. Mama said she thought Sarah was working too hard, and her digestion was affected. Sarah writhed over this anatomical turn and then felt little better when they began to discuss her music. "Here I am, trying to hear his voice secondhand," she chided herself. But when her mother called out to say that Alan wondered if she'd like to go over to the Kanes' for a fourth hand at cribbage, Sarah said no, she was sorry, but tonight she had to study like anything. So she went early to her room and gazed at the wall.

On Saturday Mama took Lucy to St. Paul to do some shopping. Archibald begged to go along and promised to spend the day in the public library. Sarah said she would help Anna do the cleaning. So she put on an old cotton dress, shrunken and faded. She decided the woodwork in her own room should be washed, and she did a thorough job. Then she took everything out of her closet, which led to sorting and trips to the attic. From the attic she brought down a little old rocking chair and scrubbed off the paint with lye. Her hands were red and puffy and she ached in every bone. About four o'clock, when she should have drawn a hot tub and called it a day, she decided to wash the dining-room windows. Anna had finished the baking and gone off to her niece's for supper. The house seemed chilly. Sarah opened the furnace damper, put on Anna's old brown sweater, caught sight of a smudge on her face but let it stay there. Then she climbed the little ladder and began on the windows.

The doorbell rang. Ordinarily she would have climbed down quickly and hurried to the door. Day or night, regardless of inconvenience, a bell was a thing one answered. She'd never heard of anyone's ignoring a bell, except, of course, the Riveras. Adolph was as likely as not to say, "I think Madam is reading, but if you will leave your number, please, I will give it to her." All this Sarah thought of as she finished applying the Bon Ami to one pane. Even if the bell meant a telegram, the news could wait until someone came home to whom news mattered. Let it ring. And it did ring, on and on. She continued to polish defiantly.

The next thing she knew a voice behind her said, "Sarah!" She turned abruptly, lost her balance, grabbed at a masculine shoulder, and fell awkwardly into Alan's arms. They were strong arms with a mind of their own. They held her close. The cheek laid against her temple was cold and faintly rough. After an eternity of pounding heartbeats she felt her head tipped back, her chin cupped in a firm hand.

"Look at me, Sarah." The whisper was harsh, even commanding, but she did not look. She could not bear to. When finally she looked up she was lost completely. "Don't you like what you see?" he asked, and then drew her to him before she could answer. She shut her eyes and hid her face against the rough tweed of his coat, but he would have none of that. His lips found her cheek, her hair, her eyes. Her mouth.

Much, much later Sarah said, "Oh, Alan, I look a fright."

"You look beautiful, but you act a fright. You've kept out of my sight for eight and three quarter days. I would have found you today if I'd had to make a house-to-house canvass."

"You walked right in."

"I certainly did. I'd met your grandmother, and she told me you were home alone cleaning house. I meant to find you if I had to come in through a cellar window. Gal, you do look tough." He held her off at arm's length, but when she would have broken away he drew her firmly back to him. "But you're the loveliest person I've ever known. I never dared think a girl like you would marry a chap like me."

"Marry!" said Sarah, aghast. "You mean—this is—Why, Alan, are we getting engaged now?"

Then he laughed, and heartily. "I don't know what your custom is, but for me, whenever I kiss a woman the way I've been kissing you—and intend to go on kissing you—and right away—like this—and this—and this—why, then I marry the woman at the first possible moment."

Sarah sighed. That is, after she got her breath she sighed. "I always meant to wear white when I was proposed to. I meant to wear something white and filmy, with maybe a touch of blue, and I meant to have a full moon and probably honeysuckles."

"You can wear white, all right, but the flowers will be orange blossoms. Sarah, do you think we have to wait till we're through college? That's too damn conventional."

On and on they talked. The furnace, turned up by Sarah when she began the window washing, did its blazing best and the thermometer shot to ninety, but they did not notice. Eventually they moved to the kitchen, where they intended to get something to eat but instead were drawn into settling the matter of Sarah's career. First they'd take their final year of college and be married. Then if Sarah could find the right teacher in Boston, Alan would go to Harvard Law School. Otherwise, he'd take Yale and she could commute from New Haven to New York for coaching, or whatever it was a pianist needed to get ready for the concert stage.

Sarah was in true distress. "Something tells me I've got to go on, Alan! Not just that my father expected me to, but because I can't stop. And still, I do think a man ought to have a wife whose mind is on her home."

"I want a wife whose mind is on me, not on the house. We'll get us a couple of servants. They can run the house while you spin off on tour."

"After all, a concert tour doesn't last the year round."

"Think of the months we have right now, here together."

Neither of them mentioned the war. Not because they hated to intrude upon their own happiness, but because the war never entered their minds.

They were still sitting in the kitchen when they heard Lucy, Archibald, and Mama come into the front hall. Sarah had only time to grab up the teakettle, which had almost boiled dry, and to say, "Let's don't tell anyone yet. Let's wait." She sped into the pantry for tea balls.

"Wait nothing," Alan said. "I'm telling the world." He got as far as the dining-room door. "Welcome home, everybody. Something happened while you were away. Something tremendous. What do you—"

"A fire!" yelled Baldy hopefully. "It's hot as a furnace in here."

"A fire!" Mama repeated, throwing down her hat and rushing to the kitchen.

It was minutes before Alan had his say. "Won't somebody listen to me?" he begged. "Yes, we did let the furnace get too hot and no, we never noticed it. Lucy's right—Sarah is crazy, but not because she stands there dropping the eggshell into the skillet and throwing away the egg." Everybody looked at Sarah, who had done just that thing. "She's got a good reason for being crazy. What I mean is, I've got better proof that she's crazy. I mean—thing is—"

Lucy helped him out. "You're engaged!"

"That's right." Alan went over to Sarah and put his arm around her. "Face up to it, Sarah. Maybe we should have asked you first, Mrs. Duncan. In fact, when I left home this afternoon that's what I was going to do. But you see—"

Mrs. Duncan couldn't see because she was weeping. "Already I've lost my oldest daughter," she sobbed, "but don't think I'm unhappy! It's wonderful. You're a very lucky girl, Sarah. I know a fine man when I see one." Drawing Sarah to her, she stood on tiptoe to kiss her tall and blushing daughter.

"A smacker for you," Lucy said inelegantly, and gave Alan a fine big kiss on the mouth.

"Gee, Lucy, I hope in your family people greet each other that way several times a day."

"We know an occasion when me meet up with it."

"This kind of occasion doesn't happen often," Alan said happily.

"I'm pleased as Punch," Lucy went on, looking as starry-eyed as any to-be brother could wish. "You're a very lucky man, if I do say so as shouldn't."

"Will someone tell me what this is all about?" Archibald demanded.

"In words of one syllable," Alan began, but Sarah interrupted.

She put her hand on Archibald's shoulder. "It means—you're going to have a brother."

"Am I?" Archibald asked with almost incredulous delight. He turned to his mother. "When will he be born?"

"Not that kind of a brother!" said his horrified mother.

"She means a grown-up brother," Lucy said.

"Me," Alan said. "Just me, old fellow."

Finally Archibald got the matter straight. "How soon will you move in?"

It was an hour later when Sarah came downstairs, ready to go tell Grandma and Grandpa. Lucy said, "Your face is just shining, Sarah." Lucy was being her sweetest self tonight, and a warm wave of appreciation drew Sarah to her. Maybe she'd never made enough of a pal of Lucy; in some ways Rachel had been her real sister. If Rachel hadn't gone away for the week end Sarah would have called her over before now. She promptly resolved to make up for lost time while she still had a year at home. Aloud she said, "If my face is shining, it's the terrific scrubbing I gave it." But she thought, someway, that Lucy understood the thing she hadn't said.

When they arrived, Grandpa had just come home from his study at the church; he still had his muffler and overshoes on. Grandma came in from the kitchen, wiping her floury hands on her apron. "You're just in time," she said. "All day I meant to bake doughnuts, and it was nine o'clock before I got around to it. You know how your granddad likes fresh doughnuts for Sunday morning breakfast."

"I thought you made them for me," Alan said. "I thought we had a sort of understanding that the doughnut jar would never be empty."

"They were for you." Grandpa set his tall overshoes on the register to dry for a moment. "Right after dinner she said, 'I don't know what Alan will think if there isn't a doughnut in the house tomorrow."

"Why, listen!" Grandma said, as fussed as a girl.

"To the kitchen!" Alan said. He found a good fat doughnut already rolled in powdered sugar. Then he took Sarah's left hand in his. "Hear ye! Hear ye! With this ring, I thee—Grandma, turn around and watch this. Something is happening to your granddaughter."

Grandpa caught on first. He rubbed his hands together and beamed. "It's already happened," he said.

"Aren't you even surprised?" Sarah asked him.

"After all, I have normal powers of observation," Grandpa told her. "But I will admit that your grandmother knew it first."

Grandma drew Alan down and kissed him. Then she kissed Sarah. There was a sweet solemnity in her kisses that gave Sarah a sudden stab, as though this were the wedding ritual. For an instant no one could speak. But Grandma turned quickly and went to the cupboard. "Two sizes of plates, cups and saucers, and sauce dishes," she said. "There's a set of six like this. Real Lowestoft, pink rosebud pattern. Day before yesterday I went up to the attic and got them out. I said, 'I'm going to give them to Sarah when she's engaged.'"

It was well after ten when they left for Alan's home. Mr. and Mrs. Kane were in the living room, chairs drawn up before a snapping wood fire. Alan came in with a whoop, drew Sarah's arm through his, and stood in the doorway in the exaggerated posture of a bride-and-groom tintype. "Guess what!" he said.

"We knew," his mother told him. She went to Sarah and took her in her arms. "I am completely and perfectly happy," she said. "If I'd sat down and drawn you to specification, I couldn't have chosen a more perfect wife for Alan."

Sarah looked incredulous. Suddenly her eyes filled with tears. "You don't really know me, and I was afraid you might think—"

But Alan's father had finally got his writing board, his books, and his manuscript pages safely stacked on the floor and was ready for his turn. "Sarah, this is the biggest day since Alan was born." He kissed her on both cheeks. "Now I'll have someone to play for me when my ideas go stale. How soon can you move in?"

"That's what Archibald asked," Alan told him, drawing up two more chairs by the fire. "We want to be married a year from June, the day after we graduate from college."

"Isn't it a little early to set a date?" his mother asked lightly.

"I know I won't be through school," Alan admitted, "but three years in law school is a long time. I'll go to Harvard and Sarah can study in Boston." There was determination, even doggedness in his voice.

"You don't understand," his mother said quietly. "I just don't want you to be disappointed. There's the war."

"The war?" Sarah asked vaguely.

"The war," Alan said with a cheerful shrug.

"The war," his father answered slowly, with such a weight of inevitability in his voice that the mood of the occasion was changed. For the first time the war came into the room where they sat, so that Sarah could feel it stalking the shadows of the sun porch beyond, lurking behind the drawn curtains, peering like a ghostly face from the mirror above the sideboard in the dining room as the firelight cast a distant reflection.

"We will be in it soon. Soon." Mr. Kane leaned back and looked into the fire. His right hand beat a rapid tattoo on the padded arm of the chair. "I see no way we can keep out."

"Why—why, we just don't have to go in," Sarah said. "I know that in this modern age any country's problems are every country's problems, but still, we don't have anything to fight about. There isn't anything we want from anyone. There isn't even anything they're trying to get from us. We have interest and friendship on both sides. What good would it be for us to mix into the war?"

"None," Mr. Kane answered sharply. "Of course we will persuade ourselves that vast good will come of our aid, but actually it would be far better for civilization to let this struggle be settled in Europe. However—it won't be."

"Maybe it will be, Dad." There was determined cheerfulness in Alan's voice. "The German government isn't having such an easy time at home right now. Maybe this winter will tip the scales, and when the German people see the inevitable outcome, they'll clean house at home and call off the war."

"Not a chance." His father took up a piece of paper and began to sketch the map of Europe. "Here's the way things stood in 1870—" And then followed a crisp history of European relations in the last half century. Sarah listened raptly, aware that she had never before heard such keen analysis of world forces and political motivations. Half an hour went by and the floor was strewn with charts of economic trends and trade balance. "As surely as we fight now we will fight again before another quarter century has elapsed," he concluded.

Sarah leaned forward eagerly. "Then those who realize our fighting won't really help in the long run, they ought not to go. It's their duty to explain these things you've been saying."

Alan took her hand in his. He knew she was speaking about him, to him, for love of him. "It won't be that simple, darling," he said.

"No, it won't be that simple," his dad agreed. "When a man in drowning, you jump in after him, even though you know you may both go down."

Mrs. Kane had sat silent through all the discussion. Now she spoke up. "Maybe we had to say all this." She smiled at them. "Maybe we had to say it now. But we've said enough. Surely we can take our joy tonight. Alex, how about some sherry?"

So the mood changed again and the cyclorama of happiness rolled back in place. When the sherry came they toasted the future, Sarah's and Alan's, and then they drank *skaal* to the four of them with years of books and music and cribbage ahead.

Conversation was lively; no one thought of the time. Mrs. Kane wished she could have heard the Schola Cantorum in New York; Kurt Schindler had conducted and they'd sung French carols. Someday she and Sarah might do a book of old-country carols together. But right now she seldom caught up with her husband's typing. Did they know that Countess Tolstoy did all of the old Count's copying besides looking after their thirteen children? Mr. Kane said the apple tree tent caterpillars were back in New England and a threat to the whole country. Alan said he waited for the day when he could take Sarah to Vermont in the spring. Apple blossoms on Winesap Hall—there was a picture for her. Speaking of pictures, Mr. Kane said, made him think of movies these days. If he had money he would open a good moving-picture house in Wheaton. Let him go ahead, his wife said, but moving pictures could never take the place of living artists—Ellen Terry, Forbes-Robertson, Duse. And what about Maude Adams? Alan wanted to know. If *A Kiss for Cinderella* came on tour at all, it would make the Metropolitan Opera House in St. Paul, and the four of them would go on a toot. But Mrs. Kane would just as soon stay home and read a gook by the fire these cold nights. She had a wonderful book, *The Purple Land*, by W. H. Hudson.

Sarah said less than the others and yet, someway, she felt as if she were the center of the conversation. Each of the three made a special place for her. Except for the Riveras', she had never seen lives so full and complete and satisfactory as the lives of Alan's parents.

It was nearly two o'clock when Alan took her home. The night was clear and cold and the stars seemed almost too near and metallic, as if someone had made an oversized Orion with artificial jewels in his belt. The snow squeaked beneath their feet and the shrill staccato of their footsteps echoed against the sleeping houses. "Tell you something, darling," Alan said, "something I just thought up. Something nobody in the whole world ever thought of before."

"What?" Sarah asked. "What" was a plain little word, but she couldn't bring herself yet to say a word like "darling" or "beloved." The thing that surged in her heart was still shy. "What do you know that's original?"

"This is the happiest day of my life!" He stopped right there in the middle of the street and kissed her forehead.

"That was yesterday," Sarah said. "Yesterday was our special day. This is tomorrow already."

"Today is more special than yesterday," he insisted. "Today has yesterday to lean on. By and by we'll have a whole wall of yesterdays to close about us like a high garden hedge around Paradise."

Sarah said, "Maybe you should take up poetry instead of law, Mr. Kane."

"All lovers do," he told her loftily. "There's such a lot you have to learn about love, Miss Duncan."

Sarah said, "I'm a quick student, Mr. Kane. You're going to be surprised how fast I learn."

Twenty-three

I f Sarah had followed her inclination she would have put off telling the Riveras about her engagement, although Mrs. Rivera was the one person with whom she most wanted to talk. She was embarrassed by her own happiness. Then, too, they might fear for her career. Not that they would consider it important whether or not a woman had a career; only that one must fulfill oneself. One must take no side roads once the destination had been glimpsed. Sarah told Alan she would like to go to the Riveras' alone right after Sunday dinner, but she hoped he would come later for tea. She walked slowly, although a late February snow, almost as penetrating as sleet, was driving against her. In her mind she turned over different ways of approaching the subject. She couldn't dash in with girlish enthusiasm, although if the truth must be told, when she'd wakened at dawn she had felt such exhilaration of joy that she might have danced naked on a hillside of violets or ridden off to sea on a white albatross.

What she did was to walk straight up to Mrs. Rivera's sitting room, wave Hortense out of the door with an air of great secrecy, walk over and stand before Mrs. Rivera, and announce, "Alan and I are engaged." Mrs. Rivera said nothing at all. The two women looked at each other, a steady look. Finally Mrs. Rivera said, "It's a long road." Her tone was not sad, but certainly it was not gay. Rather, wonder filled her voice; hers was the simplicity that dares to wonder at the wonderful.

"I can walk a long road," Sarah said.

"You certainly can walk it. And with a good swinging stride. Where is the lad?" Her tone was light now. Joy winged around their heads.

"He's coming a little later," Sarah said happily. "He's—wonderful."

"As if you were any judge! But just the same, he'll go a long way in his life. Farther than his scholarly papa. Sometimes you will have your hands full to keep up with his many interests."

"But my music!" Instinctively Sarah put out her hand, as if love were a galloping steed.

"My guess is that you'll have your concert fling and then, just when your name is becoming known across the land, just when you ought to take on a European tour, you will suddenly decide to have four bouncing babies with a summer home at Nantucket." Mrs. Rivera laughed up and down the scale with the lighthearted abandon which was so real a part of her. She laughed until tears stood in her eyes. "I laugh at the picture of your skirts clutched by sticky small hands. But I laugh more at your face now broken into two halves like the mask of a jester who must smile from one side and scowl from the other."

Her laughter drew Dr. Rivera into the room. When he heard Sarah's news he was pleased completely and kissed her joyfully on both cheeks. "This is the right way to take on marriage," he said. "Now you can map your career straight from the beginning. And Alan's career also. A settled mind is a fine thing for professional advancement." His words spilled over each other as he stacked up the future in this shape and that. Sarah knew he was keeping back something but could not think what. When he said, "Since Europe is out, perhaps a South American tour is best for Sarah Duncan Kane," then she knew. It was the war.

When Alan came and congratulations had been taken care of, they talked about war, but it was the imminent war with Mexico. "I don't see how we can get out of it," Alan said.

"I don't see how we dare get in," Dr. Rivera answered. "Our days of peace with Europe are numbered. The French Army was never at such low ebb, but the Russian Army is lower. Lloyd George's government may be more energetic than Asquith's, but too much time has been lost. Joffre's army is good for about one more major encounter, and he has no more reserves. Either America goes in within a month or we will have peace by negotiation."

"Not that!" Mrs. Rivera said sharply. "There is no temporizing with Huns."

"Peace is—peace," Sarah said hopefully. "Almost any good thing can be worked out in peace."

Alan said, "Doesn't anybody care that a man starves here in your midst?" He simply was not going to discuss the war at all times and places, and especially not at this time and place. Sarah felt suddenly as if Alan were a sacrificial animal who understood somehow that it was his slaughter under discussion and intended boldly to avert the slaughter by diverting the discussion. As the tea-things arrived they fell to discussing a date for the announcement party. Subject to her mother's approval, they decided on April first. Alan said it could not be earlier for a very, very good reason which he would explain to Mrs. Rivera alone.

The next big item for Sarah was writing to the Duncan grandparents to urge them to come for the party. She wrote pages of arguments. Grandfather's answer was short. Of course they would come. She needn't have said more than name the date.

All of March Mama spent her waking moments refurbishing the house and then spent the moments she should have been sleeping in planning the details of the reception. "I want to have all the people Sarah will remember happily in later years." The three of them—Mama, Sarah, and Lucy—were in the kitchen, where Mama had just set the girls to polishing silver.

Lucy said, "And the high-brows who will impress the Kanes."

"Why, Lucy Duncan!" Mama answered in a shocked tone.

"Good night! Mama, don't take me so seriously." Lucy patted her mother's arm as her mother turned to go upstairs after the silver dresser set to be polished. "I know a family affair when I see one, and I know who shouldn't intrude."

Sarah, who was sitting on a high stool at the kitchen table, caught a note in Lucy's voice. "By the way, Lucy, don't you have any special friends you'd like to invite? I mean, someone besides the friends we all have in common. You get around more than we do."

"Oh, I do!" Lucy whirled around to her. "I really do and I'd love to ask them, but I just don't know how Mama'd feel. Or you, either, or Grandma and Grandpa."

"You needn't worry about us," Sarah told her. "If they're your friends, that's enough."

"It's the Baers. Bert Baer and his sister Frannie. They've been awfully nice to me. Just last week Frannie invited me to the most beautiful luncheon I ever saw. They have a butler at the door just like the Riveras have, and Frannie knows an awful lot about old silver and period furniture. You'd like Frannie, I'm sure."

Lucy's words tumbled out as though they'd been crowding a revolving door. Sarah's face expressed only forthright interest, so Lucy hurried on. "Oh, Sarah, I know Mama will think they're kind of a fast crowd, but really they're good as gold. And just as generous as anything. Old Mr. McGinty—"

So that was it. Lucy was talking about the McGinty crowd who had given the Valentine party from which she had returned with the chap in the bowler hat. Sarah thought fast, so fast that she picked up Lucy's broken sentence almost without a pause.

"—old Mr. McGinty is our leading advocate of public parks and Grandpa's right-hand man when it comes to better schools. Of course I know the McGintys. Or anyway, I know who they are."

Lucy sighed such a long frank sigh that Sarah laughed. "After all, Lucy, the McGintys are Society, and even in Wheaton

I think you ought to do your sister the honor of thinking she'd recognize Society when she heard the name."

"You're wonderful, Sarah. Honestly, you're wonderful. I should have known you'd like real people even if they did live in kind of ornate houses." Lucy reached for the silver polish and began furiously on the bottom of the teapot. "In a way, they're my kind of people, and I might as well be honest about it. But I can't bear having to go on keeping my friends and my family apart."

"You shouldn't have to," Sarah said slowly. "In a way, our kind of people are snobs, I guess. We're middle-class proletariat, proud of our education. We look up to people with more education and we look down on people with less. Maybe it's partly because the McGintys are successful without education that we kind of scorn them."

"No, it's more than that," Lucy said firmly. "Grandpa's a better man than old Mr. McGinty, and he would be better even if he wasn't a minister. You're a better person than Lenore. She's Jim's new wife. He and Shirley were divorced last year, and she married a banker from Tucson the very next day. Then he married Lenore. She's nice, though. She talks beautiful French and she's been everywhere. She has the prettiest hair I ever saw, sort of burnished red; but she's got a vile temper and throws a tantrum like a child. Just the same, she brings out my motherly nature."

"Who's Frannie Baer?" Sarah asked. "And who's Bert? Does he bring out your motherly nature too?"

Lucy stopped polishing and laid down the cloth. She was so quiet that Sarah laid down her cloth also and the two girls looked at each other. Finally Lucy spoke slowly. "Bert Baer fascinates me. Maybe that's the best way to say it. He's so handsome he takes your breath. And he's so—so confident. Sometimes I think no one could really be as sure about anything as Bert is about everything. The only thing he isn't quite sure of is me. I keep him guessing, but it's hard because I'm really weak as water in his hands."

"It's time we met him," Sarah said firmly. "Maybe he'll seem different when you see him with the family. Maybe better, maybe not so good."

Lucy smiled, but not happily. "Sometimes I think it wouldn't even matter if I found out he was a bounder. I'm not a bit sure he isn't. But neither am I sure he is." She sounded so uncertain that Sarah wanted to go put her arms around her and say, "Listen, little sister, love isn't like that. Love's certain and sure and forever," but that sounded like something out of an autograph album. She did better; she turned on the faucet, ran a drink of cold water, and spoke in a matter-of-fact tone. "You make me downright curious to meet him. Is he related to the McGintys?"

"He's old man McGinty's grandson. His mother married into the Baer beer business. Frannie is his younger sister. She's married but isn't living with her husband right now. She's only nineteen and very smart, but I think she's not as happy as she is gay."

"We'll invite them all," Sarah said. "At an engagement party I guess a person can invite whomever she wishes."

While they were still talking the phone rang its staccato signal that someone was calling long distance. It was Uncle Louis calling from Nemaha. He and Aunt Ellen had just got the notion they'd drive Grandfather and Grandmother to Wheaton in his new seven-passenger Packard, so he was working on Aunt Ag and Uncle Bill to come along. "Might as well fill up the car."

"I should say so," Mama answered gaily. "Bring Ern and Arn along too. And what about Milly and John?"

In the end it was only six who were coming—Grandfather and Grandmother, Uncle Louis and Aunt Ellen, Uncle Bill and Aunt Ag.

"I'll move in with Sarah," Lucy said. "And Baldy can move in with you, Mama. Or should some of them go to Grandma's? Except it's hard for Grandma to get up and down stairs with her rheumatic knee."

"We'll manage right here," Mama said with a fine little snort. In a way, Mama responded to trouble like a fire horse to the siren.

The big question was where would the party guests lay their wraps, with house guests in all the best rooms? But like a lot of knotty questions this one never had to be answered. Mrs. Rivera called in person with a plan. It would give her inestimable pleasure, she said, to have either the house guests or the announcement party in their home. After all, Enrique was Sarah's guardian, and Sarah was the only daughter they could ever know. When she said that she caught her breath, and Mama responded gallantly to the almost imperceptible catch. Mama said that if Mrs. Rivera honestly felt she could manage to have the tea at her house, she and Sarah would be more grateful than they could ever say. Only Sarah knew that it was hard for her mother to give up the tea. Her mother was sentimental about such things. However, in Mama's eyes the Riveras were people to be pitied because they lacked both church and children. It was automatic with Mama to reach out a hand to help the needy. Sometimes the helping hand bore a cherry pie or again it might bear an engagement tea.

Sunday morning, April first, was as sunny a day as spring could offer. A determined south wind had dried up the bedraggled traces of a hard winter and coaxed out a golden halo on the maples. On this day of days Sarah wakened singing. Not singing aloud, but singing all over, the way she occasionally felt as a child when her body wanted to leap from the bed and dance on the bedposts. But her mind cautioned, "Hold back the day if you can; it will too soon be gone."

Just before time to start to the Riveras', Alan happened to be alone with Sarah in the kitchen. It was the only time in three days they had been alone. "I hope you've missed me," Sarah said blithely.

Instead of answering, he drew her to him and kissed her softly several times. Whenever she started to speak he kissed her again. "What I want to know is, why don't we get married this afternoon, sweet, while we have the families together?"

Sarah said, "Silly!" and kissed him of her own accord, a thing she seldom did.

"Maybe it isn't silly, Sarah. Life's so uncertain. We pooh-poohed Mexico, but I may be down there before we can call another gathering of the clan."

"All right, let's!" she agreed, refusing to match his serious tone.

"I could whip up a dress out of a couple of lace curtains, and for flowers I could carry the lilies of the valley off Aunt Ellen's new hat. But the ring! We couldn't be legally married without a ring, could we? And I don't think your mother'd be happy if you didn't put something on my finger publicly."

"The public be damned, but I do have something for your finger, now that you insist on it." From his pocket he took a small box, lifted out a ring with an emerald. "The stone was my great-grandmother's, but I wanted to have it reset. That's the secret Mrs. Rivera and I had—the reason we had to wait until April first for the party." He took her hand and slipped the ring on slowly. "With this ring I thee adore, forever and ever, amen. Why couldn't we call this the wedding, darling?"

Now Sarah looked at him through tear-filled eyes. "It's a *fait accompli* with me," she said slowly. "I couldn't feel more completely and world-without-end yours if we had a service a week long." With the back of her hand she brushed the tears from her eyes and looked at him with such candid devotion that Alan felt his own eyes sting.

"Let's scrap this business of waiting for graduation and assert our rights. I'll drag you off by the hair, you scream, and then when everybody runs to the rescue we'll whip off to a cave of our own and have clam chowder over a campfire for twenty-one meals every week."

Sometimes Sarah wondered what decision they might have come to if good old Uncle Louis had not come bouncing down the back stairs. Aunt Ellen, he said, needed some hot water with which to take one of her blue pills, and she would like to leave for the Riveras' in the last car if they didn't mind. No one did mind—a thing that caused her to be ready somewhat earlier than she'd planned. The family gathered in the front hall. Aunt Ag was dressed in a gray-flowered silk which fit over her new corsets like a tight slip cover over a well-upholstered chair. Sarah hugged her and thought how wonderful to be a shapeless fifty with the faint scent of something like geraniums in one's hair and undaunted joy in one's eyes. Uncle Bill in a black suit, bereft of his corncob pipe, looked little and lost, but his eyes still twinkled. "What's that hunk of green glass on your finger?" he asked.

Sarah held out her hand. While everyone admired the ring, Archibald squeezed his way to the center of things and held her hand so that the light would play on the emerald. "It's just a little chunk of beryl," he said, "colored by traces of oxide of chromium."

Alan, chuckling, corrected him. "You would be right if that were a Colombian emerald, but it's an oriental emerald, which means it is a rare green variety of corundum." Archibald was disgusted with himself; seemed as if every time he thought he knew something, it was the wrong thing. He turned to Rachel, who had just come in the back way. "Sarah has a new ring," he told her. "Who gave it to you, Sarah?"

Everyone laughed but Rachel; like Sarah, she came near to crying. She stood on tiptoe to kiss Sarah fondly. Caresses between them were extremely rare. "You've got used to your ring," Sarah said, "but I still can't believe mine's real."

"No, I never get used to mine either." Rachel twisted the little circlet of gold and blue enamel on her finger. "That is, I never get used to what it means. And today it seems to me I'll just burst with wanting Leslie here."

In time the cars were filled and the family cavalcade set forth. Sarah said happily, "We make a wonderful procession, don't we?"

"Just like a funeral," Archibald cheerfully agreed. "But a fire engine would be better. When I get married I'm going to have all the main people come in fire engines."

No mention had been made on the Rivera at-home cards of the tea's reason for being. Flattered at being asked, practically everyone who was invited came. At first there was a leisurely handful of relatives and friends, Mr. Kane and Grandmother Duncan hobnobbing together, Aunt Ag and Grandma Vanderiet swapping recipes for pickled pigs' feet. Then all at once people arrived in swarms and coveys with a buzz and flapping peculiar to the mob phenomenon of a well-bred reception.

Grandmother Duncan was the real belle of the occasion. Still a little brown bird of a woman, she made a nest of tranquillity for each one who talked with her. People sought her out, both those who knew her and those who wondered who the quiet little bright-eyed woman might be. Grandfather drew people to him too. He stood leaning lightly on his cane, watching the scene with such evident enjoyment that people stopped to find out what he was smiling at. They went off again, smiling also, not knowing they themselves had probably been the reason for his smile in the first place.

A string quartet appeared at the far end of the drawing room. Sarah recognized the first violinist of the Minneapolis Symphony. Here would be music worthy of the day. At the sound of the tuning of strings, voices ceased, people found chairs, or leaned comfortably against the wall. Some of the young people sat on the wide hall stairs. Wheaton prided itself collectively on knowing its music. "This is the reason we came," people said to themselves. "The Riveras have brought this music here for us."

Just as the quartet finished their final number, which was the Sibelius "Spring Song," Dr. Rivera stepped into the curve of the grand piano and faced his guests, bowing with grave formality. "My dear friends," he said—and then suddenly his voice was hoarse. He had to clear his throat and start again, and in that instant's quick emotion the crowd drew near together, although they did not move. "My dear friends, today I have the great honor to announce to you the engagement of marriage between my ward, Sarah Duncan, and Alan Thomas Kane. Also, I have the great joy to tell you that the wedding will take place a year from June on Midsummer's Day. They did not specify that day, and I will give myself this birthday present." He bowed. "At this time I shall be happy to have you congratulate me on my birthday a year hence. Oh yes, and the prospective groom, he will bashfully receive your congratulations also. As for the joy to be wished upon the head of our Sarah—if anyone has enough words for that, will they please to withdraw and write a new dictionary of the English language?"

Almost as if they had been rehearsed for the occasion, the families fell neatly into line near the fireplace. Congratulations sped around the circle like hummingbirds on iridescent wings. Friends found new meaning for old words. After the fashion of her grandmother Duncan, Sarah grew more speechless as excitement mounted, but she had never looked so lovely in her life, a thing which Alan's eyes found a way of telling her over and over.

"Sarah, this is Frannie Higsby," Lucy said, presenting a svelte little brunette in Paris-made black. And then before Sarah could do more than take the small gloved hand Lucy said, "And this is Bert Baer."

He was, as Lucy had said, very handsome. Not too tall, not too thin, smooth brown hair, cynical blue eyes, and a profile that might have come off a Gibson calendar. But it wasn't in his features that the magnetism lay, nor in his words, which were conventional enough. In the space of three seconds Sarah was immensely disturbed, but whether pleasurably or painfully she could not say. After Bert came Jim McGinty and the red-haired Lenore. Then Mr. McGinty, beaming heartily, unabashed by his own sentimentality. "I wiped away a tear," he told Sarah, jerking a thumb in the direction of Dr. Rivera. "It's a weakness I have. And what I say to you, young man"—this to Alan— "is that if your bride is half as sweet as her little sister here, you are to be congratulated. Indeed, sir, you are to be congratulated." With that he tucked Lucy's arm through his and turned toward the dining room.

"He's really fond of Lucy," Sarah thought. Later, watching Lucy in the dining room with Frannie and Bert, she felt the same affection. "They cling to her in a way. She's surer about life than they are, and they depend on her." They were charming guests. Bert went out of his way to chat with Miss Moseley and later, punch cup in hand, he came back to Sarah. "It's a fine occasion, Miss Duncan, and this is the way life should be. One hates to think of the fellows off in trenches." Then suddenly Sarah had the key to Bert's charm. He was afraid and he wore his sophistication as a small boy might play dress-up in his father's tuxedo. What besides the war he was afraid of, she could not tell, but definitely he leaned on Lucy even while he badgered her lightly.

Mrs. Kane, standing beside Sarah, said to him, "You'll look well in uniform, Mr. Baer," and Sarah thought he blanched. The remark wasn't like Mrs. Kane. She had spoken absent-mindedly. Sarah followed her eye and caught sight of Archibald wedged between the door leading from the butler's pantry and a small table bearing a tray of ices. She went over to him. "Archibald, are you eating too much?" she asked him in real big-sister fashion.

"I expect I am," he said. "That's why I'm right here by this door. As the Chinese say, 'A wise bird selects its tree.'"

The last guest to depart was Miss Lillie's mother. Miss Lillie had amazed herself by defiantly going home at what she considered to be the proper time, but her mother had waited for a third cup of tea and a nibble of everything she could pile on her plate.

"She is a hellcat," Mrs. Rivera said amiably as the door closed behind her and the family were alone. "I live for the day when Miss Lillie is free, and I hope only that I do not send to the old one's funeral a wreath of sulphur bombs."

"My love! My dove!" Dr. Rivera remonstrated. "Now all of our friends will know the volcanic nature of our home. A nest on the crater's edge, is it not?"

"It is not," Alan answered. "Or if it is, then I want to sink our foundation in lava also. Sarah, let's drink a toast to ourselves. May such happiness dwell under our roof as dwells under the roof which covers us now."

Grandfather Duncan, with his honest eyes on Mrs. Rivera, said, "Here today I have met the one rival Dorcas ever had," and the only person more pleased than Mrs. Rivera was Grandmother herself.

After the families had gone—with Aunt Ellen the least ready to depart—Sarah and Alan joined the Riveras by the fire. Curtains were drawn; a fire snapped on the hearth, and the four were gathered into its circle. "In all my life I remember only one other day that was perfect," Sarah said. "I was seven and my mother had gone to convention and taken Lucy with her. Father and I were keeping house alone. We had chocolate peppermints before breakfast and we walked barefoot in the grass. By and by it rained and we made a fire in the fireplace and lay on our stomachs and made up a story about a princess who could only hear the voices of those who loved her. Finally we had to quit because all the good people in the story got married and the others got measles. That night my father taught me to stand on my head. And now—this minute—I think my father is listening and chuckling. If he could speak he wouldn't know what to say except *thank you*"—she leaned over and laid her hand on Mrs. Rivera's arm—"and neither do I. There isn't one thing that could make our engagement more perfect."

But there was one thing and it happened a few days later. A letter came from Marcia Furness. She had read in the Wheaton paper the report of Sarah's engagement. "Do you remember me? I am the thin woman to whom you gave horehound drops in the drugstore on the day my husband was buried. I have thought of you many, many times. Indeed, I have a little file of clippings cut from the Wheaton paper—the things you've played here and there, the places you've gone. Someday I mean to see you again, long-legged one. But not this spring because I am trained for Red Cross work and expect to be off the minute we enter the war." She told about her work. And lastly she sent a message to Alan: "Tell him it isn't the big things that make or mar a woman's life—not the spectacular events, nor even the noble attitudes. It's the sudden kiss when she's tired and maybe haggard or haggish; it's the clipping or the joke brought home to share; it's the camaraderie beyond words. I know. I had them all and I wish them for you."

Twenty-four

O n April sixth the United States entered the war. In spite of headlines and common talk, the war had never been farther from Sarah's mind than in these recent days. For one thing, she was practicing with double vigor, partly in order to prove to Koenigstein that love would in no way imperil her career, and partly because she had a tremendous drive to practice, as if new cylinders had suddenly come into play.

"Everything I do, I do better now," she told Alan.

"It's always going to be like that," he promised her. "Together we'll each be more than we could ever be apart." But for himself, he looked tired. His own work was heavy and he spent considerable time on special bits of research for his father; it was part of his tutoring. But there was something more that Sarah could not define; as if he were yoked to the burden of the world. When he was alone with her he held her gently in his arms, his cheek against hers, saying nothing.

All morning on that momentous day, Sarah practiced at the church. Someway she had felt like playing in a big room and she had herself a wonderful time. At noon when she dashed over to Grandma's to get a sandwich and a glass of milk she thought it was odd that no one was there. Come to think of it, had she heard bells ringing during the morning? Probably the high school boys were celebrating something.

Then Alan arrived, his eyes dark with excitement, but he didn't say anything until after he had kissed her fervently— eyes, forehead, and then lingeringly on the lips. Finally he said,

"We'd be headed for the recruiting office, except that there isn't a recruiting office in town yet."

"We'd—what?" Sarah asked.

"Recruiting office." Then he realized her lack of comprehension. "Don't you even know we're at war?"

They walked into the country, fast and far, coming back by way of the lone pine on the hill. Leaning against the pine, Sarah said, "I always feel as if it were here that my father died. You see, it was here that I finally took it in, his being gone."

Alan said, "I don't need to ask you to look after my father and mother for me. They'll be devilishly lonesome."

"So will I." Then she smiled ruefully. "Don't mind me. I'm just luxuriating in feeling sorry for myself, left to walk alone on fine spring days."

"I wish I could be sure you'd continue to walk alone." Alan tried to look jealous but could not cover his pride in her. "Not only to walk alone on fine spring days but also on fine spring nights when the moon is full and lilacs are abloom on the campus."

"If I were you I'd sit up nights worrying about me. Already the thought of Shorty McKnapp in the moonlight sets me agog. 'Shorty, my Shorty, our chance has now came; while Alan's away, may I be your dame?' 'Nay, nay,' crieth Shorty, his head in a whirl, 'I will not make off with a true soldier's girl.'"

Alan laughed, but she doubted if he'd heard her. Suddenly he blurted out a confession. "Sarah, I don't like shooting. I mean I don't like any kind of shooting. When I was a kid I'd never go rabbit hunting. Could no more have potted a small furry thing than I could have killed a man." He didn't mean to say that. The words slipped out. Kill a man—there was a thing past even thinking.

Sarah said, "I know. I understand." But she didn't understand. She didn't yet take in the fact it was war he was going off to. She said, "The shooting will be over before you get out of training. Then when we're very old we'll tell our grandchildren that it never pays to cross bridges before you get to them. We'll say, 'Once your grandpappy almost fit a war and your grand-mammy cried her eyes out, but do you know what? All he learned in the training camp was how to shoot craps.'"

Thus their conversation swung, pendulum-like, from the stark to the foolish, and it was the nonsense they remembered longest. In the late afternoon they returned by way of the Riveras'. When Mrs. Rivera heard them in the lower hall she called, "Come see my surprise." Her voice was gay. They went up to the sitting room. "Oh, it's you," she said. "I thought it was Enrique. I have such a tricky letter case for him. It's waterproof, and there's even a vial of invisible ink." She spread out her treasure like a child. While they were admiring the complicated little case the doctor arrived. He came directly upstairs, still wearing his topcoat. His face was gray and drawn.

"You've already told her. I thought she might not have heard."

"Big silly, I've known for hours." Her tone was matter-of-fact. "I've almost finished the packing." She indicated the door leading into his room.

"What packing?" He went to the door and opened it.

"Your packing, of course. You didn't think Washington had wired for me too, did you? Not but that I should be useful enough over there. I would get me a tank, but upholstered inside, you understand, and I should have tea for the generals each day at four. Firing or no firing, I should expect them to be prompt." She laughed heartily.

"Do you mean a message has come from—" The doctor turned from the packed bags to the sheaf of papers clipped together on his desk.

"Nothing has come," she told him. "No one in Washington knows you exist, I think. Does that not puncture your pride, my grown-up boy waiting for his uniform? But need one be invited to join an army? Even in the slow-moving Washington someone must know that an army needs surgeons."

For a moment he did not answer. His face worked nervously. He stood facing her half across the room. Then he turned slowly from Sarah to Alan and back to his wife. "Carlotta, you are magnificent. Only—magnificent. You expect me to leave at once."

"Now hear the man brag on his wife publicly," Carlotta said to Alan. "He has no taste." Then she turned to her husband. "And what did you think, slow-witted one? Have I not seen you perfecting the instruments for two years? Now you shall be off to use them in God's mercy. And I—I shall have time at last to read what I wish to read, and to plant new iris where I wish iris to be planted. Sarah knows I have waited a long time to have my own way about the garden."

The doctor turned to Alan. "Was there ever another woman like her?"

"One," Alan told him. "And I'm going to marry her the day the war's over."

On the way home he said, "At heart I'm just a selfish young male, Sarah. I don't want to wait till the war's over for us to be married."

Sarah stopped. They were on the corner by the church. A red fire hydrant which needed paint was topped by a small blue sweater and a jumping rope. Four little girls playing hopscotch on the sidewalk yelled for them to hurry past. The four were always plain in Sarah's mind; it was a broken piece of blue glass which the smallest child tossed at square number seven. As they walked on Sarah said calmly, "Why should we wait? Today is ours and maybe tomorrow. That much we know."

Alan said, "Thank you for that, but you know, of course, I won't take you at a time like this."

"Why not?"

"You know why not." Then Alan stopped and smiled down at her. "But why should you know? I don't really know myself. My mother would say this is no time for the sane-minded to be catapulted into rash action. I think she believes that you get

236

what you demand of life if you demand staunchly enough; as if the soldiers will come home who are expected to come home."

"She's right in a way," Sarah said. "And we'd hate being panicky."

That evening Sarah was at home alone with Archibald. Anna had hurried off to see her hotheaded nephews. Mama had gone to a meeting of the Red Cross called by telephone. Lucy had left to spend the night with her effervescent chum, Kitty Lou. Sarah said to Archibald, "I'm glad you're eight instead of twenty-one."

"I may get in," he told her excitedly. "All the better minds say this may be a long war. Unless we get peace by negotiation, of course. Do you know what, Sarah?"

Obviously she did not know, so he went on:

"All day beneath the hurtling shells
Before my burning eyes
Hover the dainty demoiselles—
The peacock dragon-flies."

"Why, Archibald Duncan, did you make that up?" Sarah could believe anything of Baldy.

"Nix," said Archibald. "I found it in Grandpa's *Outlook* magazine."

"Do you have the slightest idea what a demoiselle might be?" Sometimes it was well to put the boy in his place.

"Sure I do," he told her in disdain. "In this case it is probably one of the Calopteryx. They hold their wings vertical when at rest. But it could mean a Numidian crane with white plumes behind its eyes."

Sarah thought again. It was well to put him in his place if one could. Personally she had thought a demoiselle was also a damsel, but she wasn't going to run the risk of asking.

On Sunday Lucy telephoned that she and Kitty Lou were going to St. Paul and would return on the noon train Monday. Mama took it for granted they were off to buy the spring suit Lucy had admired in a *Pioneer Press* ad. She began to argue with

237

Lucy, but all Lucy answered was, "Mama, you're sweet." On Monday Mama, Sarah, Archibald, Grandma, and Grandpa had just finished lunch when Lucy came in. Grandma and Grandpa often came for lunch on Monday because Grandma was usually tired after washing, even though Grandpa helped hang out. Lucy was not wearing the new suit and she did not have a suit box in her aims. She had only her pocketbook.

"I have something to tell you all," she said, "and it is probably going to be a shock, so I'm glad you're all here together. This morning Bert and I were married."

No one answered. They just sat staring. Lucy's eyes were on her mother's face, where incredulity gave way to gray grief that seemed to shrink and pinch her features into stark caricature. Sarah, seeing Lucy pale, turned to her mother, who had begun to tremble as she tried to speak. No sound came, although her lips were working. Grandma, her eyes on Lucy, was flushed with the quick anger she liked to call righteous indignation. Grandpa looked purely sad, but as if he were standing across a distance, too far to make it any use to reach out to them. Archibald was dismayed, frightened, cut off. Sarah hated herself for her next thought, but it was there. "If I could put this suffering into music, it would shake the world. Each one is being tortured for the other. We're an unresolvable dissonance—all off key, torn from our major. We can't find our way back." Her hands worked convulsively, as if they hunted an unseen keyboard. "Why isn't my sympathy real like theirs? It's my own family I'm trying to put into notes! But notes are more important than particular people. Music is everybody. Either we all find our dominant or—" Suddenly she leaned toward her mother, joy in her eyes, exhilaration on her face. "Look, Mama! Listen! Everybody, listen! The dominant is love!" They had all turned to her in astonishment. "What I mean is—Lucy married him because she loved him. All we have to do is to find our places. Tonic, subtonic, I mean, you see—" Plainly they didn't know what she was talking about, but something was *all right*.

238

Sarah began again, slowly, as if she were explaining to children. "She married Bert because she loved him. There's a war. They'll be separated. Days matter. Even minutes matter. By the time we'd invited relatives and fixed up a wedding, a week would have gone by; they would have been losing each other every hour they waited."

Grandpa was the next to ease into speech. All he said was, "Well, well, Lucy," but it might have been an oration. Everyone felt better. Grandma went over and kissed Lucy, patting her shoulder a good deal as if Lucy had fallen and hurt herself.

"There, there!" she said. "You were swept off your feet. The stinking scoundrel overpersuaded her." Grandma had to have a villain in every act that went contrary to her planning, and "stinking" was the worst word she knew. Somehow the word tickled Lucy. She laughed and hugged Grandma. "Grandma, you're going to love Bert. I prophesy you will. He went to school in New England and he says you're the cream of our crop. You and Bert will really get along."

"Never!" Grandma said firmly. But she patted her hair into place.

Mama took Lucy in her arms. "My baby girl!" she said. "Married. I just can't take it in, that's all. It was a shock."

"Where is he?" Archibald asked practically. "When do we throw the rice?"

It was a distinct disappointment to him that the next few days' festivities provided no legitimate place for rice, but he bought a few boxes with his own money and managed to throw a little every time the young couple came or went from the house. They came and went often. By six-thirty that evening Mama had a buffet supper for the immediate families.

The supper was gay. Alan took care of that. He teased Lucy about her lack of appetite; he ribbed Frannie for putting cream in her coffee, country style; he talked French with Lenore. Sarah had never seen him take an occasion in his own hands and toss it about in this fashion. Bert, too, was completely charming.

What would Lucy do when he went off to war? Lucy's eyes were shining. She and Bert had a subtle sign language that was sweet. Plainly they were in love, and yet Lucy was covering something. Jim and Lenore entered into the banter, but sometimes there was a sharp note in their tones to one another. Mr. McGinty was aware of this sharpness. He almost seemed to be placating Lenore. But Grandpa liked the tall red-haired girl who patently seemed amazed that a minister could know so much about politics, current books, even boxing scores. Grandma felt the edge of Lenore's superiority and took pains to make literary allusions she was sure were over the young woman's head.

After dinner Mr. McGinty automatically drew forth a cigar from his pocket, but at a poke from Frannie he replaced it. Pretending he had not seen the gesture, Grandpa said, "Wouldn't you like to smoke, Mr. McGinty?" Ordinarily Grandpa would no more ask a guest to smoke than he would urge him to overeat. But the spirit was more than the body, and definitely this was a time when Lucy's new family must feel at home.

They all went into the parlor, which Sarah had taken pains to disarrange comfortably. Magazines were on the coffee table; flowers in the vases; the evening paper, unfolded, lay over the back of a chair. Lucy walked about nervously. "Sarah is going to play for us, aren't you, Sarah?" Definitely Sarah was not. The room was full of crosscurrents, which always made playing hard for her, harder even than the apathy of disinterest. Alan said, "Of course Sarah will play for you, Lucy. What will you have?" Sarah shook her head. It wasn't like Alan to force her against a mood. He paid no attention and drew out the piano bench. Lucy said, "The Liszt Rhapsody No. 13." Where she had picked up the name Sarah didn't know, for Lucy was no musician.

"Not that," Sarah protested. "I can't begin with that."

"Then the Bach-Saint-Saëns," Alan suggested, "Gavotte in B Minor."

Sarah played. Lenore leaned back and kept her eyes on Sarah, but she was not listening; her toe tapped the floor. Sarah caught an impatient glance between her and Jim. "They're wondering how soon they can get away. Well, darn their hides, I'll make them want to stay." So she struck up Chopin's "Grande Valse Brillante." As she finished Jim moved his chair where he could get a better look at the keyboard. "One Chopin calls for another," he said. And then Sarah was off. She herself thought she had never played more brilliantly. If Lucy wanted to put her family's best foot forward, then she should have the best, and for an hour Sarah gave it.

It was Archibald who broke the spell by saying, "In China there are some strange wedding customs. A person called the middle man arranges the engagement and the bride never sees her husband until she arrives at his house to stay."

Mr. McGinty said, "You don't say! Tell us more, young feller."

"For days before the bride leaves home she scarcely eats or drinks. You see—"

Grandpa broke in. Sometimes Archibald's information was too physiological for parlor conversation. Grandpa said, "China doesn't have a thing on America when it comes to curious wedding customs. Once I was called to an Indian reservation to marry a chief who—"

Then Grandpa was off on a riotous yarn. But Mr. McGinty could match it with his stories of weddings in the Ireland he knew as a boy. He was a born teller of tales, and his audience had such a good time that they even forgot they were listening. Finally one story had to do with a soldier, and Bert, with a mock buttoning on of sword, remarked, "These days, it's likely to be hail-and-farewell-to-the-bride for a lot of us."

Sarah saw a haunted look in his eyes. Did Lucy know of his hidden fear? Perhaps he didn't know himself.

Grandma said, "I read in the paper that the Army wants single men."

Alan nodded. "I read we may even have a draft later on, but that married men will be called last."

"So I'll miss out on my career as a general, will I, because I married me a little blonde wife?" Bert's voice was almost shrill with relief. "See what you did to me, honey?"

Sarah saw how his eyes clung to Lucy's. So Lucy did know. That's why she had hastened to marry him, not just to protect him from the war, but to protect him from looking at his own abject fear.

The party broke up gaily. Everybody, even Lenore, had had a wonderful time. Bert kissed Mama good night, which pleased her a lot, but just the same, when they had all gone she went out to the kitchen, sat down by the table, and began to cry. "They're all very nice, but they do belong to a fast crowd," she sobbed. "If I thought my little Lucy would ever take a drink, I couldn't bear it. Better to see her dead, lying in her coffin."

Alan was shocked at Mama, but he was gentle with her. "Now look here, Mrs. Duncan, an awful lot of good people take a drink. My father likes his port and sherry, and when Sarah and I have Thanksgiving dinner with my parents I shall expect her to down her glass without a whimper." He turned with mock severity to Sarah. "Do you hear that, Sarah? Nary a whimper."

"I've already drunk it and I like it very much," Sarah told her mother matter-of-factly.

Archibald, who was half asleep over a bowl of bread and milk, opened his eyes wide. "Have you really, Sarah?"

Mama cried on softly. "You're different, Sarah. You might make mistakes, but you'd never be wild."

"Now I'm hurt," Sarah said. "And besides, Mama, you're crazy in a nice sweet way. If anybody in our family has a wild streak, it's me, and sometimes I feel it's likely to come out any day. Maybe I inherit it from Grandfather Duncan. He had a very wild youth."

"Why, Sarah Duncan!" Mama said, drying her eyes. "What a way to speak of your own father's father."

"What did he do, Sarah? Could he shoot the stopper out of

a bottle of champagne? Did he drink beer out of wild women's slippers?"

"Why, Archibald Duncan, what have you been reading?" Mama took her immediate problem in hand and hustled him off to bed.

If the McGintys had any wild orgies in mind, their intention was not apparent at the tea dance which they gave three days later. Half the society names from the Twin Cities came down for the occasion, as Grandma was the first to point out, and everyone behaved as well as they looked, which was very stylish indeed. If Sarah hurried Mama away to attend a recital at the college, Mama did not know she was being hurried. And the next day when Mama read in the paper that many guests stayed until a late hour, she said, "I'm glad Lucy has such nice friends."

Beneath the froth of festivities whirling around Lucy there was always the deep current of apprehension over the war. A group of the younger chaps had already enlisted and others were on the point of going in. Much to Alan's surprise, his father strongly advised his waiting for the draft. "It's sure to come in a few weeks at most. Better finish your school year." His mother had the same conviction, but more strongly. The war was a duty no one must evade, but definitely it was a side excursion from life's main path. One must take the detour in stride, gallantly, but in order.

Attending college classes day after day seemed to Sarah a futile procedure, like trying to eat while under anesthetic. What did the nineteenth-century drama have to do with the horrible living tragedy in which Alan was soon to play a part? Who cared about the skeletal structure of *felis lybica domestica* while the vibrant bodies of boys like Alan were being mangled every hour? Still—one had to go through motions. And of course one had to keep talking about things that did not matter in order to keep from mentioning the things that did.

In the last hurried weeks of school she found herself wanting to spend more time alone. Best of all she liked to stand in the open window of her own room, looking out into the elm and beyond, at the time when the first breath of morning moved across the sky. She did not think or even gather impressions but merely waited for an unnamable moment of peace that sometimes came and sometimes did not come. Wishing could not bring it, only waiting with a kind of passive expectation. When it came it was as if all the pieces of herself, broken apart in yesterday's activity, were instantly set in place. Sometimes she wanted to tell Alan about the small full moment, but she didn't for fear he might feel left out. Of course he wasn't left out because, being complete, the moment included him. One day she realized that if she could tell him, if there were a way to catch up the moment in words, he would understand! And so, after that, there was no need to tell him. She loved him very much then, with wonder.

They did not have much time alone. At school or walking in the country, there were always people about or likely to appear. At Sarah's house Mama had a way of wanting to talk with Alan; she leaned on him, Sarah thought, as she had not leaned on anyone since Father died. Alan liked it. At his house his mother took pains to leave them alone, but Sarah felt Mrs. Kane's vast inner grief, all the more apparent because it was so perfectly covered. Even when Alan wanted to keep her to himself, to sit in the garden under the stars with lilacs scenting the night, Sarah managed excuses to draw his mother out with them. But when she and Alan were alone in the beautiful night, sitting in the lawn swing, screened by the lilacs and high-bush cranberry from any passer-by, then she ached with the joy of his nearness. If this was the pull of sex, it was a force beyond all telling; every nerve and muscle cried out to him, to be nearer and nearer until she would be absorbed into the fiber of his body. Clothing was a barrier, but skin would be a barrier too. All physical manifestation was a barrier. Fire called to fire for mutual consuming.

It was the night of June second, three days before the draft, when Alan said, "What are we waiting for, Sarah? A stupid ceremony? If that's it let's have it tomorrow. Let's have it right here with the night for a backdrop and the sundial for an altar."

Sarah said, "It's silly to wait, isn't it? It's like telling a tree not to bloom when its buds are full and the sun warm on them. But—"

"But what?" He kissed her hair, her eyes, and when she would have answered he silenced her mouth.

"But marriage is more than love. Isn't that true?"

"Yes, it's true in a way, I suppose." He answered apathetically, drawing away from her. "Marriage is budgets and furniture and a house to live in."

"And babies," Sarah said firmly.

"Wouldn't you like a baby, Sarah, if it came?" He took her hands in his and kissed the palms tenderly.

"I would love it," she admitted. But she sighed in such distress that he drew her to him gently, her head on his shoulder.

"You mean your music?" When she did not answer at once, he tipped her head back so that he could look into her eyes. "Don't be afraid to say so, darling. If my career were at stake I'd be frank enough to tell you I'd rather wait a year for you, or two years, maybe even five, than to have to look right at the fact that in marrying you I'd run a big chance of never being tops in my profession. You see—I mean to be tops!"

"You will be. Anyway, that's one thing we don't have to worry about. With me it's different. I've got to prove I can do it. I have to make my place before I can give it up. Don't you see? A person can't sacrifice something he doesn't have. And then when I do step out of what you call my career, it won't be any sacrifice." The words spilled out rapidly now. This thing she was saying was a thing she hadn't before known herself; it was being revealed to her in her words. "Maybe I'll never have to give up music for babies; maybe they'll grow along together, some years babies more important, some years music. But there will be a time when I can choose. I mean, there will be a time when if I must choose, it won't even seem like a choice. It will be plain then that you and they matter most."

"And we don't matter most yet, do we?" Alan spoke slowly, sharply. "Oh, darling, that was a nasty thing to say. I know that if I needed anything of you—anything at all—you'd give it in an instant. Yes, and you'd never be sorry for yourself afterward, either."

"Do you *know* that, Alan?"

"Of course I know it."

"Well, it's true."

He spoke in a lighter tone. "But right now I don't need any more than I have—the most wonderful woman a man ever came back to. Besides, if I could battle you into marriage tomorrow I'd still have Mother to battle, and somehow that's one battle too many for me."

"Why doesn't she want us to be married before you leave? Rachel and Leslie are going to be married. His father wants them to be."

"My mother thinks weddings should be prepared for. A house found and furnished, stocks of linen and silver. She'll expect you to have chests of things, woman. And a cookbook with recipes you've tried and marked."

"Not really!"

"Very much really. But there's something deeper than that. We planned to be married when we finished college, and I think she feels that a change in plans would signify that we didn't trust the future."

"You mean—she'd think we didn't believe you were coming back?" Sarah sat up straight and looked at him in amazement. "Of course we know you're coming back!" She stopped short. "But what if you weren't?" The words were wrung from her. She had never put the thought into words before. "What if we knew you weren't?"

"Then I'd say that my cup was full with this night, dear. We've had these hours with no reservations between us except those that belong to time. I'll never wish I'd had all of you

246

because I have had all of you—all that belongs to us now. It's like you say about the tree. Buds can't be held back from flowering, but neither should they be forced beyond their moment. I want our life together to unfold in its fullness. This is an honest thing I'm telling you, and you must remember, no matter what."

Sarah made no answer for some moments. And then she said firmly, "No matter what."

It was very late when they walked home to Sarah's house. The milkman had started on his rounds. It seemed strange that people sleeping in dark houses were having the new day made ready for them in the practical fashion. Alan said, "See you in the Commons at noon. Just two weeks till exams."

But he did not see her in the Commons because at five that morning, just as he was falling into deep sleep, a telephone call had come from one of his father's former colleagues. If Alan would enlist at once, he'd see that Alan was sent to Camp Devens, where an officers' group was being selected for immediate training. And so at eight o'clock, as soon as the enlistment office opened, Alan enlisted. Later, when Sarah asked him why he didn't wait the two days for the draft, when his number might not be chosen and he might have had weeks at home, he looked at her vaguely. "It never occurred to me," he said.

Sarah never knew what happened to those next two days. To be sure, if one parceled out the duties against the hours it would have been theoretically impossible to have accomplished the final examinations, the packing, sorting, storing, the round of good-bys that were crammed into sixty hours. She was with him most of the time. They were gay when together. For that matter, they were gay when apart. Slap-happy, Lucy called it; you'd think they were off for the circus, she said. War was serious business, even if this one did bid soon to be over. Bert prophesied that Alan would never see service. Look at the British offensive in the Argonne region, he said; the Wotan Line was likely to crumble any minute. Vimy Ridge had been taken. America's entrance into the war had given the British a shot in the arm. The

American flag was now flying from Victoria Tower in the Houses of Parliament; first time that ever happened, Bert said. If the President had let Teddy Roosevelt raise his own divisions the way he wanted to, the war would be over by the Fourth of July. With Teddy for commander, Bert said he couldn't have withstood joining himself, but he knew he shouldn't leave Lucy quite yet. After all, there would soon be another draft; time enough. These were the things Lucy told Sarah as they walked over to the Kanes' for a garden buffet the night Alan was to leave.

A garden buffet at a funeral, Sarah thought; almost like a wake. Why must everyone be so horribly normal? Why couldn't she throw herself in Alan's arms and plead with him to go away with her and hide, away to the crags of the Rockies, away to the South Seas, off to the wilds of Alaska? Their lives were their own; there wasn't anyone they wanted to kill. Why must Alan's mother look so calm and speak with such determined cheerfulness when everyone knew her smile was a mask, a ghastly civilized deception.

Sarah rode with Alan to the ten-forty train. They held hands in the car so tight that both were in pain. At the station everyone made wisecracks, not very funny, through dry lips. Alan kissed Mama and Lucy. Then he kissed his mother. Last of all he kissed Sarah. Sarah heard a sob tear at his throat, but he was smiling. She was smiling too. It wasn't hard for her to smile; how could she cry when her throat and head and heart had turned to stone? Tombstone. Perhaps that was how tombstones were made—of petrified hearts. Nonsense. Alan would be home in six months. Probably in three. Next June they'd be married and these same people would see them off on this same train for a honeymoon in New England. That was the real thing. This was emotional hallucination.

Now he was gone. The train was pulling around the bend; the fluttering of white from the back platform was Alan's handkerchief. It fluttered out. Lucy said, "It's really chilly, Bert. You should have worn a topcoat."

Twenty-five

When Leslie first came home from Williams, Mr. Sando had come to see Rachel's mother, whom he had never met, to discuss the wedding. Rachel reported the call to Sarah. She had met him at the door and taken him into the parlor, but he had walked right through the parlor to the big cool dining room where Mrs. Rand was sewing. She made a pretty picture, Rachel thought, with her crisp hair knotted on top of her head and her blue house dress open at the throat.

"I just wanted to say, madam, that a wedding is a very expensive affair and that I wish you would let me take over the financial responsibility. You furnish the brains and beauty and I'll take care of the practical end."

According to Rachel, Mrs. Rand had stood up and said, "Do sit down, Mr. Sando." But her tone was cold and firm. He sat on the edge of his chair. "I am able to take care of my daughter's wedding," she had told him. "We would like to submit our plans to you, of course, but we do not need your help." Then she turned to Rachel, who was still standing in the door. "Rachel, will you make Mr. Sando a cup of tea?"

So Rachel had gone out. She was never unhappier, she said, in all her days. Plainly their two parents just wouldn't hit it off. She put the kettle on, got out the best cups, and then cried into them so that she had to go wash her face and was sure she'd never been so slow in her life. When she finally picked up the tray to go back to the dining room she was positively shaking.

But her tears were altogether wasted, because her mother and Mr. Sando were laughing heartily and having a wonderful time. "Sarah, it was a thing I'd never seen before; my mother was being coy with the big man. Unconsciously, you know, but she was definitely different."

After that, wedding preparations seemed to fly on their own wings. Mr. Sando came daily to the house. He also came each evening. He had many good suggestions. One of them was that instead of engraved invitations Grandfather should announce at church that Rachel and Leslie were being married and that all of their friends were invited. The result was that on the night of the wedding the church was packed to the last seat. No girl in Wheaton had more friends than Rachel.

The decorations were tall white candles and yellow roses. Grandpa read the long Episcopal service from a white prayer book. As a child Sarah believed that Grandpa had written the service himself for all of Christendom to use. This night he said the words as if they were new words, made only for this particular wedding. Something in his voice caught hold of the congregation, so that Colonel Clemmons's paper reported, "There was not a dry eye in the house."

When the garden reception was nearly over, after Rachel had tossed her bouquet and gone to change for traveling, Leslie took Sarah aside. "Come out to the back porch," he said. "It's the only quiet place." They stood by the cistern pump. "You're her best friend," he began without preamble. "Maybe you're my best friend too. No one, not even Rachel, understands me just the way you always have. You're more like a man. Maybe you can take a blow. Someone's got to stand by her."

"Whatever are you getting at?" The light from the kitchen fell across his face and she saw it was drawn and white. "What are you talking about?"

"I married her under false pretenses, in a way. I couldn't bear to disappoint her. She would have felt disgraced."

He stopped short. Sarah drew back. Was he going to say he

loved a girl out East and hadn't the courage to let Rachel know? "What is it?" she asked shortly. "What have you done?"

"She thinks I'm going to enlist at the end of a ten-day honeymoon. She thinks I'm going off to war like all the other chaps who are good for anything. But I'm not. Of course I'll try, but they won't take me. You see—I had a double hernia as a child. An operation patched me up, but I've never been able to go out for athletics. And my eyes, the damn astigmatism gets worse. I know they'll throw me out. They'll laugh and say I'm unfit." The last word was nearly a sob.

Sarah began to laugh. She couldn't stop laughing. She felt hysterical, and plainly Leslie thought she was hysterical, which only made her laugh the harder. "Leslie! Leslie! Rachel's got too much common sense to feel disgraced. She knows you want to go. I'll wager she'll only feel relieved. She'll be terribly glad, almost giddy-glad, that her brand-new handsome husband is going to stay with her. It's a boon from Fate without her asking for it."

Leslie shook his head. "No bride wants to tell her world that her husband has a hernia."

This time Sarah's laughter brought Rachel herself to the porch. She had come down the back stairs and heard their voices. "What's going on?" she demanded. "Is my husband already flirting with my best friend?"

"We're laying a bet," Sarah told her. "He has a surprise for you which he isn't sure you'll like. But I'm saying that if you don't like it, if your heart isn't overflowing with gratitude when you hear it, then you are to wire me collect from Niagara Falls."

"Of course I'll like it, whatever it is." She slipped one hand through Sarah's arm and the other through Leslie's. "I just wish you were coming on our honeymoon, Sarah. If you could come along and if there wasn't any war cloud hanging over all of us—" She turned from one to the other and laughed. "Oh, dear, sometimes I almost wish Leslie would fall down and break a couple of legs so he couldn't march and I'd have to nurse him."

"You see?" Sarah turned to him. "We women are all human. And someone has to raise the next Liberty Loan."

"You're both crazy," Rachel said happily. "It's time for us to go be riced."

The two-week honeymoon ran into four. Leslie's rejection was followed by a trip to Washington to sign on a dollar-a-year job as some kind of district publicity director for government activities in his section. Mr. Sando paid his son's salary as part of his own war effort. Also, he bought the young couple a house on Elm Street not far from Grandma and Grandpa, a sweet six-room cottage with cedar closets, built-in washtubs, thermostatic heat control, and a flagstone walk. But the big excitement for Rachel and Leslie was not the new house, nor yet the fun of entertaining their friends. Their big moment came on a Saturday afternoon in late July when their parents arrived together, rang the bell, walked in, stood before them half defiant and half sheepish, and announced that they had just been married by the justice of the peace and were starting on a business trip to Spokane by way of Yellowstone Park.

Rachel declared to Sarah that Leslie had simply collapsed, while Leslie insisted that Rachel had sat with her mouth open, her lower jaw swinging on a hinge, while she hunted for something to say. His father radiated satisfaction; now he would have a home and a woman in it, a fine generously built woman whose crisp flyaway hair was a delight to see and whose gooseberry tarts would melt in your mouth. No more sewing for Rachel's mother until she got ready to make baby clothes for Leslie, Junior. At that sally, Mr. Sando laughed heartily and told his bride they must be going. And off they drove in a brand-new Cadillac, leaving the town to gape and splutter happily.

Sarah went often to see Rachel and Leslie, partly because their happiness made the world seem more normal than the newspapers would allow one to believe. Partly, too, because here was a place where she could read Alan's letters aloud, except for the special passages meant only for her. To be sure,

252

she often read pages to his mother, but even there she had to omit his descriptions of bayonet practice and belly-crawling with real bullets whining overhead. He did not write his parents about the less comfortable aspects of camp life, such as mud a foot deep in his sleeping tent when a torrential rain beat the carpenters to the draw. "But with you," he wrote to Sarah, "I know you can take it, whatever turns up. Not only take it but use it. You have tremendous capacity for absorbing reality. More than I have. Sometimes I feel as if you saw another dimension to life. A time is coming when you'll open the door and walk right into that larger habitation. After that, you'll make music! Maybe the most I can ever do for you, darling, is now and then to furnish a theme, at best a new harmony, at worst a new discord. But remember, a discord is only an assortment of notes that present a challenge for rearranging."

Sarah knew what he meant; she herself sometimes had a feeling of being on the edge of understanding, at the margin of revelation. If she could ever stay the moment and look into its heart, she would know the meaning of meaning. But she could not stay the moment; it had to be caught off guard, saluted on the wing. Even so, tenuous as it was, these fragmentary glimpses set her music vibrating for days, as if the piano were charged with a magnetic current.

The current had caught her the day Dr. Rivera went overseas. She was at the piano, working over the "Revolutionary Etude," when all at once she wasn't working, she was effortless; effortless but being drained of all she had. No! Not drained, for nothing went out of her; it only went through her, feet to head, head to hands; it went through with such charge and fury that she could not contain the half of it; neither could she pour out the half of it. With Chopin she pleaded with the conquerors of Warsaw and then scorned the pleading and knew that Poland itself had the answer, that all free men had the answer. The answer lay within. She was playing it out now so that anyone who listened would understand. Even those who did not listen would understand; a resonance of meaning was charging the air. If she could go to France with her piano she could play to the hearts of the men who were fighting, so that all frailty would be lifted from them as the fog of early morning is lifted by the sun. They would be strong with the sun, invincible, supreme. Surely, surely, those who fought, believing in justice, would achieve their end and in spite of battle wrest a lasting peace from the hands of Fate.

This was the point she and Grandpa were continually discussing. Stubbornly he held that the means must always match the end; they must be of one kind. "The contention that the ends justify the means is futile," he insisted. "Such a premise can't support the superstructure. It appears to work in the short run, just as pillars which are not quite true may support one story or even two. But the higher the pillars go, the more apparent their misalignment."

"Grandpa, you're being oratorical," Sarah chided him. "That isn't even a good metaphor. I could think of a better one myself. If I believed completely in your point of view—which I don't; I only half believe—I'd say that going to war to bring about peace is like planting corn and expecting to harvest wheat. The completed pattern is in the seed."

"That's better," Grandpa agreed. He leaned back in his swivel chair and looked around his study, turning slowly from one panel of shelves to another. "So many of those who speak here have said the same thing, but because they're dealing with imponderables like hate and love, we don't catch on how practical they are." He picked up the New Testament lying face down on the desk, found a page and read, "'You cannot gather figs from thistles.' It's just a law of life. We'll never gather international accord from wars. Once we've planted figs and believed in figs, we have to cultivate figs. We can't suddenly decide that figs grow too slowly and so for a time we will reclaim our land with thistles. Once the thistles are full grown—and in a war hate surely takes on its full dimension—then the figs are already crowded out. At best a few seeds are salvaged, and from them mankind starts over."

Sarah sighed. "Honestly, Grandpa, I have to keep from thinking about the meaning of the war. I have to concentrate on victory and hope that a miracle will save us all from reaping what we're sowing. But I do think that boys like Alan will come home fired with something they didn't have before. They'll be practical about justice. I mean, they'll go right after child labor legislation and anti-lynching laws and improved public health and all the basic good things of life. They'll understand that people *have* to care for others. Don't you think so?"

Grandpa shook his head. "That's your figs from thistles again. They'll come home schooled in the ways of destruction. Right now they're being instructed in the language of hate. I'm afraid most of them will just come back tired and ready for a fling; that is, those who aren't maimed or blinded or otherwise broken."

"You old pessimist, you! You've got to trust the younger generation."

"Bless you, I'm no pessimist. I'm a staunch old believer in ultimate good, and that's why I hate to see us waste time kidding ourselves that there's any other way to approach brotherhood except heading for it. My next Sunday's sermon is on forgiving our enemy now." He walked over to a shelf and took down a worn volume. "Schiller knew. 'Forgiveness is the recovering of an alienated property, hatred a prolonged suicide.'"

It was on the way home from Grandpa's that it struck Sarah odd that so many of the boys who were leaving for training camps wanted to talk with Grandpa before they left. Believing as he did that the war was futile and wrong, how could he buck them up? Still—they wouldn't be coming to him unless he gave them something real. They wouldn't be writing to him and asking him to go see their folks unless he'd sent them off with something to hold onto. She turned around and walked right back to Grandpa's study. But he had left the study. He was out in the vacant lot at the other side of the church, hoeing his tomatoes. Standing there in the sun, she propounded her question. "What do you say to the boys? You can't tell them they're fighting a useless war, maybe a wicked war."

Grandpa leaned on his hoe. His face was lined and worn, but also, she thought, it was brown and healthy. He looked younger, in a way, as he got older. As things got more uncertain, he looked more sure. A person could even say that as more sorrow came his way he got more joyful. It was that old business of seeing something most people didn't know about. He took his time about answering. "I tell them to hang onto love, that's all. I tell them and tell them and tell them. I tell them with stories and with texts and then—well, I tell them! 'Hang onto love; it will hang onto you.' God is love, I remind them. 'You can't get lost from Him.'" He smiled, then chuckled. "So long as they can love, then hope and faith and mercy and the rest will take care of themselves. I tell them what Plato said about love's being born at the banquet of the gods. I tell them what Plotinus said about love's holding the soul in its place so that it can never fall from its sphere. 'It is closer held to Divine Mind than the very sun can hold the light which radiates from it.' I tell them about a fifteenth-century monk who knew as much about love as anybody I've met up with. 'When you can no longer think,' he said, 'you can still love.' In fact, he said, 'By love may He be gotten and holden; but by thought never.' And finally I give them a copy of the thirteenth chapter of Corinthians. 'Love suffereth long, and is kind; love envieth not; love vaunteth not itself, is not puffed up, doth not behave itself unseemly, seeketh not its own, is not provoked, taketh not account of evil; rejoiceth not in unrighteousness, but rejoiceth with the truth; beareth all things, believeth all things, hopeth all things, endureth all things. Love never faileth.' You see, I've typed this chapter on cards, and at the bottom of each card I sign my name right after Paul's. I write, 'I've tried it and it's true.'" Suddenly he stopped. Sarah couldn't take her eyes from his face. It was lighted with the same fire that sometimes flared up in her at the piano. As long as he had that, it didn't much matter what he said. Words were no more help than notes. But his words were all right; they made a record, and in looking at the card perhaps the boys could recover some of the other thing. She didn't try to tell him what she was thinking. Indeed, when she finally spoke it was to say, "I guess I'll stay to lunch if Grandma has plenty." Grandpa didn't know she'd changed the subject. He had gone back to hoeing.

At the Kanes' most of the conversation was about Alan and the war. Mr. Kane read six daily papers: the New York *Times*, Boston *Transcript*, St. Louis *Post-Dispatch*, Washington *Post*, Emporia *Gazette*, and the St. Paul *Dispatch*. Since his wife and Sarah did not read six papers, he took it upon himself to keep them thoroughly posted. Anything he lacked in intellectual approval of the war he made up for in emotional participation. Days were dark, he admitted; the war might still end in a draw if the participation of the American Army was not speeded. Every day he wrote to Alan. It was important, he said, that in Alan's grueling concentration upon training he should not do as so many others did and lose sight of the main lines of the war. Alan thanked his father, but it was plain that he was too busy felling trees to think of the forest.

His day was a stiff one. There was no time for letter writing, and yet he usually managed to write a running account of the day's incidents. In the beginning the monotony of squads right and left had worn him down. He never could get serious about folding blankets three times and placing them in a neat stack, folded edges to the left at the head of the bed, until a cocky corporal had made him run up and down the half-mile track eight times for carelessness in folding blankets.

The Kanes had a new hobby—a camera. Mr. Kane had bought it in order to take home pictures for Alan. Mr. Kane's impatience in waiting for his pictures to be developed caused Mrs. Kane to set up a darkroom and learn to process the pictures herself. It was a good diversion, Sarah thought. Mrs. Kane's hours at the Red Cross headquarters were fantastic, and in her spare time she knit incessantly.

Mrs. Rivera's hands also were seldom idle. Besides her Red Cross knitting, each morning she brought her map up to date. With complete absorption she drew and redrew battle lines, using a fine gummed tape of various colors. Whenever Sarah came she reported Army movements in the dry voice of a seasoned poker player, pronouncing French, Belgian, Italian place names with ease and often describing topography. No emotion whatsoever colored her reporting. But Sarah found out that this emotional detachment was schooled.

Another new occupation kept Mrs. Rivera's hands busy. She had taken to practicing on the piano. The first Sarah knew of it was one August morning when Mrs. Rivera greeted her with the announcement, "I have had my piano moved to the drawing room so that we might play some two-piano numbers. That is, if you would care to play." Sarah managed not to say, "For goodness' sakes!" Instead she said she'd bring some books over that very day.

"There is a nice thing by Anton Stepanovitch Arensky here," Mrs. Rivera went on as calmly as if she'd been playing with Sarah every day. "It is a waltz with chromatic runs for nimble fingers. Shall we begin?"

She took the part with the most runs, too, and executed them with such fine flourish that Sarah wanted to shout, "You amazing, astounding, flabbergasting woman!" Instead she said, "My chords should be bigger; I'm not giving them enough. Shall we play it again?" Mrs. Rivera was obviously more pleased to be taken for granted than to be praised. It was like a game in which the surprise card must pass unnoticed. After the waltz she brought out Edward Schütt's "Impromptu-Rococco," Opus 58, No. 2. "Shall I take the second piano?" she asked, and then dashed off her part flippantly, saucily, and wished for more.

Sarah could restrain herself no longer. "I just wish that Dr. Rivera were here."

"Rivera? Rivera! That name sounds familiar. Ah yes! A charming man, they say. A very great surgeon. I am told on good authority—very good authority, you understand—that on brain surgery he is one of the greatest in the world. I am told that he does operations which before this war, before his arrival in France, would have been impossible. No one had the instruments to perform the operations, nor yet the audacity to use the instruments. I would like to meet such a man sometime. Who knows? Perhaps next year he will come here and we will play for him, you and I, on our two pianos."

After that Sarah went often to play on the two pianos. Sometimes Mrs. Rivera read aloud pages of her husband's letters. One week end he had operated for sixty-one out of seventy-two hours. He had performed an eye operation for a German officer who had interned with him in Vienna; had saved the nose of a second lieutenant whose mother had once come to Wheaton to be operated on for brain tumor. Again he wrote, "I am sending you by special post the odor of a thousand roses blown across the warm night. Would that I could catch such fragrance and let it bear my love to thee—to thee and Sarah. You two will know, as I do not, how roses dare to bloom on the edge of carnage." Another time he said, "Tell Sarah that I desire her to give a command performance of Brahms tonight. The heart alone is not enough; we need music of intelligence, and such to me is Brahms. A very philosopher of music is Brahms, and he speaks to my condition."

Notwithstanding the fact that Sarah shared her days with many people, and notwithstanding the long hours she spent at the piano, she was intensely lonely. To miss a person as she missed Alan was almost a physical illness, an inward fever which nothing cooled. No matter how intently she bent her mind to other considerations, he was always there, nearer than thought. When his furlough might come he had no notion. It was no use, he said, in being led into bright expectations by camp gossip. Toward the end of August he thought it might be Thanksgiving before he saw her. And then, one day in September, he walked in.

He walked into the parlor, where she was working over and over a single passage of "The Fire Bird." Faster and faster her fingers flew except when she would pause to play a run slowly, rhythmically, as if she were a beginner seeing it for the first time. Finally she was aware that someone had been in the room for quite some minutes. She turned around ready to remonstrate—and it was Alan! She did not move; she did not speak; her mind was numb. This was Alan and yet not Alan. This man was taller than Alan, very brown, very straight, very strange. On his shoulders were the bright new bars. When he started toward her she wanted to run; a strange man should not look at her the way he was looking. And then in an instant he was Alan. No other arms could fold her in so closely; no other lips could make her heart race in her throat. Her whole body quickened to his touch, and her spirit sang out higher than any notes ever written on a staff. It was minutes before either of them spoke.

Then Alan said, "Two weeks, darling. Tomorrow Grandpa marries us and then we go away for thirteen days by ourselves."

For a time they thought it might be true. No one mattered so much as themselves. They would get a license this very afternoon. They would ask his mother to have a family party this very evening; they would share all they could share. And then they would be gone. He knew a place in Canada, a hunting lodge his father used to go to. Yes, they would even come back a day early and see the family once more before he left. No one was home at her house, so Sarah walked home with him; it was his parents they must consider most; he was all they had. When they neared the house Sarah said, "You can't just walk in on them this way, like a shot from the blue. I almost fainted myself. Let me go ahead and tell them I've heard you're coming very soon. And then in five minutes you come!"

Even so, with some preparation, his mother broke into dry sobs as she threw her arms around him and his father cried openly. Here was another kind of love, Sarah saw; parent love was tremendous too. It all but overwhelmed them, making them ask foolish questions about food and clean clothes, making Alan tell incidents of camp life that no one cared about. All at once Sarah saw Alan throw back his shoulders. "Well, Mother, I have real news for you," he began. But Sarah motioned to him not to tell them now. Wait. Surely it would be easier in a little while. But there never came a time to tell them, not all afternoon. His mother planned each day full. She called Flossie in and ordered his favorite meals. In every plan she included Sarah and did not see the numb heartache which made them answer in monosyllables. "Never mind, I'll tell her before I go to bed tonight," Alan whispered when his mother went to telephone to all the family to come at once for a picnic supper. "We'll get the license first thing in the morning and herd the family over to your house and be married before they can catch their breath." She nodded agreement.

In the morning he arrived at her house before breakfast. She had been up a long time. Who would sleep on her wedding day, especially such a day of autumn ecstasy? She had told her mother, and her mother had acquiesced. To be sure, she had shed a few small tears over having a second daughter married without a wedding veil. What was the world coming to? Nevertheless, she was in high spirits and already had Anna polishing the silver for a wedding breakfast at high noon. But when Alan came in Sarah knew before he spoke. His mother thought these hasty war marriages extremely poor taste. Marriage was a long-time venture to be entered into with dignity and fully drawn plans. Where would Sarah live? What would she do? What if—such things had to be thought of—what if there should be a baby? Would that be fair to Sarah? To the baby? To any of them? And besides, what would be gained by a wedding except—she hated to say it, but after all the thing was plain—except the physical relationship? And they weren't the kind of young people who put that first.

"Do you know how I answered that, darling? I told her I was that kind. I wanted you and I wanted you now. From the marrow of my bones to the halo on your soul, I wanted to marry you today."

"What did she say?"

"She didn't say anything. But I left her in tears. This is the third time in my life I ever saw my mother cry." His voice was ragged with distress.

"We can't do it, Alan. It isn't worth it."

"To me it is."

"Not really. We'll live with our families a long, long time and we don't want to start our own brand-new family by hurting them."

Stubbornly he stuck to his decision, but both of them knew that much of the joy had gone out of the honeymoon. No matter how perfect everything might be, no matter how happy they were together, a kind of misery would tug at his heart and therefore at her heart too. They made no more plans.

Sarah found out that fourteen days are only one deep breath for love, and sometimes the breath is a smothering one. They might be dancing gaily over at Lucy's, where the young married crowd had a way of gathering late in the evening, when suddenly Alan would hold her so closely that she couldn't move. Then they'd go out onto the porch and stand watching the moon through the vines, saying nothing. There was nothing to be said. By day they picnicked and took long hikes into the country. One rainy day they went fishing with Grandpa and cooked their catch in an old log cabin, forsaken and windowless since settlers' days. On another gold-and-russet afternoon they took a spin to St. Paul and leaned over Minnehaha Falls, quoting *Hiawatha* to each other; then drove to Como for dinner and came back in town to see a revue. Most of the time and at most of the places someone was with them. It was hard to leave out Alan's parents; often it was impossible to leave out Archibald. It was even hard to refuse Grandma's repeated invitations; every single day she made fresh doughnuts, expecting Alan to drop by. Everyone tried to show them a good time and succeeded thereby in keeping them apart. Not that there was much talk when they were alone. All the thousands of little things Sarah had planned to tell him seemed to fade from her mind at the touch of his hand. About the future, which should be the gossamer stuff of lovers' talk, they had little to say. Not that they doubted the future, but that an impenetrable wall seemed to fence it off from them.

Their last evening was a cold one. Already in the tang of October the chill of winter was apparent. They stayed home at Sarah's, shut themselves in the parlor, and made a fire in the fireplace. A faint sense of guilt that they should have been at Alan's house with his parents clouded the evening but drew them closer together. Much of the time they just sat, holding each other's hands lightly, afraid of the depths that drew them. Afraid and hurt at being afraid; what had they to fear, two who loved each other from everlasting to everlasting?

"If you should set this night to music, people could not listen," Alan told her.

"They could not get enough of listening," Sarah said. "They would put it on a record and play it over and over by day and night."

"It is the only music I shall ever hear, darling, until we are together again."

"How can you say 'together again' as if mere distance could keep us apart?"

"You are with me all the time, waking or sleeping, no matter what I'm doing, no matter what I'm saying."

"It's that way with me too."

When it was two o'clock he left her and at five he was back again, ready to take the very early train. "I've already told Mother and Father good-by," he said. "Sarah, will you ride as far as St. Paul with me?"

She went. But everywhere there were people. And if there had been no one, there still was nothing to say. In the new Union Station she kissed him at the gate before he went down to the train. Third gate from the left, it was. A spot forever marked by anguish without tears.

Twenty-six

Going back to college seemed a profitless proceeding, but Sarah dug in. An R.O.T.C. unit had practically taken over the campus, and the youthful reserve officers were very lively. Nevertheless, the halls seemed empty; everyplace she looked Alan's absence was conspicuous.

Koenigstein was having a difficult time about his name and nationality. German music was withdrawn from public programs; Wagner, especially, was anathema. German-Americans were asked to give up public positions, and if they showed rebellion or animosity they were sometimes ordered to move out of rented property and then found difficulty in procuring other living quarters. The five young Koenigsteins—Hans, Fritz, Ludwig, Gretchen, and Wilhelm—were obliged to change their first names if they wished to stay in public school. A committee of neighbors waited on Papa Koenigstein and his plump wife Elsa, requesting that the name Koenigstein be changed to Kingscup, whereupon Koenigstein flew into a fury and chased them out of the house with a broom. His name meant something in the world of music, and besides, it was printed on his naturalization papers; if it was good enough for Uncle Sam it would be good enough for him the rest of his life. He lost two thirds of his pupils and had all the front windows of his house broken on one of the coldest nights of early winter. There was no telling what might have happened to him had not his good Irish friend, Victor Herbert, happened to come to Minneapolis. The bond between the two had been hardy ever since they had shared a flat when Herbert was violoncellist of the Strauss Orchestra in Vienna. It was only after Victor Herbert had given reporters a story about seeking Koenigstein's help in scoring songs for *Babes in Toyland* and *The Red Mill* that pupils began to return. Of Herbert's stories, Koenigstein said, "Bah They are more useful than true," but he was pleased to be spat at no longer by his neighbor, Tim Kelly.

Sarah never missed a lesson and memorized with such dispatch that Koenigstein was moved to pleasure in spite of himself. For the first time he began to talk about her future in terms of greatness. "And so they say a woman does not have the strength for Tchaikovsky in B-flat minor. Brilliance in feminine hands becomes toneless. Bah! So Paderewski alone can play out the heart of the new freedom. Bah! There is coming, I say, a woman who will be remembered!"

After that Sarah added evening practice to her long days. She was aware that Mrs. Rivera often followed her with anxious eyes, but certainly it was better to play out one's heart than to let it corrode with longing. Not that there was anything unusual in being deprived of a sweetheart; half the girls in America were living on letters. Alan's letters were encouraging, too. He would surely be home again before Christmas. Moreover, he felt optimistic about the war. Perhaps he would never see action. And if he did, there was Babson's statistical report that out of one thousand men only sixty are killed and one hundred and fifty wounded. Let Sarah get her lessons like a good girl so that she would be free to make the most of the short days he would have with her. Then one day a special-delivery letter announced, "Word isn't official yet, but something tells me that my legs will be under the family table for Thanksgiving dinner. I sniff a change blowing our way."

So Sarah walked out into the country to get some of the trailing pine still accessible under the snow. She returned bright-eyed, joy coursing in her veins. Coming in by way of the Kanes' kitchen to sort over the greens, she saw Flossie taking an apple pie from the oven. She opened the dining-room door and heard the voices of Mr. and Mrs. Kane out on the sun porch. "'Over the river and through the woods,'" she sang out. "'Hurrah for Thanksgiving Day.'" And then she stopped in the doorway. Mrs. Kane was standing motionless by the window while Mr. Kane folded and unfolded a piece of yellow paper.

Alan had gone overseas.

It was Grandpa's trouble, Sarah said later, that made a man of her. All at once she took herself by the scruff of the neck and shook herself into common sense. Loneliness could not be wallowed in. While it was Grandpa who lifted her from the emotional bog, it was not through any intent on his part. A committee of good sisters from a local lodge had called in person to ask permission to use the church for a bond-selling and enlistment rally. They especially liked his church, they said, because of the arrangement of the balconies from which they intended to have flags dramatically unfurled at the high moment. Their request was purely perfunctory because they had already announced their plans to the newspaper: two buglers would stand in the choir loft to call the meeting to order and, as a final thrill, taps would be sounded from the bell tower when the meeting was over.

Grandpa said, "Your plans are excellent for such a meeting, ladies, but it seems to me that a house of worship is not exactly the place to raise either bonds or recruits."

The argument was on. For the women, this was a holy war and God was on the side of the Allies and the right. For Grandpa, no war was holy and only God knew whom to bless and in what measure. So the women went into battle formation. They took their cause to the newspaper where the editor, Colonel Clemmons, gave them front-page space. Other delegations called on Grandpa, and things might have gone badly right then had not help come from an unexpected quarter. Mr. Ramsey publicly gave it as his legal opinion that there was no reason to force the Christian Church to house a secular meeting when everyone knew that the Episcopal Church had never permitted any kind of civic gathering in their sanctuary. Whereupon the battle shifted ground. Mr. Ramsey's most formidable rival was the leading vestryman in the Episcopal Church. The vestryman tried to make the point that historically Episcopalians had been more respectful of the house of God than Christians, Methodists, and their ilk. Unfortunately for the vestry-man, a Methodist banker spotted that word "ilk"; he was a man of parts and he did not intend to be called "ilk." The Methodists swung to Grandpa's side. It was very confusing, but things gradually quieted down without Grandpa's having to call a special meeting of his board.

Even the original delegation of women subsided, because their rally occupied all of their attention. But they had not forgotten or forgiven. Just before Christmas one of them came to Grandpa with the glad news that she was taking a collection for a red satin banner to be hung in the front of the church, bearing a star for each boy who had joined the armed forces. "Blue stars so long as they are in this country, silver stars when they go across, and then"—a note of rapture in her voice—"when they are killed we replace the silver stars with gold."

Grandpa said gently that loyalty and remembrance were highly commendable but that a church was not the place to celebrate a victory of war or do honor to the victors. Why should there be a star for the boys who went to fight but no star for Leslie Sando, say, who raised bonds? And if a star for Leslie, then why no star for Rex Coulter who, though crippled, was doing distinguished social service work in the slums of Chicago? Why not a star for an honest farmer who helped to feed the hungry world? If there were to be stars on a banner in the house of God, should they not honor all who tried to build brotherhood in this world? For all or for none, he said; no special distinction, certainly, for the soldier.

So the fat was in the fire again, and it soon spluttered all over the town. Practically everyone told everyone else that they knew Grandpa was not a disloyal citizen but that this was a war to protect the children of Belgium and the homes of France; this was a war to end war; if God were not on the side of the liberators in this war, where would He be? Grandpa must be made to see the light. But Grandpa felt that on this question he had to walk steadfastly in the light he already had. Nevertheless, Sarah knew that he continued to seek more light. One night after choir practice she had gone back to the church for her purse, and there she had seen him on his knees by the communion table. A shaft of light from the street lamp gave his face a chiseled look. He had not heard the door open and he did not move. It was cold in the church and he had forgotten his overcoat. She wanted to go down and kneel beside him, but instead she went out quietly. Surely in this need the Lord would speak to him as He spoke to Moses, "face to face, as a man speaketh to a friend."

Grandpa did not mention the war in his sermons, but just the same more and more people were coming to his church. He made it seem as if in these hard days the way a person lived mattered to God. But in spite of the continually growing congregation and in spite of the way the boys home on furlough streamed in to see him, the Church Board held a special meeting and gave Grandpa a document of *whereases* which told him point-blank that the board and not the minister would decide what kind of banners might be hung in the church, and whereas this was a people's war the people could have stars where they wished. In conclusion, they expressed their appreciation of Grandpa's leadership and hoped it would continue, under the grace of God.

The next Sunday when he walked onto the platform there stood the new service flag. Grandpa did not appear to see the flag, but the congregation saw nothing else. He preached on one of his favorite texts, "Speak unto the children of Israel that they go forward," and he laid the needs of the world before them, especially the needs of the hungry and homeless. When he finished he sat down. The invitation hymn was sung: "I Am Coming to the Cross." Grandpa stood again, head up, and his tenor rang out strong, as usual. Just before the benediction he read his resignation, including a short statement of his views. Then he blessed them all in words to which they were accustomed and went out the back way instead of going to the front of the church to shake hands.

The next week was probably the longest week Sarah ever remembered. On the following Sunday, Grandpa's resignation would have to be acted on by the congregation. In the meantime the town seethed. Every kind of organization took a stand, which was rather bewildering to people who belonged to a dozen organizations and found them all taking somewhat different stands.

Colonel Clemmons stated the issue clearly in his editorial. Was the Reverend Vanderiet patriotic or was he not? But the president of the new Kiwanis Club clouded matters by calling attention to the fact that ever since the war began the Reverend Vanderiet had been unintentionally aiding the war effort by his unsurpassed ability to build private and public morale.

Sarah, powerless to help her grandfather, took advantage of a blizzard to stay home and type up parts of Alan's letters for her overseas scrapbook. Alan must have gone very quickly to the front, or near the front, because his letters made mention of hard facts only associated with fighting areas. His battalion was among the replacements heralded by the newspapers as filling a desperate need in the French ranks. New troops, the papers said, inadequately seasoned, were better than no troops. Alan mentioned the acrid smell of powder which stung the throat. "Amazing, too, how quickly we are learning to distinguish the different kinds of firing. Howitzers and French guns split the air in different keys, and our own artillery has its distinguishing dissonance. One part of my mind listens for the diversification of pitch and rhythm, but you can bet your neck that direct attention does not wander from the drill officer's instructions: 'duck, flat—hide—scram—mask—

barb wire.' After our first skirmish we had an off-the-record lecture from a tough little major; if I could spell some of the terms he used you still couldn't find them in the dictionary. However, isn't communication of ideas the first duty of anybody's spoken word? The major communicated!

"No one told us that the front offers such splendid displays of fireworks. There is so much they did not tell us! After one's ears become accustomed to the infernal racket it is good to lean back against the cushioned night and enjoy the pyrotechnics. Last night Fritz gave us a first-class display, even to colored rockets and fascinating pinwheels. I quite wished you were there beside me, safe in the curve of my arm, enjoying the arabesques and curlicues whirling above us."

In a new company which was shifted to his battalion an old friend turned up. Bob Winters had been in prep school with him. They had swum and sailed together summers. Sarah felt that she knew Bob from Alan's talk of him. When Bob left Yale for the Army he had a sweetheart named Elise who lived in Virginia and went to Sweetbriar. Alan had planned that the four of them would get together sometime. It was a great satisfaction to the Kanes to have Alan and Bob together. Alan asked Sarah to write to Bob, and she did. Bob answered. It was nice having someone over there to tell her about Alan; how well he was liked by his men, what an appetite he had, the way he talked of her whenever the two of them were together. Things were getting tougher now. Mr. Kane, reading the boys' letters, said that obviously they were seeing action.

"Ho-ha-hum! Lice are a lousy invention," Alan wrote. "Was it David Harum who allowed that a dog needed fleas to keep him remembering he was a dog? Maybe these little flippers are a worthy device to keep our hands and minds in action when otherwise we might slip into the sloughs of philosophy.

"A gray day. Gray mules, gray motor trucks trudging down a gray road. Gray smoked walls of half-destroyed houses, an arched bridge of gray stone. Gray soldiers in the murky half light of early morning, picking lice from their shirts.

"Shall I tell you something funny, darling? Once in fifth grade I got a prize in geography. I could locate more cities, more bays and fords, more mountains and rivers than anyone else. I was so young that I imagined places to be important. But actually, who cares who owns the river in which one drowns? Who cares for the name of a mountain on which one crashes? Who wants to know the map name of the soil that drinks one's blood? Spilled blood has a sweet smell, did you know that?

"Sometimes I sense what Grandpa means about non-violence. Wars will go on until sometime some nation which could win if it wished refuses to fight. That nation will be invincible. But in the meantime, men like Grandpa are bound to be persecuted."

When Sarah read that paragraph to Grandpa, somehow he did not seem too greatly harassed by the storm that raged about his head. When Mama wrung her hands and Grandma was unable to eat, he told them to remember Socrates, who made up his mind on public issues while he was in good standing and then when the shoe pinched did not try to escape barefoot. Grandma told him not to try to be funny about Socrates; in the end he had to drink hemlock. "Well, at least he didn't spit it out," Grandpa declared cheerfully. He simply refused to argue or to be cast down. Did he really think his people would refuse his resignation? Colonel Clemmons said that if they did, Wheaton would be an object of scorn in the Associated Press.

On the momentous Sunday there was no standing room in the church. Grandpa preached a rousing sermon on the text militant: "And the Lord, he it is that doth go before thee; he will be with thee; he will not fail thee; fear not, neither be dismayed." At the close of the service the chairman of the board, good-natured Mr. Benson who owned a hardware store, called for a vote of the congregation on their minister's resignation. Should it be accepted? The ayes had it. Then Grandpa pronounced the benediction in a good firm voice and went out while the organ was playing the response. Many voices were strident as people left the church. Others were choked with weeping. In almost every family Grandpa had baptized or married or buried someone. But many who loved him most had voted aye for conscience's sake.

That night the family got together. What would Grandpa do now to earn a living? Even the house he and Grandma lived in belonged to the church. No other church would want to hire him; they would not dare. The next morning Mr. Ramsey called on Grandma and Grandpa. Sarah happened to be there. Mr. Ramsey's lips were as tight as ever, his back as thin. He said, "Brother Vanderiet, in my opinion your point of view is sadly biased by impractical idealism. People are not yet ready for the millennium. I voted against you. But yesterday evening I took the liberty of convening the board to suggest that as a gesture of gratitude for your long and faithful service you should be allowed to live in this house until a new pastor is called. It is my judgment that it will take the best part of a year to find a suitable man." Sarah almost hugged him but he walked out of the door as stiffly as he had come in.

Grandma said she wanted to move right out of the house, regardless of the motion; Grandpa said nonsense, they would pay rent and remain. Mama said there was no need for either of her parents to worry about finances; Dr. Rivera would gladly arrange for her to draw ahead on her annuity insurance and Grandpa could pay her back later. Grandma said this was the time for Grandpa to take a vacation and write a book of sermons, just as she had always wanted him to; she would be the one to get the job. And so she did. Asking no one's leave, she got herself appointed Wheaton's representative for a children's encyclopedia and was already embarked upon her door-to-door career before any member of the family knew what she was up to. Nor would she desist. She liked the job. She didn't even mind having a door shut in her face; it just showed which people lacked breeding. Often the people who invited her in made a great fuss over her. She made it a rule not to discuss Grandpa's position on the war.

Bert came home from a trip and met his wife's grandmother toting her big sample book. Lucy had not written him about Grandpa's fight; all talk of the war distressed him, although he was forever bringing up the subject. He got the story firsthand from Grandma. That afternoon Grandpa's bank called to say that five thousand dollars had been deposited to his account by a friend who wished to remain anonymous. Grandma was in a quandary. She suspected that money of coming from the McGinty-Baer treasury, and everyone knew that Baer money had been made in beer. It was Lucy who finally solved that dilemma.

"If the money came from Bert's people, he hasn't told me," she insisted, "and I don't want to ask him. If he wants to do something anonymously, he ought to be allowed to do so. Besides, Grandma, this money was probably made in the barrel business. The Baers were already into the barrel business before anyone else seemed to see that prohibition was inevitable." So Grandma gave up the house-to-house calls, but she still took orders over the phone.

Lucy came more often to Grandma's these days. She was expecting a baby the first of May. "Bert wanted a baby so very much," she said. "You see, he might have to go any time." Again Sarah felt that somehow Bert wanted Lucy to have a baby so that he would be less likely to have to leave. She wished she didn't sense this thing about Bert. He was such a likable chap; even when he had had too much to drink he was gallant and charming. If he had a conviction against war and came out and stood shoulder to shoulder with Grandpa, it would be different. But he stood shoulder to shoulder with the committees who got the town band out every time a group of boys went off on the train. He told them all he'd see them in France. Just as soon as he got the new barrel business on its feet—a business now rated highly necessary to the war effort—he'd see them Over There.

Rachel, too, was going to have a baby. Lucy wanted a little daughter and Rachel wanted a son. Her baby was not due until June, but by March she navigated with difficulty like an overloaded ship. Sarah worried over her and wished Dr. Rivera were home, but Rachel was not worried. She was never so happy and, she said, never so well. She loved every minute in her new house, cooking for Leslie, sewing fine seams, and waiting for Sarah to drop in.

Sarah was pleased that Alan seemed to miss her music as well as herself. It amazed her that he could remember so vividly not only the names and opus numbers of things she had worked on but also separate passages.

Billeted in this quiet village which scarcely shows the ravages of fighting at all, we seem to be in another decade, maybe another incarnation. Last night the moon was full. Laced shadows of branches, still bare of leaves, were silhouetted against the stone walls of houses. The air was balmy and we sat outside and smoked. Bob said it was a night for Beethoven and he'd take his strong and mighty, maybe the "Emperor Concerto." I told him nobody, not even Paderewski, could play it the way you could. But me, I'd take mine happy and melodious under the moon. I'd take the G Major Concerto, I said; is it number four? The one that has the wonderful runs in the second movement, where the piano and strings talk back and forth. The strings get insistent in their wooing, but the piano is gentle, leisurely, calm, sweet. You'll know which one I mean.

There is a large blond Englishwoman in this village, Lord knows where she came from or why she's here. We met up with her outside the canteen. She's a self-confessed grandmother who wears white slacks with pink underwear showing through, and her first comment to us was a remark about the queer costumes of the natives! But from here on she can dress as she likes without a snort from any of us because she can play the piano. I mean play! Sarah, even you'd say she can play. Without preamble she plunged into the Rachmaninoff Concerto in D Minor. Whenever the orchestra was

274

supposed to come in she would describe the passage. Sounds like a lecture in public school music, doesn't it, but actually she made you feel the instruments. On the long piano solo with the soaring arpeggios and swift plunges into the bass, she likes to show off her piano gymnastics, but she has what it takes. Seems she knows Rachmaninoff. He'd told her all about his first trip to America, back around 1909, when he toured with the Boston Symphony under Max Fiedler; told her about practicing with a dumb piano on his way over on the boat because he didn't remember his own concerto very well. I told her you'd had some coaching from him when you were a mere child prodigy. She was much interested. Or was she? She began to tell us how good she was herself at twelve, and by way of illustration played a chromatic étude of Chopin. We were all set for a swell evening when little Piedmont came in to tell me that one of my men had tried to blow his brains out. Lordy, how I ran! The guy had only nicked his right ear, but he'd scared hell out of himself. He belongs to some odd sect in South Carolina, and when he'd heard his mother was dying of tuberculosis he thought he'd beat her to the pearly gates and hold out a welcoming hand.

In April he wrote, "All of one's senses are quickened by peril. The taste of one's own saliva with the tang of fear in it is quite different from the sharp salty taste that follows simple exertion. There is an especial sapidity in the tender ends of new blades of grass; there's the stale taste of a chewed matchstick and the insipid sweetness of French canned cream. But tonight we had a new experience in taste—fresh mutton stew with little onions in it. Where the cooks found the mutton I wouldn't know."

Earth—the beautiful earth! I don't mean our noble planet, either, but just the black dirt beneath my feet, beneath my belly, into which I bury my face. Yesterday I clawed into earth in which, last week, the roots of orchard trees had been embedded. Small roots remained alive, although the parent trees were gone now and had no need of them.

Don't tell me that animals don't have a psychological pickup as quick as any human's. Yesterday half an hour before we opened fire—on a morning that was just like any other sunny morning so far as man or beastie could see—the rabbits started running across the field where we expected to advance. They were scurrying ` desperately, as if they must get someplace while there was still time. Later, when we were advancing as we could and dodging for cover, I came upon their warm soft bodies, many of them, unscathed but dead. They died of fright, I think; the breath was terrorized out of them. Perhaps we men have a right to tear each other to shreds; we made up our minds by way of our own free wills. But the animals have no say. Whenever I hear wounded horses screaming in elemental anguish I am filled with fearful loathing of myself and of the whole human race.

The first of April, when Sarah walked into Koenigstein's studio to take her lesson as usual it was a much excited maestro who advanced, arms open, with a torrent of reproof pouring out upon her.

"So slow you come, I suppose the time of people waiting for you makes no difference so long as you buy a new spring bonnet. What is a career, anyway, or what is a teacher?"

"I'm not late," Sarah remonstrated, pointing to his big clock.

He ignored the clock. "Of course you are late. For two hours I wait, I wait, I wait. The Summer Civic Orchestra will have their opening concert as a part of the university commencement and I—I, the spurned and spat-upon Koenigstein—I am now asked to suggest the name of a piano soloist. With an all-Minnesota orchestra they wish to have a Minnesota artist. What do you say?"

Sarah's brow was puckered in thought. "Talmadge is good," she said. "I don't know if he is good enough for that orchestra, but he's a graduate of Minnesota, and he'd make a handsome appearance. And what about your protégé from Zumbrota? What about Stanly Kliscz?"

"Ninny! *Dummkopf!*" he chided. "It is yourself I am asking. Would you like to make your debut on May twenty-ninth with the Civic Orchestra?"

Finally Sarah recovered and they began to make plans. "What is the concerto to be?" she asked, so excited she was pale.

"It is to be Beethoven. And I think it is out of tribute to me, a sort of apology they are fixing up." He strutted a little. "And maybe, too, a sop to the German-American voters!" He shrugged his shoulders. "But it is a Beethoven concerto they asked for. Which do you choose?"

Sarah pondered. She was especially fond of the Fourth, but then again—"Bah! And fie upon you!" Koenigstein said. "There is only one for you. The 'Emperor'!"

"The 'Emperor Concerto' for me?"

"And why not? Is it a schoolgirl I now deal with or is it a concert pianist?"

So Sarah went to work on the concerto. Except for writing to Alan and attending classes, all other concerns faded from her mind. Lucy's baby, born in the middle of April, was a fine big boy weighing nine pounds. By the time Sarah reached the hospital Lucy had forgotten she had ever thought of a daughter. The baby was promptly named Bert for his proud father, who was very pleased, very sentimental, and already very drunk. He gave Lucy a ruby pendant to celebrate the day and would have taken Sarah off to buy another if she had been willing to go. But she had to get back to her concerto.

Alan's letters came regularly. She felt very near to him these days. It was as if their spirits, by sheer effort of will, annihilated distance. Indeed, the sense of his presence seldom left her now. Together, like this, there was nothing for either of them to be afraid of, ever. She always carried one or two of his letters with her, ready to read paragraphs aloud to anyone who wished to hear; the pages she kept to herself were worn thin.

Gas is a diabolical invention. It creeps so silently, soft-pawed as a kitten. It settles into the hollows which are our only hide-outs from shells. Those who are caught without their masks on are suffocated. And those with masks on feel as if they must suffocate, so that there is an almost uncontrollable desire to tear off the mask and take a chance. The curly-headed boy with the big feet who talked so much about his grandmother—remember?—he tore his mask off too soon and has been taken to the hospital.

Every individual knows he must die sometime, but how few of us ever think of the dying process. Looking on from the outside, there seems to be a strange withdrawal of life, a timed recession of the vital energy. You see it in the fatally wounded who are stupefied by their pain. Death comes first in the eyes; even though they are looking around them, taking in the scene and the people, still there is an abstraction about them, an inward knowing. Then the skin grows tired and ceases to function save as a covering for the skeleton; the skeleton comes out to meet the skin; bones seem to show through even in a fat man. The nose grows sharp, the teeth turn to chalk. I wonder how dying feels from the inside. To know that one is caught in the final process must be a fascinating thing. And I wish to know. When my time comes I do not want to be flung beyond our three-dimensional consciousness without warning. A man deserves to proceed with dignity from Here to There, adjusting his inward eye to new dimension as he goes. Now don't think I'm getting morbid, darling. I never felt farther from death than I do this minute, sitting snug and warm in the kitchen of a fine stone farmhouse, expecting to leave for Paris before the week's over. I intend to live to be an old, old man and to die in my good bed with you sitting beside me in your wheel chair, holding my hand and looking very vigorous for your ninety-seven years.

The first of May he was made a captain, and in the reorganization of the battalion Bob was transferred to his company as first lieutenant. They were pleased as Punch. "But all is not going so well with Bob," he wrote. "Elise has broken their engagement and is going to marry a flier from her home town. I think Bob has been afraid of it all along. Gosh, darling, maybe I ought to worry about you, but I never do. You are the air I breathe and the food I eat."

We've been brought back of the lines for a three-day rest. Great business to wash one's clothes and bathe in a rain barrel and sleep in clean straw and have plenty of hot food. But I wish we hadn't come. It's this way: Bob and I got leave to go to a field hospital to see a chap named Perry Porter who'd been in officers' training with Bob. He'd been wounded badly. Well—we saw him just before they loaded him onto a stretcher to take him to some special hospital. He'd lost both legs and both arms. Instead of being a six-footer, he'd fit in a baby's crib. He was Phi Beta Kappa from Cornell, an engineer; married two weeks before he left home. Now they say he'll go back to his bride in a basket. But not if he has his say. He tries every way to finish the job for himself, but without arms a man can't cut his own throat. Listen, Sarah! This is a war to end war. It must never happen again. You and I and the rest of our generation, we've got to carry the load for these lost arms and legs.

New recruits, French. Too young, too green. Under fire, they can't keep their food down. Thank heavens our company is past that. It's dangerous to have to vomit as you run. They say that American reinforcements are coming up in a big way. Soon we will have an American army and take on complete identity. Even now it seems to me we dominate the French, although we are only regimental fill-ins being seasoned to our task. The old French troops are canny and quick; they do by instinct the things we have to think over for a fraction of a second. That fraction of a second is too long. Often we owe our lives to their automatic responses. But just the same they are tired, not only in body and mind but in soul. We guess our battalions must be coming soon and thick; today we came upon twelve dozen new coffins stored in an old barn. They were made of pine and smelled like Christmas.

The day of her concert Sarah was up with the sun, leaning out of her window and drinking in the crisp golden morning.

She took her bath cold, flew back to her room, and felt like turning cartwheels. Catching sight of herself in the mirror, she grinned sheepishly and then shook her fist at the grin. "You're a homely old mug, all right, but you have a nice mop of hair atop you." She let her hair down and brushed it vigorously. She caught another glimpse of herself full length and nude. "Tall girls shouldn't get too thin. Alan won't want a clothes pole." Just the thought of Alan sent her spirits skyward again. What a day this would be if only he could be sitting in the front row trying to keep from looking conspicuously proud when she took a bow.

She intended to make him proud. The rehearsal had been a pippin. Everyone said the orchestra made a favorable showing alongside the regular Minneapolis Symphony; indeed, for this occasion, they had much the same personnel. At the rehearsal she knew she hadn't looked very impressive when she arrived among them. She'd come out of the rain and felt a little frightened as well as dampish. But Mr. Gullich was a real conductor. He was the first of the long line of great conductors for whom she meant to play! This seemed like a big occasion now, but someday she'd look back and say to reporters, "My first appearance with an orchestra—let me see; it was in Minneapolis, on May 29, 1918. I played this same 'Emperor Concerto.' That took nerve, did it not?" She would then laugh at her own temerity. "My husband was overseas at the time. Yes, the placid gentleman you met in the library, but then he was thin and hard and brown and—" The make-believe faded. It wouldn't do to keep Alan in mind so vividly; the thought of him made her heart turn over and her wrists go weak.

Most of Wheaton, it seemed, was going to the concert, or at least all of Wheaton that mattered to Sarah. Mrs. Rivera had invited Miss Lillie and had managed, skillfully, to impress Mrs. Tower with the length of the program so that the old lady had actually preferred to say home. Grandma and Grandpa, Mama and Archibald were driving with Bert and Lucy. All of the McGinty clan would be there. Professor Richter was bringing two carloads of students, and Miss Moseley was chaperoning one of the cars. Colonel Clemmons knew a news item when he saw one and wrote an editorial on the future of Wheaton's celebrity, Sarah Duncan. He also managed to bring in the future of Wheaton's great newspaper.

Only the Kanes would not be there, and that was a thing of sorrow to Sarah. Mrs. Kane had had a severe case of grippe which had left her with pleurisy. For some unfathomed reason she remained extremely weak; even sitting up in bed tired her. Her husband would listen for both of them, she said. But Sarah remonstrated over Mr. Kane's leaving his wife. If she couldn't have both of them she didn't want either. And so it was settled; Mr. Kane would remain at home also. "No one will be more present than we two," Alice Kane said, "except, of course, Alan. No matter where he is or what he's doing, he will be in the front row center." Her eyes filled with tears; tears came quickly to her these days.

Sarah squeezed her hand. "Only one face will be plain to me, and you know whose face that is. All the others will be a pleasant blur."

"There is a small thing we want you to have, my dear." Mrs. Kane reached under her pillow for a tiny old-fashioned jeweler's box. "It's a pin that belonged to his great-grandmother; a little violet made of amethysts." She laid the pin in Sarah's hand. It was an exquisite bit of jewelry, delicately wrought of gold, the leaves inset with green enamel and each petal of the flower formed by a single stone.

"I'll wear it as my talisman," Sarah promised. "I'll always wear it when I play a concert. We're a-borning a tradition this minute."

In spite of the talisman, in spite of the lovely new gown of yellow chiffon beaded with seed pearls at neck, wrist, and belt, in spite of Koenigstein's bragging and Mr. Gullich's evident pleasure, Sarah was nervous when she arrived backstage. She paced the floor, felt like a fool, stopped pacing, and felt a bigger fool. She looked at her hands and they appeared enormous. So long were her arms that if she sat on the stage she could easily reach across the auditorium to play a piano in the balcony. Moreover, her hands were cold; her feet were cold also. Her nose was cold, the top of her head was cold, chills ran down her spine. For the fifteenth time she looked in the mirror, unaware she had looked before, and wondered how any human could have such an inhuman nose.

A boy's voice called, "Miss Duncan!" She went out where the men of the orchestra were taking their instruments from their cases. The boy was a Western Union messenger, a mere youngster with a thin freckled face; in his hand was a sheaf of telegrams. He flipped through the telegrams in search of hers. Sarah saw an envelope with the black border that the government now used to warn relatives of bad news. Her heart stopped beating and the voices of the musicians grew dim, but already the boy had found her envelope and it was a plain one. Nevertheless, she grabbed for it and tore it open with shaking hands. "WHEATON, MINNESOTA, 11:40 A.M. MOTHER AND I ARE THERE WITH YOU AND ALAN, PROUD BEYOND WORDS. ALEXANDER KANE." The blood came back to her heart. She was warm now. Everything was going to be all right. She found a chair and thoroughly enjoyed the first half of the concert.

She continued to enjoy herself when her cue came to go onto the stage. These were friendly people who packed the auditorium; they waited for her with confidence. Confidence welled up in her also, confidence and something more. Many of these people were lonely; their hearts were overseas where hers was. They were troubled and anxious; some were afraid. She would give them courage and tranquillity; she would give them—Beethoven. She stood by the piano acknowledging their initial applause, aware of something real and warm which swept from them to her but unaware that her tall, slim serenity had already sounded the keynote of her music.

With the first swift runs she felt buoyed up, assured. By the time the orchestra took over she was already a part of the music, and when the piano again led out it was as if the thematic ideas were being born afresh in her. In the second movement, especially, she had an excited anticipation in waiting for the music to unfold, as if she did not know what was coming next, and then with the first sure descending melody the answer rose from within her. All during the third movement she felt she had little to do with the music except to let it flow, and flow it did in syncopated figures of descending chords that woke some tutelary goddess in her fingers. She was loath to have the music end. Without it they would all, players and audience, be small again; small and solitary. But never so alone as before; they were sharing life's real splendor, a magnificence of spirit.

The last note had died away and the conductor had lowered his baton before the applause broke over her, wave on wave. Over and over she acknowledged it, and when she left the stage they called her back. The orchestra stood and Sarah was so touched she could have hugged them to a man. She wanted to call out to them all, "Look, you dears, that music wasn't mine. It was yours and yours and yours, all of you together. Yours and Beethoven's and our boys' across the seas." But no words were needed; they understood, and that was why their applause continued. She had made them greater than they had been before.

Backstage, Mrs. Rivera was waiting and Adolph stood at the door. There also was the same freckled-faced messenger. He held out another envelope. "They said not to deliver this one until you was through playing. It's over now, ain't it?"

"It's over," Sarah said, tearing open the envelope. She read the message aloud, "WHEATON, MINNESOTA, 1:10 P.M. MOTHER HAS SEVERE RELAPSE CONDITION CRITICAL BEST RETURN AT ONCE."

Adolph drove them home. He drove fast, and neither Sarah nor Mrs. Rivera had anything to say. When they drew up at the

Kanes' front door Mrs. Rivera would have waited in the car, but Sarah took her by the hand and drew her up the walk. The door was open and they went in. There was no one downstairs, but as Sarah started up the stairs Mr. Kane appeared in the upper hall. This was an old man, stooped and broken. Slowly he came down to them. No one spoke until he reached the bottom stair. His mouth hung open almost foolishly; he tried to find words but found only broken sounds. Sarah gripped his arm.

Finally he blurted hoarsely, "Alan was killed in action."

Twenty-seven

Oddly enough it was her mother who helped Sarah most through the next few days. When she first reached home late that night and her mother threw her arms around her and began, "My poor dear! My darling, your mother understands!" Sarah felt an impulse to push her away and run to her own room where she could lock herself in. Restrained by effort, she said, "Mama, I can't talk. You know it's always this way with me. I just can't talk."

Her mother stopped patting her shoulder. "Your father was like that." There was remembrance in her tone. Some people, at a time when you'd think they'd want consolation, didn't want anything at all. From that moment she not only ceased to proffer verbal comfort but she kept other people from intruding and did it in a common-sense fashion that was in itself comforting

In the middle of that first night, as Sarah lay awake, too numb for tears, it occurred to her that her mother, too, had lost the one person who meant more than all the rest to her. Still, her mother had children left to love. Children! Sarah sat up in astonishment. She'd always taken for granted the children who would someday be hers, just as one took for granted growing up and having a checkbook, getting married and having "Mrs." on one's calling cards. How crazy a young mind was, lumping together the unimportant little side issues and the things that mattered terribly. She lay down again. Now there just wouldn't be any children. Suddenly she began to cry. For those who never would be, she could cry. It seemed as if Alan were weeping with her.

She turned to put her head against his shoulder. There was only the empty night.

Next morning the word about Mrs. Kane was slightly more encouraging. Sarah went to the Kanes' right after breakfast. Mrs. Kane knew her and began to talk volubly about Alan's childhood, turning her head constantly from side to side. By and by the doctor came and gave her something to make her sleep again. Sarah went to the library with Mr. Kane. He said, "It is a good thing that people are able to have funerals for their dead; it gives them something to do."

Sarah said, "Would you like to have a memorial service of some sort?"

"Would you?"

"We wouldn't want to have it now with his mother too ill to come, and later—well, there isn't any special time, is there?"

He shook his head. "But I wish I knew how he died. I wish we knew."

"Bob will write. I know he will write as soon as he can."

"If he wasn't killed also. We will just—wait."

Grandpa came with a squib he had cut from the newspaper. Tucked away in an inner page under long accounts of the way the Germans had gained ten miles, crossed two rivers, captured Soissons, and taken twenty-five thousand prisoners, there was a quiet little dispatch from General Pershing.

This morning in Picardy our troops attacked on a front of one and one fourth miles, advanced our lines, and captured the village of Cantigny. We took two hundred prisoners and inflicted on the enemy severe losses in killed and wounded. Our casualties were relatively small. Hostile counterattacks broke down under our fire.

Grandpa said, "I believe this was Alan's situation, and if so, it's the first real American offensive. There's a comment on the editorial page which quotes the London *Evening News*. Listen to this:

"Bravo the young Americans! Nothing in today's battle narrative from the front is more exhilarating than the account of their fight at Cantigny. It was clean from beginning to end, like one of their countrymen's short stories, and the short story of Cantigny is going to expand into a full-length novel which will write the doom of the Kaiser and Kaiserism. Cantigny will one day be repeated a thousandfold."

Sarah nodded. "Pershing says the casualties were relatively small! Relative to what? For me, the continent of Europe would not be missed so much." There was no bitterness in her voice; only wonder.

Plainly Grandpa had more to say, but he did not know how to begin. Sarah helped him. "I know the things you want to tell me, Grandpa, and I believe the way you do, I guess. Life just wouldn't make sense any other way. I'm not troubled for Alan; I'm just troubled for me."

Grandpa leaned against the door. "I have a friend who's helped me through a lot. He's the most humorous friend I have, probably, and he has tremendous common sense too. Chap named Chuang-tzu; lived a couple of hundred years B.C. This man Chuang-tzu lost his wife who had been a particularly companionable sort. The next day a friend came to mourn with him and found him sitting on the ground singing and keeping time on a brass basin. The friend was shocked. He was very much shocked. He reminded Chuang-tzu what an estimable woman his wife had been and what a fine mother to his son. Not to shed a tear would be surprising enough, he said, but to sing was a most excessive and unusual demonstration. Then Chuang-tzu answered him, and I'll tell you exactly what he said:

"It really is not singular. When first she died I could not help being troubled by the event. But then I remembered she had always existed before birth. She had neither form nor substance then. Substance was added to spirit and substance took on form, and she

287

was born. And now change comes yet again and she is dead. The relation between all this is like the procession of the four seasons. There now she lies with her face turned upward, sleeping in the Great Chamber of Eternity. And while this is so, if I were to fall to weeping, and sobbing, I should think I was ignorant of the law of Nature. I therefore restrain myself."

"It's a wonderful story, Grandpa. Alan would love it himself." Sarah smiled, almost happily. "He had such regard for the way you wander about in the centuries, hobnobbing with all kinds of people. I'm sure I'm going to come to a time when I can think of the procession of the seasons, life, death, and life again, but right now I can't imagine there will ever be a minute I won't miss him."

Grandpa nodded. "Don't cling to your grief, though."

"The thing I cling to is a sentence he wrote in a letter about its being up to us to validate the sacrifices already made. Do you remember that letter? It was the one where he told about the young officer who'd lost both his arms and legs. Alan said that people like us, him and me, had to make good those legs and arms. That's the thing I keep thinking of now, how I'm going to make good on the job."

In the days immediately following she had to keep her mind on the immediate present because each day brought a new anxiety. Archibald came down with the measles and was very ill. Then a letter came from Nemaha saying that Grandmother and Grandfather were both down with this influenza. Aunt Ellen was taking care of them because Aunt Ag had thrashers. Mama felt she ought to go, but Archibald was too ill to be left. Sarah would have gone in a minute, but Rachel's baby was due any day now and Leslie's work often kept him away overnight. Rachel's concern for Sarah seemed to have obliterated everything else from her mind; she didn't even talk about the baby.

"How do you feel today?" Sarah would ask her.

"I've quit thinking about how I feel, Sarah. I'm just a part of Nature now, letting the inevitable have its way. Look at the size of me." Then she'd laugh. "My, but I'll be glad to see my feet again. Seems like I ought to get a telephone so I could call them up and find out how they're doing."

Sarah laughed, too, and that pleased Rachel immensely, but just as suddenly tears rolled down Sarah's cheeks. Rachel wiped them away. "Don't, dear, don't."

"I don't mean to. It's all right. Really it's all right. Let's think about today. Maybe this is *the* day. Maybe by this time tomorrow you'll be holding Leslie, Junior."

Sarah was right about the day. Rachel went to the hospital at noon. When Leslie arrived at six o'clock the doctor came to the waiting room looking grave. "Would you step into the hall?" he said.

"Come with me, Sarah."

The doctor wasted no words. "Things aren't going well. She tends to hemorrhage."

Leslie went white. Sarah had to ask the questions. "Can't you operate? Can't you take the baby?"

"Not and save it. Not now." The doctor shook his head.

"Is it still alive?"

"Yes, its heart is beating strongly." His crisp tones did not cover his concern.

Then Leslie broke in: "Never mind the baby. Just take care of Rachel."

"If we must choose, we shall, of course. But I'm not sure we can choose." He left abruptly.

Then Sarah and Leslie waited alone. They seldom spoke. As the hours of the night went by things came clear to Sarah in the silence. No one advanced an argument about life and death; indeed, she did not have a clear-cut thought. But where before she had felt lost, she now felt serene. The place where Rachel was going, where Alan had gone, seemed more real than this hospital. "Place" was a foolish word, but it would do as well as any other. Actually she supposed the place was right here; if the limitations of the senses could be lifted for a moment, everything would be one. She felt as if her tranquillity were a luminous thing enveloping her and Leslie, both. Enveloping Rachel also. She could feel it pulsing like light waves out from her toward the delivery room; she seemed to know when it arrived and stood over Rachel like an iridescent cloud. Rachel smiled. Sarah smiled, too; gratitude swept through her. Imagine knowing all this about life! Its oneness, its grandeur, its elation! She leaned back with a sense of limitless wonderment.

A nurse stood in the doorway. "Mrs. Sando is doing well and you have a fine baby girl, Mr. Sando. She weighs seven pounds fifteen ounces, and she has a lot of dark hair."

When Sarah reached home in the early morning Mama had just hung up the telephone. Grandma Duncan's influenza had turned into pneumonia.

"I'll go," Sarah said. "Archibald would rather have you here."

She had only half an hour before traintime. Anna insisted on making coffee and scrambling eggs while she packed. "Troubles never come singly," Anna insisted. "Always in threes. First Mr. Alan and then Baldy and now your grandma. The first one sets the pattern, too. We got dark days ahead."

"Nonsense, Anna, don't you let Mama hear you say a thing like that. This time next week Archibald's going to have you running your legs off bringing him food."

When Sarah reached Nemaha, Uncle Bill met her at the train. "Sarey, it's going to do everybody good to see you, specially Pa."

"How's Grandmother?" Sarah followed him to the car.

"She ain't doing good at all. Doctor's there now." Uncle Bill sat straight behind his wheel; he still preferred horses, but a Ford made better time.

Aunt Ag met her at the door and gathered her into her arms as if she were still a child. "Best hug in the world," Sarah said.

"We've been thinking of you," Aunt Ag told her. Then, anxiously, "Sarah, I feel like we shouldn't try to hold Ma back.

Seems like she's been awful tired all winter, and maybe this is her time to slip out quiet-like without much pain."

Grandmother looked very small lying against the big white pillows. Sarah's first thought was that she'd never realized what a little woman Grandmother was. And how she'd stood up to life through all these years. Her breath came raspingly. The doctor had a stethoscope on her heart. He was an old fellow with mutton-chop whiskers; he looked like someone out of Dickens. Aunt Millie whispered that he was a specialist come all the way from Lincoln. Sarah slipped in to see Grandpa, who had the influenza. The parlor had been turned into a second bedroom. He was awake and listening for her. He said, "I knew it would be you who'd come, Sarey, and I'm glad you did."

Sarah explained about Archibald.

"Let me ask you," Grandfather said directly, "do you think it's your Grandmother's time to go?"

Sarah was surprised at her own answer. "I think maybe it is, Grandfather."

After a while he spoke again, slowly. "I'm glad it's her, first, Sarey. I wouldn't have wanted to have it her that's left alone."

Toward morning Grandmother seemed to breathe easier. Sarah and Aunt Ag were alone in the room with her. For some reason Sarah walked over to the window and ran up the shade. The first lovely light of day poured into the room. Grandmother turned her head and saw Sarah. She smiled. Then she lifted her hand a little and gestured toward the window. "Did you ever see such beautiful light?" She closed her eyes and sighed.

Aunt Ag turned to Sarah. "I do believe Ma's going to get better. Go tell Pa."

Sarah started for the door, but she turned again to look at Grandmother. She was perfectly still now. Aunt Ag turned too. They both bent over the bed. "Just—like that!" Sarah's eyes were wide.

Aunt Ag was crying softly, the whole hulk of her shaking with little sobs. "I'm glad," she said. "I'm glad it was easy. For some it's like that—just a little step."

They stood together for a moment at the foot of the bed. Out of her childhood forgotten words flashed back to Sarah. "After Countee Cullen's grandmother died he wrote a little poem for her:

"This lovely flower fell to seed,
Work gently, sun and rain—
She held it as her dying creed
That she would grow again."

Aunt Ag nodded and smiled through her tears.

"He was a colored poet," Sarah said.

"Color don't matter."

"When I look at her, I wish I had back every mean thing I ever said."

"Me too."

"Her kind's—great."

"You're a lot like her," Aunt Ag said. She came around to Sarah and pulled down her head and kissed her. "Now we'd better tell the others."

A week later when Sarah reached home, Bob's letter was waiting.

Somewhere in France
June 2, 1918

Dear Sarah:

Only two other girls I feel I know as I know you. One is my sister, Sue, and the other, Elise, of whom Alan has told you. Knowing you so well, I needn't write any introductory words and certainly I shall not try to offer sympathy. You want to know about Alan's death and I shall tell you.

They inform us now that our attack of May 28 at Cantigny was the first direct attack of the A.E.F. We were in open country. Under direction of the superior French Command, we had been well rehearsed. Early in the morning our artillery opened up and gave the enemy all they had for at least an hour. Then we were ordered over the top. The barrage constantly preceded us and we had a fine unit of flame throwers and engineers as well as twelve French tanks. Toward the end of the attack—which lasted less than an hour— there was hand-to-hand fighting because the Germans were sheltered in several caves and in a sizable tunnel. Our baseball training helped in the hurling of hand grenades.

Alan and I were near together, running across an open stretch. He had just turned to me and waved his hand because I had so often expressed a hope that in tough sledding we might be near together. Then one of our men stumbled just in front of him; an arm was torn off and Alan stopped to turn him over and get his face out of the dirt. Before he could straighten up Alan was struck through the hip and fell. I saw him fall but could not stop. It seems incredible to write the words, but we had to go on. Next I saw him he was in the front-line dressing station.

At first I thought he was not hurt too badly. He was propped up slightly on a cot and was neither moaning nor writhing. He did not seem to be in pain. Indeed the surgeon told me that he never was in pain as the shrapnel had splintered the spine in such fashion as to cause paralysis. It is no comfort to know that if he had lived he would never have walked, but so it was. His big trouble was internal bleeding. The surgeon and two assistants felt that operation was absolutely pointless. At my insistent request the senior surgeon was called in, perhaps an hour later, and corroborated their opinion.

Alan did not speak. I thought he could not speak, but I spoke to him several times, asking if I could do anything for him. He shook his head slightly. I felt completely sure that he knew the state of affairs. When I saw that he had not much more time I leaned over him and asked, "Can you give me any indication of anything you would like to have me do? Could you write a message if I held your hand? Anything you want to say?"

And then do you know what he did? He smiled. Not a wan smile at all, but a good wide grin, and he said, "Something significant, eh?" I do not know whether he might have spoken before but felt there was nothing to be said or whether speech just then came to him. In a moment he said, "But of course I should send a message to my mother. Tell her she's a brick. Tell her it's her kind who must carry on. Our generation won't be much good and the kids are too young. She'll know how to do it." He stopped speaking as suddenly as he had begun, but in a few moments he said, "Tell Dad his book had better contain wisdom as well as fact. We can't have this kind of business ever again."

After that he seemed to shrink into himself and his eyes were closed. By and by he opened them, though, and seemed to pull himself back to smile at me. I leaned close to him and said, "Sarah? What about Sarah?" Then there was such a look of pride in his eyes, such a look of complete devotion and satisfaction that I shall hold fast to it all my days. "Nothing," he whispered. "Nothing at all. She knows everything I could say and more." He closed his eyes, and I was sure he had gone over when he looked up once more and spoke out strongly. "Tell her to live," he said. "Tell Sarah to live big. Tell her to take it all in and give it all back. She couldn't be miserly with life if she tried. I want her to be—magnificent." After quite a pause he added in a very faint whisper, "She's sweet. Sarah's sweet."

We buried him, Sarah, in a coffin of fresh pine. Chaplain Weston said the service for him and nine others. The sun was shining and a brown-and-yellow bird, smaller than a lark, chirped along a furrow of earth. I felt Alan's presence strongly. I mean I felt that he was still strong, that nothing had gone out of him in passing, that he had taken the final step in stride and knew he had a destination. I've never figured much about what lies beyond, but increasingly my hunch is that the chaps who insist that individuality is independent of the body have caught up with the facts of the case. Nobody can tell me Alan isn't still going about his business and that it's a very necessary business for him and for the rest of us.

When I return I shall come to you.

Bob

294

Twenty-eight

In the slow days that followed her return from Nebraska, Sarah found that it was one thing to have a high resolve "to carry the load for those lost legs and arms" and quite another to find a way of doing something of real service. At night she felt frantic about it. She couldn't meet another day of merely routine affairs.

Mrs. Kane was getting better, able to sit out in the sun, but she looked old. Her features were sharply drawn, her voice colorless; her hands moved restlessly all the time, and she did not try to knit. Mr. Kane hovered over her. His writing had been laid aside; a masterpiece on the history of neutrality did not seem important now. One afternoon Sarah went to see him at a time when she knew Mrs. Kane would be sleeping. "We can't let Alan down," she said sternly. "I've got to find something worth doing. And you've got to go on with your work. Alan said you'd have to write with wisdom now."

He looked at her vaguely. "I don't have any wisdom."

"Then get it!" She spoke sharply. "It's people like you who have to get it because—because—well, because there aren't any other people but us." Then she slumped into a chair. "Oh, I know I sound young and moral. Who do I think I am?" Her hands were clenched in her lap and she looked at the floor to keep from bursting into tears.

Mr. Kane got up and walked slowly over to her. He looked down at her. "You're the young generation, that's who you are.

You're the crippled generation. At best your generation can only limp along, and most of the time you won't know where you're going because half your brains have been shot out. That's why my generation has to get in trim, as you say. Sarah, listen to me. Look up here at me."

She looked up. His eyes were dark with the intentness of his words. "I pledge you that I'll find such wisdom as I can and that I'll get back to work."

Sarah put her arms around his neck as if he were indeed her father. "You'll do all right. But what can I do?"

He patted her shoulder and held her with such tenderness that some of the ache went out of her and she felt spent but inspirited again.

The next day when she came she found Mrs. Kane sorting table linen. "Sarah, we're going back to New England. Shall you mind terribly?"

"Back—permanently?"

She nodded. "We own a farm in Connecticut, one we bought just before we came out here. Alan never saw it, and so it has no memories. The house is falling to pieces, but the barn's wonderful. It's the original old barn. I'd like to make the first floor into an apartment for us, and on the second floor I'd like to have three or four big bedrooms for boys coming back tired. Not for the wounded who need hospital care but just the worn-out ones. There's a wonderful view to the south, and west of the barn is a field of white clover." Her eyes shone; there was color in her cheeks.

"You're wonderful, Mrs. Kane. Alan would—well, if he were here, he'd—he'd—"

Mrs. Kane smiled. "I just wouldn't be surprised if it were he who gave me the idea, dear. I woke up in the night with it already planned out."

"We'll miss you. Goodness! I can't imagine Wheaton without you."

"We'll miss you too. Terribly. You know that."

Sarah tried not to sound as lost as she felt. "Of course when I go to New York to study I can see you often."

"There are a few things I want you to have, Sarah. Things that would have been Alan's. Even some linen and some old silver. And there's something I want to say right now while our grief is fresh and the idea of your marrying someone else seems preposterous." She laid down the napkins she had been counting and spoke intently. "I want to say that we hope you will marry. We hope you'll find a man worthy of you and that you'll love him a great deal. He won't be like Alan and you won't love him the way you loved Alan. But you've got to live big, as Alan said, and marriage is part of the fullness of living."

"Not for me, I think. But thank you and thank you for saying it."

Over at Lucy's life did not run smoothly. Sarah dropped in frequently to help with the baby. When Lucy was upset he seemed to pick up her mood and grow fretful. Frequently Lucy had two babies to look after because Lenore was often away, leaving her bouncing red-haired baby boy in the care of a slow-witted nurse-girl. At such times Lucy stepped in. Mr. McGinty seemed exceedingly grateful to her. Bert was grateful, too, when he was home. His business took him away often and he always returned looking haggard.

One morning Grandma called Sarah on the telephone at four o'clock. Fortunately Sarah got the phone on the first ring before it wakened anyone else. "Please come over, Sarah, as fast as you can. No, nobody's sick. Grandpa's still asleep. You've got to get here before he wakes up."

Sarah ran. She was glad to have a reason to run in the early morning. When she reached the house Grandma was waiting on the front porch, broom and bucket in her hands. Then Sarah saw what had happened. Someone had painted "Traitor—Slacker—Yellow Dog" in huge yellow letters across the front porch.

"I heard someone moving down here. Ordinarily I would have called out, but your grandpa doesn't sleep so well lately, so

I just came down. I saw them quite plain—two boys and an older woman: They ran off dribbling the paint. See?"

Sarah saw. She saw not only the yellow paint but the vindictive eyes that sometimes met Grandpa on the street. Also, lately, she'd been noticing the way Grandpa and Grandma came late to any kind of public meeting and left early. This yellow paint was an outrage. But it was also supremely silly; a man like Grandpa being treated as if he were a menace to society. Well, if it was silly, why not laugh? She did laugh.

"Golly! Grandma, it's really funny when you think of it. Foolish, stupid people who can't see that Grandpa's working for the same thing they're fighting for! I bet the angels laugh."

"It won't be funny for him to walk out and see it." Grandma was scrubbing again, but to no avail.

"He won't see it. Let's paint the porch before he wakes up. He has the gray paint out in the garage and he'll think we painted the porch to surprise him."

Sarah found a sharp piece of glass and three sheets of heavy sandpaper. She scraped while Grandma began to paint. They worked furiously. Three hours later they had just hung out a sign, "WET PAINT," and were cleaning off their brushes when Grandpa opened the front door. He never knew they had painted the porch for any other reason than the fact that Grandma got tired of asking when he was going to get it done.

At Rachel's, happiness bloomed with the roses and contentment glowed on every shining windowpane. The baby was dainty and pretty and amazingly good. They had named her Sarah but called her Sally. Sarah herself, whose motherly nature had always been more of a notion than an actuality, was never so content as when tending this tiny sweet-smelling bit of perfection. When she held Sally her own mind ceased to struggle and she felt as acquiescent as a field nursing the grain at its bosom. Being Rachel's baby, Sally was almost hers.

But when Leslie came home with his war talk Sarah was distraught again. If he could be useful, why couldn't she? He was a whiz on Liberty Loan drives. He poured enthusiasm into people. "Our boys are arriving in France, three hundred thousand a month now," he would say, and just the way he said it made one hear bands playing "Tipperary" and see the flags of the Allies floating in the breeze.

"You find something for everyone to do but me," Sarah complained dolefully one night. "Up to now I was sort of needed at home, but with the Kanes leaving and Archibald well and Lucy taking on an extra maid, I could go off. But I'm just useless, not trained for anything."

"You're trained to play the piano," Rachel said, "and maybe you ought to be taking up your lessons again, Sarah. You know yourself that there's nothing the world is going to need more than music."

"There's nothing the world needs now more than music," Leslie said. "You should visit the camps I've visited. Why, the way the boys pour into the canteens when someone good sits down at the piano is—Sarah! I've got it! You should go play to the boys!"

It seemed preposterous when he said it. An unknown somebody didn't just walk up to a canteen door and say, "Here's me. I can play the piano, I can."

But nothing seemed preposterous to Leslie, not if it might help to win the war. He knew a man who knew a man, and off he went on the scent. When red tape snarled, he got a higher-up to snip it. Exactly ten days later Sarah found herself engaged by the Y.M.C.A. as a hostess entertainer. From that day to the end of the war she was lent around among so many different groups that she never knew whether she should wear a Red Cross pin, a Knights of Columbus button, a Jewish Welfare insignia, one of the famous triangles of the Y, or wave aloft a Salvation Army doughnut.

Leslie was right about the need for music but wrong about the kind of music. "The men want to be amused," he had insisted. "Make them laugh. That's the big thing; make them laugh."

And so she learned to make a fool of herself hilariously and not to mind—much. She could stand with her back to the piano and play a gay accompaniment to a set of limericks. She could play different tunes with the left and right hands. She could play just about any song the men could suggest. And then one night she discovered her real usefulness.

By that time it was the end of August and she was overseas. The place was a huge Y.M.C.A. hut packed to capacity. The men were back from trench sectors, seasoned battalions as the new American Army reckoned service, leaving again next day for the front. Sarah performed all her stunts. The men were hilarious but restless; they were applauding the girl herself more than her program. They liked her tall slimness and her wide smile. Sure, the stunts were fine too. Then a tall Texan toward the back of the hut called out, "Say, miss, play us a real piece." Sarah hesitated. Three or four others took up the cry. "You can do it." "Concert stuff, you know." Then someone called, "'Liebestraum'! Do you know 'Liebestraum'?"

So she played "Liebestraum." Remembering Alan, she played out her heart. And then the hut fairly shook with the applause. She played Rachmaninoff in C Minor. Koenigstein, of all who had given her advice, had been the only right one. When she'd gone to tell him good-by, he had said, "Give them the best, Sarah. Try to get things they've heard before, but don't play down. Play up." After all, the boys weren't kidding themselves. It was death they would encounter. Only the best could talk their language.

In those next three months people came and went so rapidly that in Sarah's mind their faces ran together like a composite photograph. She danced ten thousand miles, and all of the boys, even the obviously tough ones, were good guys. She made coffee in cups, pots, kettles, urns, and once in a tin bathtub heated underneath by charcoal. She helped to fry doughnuts so near the front that she had to wear a helmet. She wrote letters for chaps whose names looked as if they'd been made from a handful of alphabet macaroni spilled out helter-skelter. She sent home watches and pictures and money for boys ordered off so fast they couldn't even address an envelope. She drew up wills in legal fashion and stamped them with the day's ledger stamp in lieu of something more official. She explained to the sullen ones and the bitter ones and the heartbroken ones that all women weren't double-crossers because one girl had thrown them over. Sometimes she felt that she succeeded a little in leaving them something to hold to.

Home seemed far, far away. The present was the only reality. Strain, struggle, danger; humor, pity, hope. But occasionally a letter from home brought a surcease from present anxieties. Archibald wrote long, amusing accounts of daily life and four-syllable commentaries on the international scene. Also, he sent a technical report on his mother's high blood pressure, paraphrasing some medical work without benefit of a spelling book. His conclusion was that Sarah need not worry about Mama. Mrs. Rivera wrote that Miss Lillie Tower's mother had died, and after the funeral the executor from the bank had produced all the savings she had purported to lose when she broke Miss Lillie's engagement to the young grocer. At last Miss Lillie was free while still a young thing of sixty-four; she was buying a car and going on a trip to the Red Cross headquarters in Washington, D.C. Two of the teen-aged Koenigsteins would be her chauffeurs.

Miss Lillie's own letter was almost laconic on the subject of her fortune. "From my point of view it's a goodly sum, Sarah. I tell myself that my mother planned it this way—so that my latter years would be free of financial pressure. I tell myself that she really believed I would have been a handicap to a man and that all she did, she did in love. That's what I tell myself by day. At night when the heart is more open to recollection I—go to sleep.

"You'd never know the Rivera household. That huge dining room has become a Red Cross workshop, and except from midnight to 6 A.M. it is always full of women working in shifts.

They say Mrs. Rivera works the clock around, and it must be almost true because materials are always cut and ready when the morning shift comes on. Working girls put in two hours before they go to their regular jobs at 8:30 A.M. She's really tremendous—Mrs. Rivera—and although she is thin I think she looks very well. They say she reads parts of your letters aloud to the girls, so whenever you have to skimp on letters, leave me out and write to her."

It was not Mrs. Rivera but Mama who wrote about the citations Dr. Rivera was receiving. "There have been two articles recently. One in a scientific journal and the other in the New York *Times*. I am sending the *Times* so you can see for yourself." Sarah never received the paper, but she didn't need it. Dr. Rivera's work on the brain was common talk. Twice she had arrangements to go to see him, but both times she was ordered to a different place. Once when she was in Paris living with the Y.W.C.A. at the Hotel Petrograd and playing two concerts a day, he was in Paris only a few blocks away, but neither knew of the other's presence. That was the war for you. Ships not only passed in the night, but they passed without salute.

Some of the passing craft deserved salutation. A few of the lads lingered in her mind. There was Tim whose wife had died giving birth to her baby; he wouldn't tell his platoon lest they be depressed on the eve of departure for the trenches. There was Harvey who talked with a Georgia drawl and showed her the picture of his mother and sisters standing on the verandah of a white-pillared house; he asked her to marry him after her third concert and meant it. The next week his buddy wrote that he'd died in a gas attack. There was Ned with the big black eyes, black curly hair, wide smile, and the best stock of English ballads she'd ever met up with. He came every night, danced like Apollo, and left the girls swooning. Two months after he left Tours she had a post card from him. He was learning Braille. There was George, squat and squint-eyed, who gave her pointers on Tchaikovsky and was right. Buck-eye took her sight-seeing

think of the future, he said. What future? Sarah wondered. Alan was not among the cheering troops returning home. There was no music in her, and she doubted if there ever would be again.

Twenty-nine

E ven on the trip home Sarah could not throw off the mood of desolation. For one thing, the ship was horribly crowded. If she walked the deck or stood by the rail looking out to sea, someone always appeared in hilarious mood. She would have been glad to enter into the soda-fizz levity of the younger nurses, but definitely she belonged to the tired group.

Arriving in New York, she automatically fell into the line of those who were sending telegrams home and then dashing for train reservations, but when her wire was half written, she laid down the pencil. The family were not expecting her and she did not want to arrive home in this state. Night found her tucked into a small hotel room high above the noisy city. The anonymity, the aloofness pleased and stilled and comforted her. For nearly two weeks she came and went as she wished, shopped with growing interest, wandered through the Metropolitan Gallery, and finally on a cold night in mid-December went to hear the *Messiah* sung by a famous choir. The contralto had a peculiarly true and vibrant voice. Sarah felt an expectancy stir within her. She was waiting some assurance. It came when the singer poured the balm of an ancient promise upon them: "He will feed his flock as a shepherd and gently lead those that are with young." All at once she realized she had been suffering grave misgivings for the brave new world that was expected to rise from the ashes of the war. Even before the confetti celebration of the Armistice, mistrust had been corroding her mind and she did not know how to take up where the war left off. But now she knew that somehow life would again flow strong, not only for her but for the whole maimed world. When she stood for the "Hallelujah Chorus" it was not elation she felt but comfort. Tears ran down her cheeks.

Home seemed strange. Its familiarity made it strange. Everything was just where it had always been. Anna still forgot to fill the salt shakers, Archibald left his skates in the middle of the hall, Mama's kid curlers were strung around her room. They visited a lot, she and Mama, and she explained details of Army life that Mama had not got straight from her letters. Mama said, "My goodness, Sarah, you've seen a lot of life." But Sarah hadn't really told her much.

Over at Lucy's a huge wing had been added to the already commodious house. Bert's mother was home, looking dragged out, and the housekeeping devolved on Lucy, who was surprisingly efficient. Bert was haggard and thin after his illness; moreover, he was afraid to touch liquor and had a lost look. Everybody pampered him, trying to make up for his lost love. He was wonderful to Lucy. They had bought a moving-picture camera in order to keep a record of little Bert's days.

Rachel was blooming. Already she was pregnant again. "Les said you'd be scandalized, Sarah, with Sally only five months old. And listen! Did you know there are twins in his family? His grandmother had two sets. There were twins in my grandfather's family too. Wouldn't twins be wonderful?"

"Make it twins, and I'll marry me a concubine," Les said. "You'd be so tied down we'd never get to a concert."

"The concubine might have twins also," Rachel answered calmly, "and then look who'd have to walk the floor nights."

Mrs. Rivera was thin but she looked ever so well. "I'm simplifying life," she said. "Come see how I've done over Enrique's rooms. We've made the upstairs sleeping porch into a wonderful home laboratory. Even a sink with running water. Having a laboratory at home will give him privacy and save him time."

This was indeed something new. Mrs. Rivera had never wanted to hear the names of ailments, medicine, or instruments before. Now her eyes shone. "He's wonderful, Sarah. Shall I tell you a secret? We're going to have a new hospital. We're putting everything we have into it. There won't be any better brain surgery done in this world than will be done right here."

"You can't guess how people talk about him over there. Everybody connected with the medical corps says his name with bated breath."

"Of course I can guess. I have clippings. My proud one does manage to send me what he calls some odds and ends of no value which perhaps should nonetheless be saved. They are merely citations and letters of appreciation from Pershing and from the King of England in his own hand and a few other trifles."

Grandpa had finished his book of sermons and it was to be published. Grandma simply bristled with pride. She managed to make some mention of the publisher every time someone dropped in. Grandpa had also been offered a job at his denominational headquarters. In fact, the National Board felt that soon Grandpa's pacifism would be an asset. With the Laymen's Missionary Movement getting into swing and the League of Nations occupying people's minds, the whole idea of brotherhood without rancor would be very popular. But Grandpa was a pastor at heart and he waited for the Wheaton boys to come home.

If Christmas was uneventful, it was also less depressing than Sarah had feared. She was able to keep Alan below the surface of her thoughts all of the day, except for a moment at dusk when she chanced to look out the window and catch the blue sheen on the snow. Two days after Christmas she went to see Koenigstein. He kissed her on both cheeks. "You are growing up," he told her. "And not hard to look at either. It is time for you to go to work."

"I want to go on with you; it's nonsense about sending me off to New York."

"You are ignorant, my lamb. The fundamentals, yes, I have taught you. But you are illiterate in experience. Symphonies, concertos, great music for the strings"—he counted on his fingers— "opera, oratorios, fine organs—bah! You know nothing. Today I write to Ludwik Rydz."

"What is he like, really?"

"He is this way." With his hand Herr Koenigstein indicated height and circumference. "He is tall, large, and he booms. He has no heart, no mercy, no manners, and he gives no quarter. Either he will make or break you, and if he breaks you he will not care."

"I am afraid to go." She shrank into her chair.

Koenigstein turned on her. "It is possible, at least possible, that you may make great music."

The next day Sarah practiced for seven hours. It was the first time since Alan's death that she had felt like wading into hard practice. The following week she left for New York, and Karen met her at the train. It was Karen's idea that the two of them live together. She would be gone all day at her job on the lower East Side, and Sarah could practice to her heart's content. Sarah liked the apartment Karen had found. It was old, but it had a view of the East River. The living room was long and high-ceilinged with an old-fashioned fireplace at the north end and a bulging bay window to the south, a wonderful sunny place for the piano. To be sure, the bedroom was not much and the kitchen was less, but they had their own bath and there were two fine closets in the hall. At first glance the shabby furniture was depressing, but in fifteen minutes the two girls had things moved around and mentally refurbished.

"We'll take out everything we don't like," Karen said, "beginning with both lamps and ending with that horrible sagging armchair. Better I should sit on an orange crate."

"We can't eat on these cracked dishes," Sarah said. "I'd have dyspepsia in a week."

"But we can't spend money, Miss Hetty Green. We promised our budget wouldn't budge."

"We don't have to buy dishes," Sarah answered slowly. "I have a lovely set of Lowestoft with pink rosebuds. My grandmother Vanderiet gave them to me the night Alan and I were engaged." She paused and then went on. "There's a perfectly huge Paisley shawl, too, that we'll use in the living room. And some fine Italian linen and an English Sheffield cream and sugar set that belonged to Alan's great-grandmother. I'll have them sent on right away for us to use. You see, there's nothing to save them for. Isn't that odd? Life isn't something that's going to happen by and by. It's now."

Karen's mother sent a hand-woven rug to use before the fireplace, but it was so lovely that they spread it on an old couch to lend an elegant touch. Both girls felt that in a sense the place was more homelike than home. Karen said, "It's odd, but in a way you can't go home again. I mean when we change, home changes too—I guess you have to make home as you go if you want any."

Ostensibly Sarah put off going to Ludwik Rydz because she was busy getting their rooms in order. Then she had a slight cold, and after that she waited to get the big rented piano tuned so that she could brush up a bit. It was a dismal gray day around the first of February when Karen stopped whistling as she made the coffee and called cheerfully into the bathroom, "Up out of the suds, Aphrodite! Methinks this is the appointed day. Unless you plan to sandpaper our brownstone front, you will be hard put to find another reason not to meet the Maestro."

Sarah emerged, tying the cord of her bathrobe so tight she was likely to cut herself in two at the waist. "Not today. I am a child of the sun and could never do brave deeds with the weather against me."

"None of that, little violet. Not another shrink from you." Karen broke an egg so that it splashed.

"I guess you're right."

324

So Sarah dressed with care and started off. She treated herself to a cab, telling herself she must arrive early before his day's work began. Then she ignored the elevator and slowly climbed the four flights to his studio, hoping he would be too busy to see her today. A neat middle-aged woman with a plain flat face and a knob of plain brown hair admitted her to the outer office. "Miss Duncan," the plain woman repeated. "Yes, we have had a letter from Herr Koenigstein. I will tell the Maestro that you have come." No shade of expression crossed her face. As she opened the inner door she added the two words, "at last."

He came out promptly and briskly and stood looking at her from under his great beetling brows. He was tall, broad, stoop-shouldered, long of arm, and, as Herr Koenigstein had said, he had no manners. When he spoke his voice had a deep, guttural boom which astonished and frightened her so that she was a full half minute taking in his words. What he had said was, "Music is a side line with Miss Duncan, I see. After she has seen the milliner and the dressmaker and the masseuse and attended all of the theaters, she then comes to see Ludwik Rydz, another of the sights of New York."

"I had a cold," she said in a small voice.

"Perhaps the cold settled in your hands. Well, we shall see. Come to the piano." He led the way into his studio, which was a big room, as large, she thought, as any ordinary house. It contained two grand pianos, and at one end there was a small stage. "Sit there." He indicated the piano which had the poorest light. He himself stood in the window and lit a cigarette. The plain woman took a chair inside the door and at once began to knit. Sarah sat down at the piano feeling that her hands were as far away as her feet and wondering which to play with.

"What would you like to play?" he asked with a kind of derision in his voice.

For the life of her, she could not think of a thing except "The Spinning Wheel," which had been her first piece. Later she wished she had played it and gone home.

"But you played a concerto at a concert, did you not? Surely Herr Koenigstein did not prop the music before you." He lit another match and flipped it, still burning, in her direction.

"I played Beethoven's Concerto in E Flat," she told him weakly.

"Only the 'Emperor Concerto,' that is all !" He turned to the plain woman. "Do you hear that, Minna? She plays the 'Emperor Concerto.'" His tone was more than mocking, it was derisive. "Well, play then. What are you waiting for?"

Weak as she was, Sarah answered in an even voice: "I was waiting only for the Maestro to finish his instruction." She flexed her hands, took a deep breath, and played the opening run. Then the music flowed into her and she was not afraid. This was Beethoven; whether Ludwik Rydz liked it or not, it was still Beethoven and Beethoven belonged to her, to the least student, as much as to a master. Her chords were big and sure; she had the strength of ten.

But the Maestro had the strength of a battalion. "The pedal!" he bellowed. "She thinks a pedal is a handle bar to lean upon! Begin again, third line, page four."

She had no score, but by luck she found the phrase he meant. She gathered momentum. "Weak! Weak-kneed, effeminate," he roared. "Come out with vigor." All she had she poured into the music, but she felt she was now playing with the tread of a horse. "Too light, too fast," he roared. "It is like this—" And he sat down to the other piano and struck the chords. He was right, too; at his hands the music took on new stature. Resolve flooded Sarah; someday she would play like that. She would play so that no one in the whole world could bellow at her.

Time went by. It must have been a good hour later, she thought, when be rubbed his hands together and genially announced, "Put it away. Maybe one, two, three years later you will get it out again. Come on Thursday at the time Minna tells you, and bring all you have studied of Bach." Then as an afterthought he added, "Koenigstein should not send me a pupil so ignorant, but I will try you for a week or two." He wrote something on an old card. "Go to this man and tell him to give you the works." He chuckled. "The piano works." He walked over to her and felt of her shoulders; he ran his fingers down the broad muscles of her back to the buttocks, which he pinched. Before she could remonstrate he was pinching her arm judicially. He hurt her, but if he knew he did not care, and she was too angry to cry out. "Thursday, then," and he pushed her toward the door.

Minna rose from her seat and followed. Sarah paid no attention to Minna. She never expected to see the plain woman again, nor the Maestro either. There were others in the waiting room— four young men and three girls; also an office girl, typing—but she saw them only in passing. Although she made straight for the door, Minna was there before her. Minna opened the door and followed Sarah into the hall. "You forgot something," she said. "The Thursday appointment."

Instead of answering, Sarah asked a question and her voice was bitter. "Who are those others? New pupils also, I suppose, waiting to be insulted and go home."

"They are old pupils waiting for the lessons they should have had this morning. Only three times before has he, Ludwik Rydz, kept his pupils waiting. Your time will be half-past eleven and you must never be one minute late." Her face was still without expression, but she added, "I always sit in the room so that if a pupil should faint I may bring cold water." She opened the door and disappeared within.

Sarah looked at her watch. It was a quarter to twelve and she had come at nine.

On the way home she thought of the address he had given her, and a policeman gave her directions. She found a basement workroom and a round, mild-mannered man who answered to the name of Antoon Maas.

"So the Maestro sent you," he said, beaming at her through the heavy steel spectacles which he wore on the end of his nose.

"Then I congratulate you, young lady. Ludwik sends only the best and seldom a woman. Come whenever you wish and bring some overalls with jacket and pockets."

"What am I coming for?" Sarah asked him in bewilderment. And then at last she smiled. The man was a comic cartoon, the place was a junk shop, and she who had started out only this morning to be instructed in piano by the world's greatest teacher would now please to come to the junk house in overalls with pockets.

It was the beaming round face which then showed surprise. "To Antoon Maas? For what else but to build and rebuild pianos."

All the rest of the winter Sarah spent some of her best hours, and often long ones, in the shop of Antoon. She learned about strings, their resonance, their resilience; she found why Bach had first divided the scale into twelve half tones; she learned true pitch. She learned about pedals and the trick of striking notes without sounding them in order to pick up the overtones of a chord. She learned a thousand small related facts of piano construction, but best of all she learned to know Antoon. His passion for exactitude, his devotion to fidelity, his elation over fine workmanship were of inestimable value and she knew it.

Only once, a short time after she had begun going to Antoon's workshop, she had rebelled at what then appeared the over-meticulous monotony. The next morning when the Maestro asked her, "How do you come with the pianos? Could you now build one by yourself?" she answered, "I could not." Then she grew bold. "And why should I? One does not need to know how to service a car in order to drive it."

"And so we talk now merely of mechanics, do we?" His fury mounted. "Is it not enough that I, Rydz, say it: a musician should know his instrument?"

"It is enough," Sarah answered with the humility she really felt.

His fury was gone like a whirlwind which had become a puff of cloud. "Never mind," he said soothingly, almost sunnily. "It is an ogre's hobby and may yet stand you in some good stead. I myself could build a piano with my own two hands." He laughed like a small boy and pranced about delightedly. "Someday, who knows, you and I shall be shipwrecked on a desert island with only a box of piano keys, a few strings, and some pedals. You will say, 'Ludwik, I pine and die for a piano. What shall I do for a piano?' Then I will say, 'Never mind, my sweet one, my poor one, Ludwik will build you a piano.' And so I shall build it before your astonished eyes."

That was the first time she had seen him in a truly genial mood, and she did not know then that the name of Antoon, like Antoon's presence, always put him in a genial mood. The reason was simple: Antoon would have no other mood. Bad temper, he said, made strings draw up and lose their tone; it was because strings were more sensitive than people that so many pianos must be remade. On a good day when the tone of a restrung piano suited him exactly, Antoon's elation was the ecstasy of a cherub at the sapphire gates. Then his round face grew rounder, his eyes bluer, and he needed only a pair of wings in order to take off for realms supernal. If at one of those moments Ludwik Rydz happened to drop in on them, Ludwik would play the new-made piano. For them he played with a fire he seldom excelled on the concert stage. Antoon and Sarah, sometimes Karen also, sat and wept as he played and would have crowned him a god if for them he had not been one already.

A god, perhaps, at the piano when his ruthlessness, his pride, and self-esteem were drained away, leaving him free and great, but a very devil at times in his studio. One hour, two hours, three hours, he would keep a good student working until Minna would begin to clear her throat ominously. If he paid no attention to her throat she would then walk around the room. "Stop walking! Stand where you are!" he would shriek at her. But Minna would then walk faster, sometimes almost prancing, until his fury at her would make him forget the lesson, and when he had driven Minna from the room he would turn to the student and announce, "You see? It is Minna, my good Minna, who keeps me from killing my students and myself with them."

There was no element of Sarah's musical education too small or too large for his attention. He sent her to hear the great pianists of the day and he expected her to report critically on everything they played. "In the Beethoven Third, where did he speed the tempo?" If she turned to the piano and played off the correct phrase he would whirl around the room dizzily like a great dancing bear, but if she looked blank he would roar like a lion at bay. Orchestral music, also, he expected her to know. Not only did she go on regular days to the concerts, but he managed to get her into rehearsals, where she would sit in a corner scanning a score for hours on end. He would set problems for her: "The Bruckner in E major, where is the emotional climax? ... Elgar, in E-flat major, mark the score as you would conduct it yourself." Occasionally he would agree with her opinion. The joyous scherzo of the Schumann Number 2 in C major was a favorite with him also; Chabrier's rhapsody, "España" was both rhapsody and España; Debussy's "La Mer" was winged for the spirit's sheer delight, especially the dialogue between wind and sea! Whenever they agreed, which was not too often because frequently Sarah had never before heard the work that he dissected so minutely, then they were happy as school children with two straws in a soda. His pleasure in a bright pupil had all the pride of a big child for a precocious playmate's success.

Oratorios she must know, also, and the way to know them thoroughly was to accompany. He found positions for her. Sarah was glad for the work, not only for the opportunity to hear fine voices and to familiarize herself with the scores, but because she needed the money. Two years would completely exhaust all of her share in her father's estate. Rydz was a man of expensive whims. One day she arrived for a lesson only to be met by Minna with a lunch in a paper bag and a taxi waiting at the door; the Maestro had said she must leave at once for Boston to hear the Liszt Hungarian Rhapsody No. 2 played as it should be played. Another time it was Philadelphia she must rush to, and once to Cleveland to get the effect of solos, chant, and choral recitative in Berlioz's *Roméo and Juliette*. When she remonstrated that it was a pianist she expected to become, not a director of orchestras, he said to wait, only wait, until she heard Mahler's gigantic symphony directed again by Stokowski. Besides the regular orchestra there was the pianoforte, an organ, a mandolin, four extra trumpets, and three trombones, one hundred and ten instruments in all, and that was only half: there was also a chorus of nine hundred and fifty voices, including two mixed choruses and a boys' choir. And what had that to do with the piano? "It is great music and great music is all one. When you can contain great music, you can make great music."

Not all of Sarah's time, however, went into her work. Erik Einersen came to town, and where would he more naturally turn than to the apartment of his favorite cousin? The first time he came the girls were having a late supper in the kitchen, eating ravioli they had carried home in a paper carton. He had merely knocked and walked in. In a tweed suit he looked very different than in uniform; taller, broader, and more distinguished. Drawing back a little from his strangeness, Sarah thought that all he needed was a saber cut across his cheek to give him the final distinction. But something else was different too. Beneath his banter he seemed starkly tired; too tired to be bored. However, he was merry enough. Drawing up a stool and finding himself a bowl, he went to work on the ravioli. At the same time he called for news of everyone in Wheaton, and it was hard to believe he had never met a single one of them except Dr. Rivera.

"Dr. Rivera's hospital is under construction," Sarah told him. "Most of the staff are already there, working in an improvised annex to the old hospital. He's decided now that surgery isn't enough and he wants to experiment with psychoanalysis too. He says there's definitely something to the theory that disease of the mind may be something apart from disease of the brain, and if he can find a doctor who'll join the staff to—"

"I know about the hospital," Erik cut in crisply. "But if I must listen to other people's good works I'd rather know about the Uhrenholdt reformation of the East Side."

"You'll be sorry you asked," Karen told him, "but maybe you'd have an idea of what to do with the seven sons of Timothy O'Connell. The oldest son is nine and the youngest four days old. His mother must have been beautiful once, but she's dying of tuberculosis of the spine. Smartest bunch of kids you ever met up with. At five, Mike is—" Then the tale was on. Sometimes she paused, drawing crisscross lines with her fingernail on the tablecloth. The others did not interrupt. Erik lit his pipe; Sarah made tea. Finally Karen smiled. "Well, those are the short and simple annals of the poor. Down there I have to act hard-boiled because my supervisor expects her staff to be level-headed. But why the hell level-headed and stony-hearted should have to be synonyms, I wouldn't know."

"So long as the O'Connells have you, they'll be okay," Erik said lightly. "I know a man who knows a man who might be useful on the landlord angle. And in the meantime, here's this and this." From his billfold he drew some bills, rolled them together tightly, snapped a rubber band around them, and handed them to Karen as if they were a cigarette.

Karen thanked him and started to the bedroom for her purse but turned in the doorway. "You know, Erik, down where I work children die of measles and whooping cough and quite ordinary diseases because—"

"I know, my dear young reformer. You and I had the same fifth-grade reader. 'Who gives himself with his alms feeds three.' But I say that the gift without the giver is better than no gift at all. Do you want this too?"

He reached out his checkbook.

Karen shook her head and then laughed. If he would not be serious, then she would be cheerful. "He really would give away his last cent, as they say," she told Sarah. "I've seen him do it when he was so poor he had to carry telephone slugs in his pocket to jingle."

"You're hinting around to find out whether I've enough left to take you out to dine," Erik accused her. "I do, and tomorrow's the night." He spoke to Karen but he looked at Sarah.

She shook her head. "Tomorrow I rehearse with Evan White-side, tenor, and I want to be good. They say he takes his accompanists to Florida and practices by moonlight on the beach."

"He is a low form of life," Erik told her. "There should be a law requiring handsome singers to have plain accompanists. How about the next night?"

At a look from Karen, Sarah accepted, and both girls promised to be ready at seven. As it turned out, however, only Sarah was ready. Exactly at seven Karen phoned to say she had to go to a confirmation party for the Martinelli twins. Sarah hissed into the phone and flatly refused to budge without her, but the doorbell rang, and while she was answering it Karen hung up. In the end, of course, Sarah went. It was her first taste of genuine nightclub life. To her surprise, the headwaiter knew Erik. After that nothing surprised her. She felt as if she were someone else doing these things; everything came easy, even witty remarks, as if she were playing a part she had learned so well that no one had to prompt her even when the actors said lines that weren't in the script. She and Erik danced and she hated liking it so much, so she asked trite questions to keep him talking. Did he go dancing every night? By way of answer he quoted John Donne to her:

"Who makes the past, a patterne for next yeare,
Turns no new leafe, but still the same thing reads,
Seene things, he sees againe, heard things doth heare,
And makes his life, but like a paire of beads."

All in all she had a wonderful evening and felt sophisticated. Indeed, she felt positively regal as she stepped out under the canopy to wait for a taxi and only wished she had Mrs. Rivera's fabulous white furs.

It was weeks before they saw him again. He was tanned and seemed less tired. He'd been on the West Coast, he said, trying to decide whether to buy a casino, a pert little gold mine, or a natty dancer whose name would look well on Broadway. Karen sat on the arm of his chair while she ruffled his hair and gave him a fine kiss on both cheeks. He put his arm around her and turned to Sarah. "And she expects a man to keep his mind on what he was reporting. I'll talk to you, Sarah. You're above these womanly wiles."

Right away Sarah wished he hadn't said that and then wished she hadn't wished. Why did he have to keep stirring her to realization that she was a woman, when actually she was a musician first, second, and completely. When next he asked her to go dancing she intended to be busy but permanently. However, he did not ask her. He said he'd been thinking all this time about the O'Connells and he'd like to bring a couple of guys in for an evening. They came and kept coming. They were intelligent young men, a lawyer and an architect. Karen also brought in some of her friends. Sometimes the talk was technical for practically the whole evening, all about wage-hour bills and the possibilities of the International Labor Office at Geneva. But every evening ended in music, as any evening should.

Finally Erik brought a chap named Pete Post, short, square, and expensively dressed. "He owns a yacht," Erik said with a fatherly pat on Pete's shoulder. "But he's okay."

"I'm not bright," Pete said, crossing his eyes and letting his arms dangle loosely. "I'm not bright, but I have money, so the boys let me play."

He was bright, all right, and evidently it annoyed him that he had money and everyone knew it. There was a light strain of cynicism in him, also, which might be the reason he and Erik seemed such good friends. Pete didn't talk as much as the others, but when he spoke it was to the point. Since he got out of the service he had been giving full time to the National Association for the Advancement of Colored People.

With her usual directness Karen's first remark to him was a question. "Why? Why are you working with them?"

Pete answered shortly, "I saw a Negro boy lynched."

Karen looked at him steadily. "You can slide down my cellar stairs," she told him.

"That's what I was figuring on asking you," he answered, also gravely.

"You think fast, don't you, for one who isn't bright?"

"It's just that I'm weak about red hair."

"Mine isn't red!" She reached up to feel it, as if in proof. "It's blond."

"That's what I said. Blond hair throws me every time."

Karen went to the kitchen to make coffee. Pete went to the kitchen also. When he returned carrying the big coffeepot, he announced, "Karen and I are engaged. That is, I'm engaged. Tomorrow I will buy myself a ring. Now you guys start betting how long before Karen wears a ring too."

Karen ignored him. She always ignored him, whether he came with Erik or without Erik. He came often.

"Don't you like Pete?" Sarah pressed her.

"Sure I like Pete. But he takes my mind off my work, and I think the right man ought to make a woman feel more equal to her work. Besides, I'd never marry a rich man. Do you think he'd be working for the N.A.A.C.P. if he didn't have all that money? If he just had himself to give?" She slammed shut the ledger of the Daisy Club. The Daisies were a group of hard-boiled thirteen year-olds and her number-one headache. "Antoinette is the new president of the Daisies," she went on, "and she certainly is a daisy herself. One sister is a prostitute and another dances at Joe's Burlesque."

"I refuse to be drawn up side paths. And I still say Pete's a pippin. Next to Erik, he has the best mind of the lot." Then she added as an afterthought, "Though who am I to judge a mind? My own doesn't function."

Sometimes she felt waterlogged with trying to take in so much music. Whenever she was completely stymied she fled to Connecticut and spent a short week end with the Kanes. Their barn had indeed become a lovely place. Both front and back, the wide doors to the haymow had been replaced by sliding panels of windows which opened onto a wide hallway that ran the full length of the upstairs and became a huge sitting room for the boys who occupied the six sunny bedrooms. They were an everchanging group except for Tim, who was lame. Tim stayed on and wrote poetry that broke one's heart. After an evening of listening to Tim read Shelley, Keats, and Lanier, Sarah was ready for business again.

Before Christmas of the second winter, Rydz had put her to work on the Schumann A-minor concerto. He scowled at her as he handed her the score and said morosely, "When you've got this inside you, we'll talk about concertizing." She walked all the way home to calm her elation. A concerto meant an orchestra, and for Rydz to offer the public a new concert pianist meant one of the truly fine orchestras. Surely, though, he would want her to give a recital first. So far he'd never mentioned a recital, but he encouraged her to play for an audience whenever possible. "Go to small towns, go to women's clubs, go to high schools, go anyplace where there are people to be drawn from their chairs. Take them in your hands, the people, and do with them as you will. Audience experiences you must have even if you pay them to listen." Sometimes for weeks her music absorbed her so that grief retreated to interior numbness and then, suddenly, it would step forth again as sharp as a fresh sword thrust.

It was now her third spring with Ludwik Rydz. She was used to him, if one could ever become used to the unpredictable. He knew her, too; he knew she could stand up under his lash, and so something—perhaps Minna's presence—kept him from driving her to the breaking point. "Minna is your conscience, maybe your soul," Sarah had said to him once.

"Minna is my Poland," he had answered. "Chopin carried a handful of his native soil with him. I carry my Minna. She was my nurse. That stoic face of hers is the first face I remember. She knows me as no other woman can."

Maybe it was true. Women came and went in his life, or so it was rumored; perhaps it was because of Minna that he needed no permanent affection. Minna herself had favorites among his friends and students. When a lesson was particularly grueling she often took Sarah to an inner room and gave her malted milk with homemade sugar cookies. For the first Christmas she knit blue angora bed socks for her, and for the second a lovely afghan in shades of green. Sarah loved her and brought small troubles to her, things she would mention to no one else.

"Minna, Gomez makes love to me, and do you know, I'm half in love with the guy myself."

Gomez was a brilliant young violinist who sometimes came to play with Ludwik; together they would improvise, a thing they declared no other two virtuosos had ever done.

Minna said, "It is his violin which courts you. Without his violin Gomez would be a taxi driver."

Later that afternoon Sarah said the same thing to Karen and Erik. Erik had stopped by on his way to ship out for Europe.

"Just like that," Karen said, "he goes roaming."

"Just like that," he repeated, "he's off to see a gent named Jung."

"Who is he? A bookie or a broker?"

"He's a man who reads your mind. Think it will take him long with me?"

Karen turned and almost snapped at him, "Not these days."

Erik ignored her. "What goes with you these days, Sarah?"

"Gomez goes with me these days. I think I'm half in love with the guy."

337

"Half in love would be capacity for most women, wouldn't it?" he asked coldly.

"It is for me," she told him, also coldly. Then she made herself speak casually. "But no matter how much in love I might think I was, I'd leave when music spoke. Wasn't there a saint who stepped across the threshold with her children clinging to her skirts when she heard the holy call? That's me." She waved her hand to them and left the room.

"She means it, Erik."

That night they went, the three of them, to hear the B-minor Mass sung by a Russian choir. It was Sarah's first experience of the Bach Mass and there were moments when she truly wished to die. Anything she could get from life thereafter would be anticlimax, and anything she could give would be travesty. Erik reached over and took her hand in his. Then she felt amplified, as if her power to hear and feel were given new dimension. There was nothing personal in his touch. When they went out they did not speak until they reached the street. Then he said, "Au revoir, gals. Sorry I can't take you home. Be seeing you sometime." He hailed a cab, put them in, and left.

Karen said, "I just can't bear it. Last time he was here I thought he seemed more serious. Not so cynical. Did you know he'd stopped in Wheaton and talked with Dr. Rivera?"

Sarah shook her head. "No one's mentioned it."

"Probably no one knew but Dr. Rivera. That's Erik—the oyster! I hoped so hard he'd go back into medicine."

"After all, people have to choose whether they want life to mean anything or not." Mentally she shook him out of mind, hoping to recover the music still singing in her ears. Under the spell of Bach mankind might be important, but not men!

Thirty

Early in May 1922, on a day like any other lesson day, Sarah walked into the Maestro's studio thinking that if an opening occurred she would like to ask leave to go home for a short time. For more than two years she had not been home except for the briefest of holidays, and she was homesick. She sighed as she laid down her music.

"To sigh on a day like this!" the Maestro scolded. "Today there is spring in the air and I have news for you. Next week I go to Poland. From Warsaw I go to London, from London to Paris, from Paris to Vienna, and maybe then I go to Mars. Bedarski, my European manager, called me on the telephone that we must have summer concerts this year, and now I go."

Sarah just stood looking at him. In this blithe mood all he was doing was tumbling her plans about, as if they were of no account at all. "And you, Miss Tongue-tied, do you know what you are to do? It is time for you also to concertize. To South America you go. I have decided that you shall make your first appearance in New York on December eighth, but first you must play with good orchestras and give concerts of your own in Rio and Buenos Aires and many such places. Miguel Molena, who has managed my two tours in South America, he shall manage you also. I shall wire him that on July fifteenth you shall appear. That is the middle of the winter season in Rio."

One week later Sarah was in Wheaton. But just before she left New York, Pete had walked into the apartment, collar turned up, hat pulled down. "Tomorrow I leave for Chicago to hunt a job as a bricklayer," he announced as he dropped onto the couch.

"How come?" Karen asked. "Is somebody after you? You look as if you'd walked all night."

Pete thumped his chest. "The bright one has got himself disinherited."

"Really?" Karen's pleasure was so obvious that it was Pete's turn to ask, "How come?"

Karen blushed. "I just thought—that is—well, it's a good thing for a person to be on their own, isn't it?"

"It's a good thing for a person to study grammar," said Pete severely. Then he returned to his gloom. "On what I could earn with my two bare hands, how could I support an expensive wife?"

"That's different. I didn't know it was an expensive wife you had in view."

She was practically caroling now.

Pete looked at her for a full minute. Then he walked over to her and took her by the shoulders. "This is no time to lead me on." And in spite of an effort to maintain his usual light tone, a serious note was there. "I'm pledged to a cause, as they say in the history books, and you don't seem to understand that I've let 'em down. No more spondulix. When I take to laying bricks—Oh, damn, what's the use? I'm a washout."

"Know what?" Sarah said. "It just could be that you're more important than your money. Maybe you'll know it now. Maybe you'll mean more to your organization, too, being poor like the rest of us." She went to the kitchen and left him with Karen. When she returned he had left, but Karen was smiling broadly.

"So what?" Sarah asked.

"So nothing. He just left, that's all." But she kept right on smiling.

Before her train pulled into Wheaton, Sarah was out in the entry where the porter had opened a door, sniffing the good Minnesota air. Home was a wonderful place. How thrilled they'd all be that she was ready to go places at last. That's really what her father had in mind; Alan, too. If they were here now, waiting for her to step off the train … She pulled herself together and was the first on the platform.

Her mother was waiting, beaming happily. She looked plumper and a little flushed, but her blond hair still showed no gray. You'd never think she was the mother of a grown-up concert artist. Archibald was with her, his sharp face as excited as ever. Grandpa had driven them down in his new Ford; Grandma hadn't come because she wanted to have breakfast waiting at her house. She had a surprise, Archibald said. Sarah knew what it was: fresh doughnuts, baked this morning.

"Grandpa, you look younger than you did last time I saw you," Sarah told him.

"He's insenescible," Archibald said. "And he's going to build an addition to his church, a big plant for Sunday-school and church dinners. It's going to have a special court for volley ball."

"Why, Grandpa, you always said the church was more than a Y club," Sarah teased him. "And here you go pampering the young."

"The young I'm aiming for need a little pampering, if you call it that. Since the garment factory and the new mill came in, Wheaton has its slums."

For nearly two years now Grandpa had been pastor of the church again. None of the trial preachers had suited the congregation, and besides, as Mr. Benson had pointed out, Grandpa had proved his loyalty by helping the returned soldiers to find jobs.

The minute breakfast was over Archibald dragged his big sister to the garage. Sarah couldn't get used to his being so grown up. At thirteen he was finishing his sophomore year in high school. They said he'd run his chemistry teacher ragged with his incessant flair for experiment. Mama had drawn the line at a chemistry lab in her basement; you never knew when he might blow the house up, besides the terrible odors. But Grandma was not afraid. She was so certain that God would care for those he had singled out for greatness that she'd persuaded Grandpa to rig up a workshop above the garage, and she had used her own encyclopedia money to install a sink and put up a stove. Moreover, she assisted Archibald whenever he needed a fellow experimenter. Grandpa said it was she who contributed some of the smelliest concoctions. Grandma didn't make any comment, but she looked much pleased. Archibald said, "She's all right. She does exactly as she's told."

The day was crammed full. It seemed incredible to Sarah that in little more than two years a hospital had been built, equipped, and set to running full steam ahead, but here it was. More than a dozen new doctors had joined Dr. Rivera and his former associates. Besides his own absorbing interest in brain surgery, he wished to make a place for some kind of mental clinic.

Lucy had not come to breakfast at Grandma's. Bert was leaving the next day for the sanitarium; couldn't Sarah come see him before he went? "Everything is not sweetness and light over here, Sis," Lucy told her on the telephone, "but just act as if it were."

When she arrived Bert buttonholed her and drew her out on the porch where he could talk. "I've been wishing you'd come. Look here, Sarah, you've been around. Lucy's such a babe in the woods. You tell her that the best of men wander now and then. Tell her it doesn't mean anything. She and Bertie come first with me, and she ought to know it." He was angry. "Now she backs me into a corner where I have my choice between the cure or the law." He was very distraught and kept cracking his knuckles nervously.

Later she found out what he was talking about. On a business trip to Chicago he had had a temporary alcoholic paralysis, and the attending physician had discovered that the dashing brunette who purported to be his wife had no clear idea about his home and antecedents. It was his grandfather McGinty who had come to the Chicago hospital to get him, and it was also Grandfather McGinty who threatened him with dire legal and financial consequences if he didn't take himself in hand and straighten up. Lucy tried to be objective about the whole thing and to treat him like the sick man that he was. It was plain that her affection for him had deepened rather than waned. When the car from the sanitarium came for him she tucked him in and kissed him good-by as gaily as if he were off on a fishing trip, but when she turned back to the house she was trembling all over.

"The sanitarium's in Iowa. A wonderful place, but they wouldn't let me go along. Sarah, let's take Bertie and both go home for the night and sleep in our old rooms, should we?"

They talked half the night. Lucy couldn't see her way ahead. "Seems like all I can do right now is to hang onto Grandpa and let him hang onto God."

"Come to South America with me," Sarah said. "It seems I have to have a chaperone. Can you feature that?" Then they talked about Rydz and Antoon, about Karen and Pete and the things people worked for. Lucy agreed that everybody needed a cause to work for. She might run an ad in Colonel Clemmons's paper—Wanted: a cause, by distraught wife. They laughed and the laugh sounded the way she used to sound. It was wonderful to be here together, just laughing in the night.

It was Rachel who solved the chaperone problem. She had begged Sarah to come for lunch the very first day. "All the children are awake then, and Sally's dying to see you." When Sarah opened the door the three of them—Sally, Midge, and Martin—stood hand in hand, ready to sing a welcome song, but unfortunately Sarah hugged them so tightly that the song dissolved into squeals. "Imagine Sally's being four years old! Sally, you can't do this to me."

"Midge and Martin are going to be three," Sally told her. "Will you be here for the party?"

"Rachel Sando, there's something you haven't written me. There's another kind of party coming up!"

"Any day now," Rachel acknowledged, "and honestly, Sarah, I'm just as excited as before Sally came. Seems like I'll never get enough of having babies."

A car honked up the drive and Les jumped out. "Gosh, Sarah,"—he kissed her resoundingly—"now life can begin again."

"Seems to me life's doing pretty well by you here."

"Couldn't beat it. Isn't she wonderful?" He looked at Rachel the way he always looked at Rachel.

"With me, she's tops," Sarah told him.

"Mercy on us, you're getting me embarrassed," Rachel said. "Come in to lunch."

There was a maid now. A maid and a laundress and a woman who cleaned on Fridays. "Les certainly looks after us," Rachel said fondly. "And if there's any little thing he slips up on, Mother and Dad bring it on a platter. Sarah, if I were any happier I'd go up like a balloon."

It was Miss Lillie who should go as chaperone. Everyone fell right in with Rachel's suggestion, even Miss Lillie. They were at the Riveras' when Sarah asked her. "Of course I could go," Miss Lillie said without even hesitating. "That is, if you think I'm not too old."

"Ridiculous!" Mrs. Rivera answered, taking the matter into her hands from passports to luggage. "However old you are, you don't look it and you're strong as an ox. Besides, you understand Sarah and you understand music. You can keep her clothes and morals both in order without cramping her style."

Dr. Rivera walked over to his wife and looked at her reproachfully. "My dear, your language shocks me."

Sarah began to get ready for her trip. Under Mrs. Rivera's eye she had three concert gowns made in St. Paul. "No women are better dressed than the women of Buenos Aires," Mrs. Rivera assured her. "It has always been so. This is the time to go to town with your clothes." So Sarah went to town.

Moreover, she decided to give a home concert before she left. Everyone in town seemed to want to hear her, and the Women's Club, with the music department of the college, would be her joint sponsors. The date they suggested was May twenty-eighth, but Sarah made it June first; she could not play a concert on the anniversary of Alan's death. The four years seemed a millennium, but the only difference that time had made was that now she could stand aside and look at her loss, measuring its outreach which would become greater, she was sure, as the years piled up. One day in the study at the church she said, "Grandpa, sometimes I feel as if deep inside me there were a sentinel, more me than I am, who has never been moved by grief. Not that grief isn't real, but as if this sentinel were lovingly indifferent to pain or joy." She stopped short. "I can't say what I mean."

"I know what you mean, though. Something waits, waits silently until the inner meaning has a chance to rise."

"Now how can any part of me be so indifferent, so much above the fray?"

"We don't burst into tears when we see a child fall down and break its toy, even though the child is crying its heart out. We have a longer view. Our moment is bigger than the child's moment. We realize that a broken toy or a skinned knee, even some broken bones, are definitely a part of life. We're genuinely sorry for the child, but we aren't shaken. Maybe your sentinel has this same long view, a longer view than your mind can compass."

Sarah smiled, a quick child-smile. "Maybe God looks at us the same as the sentinel does."

"Tell you what, Sarah. Could be your sentinel *is* God. Not all of God, but God in an our-size package. Or should we say God in our-size voltage?"

"There aren't any good words for it, are there?"

"No." He sat still, inwardly absorbed. Half an hour later when the phone rang she told her mother, "Grandpa and I have had a long talk," but actually not more than a dozen sentences had passed between them.

One day Mrs. Rivera said to her, "Sarah, I want you to go see Enrique's family while you're in the Argentine. His cousin

Rodrigo will meet your ship. He's a sweet old gentleman, the head of the clan. You will love his wife, Cousin Consuelo. She is shaped like this"—she drew two curves in the air—"full sail ahead and behind. But Cousin Louise"—she drew a straight line—"no more shape than an ironing board."

"I'd love to meet them," Sarah told her, trying not to show that it was something of a shock to know that Dr. Rivera had a family after all these years of silence.

Mrs. Rivera went swiftly on. "Do you remember that once when we were in New York, back when you were a child at the time the *Titanic* sank, I told you that sometime I wanted you to know about my people?"

Sarah nodded, but the older woman did not wait for her to speak. "It's only since Enrique came home from war that I've been able to trust myself to speech. Before that I think I was always waiting for him to be snatched away also, as my father was snatched away. You see, my father was a very great man. He was a sculptor; the whole world knew his work. But also he was a patriot. He planned that there should be a house cleaning in high circles, and after that there should be democratic government even for the poor ones who live in the little adobe houses and for the children who have never gone to school. He planned that the Argentine should be one of the most advanced nations in the world. There were wonderful men planning with him; the best of our country. But at a secret meeting a sentry slept and a spy found out all that he needed to find out." Now her voice fell to a whisper, but she went on. "That my father should be killed would be expected, but he was tortured to death in a cave. And my mother was bound where she must watch. *She had to watch.*" Her voice grew strong again. "I want you to know that there are not many depraved ones like those who did this thing. They were crude men who thought they would please their masters. But still, their masters were not entirely ignorant. After that my mother had no mind. She was taken to a convent, and there she remains. She cannot speak, and I think she knows only what happens each minute. She is without memory. The dear God relieved her of her memory as completely as the corrupt officials relieved her of my father's fortune. Cousin Consuelo writes to us that my mother is well and they treat her as if she were an angel, and I think maybe she is. Her hair is snow white, but they say her face is as lovely as a girl's. I think she is happy sitting in the sunny garden mending for the sisters. Cousin Consuelo says that she listens when she is spoken to but she never answers. From the day my father was killed she has never spoken."

Sarah could not find words to answer.

Mrs. Rivera said, "Let us leave yesterday's sorrow with yesterday, shall we? And now we talk of Sarah Duncan's tomorrow."

Just then Dr. Rivera came home bringing some of the younger doctors with him. Adolph appeared with tea; everybody talked at once. They were forever arguing whether psychoanalysis was a fraud, a fad, or a science. Dr. Rivera took a midway position. "We can't eliminate it until we give it an open-minded try. Certainly there are cases of mental derangement which are plainly operative cases. For them we need surgeons. And there are cases which are plainly psychological. For them we need psychiatrists. In between lies a wide range which we treat with drugs, and for such cases we need medical men."

"But some of these medical cases could also be treated by psychoanalysis," one of the younger men broke in. His name was Paul Pearson, an exuberant pock-marked chap with the figure of the Discus Thrower. "If an added pinch of adrenalin or pituitary artificially administered can set them back in mental equilibrium, what about releasing the psychic factors that produce the mental equilibrium and thereby bring the glands into balance again?"

Some of the men hooted. "It can't be done that way," they argued, and plunged at once into case histories.

"It has been done," Paul insisted, and matched their case histories.

"Wait. Only wait," Dr. Rivera said. "One of these days we shall have our own psychiatrist and then we shall try and see. Come now, Sarah, and play us back to sanity."

So Sarah played. When she left she kissed Mrs. Rivera tenderly on the cheek, a thing she had done only two or three times in all of their years. Paul walked home with her. It was more than pleasant swinging along in the cool dusk. She felt like skipping. "Life is pretty nice," she said abruptly. "Just—trees and lawns and people on porches. Work and friends and all the new places to go. There's a good summer smell tonight, too, isn't there?" She sniffed the fragrant evening.

"That's your youth," he told her. "Now at my age the seamy side of things begins to show. I'm getting cynical."

He didn't sound cynical, but she wished he hadn't said it. Right away it made her think of Erik. So many things made her think of Erik. But that was probably because she was always thinking of Karen, and she knew Karen worried about him. At her own front porch she told Paul good night and went into the house with a most determined tread. A concert pianist had no time to worry about somebody in New York worrying about somebody else off in the middle of Europe. Especially when somebody else went to Europe of his own accord. She practiced until 3 A.M.

The next day word came that Bert Baer had run away from the sanitarium wearing only his pajamas, Rachel's fourth baby was born, Archibald blew off a corner of the garage roof, and Grandma singed her eyebrows, but to Sarah all the events were trivial. Her music was possessing her as it always did before a program. Later, when Bert returned properly clad in a suit he had bought from a farmer and sober as a judge, she was pleased but plainly abstracted. Even Rachel's nine-pound son registered vaguely. So did her mother's prolonged headache, which ordinarily would have given her concern. Life was less real than the interpretation of it which came from her piano.

Thirty-one

On the evening of her concert Sarah went early to Mrs. Rivera's to dress. Her mother had had a big tea that afternoon and wanted to lie down, and besides, Sarah's dress was at the Riveras'. It was a lovely thing of silver-colored chiffon, and she couldn't wait to get into it.

"First the make-up," Mrs. Rivera said. "Now that you are a professional, it is not enough to wear your own good skin."

So Hortense went to work with her little pots and brushes. Nor would they let Sarah see herself until the dress had been slipped over her head and all of the finishing touches completed. When finally she was allowed to look in the long mirror she gasped. "It couldn't—it simply couldn't be me."

Mrs. Rivera laughed delightedly. "It's the concert you."

"I feel like the moon sweeping across the sky with the Milky Way for a train." She sailed lightly around the room, bowing to an imaginary audience. "I'm really glad I got ready early so I can borrow your piano and play a piece in my finery. Otherwise I'd be too giddy to remember my notes."

The telephone rang. Sarah, who was nearest, picked up the receiver, still laughing lightly. "Hello, this is Sarah. I mean—"

But Anna's voice cut her off. "Sarah! Come quickly. Your mama's lying in the middle of the floor and her face is red as anything. She can't talk. Hurry!"

Sarah, Dr. Rivera, and Mrs. Rivera, all three, arrived together. Anna had Mrs. Duncan's head in her lap and was moaning rhythmically. Sarah knelt beside her mother; Dr. Rivera took her pulse. "It is a stroke," he said. "Help me lift her to her bed."

In the half-hour that followed, nurses came and two other doctors were called in consultation. One of them was Paul, and even in her anxiety Sarah couldn't help noting his swift approving appraisal of her. It made her feel a little sick in the middle of her stomach that she should have been aware of his glance when her own mother lay dying. Froth and tinsel, that's what she was at heart; just fooling herself and the world that she had anything real to speak through the piano. The piano! The audience was gathering now. They would have to be sent home.

"Sarah! Would you step here?" It was Dr. Rivera speaking. He had gone into the hall with the two other doctors.

Sarah let go of her mother's inert hand and went to them.

"We think it is only a light stroke," he told her. "Certainly she is in no immediate danger. She may sleep for hours."

"You mean—you mean she might even—get well?" Incredible gratitude flooded up in her.

"Of course she'll get well. Some of the paralysis may linger, but I think a few months' good nursing will put her on her feet." He smiled at her reassuringly.

"She'll have that!" Sarah said with almost passionate devotion. "We'll give her—" Then remembrance stabbed her. In two weeks she was to sail. She finished the sentence in a monotone: "We'll give her every kind of care."

There wouldn't be any concert tour. Everything would be called off. In a flash she saw Ludwik Rydz's anger cloaking his disappointment. He would think she should leave her mother, dying or living. He would say it wasn't the musician's responsibility to minister to the needs of ordinary people. He would be through with her definitely. She felt Dr. Rivera looking at her. His watch was in his hand.

"We must call the concert hall," he said practically. "Already it is five minutes until eight-thirty. Are you able to go on?"

If she could have spoken at all she would have said that of

course she could not go on. Of course she would not leave her mother. But his very question had surprised the speech out of her. Mrs. Rivera answered for her.

"Naturally she will go on. Call and tell them there has been a slight delay. No one must know the reason. Sarah will ride with me." She took her firmly by the hand and they went downstairs. Paul and the older doctor followed. Dr. Rivera would stay with her mother.

Anna met them in the lower hall. "Your grandpa and grandma have already left. Nobody answers the phone." She was still wringing her hands.

Sarah found her voice. "It's better that way. Dr. Rivera says she's going to be all right, Anna. She'll need a long, long rest, but she's going to get well. He's going to stay right beside her until I get back."

The high school auditorium, built for the town's best occasions, was so jam-packed to the doors that Archibald, who had been in his place for nearly an hour, announced in a resonant whisper, "In case of fire, a lot of folks will probably be trampled to death." All around him people smiled, glanced at the exit signs, then settled back expectantly to wait a proud moment. "When I first knew Sarah Duncan she was ..." or "Sarah herself told me ..." or "I always said Sarah Duncan would show the world."

And Sarah did. She was only a few minutes late in walking out onto the stage. At the sight of her the audience broke into applause which startled her so happily that her smile was practically a grin, and they loved the tall frank girl who stood before them. Just for an instant when she sat down at the piano and the audience hushed, it was her mother's labored breathing she seemed to hear. Then a numbness weighted her chest and spread to her fingers. After all, why force her fingers to play for these people? If they only knew, instead of this evening's being the beginning of a concert trip, it was the end. She struck the opening chord, and from then on her hands found their own sure way. As Bert said later, she was geared in high. And she herself was aware that she was geared in high. It was astounding. The biggest chords required no effort; the swiftest runs fell from her fingers, as if an automaton displaying a technique not her own. She was incandescent with music. Something Mendelssohn once said flashed to her now, something about playing better in London than in Berlin "because the people here exhibit more pleasure in listening to me." Let the people of Wheaton, then, have the credit for what they were listening to. But she knew it was not altogether so. Actually this music she gave them tonight was more than tonight's music; it was tomorrow's music and the music that should have belonged to the days coming after. This was all of her concerts in one. She might as well be lavish while she could; tomorrow she would be empty-handed. Tomorrow she must cancel her steamship reservation and cable Señor Molena.

After her last number the audience found their release in unprecedented applause, calling her back again and again. She came; she played encores; she bowed and smiled as gay as the gayest. The audience had no notion of releasing her so long as this current of vibrant vitality was available. Finally the high school principal came to the front and silenced them. "The rent on the auditorium has expired," he told them, "and Miss Duncan may expire also if we do not let her go." Then the people disbanded reluctantly, mouthing old superlatives with a new sense of the inadequacy of words.

Dr. Rivera was waiting for her in the living room at home. Just the sight of him sitting in her father's chair reading a book made her know that all was well. Her mother had wakened, mumbled something incoherent, and then had fallen into a good sleep. He went with Sarah to her mother's room and gave further instructions to the nurses. "She's going to be all right, Sarah. Time and care are the great physicians." Then he saw the stark look in her face. "This mustn't upset your plans. Life goes on and so must you." But Sarah felt that this was one time when there was some doubt beneath his own words. In real life one didn't step over the threshold with family responsibilities clinging to one's skirts.

Undressing in her own room, she looked around at familiar objects, but each thing seemed like only the shell of itself, as if—the reality being gone—it might crumble at a touch. "If I don't go on I'll lose my technique. I'm afraid. And my chance, too. It's all very well to say that good work makes its own way, but there are plenty of fine musicians who lack only the interest of someone who matters to get them before audiences. Rydz will be furious. He'll be through with me. Why did this happen to me? There's a connection between circumstance and character, but I don't know what it is. Here I am thinking of myself when it's my mother who's ill. She has character. She deserves care. I want to give her everything. But Rydz will grow sarcastic. Sarcasm is worse than irony. Erik is ironical. Erik couldn't operate any more—just like me—so he wouldn't play the piano with his left hand." She knew her thoughts were becoming incoherent, but she couldn't turn them off. Sleep seemed as incredible as sunrise. But almost at the same instant both came.

In the days that followed everything she did seemed to be done automatically. None of her emotions—neither pity, grief, nor regret—had any warmth in them. Rydz was as furious as ever she had pictured him; he burned up the cables, pleading, ordering, threatening. The great had to go on, he said; the people they stepped on were part of the cost of their greatness. Finally she quit answering him by wire and wrote a long letter. Strangely, it was not a hard letter to write; it seemed to be a letter about someone who didn't matter much anyway. She explained to him that her mother was not responding as rapidly as Dr. Rivera had expected her to; the paralysis of the left arm persisted, and her tongue was thick. Also, there wasn't as much money at home as there used to be; they couldn't afford a nurse by day as well as night. Moreover, she didn't feel as free as formerly to turn to the Riveras because everything they had, she felt sure, was tied up in the new hospital. Then there was Archibald to look after. He was not only high-strung and experimental by nature, but he'd reached the stage where he did not want advice from anyone; he had to be handled with finesse. She'd keep up her practicing. She wouldn't slip. By fall she'd be better than ever.

But by fall she was not better than ever. For the first few weeks she had tried desperately to catch hours, half-hours, even quarter hours, for practice. But Anna had gone off for a two weeks' vacation and had had to stay five. Her mother's progress continued to be slow, and for the first time in her life she seemed depressed. Sarah's presence buoyed her up. She liked to be told all the little comings and goings of the neighborhood. Sometimes Sarah had a wild inclination to smother Mama and run to the empty church where she could lock herself in and play the clock around. Actually she waited on her mother with tenderness. But sometimes when she sat talking to her she kept a score open on her lap, out of sight, and tried to refresh her memory. But then she'd be too slow in answering and Mama would grow querulous, whereupon Sarah would be consumed with shame and try to make the pity in her heart drive the longing from her fingers. It wasn't that she minded the cooking, ironing, shopping, nor the endless steps. Nothing her body did made any difference.

Everyone took for granted that her career, as they called it, was only postponed for a few weeks. When the weeks stretched into months they said the same things. Lucy was expecting another baby at Thanksgiving time and could not do much actual nursing, but she came every day, bringing something good to eat. One day she said, "I know this delay must be hard for you, Sarah, but at the end of five years you won't know the difference. It's just like the time one takes out to have a baby; for a while you're out of things, and then by and by you're in again." She didn't understand that having a baby was on the main line for her while any kind of time out for a musician was sheer loss of skill.

Rachel, too, absorbed in the happy routine of family life with four small children to look after, saw all other pursuits as relative. Sometimes she'd invite Sarah over for a quiet bite of supper in the cool of the evening after the young fry were in bed. "I know you must feel horribly frustrated, Sarah, but I keep telling myself that a musician has to have something to play about, and this is real life you're living now." Even Leslie added paternally, "Just keep up the good old practice, fellow, and that December concert will be better than ever."

Only Miss Lillie knew better. "I can tell by your face that you aren't practicing, Sarah. A musician can't recover lost time. You couldn't possibly get ready for that midwinter concert unless you're hard at your practicing now." Her face was contorted with anxiety.

Sarah only stared at her for a moment. Then she shook her head. "It isn't only that every minute of the day and half the night is busy. It isn't only that my mother clings to me and never wants me out of the room. But there's Archibald. He wants to quit school to go to work in a chemical laboratory. Neither Grandpa nor I can talk him out of it, and I know that if I so much as turned my back he'd be off."

Help came from an unexpected quarter; not help to free her time but to ease her mind a little. It was a dark day in late October with a biting wind snapping the last limp leaves from their stems. Anna was grumbling because the weatherman had refused to give her one sunny day to wash. Mama had decided to knit for Lucy's baby but after buying the fine blue wool had discovered that her left hand grew numb with use. She wept and knit intermittently. Archibald was home with a cold, and the house was too small for him. Sarah was doing accounts in her room, thinking about all of them and hence having to re-add her columns, when Anna appeared at the door.

"There's a man to see you."

"A man? You mean a salesman."

"Not a salesman. He's a visitor and he wants to see you very much."

Somewhat irritated, Sarah went downstairs. The strange

man came toward her with outstretched hands. "Sarah! Of course it's Sarah! I'm Bob Winters."

"Bob Winters!" Sarah felt her knees grow weak. This was Alan's friend, this was the man who had seen Alan die. She looked toward the door. It seemed as if Alan must be following him in through that door. As if there had been no reality in these long years between them.

"Sit down. I've waited a long, long time for this day."

"I'm on my way to the Coast to meet Elise. We're going to be married."

She nodded. The chap Elise had married had been killed in France. How long ago that was! As long ago as Alan. For Sarah it was a strange hour that followed. She heard herself talking about her years in New York as if the experience belonged to someone else. Even these months at home belonged to someone else. She could laugh as she talked. They both laughed, and he talked animatedly of the future.

"You're a wonderful woman," he told her as he rose to go. He came over to her and took both her hands in his. "I used to think Alan was biased by his love, maybe, but now I think he was merely exercising his usual good judgment. I want Elise to know you. You're one in a thousand."

"Don't say that!" There was distress in her voice. "You don't understand. I'm really a failure. Everything I attempt to do peters out." Now her words rushed forth. "When I was a child my father expected me to be a great painter and I threw everything I had into painting and failed. I failed Alan too. We should have been married. Then he would probably have waited for the draft and he wouldn't have been in Cantigny on that day. Now I'm failing in my music too. Everything I set my heart on has to fail."

Suddenly from behind her came Archibald's most earnest voice. "That doesn't make *you* a failure, though." Evidently he had come in from the dining room in time to hear her last sentence. He walked right up to her. "Things you do can fail without *you* failing. I mean—I mean—" He hesitated for words.

"He's right," Bob said. "I don't have any words for it, either, but he's right."

Archibald's sharp features lightened. "What I mean is, sometimes what you want to do *has* to fail so you won't. I mean, like you being responsible for me. If you hadn't failed, I would have. If you'd gone to South America, I'd about have gone nuts with Grandma and Mama always holding me back. I'd about have—" He stopped short again and went out of the room.

That night Sarah went over to see her grandfather, knowing that Grandma had gone to a meeting. Her first remark wasn't the thing she'd meant to say at all. "I guess it isn't failing at the main thing that's so tragic. It's failing at the substitute."

Grandpa laid down his book. "For a decrepit mind, you'll just have to back up and document that remark."

Sarah laughed. "I mean all I've been doing for Archibald is successfully holding him down, making him just like other sophomores, and being sort of pleased he's smart enough to be a problem, when what I should have been doing is help him find his way. His way isn't going to be an ordinary way."

So they had a long talk about Archibald and decided to ask Dr. Rivera if he could work in one of the hospital laboratories afternoons. Then Grandpa said, "Your concert doesn't seem any nearer, does it, Sarah?"

"Not a bit." She shook her head, still smiling. "I guess I'm just a small-town Prometheus, chained by small-town circumstances."

Grandpa did not smile. "And what would you be saying through the piano if you could be playing to the listening world?"

"You know what I'd say. At least what I'd want to say. I'd hope to give people faith in themselves. Faith in justice and love and beauty. Maybe faith in God." She shrugged her shoulders. "I suppose I'd hope to let the composers speak through me— Chopin shouting courage to beleaguered Warsaw, Beethoven insisting on immortal melodies when he was deaf. Maybe that sounds sentimental, but the great ones do speak of tremendous certainties. It's all there in the music."

"Well, my dear, you're saying those same things right here at home." He leaned toward her. "What difference does the instrument make?"

"It makes a difference to me. And if you expect me to say that if God wills I'll play 'Home, Sweet Home,' on a harmonica, then you're going to be disappointed, because I'm not going to say it." She rose to go.

Grandpa got up too. He held her coat for her and buttoned it as he used to do when she was small. Then he stood back and looked at her. "Some things I have opinions about and some things I know. Just a few things I know. One of them is that when we're not only willing but eager to play on any instrument at hand, then God either gives us the very instrument we crave or a better one. I don't mean one that's better *for* us, but one we'll enjoy more. It's a plain rule, like two and two makes four."

"You're sweet, Grandpa." She kissed him good night. "Even if I'm unregenerate, I'm grateful."

The next day the sun shone and autumn flung out the last banner of October's bright blue weather. Mama felt better. She was knitting more easily and thought maybe she would let Bert take her to ride in his new Buick. Sarah decided to walk over to the Riveras'. Over there teatime was always interesting and often gay since the young doctors, sometimes accompanied by their wives, had taken to dropping in on Mrs. Rivera for what they called their daily tonic. It was weeks since she had stayed for more than a few minutes, but sometimes Paul or one of the others walked home with her, and that gave her one more thing to report to her mother.

Today there was much laughing going on in the drawing room. As she gave her wraps to Adolph she heard Paul's voice saying, "My past's an open book. An expert could analyze me in thirty minutes flat."

The voice that answered was deeper than Paul's and not like any other anyplace. Why should it make her reach for her coat and draw back? If Adolph had not been standing in the drawing-room doorway waiting for her to enter, she would have slipped out again. As it was, she went in regally, hands extended, warm cordiality in her voice. "Why, Erik Einersen, what pleasant gale blew you into Wheaton?" It was exactly the kind of voice with which she might have greeted old Mr. McGinty or Mr. Sando.

He took her hands and he held them both in his while the others poured out their comments.

"Didn't you know—"

"Dr. Rivera had him up his sleeve all the time we were—"

Still he held her hands and he did not mean to let go until she looked at him. Finally she looked, but only for a fleeting glance. It was enough for him. He gave her a chair and she knew she was trembling. "No tea," she told Mrs. Rivera. She couldn't have held a cup.

By and by they made him talk about this Dr. Jung with whom he had spent so many months. And his visit to Dr. Freud, what of that? What kind of magic did he now expect to effect with his mind cures? Would medicine fall back among the lost arts? Wasn't the whole field of psychoanalysis open to invasion by all sorts of quacks? He accepted all of their questions at face value, whether the tone was earnest, supercilious, or even edgy. His answers were direct but, at first, cursory. Several times he tried to turn the conversation into other channels. Then when it would not turn he walked over by the fireplace and stood there for some time talking seriously, even brilliantly. He made no pretentious claims, but he was never unsure of his ground.

It was late when the guests rose to go. Dr. Rivera, who had come in soon after Sarah's arrival, would have detained them all indefinitely if some had not had dinner engagements. He liked to have his boys around him. Sarah loved the deference he paid them as colleagues and at the same time the kindly critical eye he kept upon them all. In the general hubbub of departure she might have slipped out had not Dr. Rivera laid his hand upon her arm. "Stay to dinner with us, Sarah. It's a long time since you have stayed."

"Oh, I can't do that," she said in sudden consternation as she felt Erik's eyes upon her. "Mama would think I'd deserted her."

"Mama knows better," Mrs. Rivera said. "An hour ago Adolph telephoned to her and your mama said that Lucy was staying for supper and you wouldn't be missed at all." She laughed at Sarah's surprised expression, so that Sarah had to laugh too.

"I never get used to what goes on in French in this household," she said to Erik. If her retreat was cut off she would once more don her robe of cordial regality.

But he would have none of it. "Karen wrote me about your mother's illness. In fact, she has kept me pretty well posted on what you have been doing."

"She's the only person I've written to," she told him, for lack of something better to say.

"Me too. She's a wonderful correspondent. If I lost my other hand I'd probably hold a pencil in my teeth in order to keep her letters coming."

This was something new in him, his being open, even casual, about his loss. She had noticed that he had held his teacup easily in his artificial hand; he even gestured with it.

"Erik, would you go back to surgery if you could?" She could have bitten her tongue out after she said the words.

But he was not perturbed. "No, I would not go back to surgery. To be sure, I'd like to have my arm. It would facilitate daily life. But"—his shrug was the old gesture, lightened of cynicism—"an arm is a small price for a deep satisfaction."

Her next words were almost mechanical because her mind was occupied with an inner consideration. "You believe psychoanalysis is more important to the world than surgery, don't you?"

"Not at all. It's just more my dish, that's all. May seem odd when I have also such a passion for the feel of an instrument finding its way with living tissue. Once I couldn't have believed myself that there was any other pursuit—profession—" He finished with a smile and the quirk of an eyebrow.

Maybe he knew she was hardly listening. So Grandpa was right! When one made the final act of acceptance, when one took what life handed out, then she reached into her treasures and brought forth something better. Except, what could be better than music? So the theory flattened out against fact, after all.

It was a wonderful dinner they had together, the four of them. Mrs. Rivera had never talked more interestingly, but Sarah, too, was doing well and knew it. All the little incidents of the summer fell into perspective and became amusing. Then the men took over and Erik drew from the older man a philosophic discrimination Sarah never knew he had. Time sped by. None of the four was conscious of moving from the dining table to the fireside. Talk flowed on until, in a moment's pause, the little gilt clock chimed ten.

Then Dr. Rivera leaned back with a sigh and smiled at Sarah. "Now we will have music. What shall it be? But Brahms, of course."

"Mozart," said Mrs. Rivera.

"Bach," Erik said. "As my friend Dr. Jung would say, Bach is like the pyramids, at all times above the expression of personal problems and personal emotions."

"I can't." There was a kind of frightened determination in Sarah's voice. "I haven't played for months. Actually, it's more than a month since I've even touched the piano."

"Why, Sarah Duncan," Mrs. Rivera ejaculated, "have you been as busy as *that?*"

"I thought I was." She felt her voice growing smaller. "It wasn't only that I had no time to play, but I had no reason."

"Do you mean no audience?" Dr. Rivera spoke gravely.

Sarah nodded. "No audience, present or future."

Then Mrs. Rivera spoke out passionately, more to herself than to Sarah. "It is our job only to make the music. The audience that should hear it will be brought to our music at the right time."

Sarah looked at her in amazement. This, too, sounded more like Grandpa than Grandpa did himself. She felt convicted, but of what she did not know. Surely one who gave up a career for a duty could not have done wrong.

It was Erik who answered for her. "Sarah can do more *with her left hand* than anybody else with two. Over in France I once saw her flay a man with her left hand and then set him on his feet again." He chuckled. "It was wonderful. Damn near killed the guy, but that was what he needed. He had to get over his colossal self-importance. Took him quite a while, too, but he's going to keep at it until he doesn't cast a shadow."

The others knew he was speaking of himself. Sarah saw that they knew. He didn't care. He was looking at her with pride, and anyone could look on who wished to.

Mrs. Rivera said, "Erik, you sound young, but you're right."

Dr. Rivera leaned back in his chair, crossed his feet, and put his hands behind his head in a way he had. "Sometimes I think the sociologists are all wrong and circumstances don't have a thing to do with character. We come in with the soul equipment we've earned, one way and another, and we make of circumstances what we will to make of them."

"He is a heathen," said his wife fondly.

He went on grandly. "Circumstances are just a by-product, a visualization of what we are. If they appear to trap us, it is only that they are uncovering a block in our being. They are dramatizing an inner situation. Some intent or knowledge within us has not come clear and so we are forced to pause and take our sights again. Maybe you think I'm just throwing words around, yes? But they mean something. Life never gives us a harder task than we can do with profit to ourselves. I'd go further: She's always nudging us, life is, toward clearer meaning.

But sometimes the only way to make our befuddlement plain to us is to tangle our feet in confusion so that we cannot rush thoughtlessly on."

His wife said, "We can see the confusion of circumstance when we might otherwise ignore confusion of spirit. I am one who knows."

"I am another," Erik said. "Looking back, I think I was frequently nudged, as you call it, toward the psychological, but I was too set on success in an accepted field to pay attention to the nudgings. However, I don't think that being blocked by circumstance always means that we are on the wrong path. Only that we are ignoring someone else's need on our way, perhaps, or are living too meagerly. Once we sort ourselves out, then we can proceed again with less encumbrance and better equipment. Or doesn't that make sense?"

"It does to me." Sarah looked from one to the other. "Archibald said almost the same thing—about my failing so he wouldn't. He was trying to point out that maybe I was delayed so that I could help him go on. And after all, what he does is as important to me as what I do! But what if I couldn't figure any meaning out of being blocked? The basic question is—" She hesitated. "Maybe I don't know what the basic question is."

Erik leaned toward her. "Yes, you do. Ultimately we have to answer three questions without confusion: who we are, why we are here, and what is our destination."

Mrs. Rivera broke in: "I can answer the first one, who we are. We are creatures of unlimited creativity—" She paused.

Her husband took up her sentence "—here to grow into full stature. Each of us and so all of us, inseparably."

"Then that takes care of the third question, I presume." Erik smiled broadly. "Destination: perfection, no less."

Sarah smiled too. "We sound like Grandpa, don't we, leaping blithely among the ultimates. A lot of people might point out, though, that all our talk hasn't changed our circumstances. But it's made my circumstances seem less permanent, less irremedial. How's that for a word? I feel as if an invisible hand had lifted a too heavy cloak from my shoulders—if you know what I mean— and I'm ready to walk to Rio and carry my own piano. Or I'll even accept another destination and another kind of instrument if I can purely be me and play it."

Dr. Rivera got up to put wood on the fire. "If you'll purely be you, you can play any instrument."

Sarah rose too. She would have to keep the talk light or she'd burst into tears. It was such great relief to feel, to believe, that meaning could be found beneath confusion, that somehow there was always a way out and on. A right way, a living way, a satisfactory way. It made a game of circumstance. A kind of holy game. Failure became exhilarating. One felt heady with excitement in hunting clues. She laughed lightly. My goodness! They'd think she was crazy. Unconsciously she had walked to the piano, and they were expecting her to play. But she only said, "I'd like to give you Debussy right now. Maybe the 'Golliwog's Cakewalk.' Only I've got to go home. Really I must."

"I'll ring for Adolph to bring the car around," Mrs. Rivera said.

"Not tonight, Mrs. Rivera." Erik laid a restraining hand upon her arm. "Tonight I'm walking Sarah home if you don't mind." He turned to Sarah. "And if you don't mind."

She did mind. Suddenly she felt dizzy again and her mouth was dry. She reached for her regality, but it didn't come. She nodded dumbly and started for the hall. "I'm sorry about Brahms, Mozart, and Bach," she called back to them. "But I'll do better next time."

"She certainly will," Erik said as they all followed her. "I give you my word, she certainly will." He took her coat. "She may have to be a left-hand wonder with a couple of jobs on her hands, but she's sure to be a wonder."

Sarah wasn't sure what he meant, but she certainly did not intend to ask. There were times when it was better to hold life back, if one could, and this was plainly such a moment.

Novelist and playwright
Margueritte Harmon Bro was
born in Nebraska in the late
nineteenth century. She lived in
China, Japan and Indonesia,
and traveled extensively through
Mexico, Argentina, Brazil and
Uruguay. Her best known works
include *When Children Ask*,
Every Day A Prayer, and *The
Book You Always Meant to Read*.
Sarah was her first novel.